# letters to molly

USA TODAY BESTSELLING AUTHOR

# DEVNEY PERRY

# other titles

**Jamison Valley Series**

The Coppersmith Farmhouse

The Clover Chapel

The Lucky Heart

The Outpost

The Bitterroot Inn

The Candle Palace

**Maysen Jar Series**

The Birthday List

Letters to Molly

**Lark Cove Series**

Tattered

Timid

Tragic

Tinsel

**Runaway Series**

Runaway Road

Wild Highway

Quarter Miles

Forsaken Trail

Dotted Lines

**The Edens Series**

Christmas in Quincy - Prequel

Indigo Ridge

Juniper Hill

Garnet Flats

**Clifton Forge Series**

Steel King

Riven Knight

Stone Princess

Noble Prince

Fallen Jester

Tin Queen

**Standalones**

Rifts and Refrains

A Little Too Wild

# contents

# prologue

### Finn

"**M**iss?" I snagged the waitress's attention as she walked past our booth. "Could I get another beer?"

"You got it." She smiled and hurried away as I downed the rest of my first Bud Light.

Drinking was necessary when my sister was cuddled up on the other side of the booth, lips locked with this new guy she was dating. *Jamie.* There wasn't anything quite as uncomfortable as watching your little sister kiss a man with tongue.

I looked over my shoulder, searching the crowded restaurant for our waitress. If this was how the night was going to go, I needed to order two more beers instead of one. The waitress had disappeared. *Damn.*

"So, Jamie." I forced myself to say his name nicely as I turned back to the booth. "Poppy tells me that you're from a ranch around here."

He and Poppy broke apart—*thank fuck*—as he nodded to me. "That's right. It's about forty-five minutes from here. You guys should come out there with me one of these days."

Jamie stretched his arm behind her and rested it on the

back of the booth. And there it was, the dopey grin. Clearly Jamie was just as infatuated with Poppy as she was with him.

I tipped the beer bottle to my lips, frowning when I remembered it was empty. As I set it down, I studied Jamie from the corner of my eye.

He was two years younger than I was but just as bulky, probably from growing up on a working ranch. He wore his hair too long and too shaggy. His green and white pearl-snap Western shirt was unsnapped one too many. And the guy was wearing flip-flops in September.

Despite his strange cross between surfer and cowboy, Poppy was enamored. She'd gone out with him three times already. Wasn't that too much? It seemed like too much.

When she'd invited me along tonight to meet Jamie and her new roommate for burgers, I'd had no choice but to say yes. Poppy was already in deep, and I had to know what kind of guy we were dealing with here.

"You're a senior?" Jamie asked. I guess he hadn't completely forgotten I was in the booth too.

"Yep." I nodded. "Landscape design. What are you studying?"

"Education. I figure working until I'm sixty-five will be a hell of a lot more fun if I get to hang out with kids all day." He flashed Poppy a wide, white smile. Then he took the unopened straw on the table and ripped the paper free from the plastic.

With a spin of his fingers, he balled up the paper. I knew before he was finished that it was going into one end of the straw.

Sure enough, he loaded the ball, grinned at me and brought the empty end to his lips. Then he took aim. One hard puff and the paper ball went flying toward Poppy's nose.

"Jamie!" She swatted the straw as they both laughed.

This guy was a goof. No wonder he wanted to be around kids all day. He'd fit right in.

I'd only met him one beer ago, but I'd already pegged him as the class clown. The guy cracking jokes and playing games. The guy who'd make a fart noise just to lighten a somber mood. He was the guy who always had a smile and made sure everyone else did too.

I liked that for Poppy.

Which meant I was going to have to get used to them kissing.

Poppy could use a good-time guy. She'd gone home to Alaska for the summer to live with our parents. She'd worked hard for three months to save some money for the upcoming school year, which meant there hadn't been much in the way of fun.

If I took a black light to Jamie's forehead, I was sure I'd find the word *fun* written in invisible ink.

"Where's this new roommate?" I asked Poppy, hoping to keep her mouth busy with conversation instead of, well . . . Jamie.

"She called to tell me that she was running late." Poppy checked her phone. "That was about fifteen minutes ago, so she'll probably be here soon."

"What's her name again?"

"Molly," she and Jamie said in unison, then smiled at one another.

"And I haven't met her before?" I'd met quite a few of Poppy's friends but I didn't recall a Molly.

"Nope. She lived in the coed dorms last year."

Our waitress walked past the table with a tray of waters but stutter-stepped when she spotted me. "Oh, shoot. I forgot your beer. Give me a few minutes."

"You know what? It's okay." I held up a hand, already sliding out of the booth. "I'll just go to the bar and grab one." Or two. *Maybe three.*

"Are you sure?" she asked.

"Yep. No problem at all. You guys want anything?" I asked Poppy and Jamie, but it was too late. In the ten seconds I'd stopped watching them, they'd returned to whispering in each other's ears and I was all but forgotten.

I walked away from the table, taking a necessary break from the happy couple. Along with watching them attempt to conjoin themselves in public tonight, I was also going to have to play nice with the roommate.

Poppy had assured me this evening wasn't her arranging some sort of blind double date. This was simply dinner and a chance to meet Jamie and Molly before I got too busy with my last two semesters of school.

Though even with a heavy class load and part-time job in the evenings and weekends, I had a feeling I'd be seeing a lot of Jamie.

I had to admit, he wasn't a bad guy. The constant touching was annoying, but call it guy's intuition, I knew Jamie wasn't in this for an easy score. He liked her.

I leaned my elbows on the bar and signaled for the bartender. "Bud Light."

He came over and checked my ID, then went to the cooler for my beer. I dropped some cash on the bar, took a healthy pull from the longneck and, in no particular hurry, began making my way back to our booth in the far corner of the narrow restaurant.

Even from a distance, I could spot Poppy and Jamie making eyes at one another. She'd never been like this around a guy before. A pang of older-brother possessiveness hit hard. I didn't want to think of her as a grown woman. I didn't want her to find a man who'd take over the things I did for her now, like changing the oil in her car or buying her Chinese food on Sunday nights. I wanted her to stay my little sister.

But at the same time, I wanted her to find a decent guy. One I wouldn't want to sucker-punch on their wedding day.

"Oh, shit," a woman cursed just as a slosh of cold beer coated my hand. "I'm so sorry."

"No problem." I switched my beer to the other hand and wiped off the wet one on my jeans. Then I looked at the woman who'd bumped into my arm.

My mouth went dry.

Framed by brunette curls was a face so stunning I wasn't sure where to look first. Her brown eyes twinkled, their flecks of gold matching the shimmer of her eye shadow. Her skin was like porcelain, flawless and creamy except for the rosy blush of her cheeks.

Her lips were painted a pale peach. Their delicate, soft color was sweet, a sharp contrast to those chocolate curls bouncing down her shoulders. Those curls screamed sex. They begged to be twisted around my fingers. To be splayed across my pillow.

"You're Finn, aren't you? Poppy's brother?"

I forced my eyes away from her hair. "Uh-huh." *Smooth, dumbass.*

"I'm Molly." She stuck out her hand, taking mine and doing the handshake for us both.

This was the roommate? *Yep.* The woman of my dreams was my sister's college roommate. *Fuck me.*

"You don't have freckles either," she said, studying my face.

No, I didn't. Poppy and I both had red hair, mine a shade closer to auburn than her ginger. We'd inherited it from our mother but hadn't gotten her freckles. None of which I could tell her because I'd forgotten how to speak.

I took a swig of my beer as Molly glanced around the restaurant. I swallowed it down, remembering I was a senior in college, not mute. And definitely better than this with women.

"We're back there," I said, gesturing to where Poppy and Jamie were sitting—and kissing again.

Molly spotted them and groaned. "Those two are nauseating right now. I ate lunch with them yesterday and had to throw a chicken nugget at Jamie's head before he even realized I was there."

I chuckled. "Poppy didn't have many boyfriends in high school. This whole PDA thing is a first for me. I'm not going to lie, I don't like it."

"I'm not much for PDA myself. Call me old-fashioned, but I'd take a heartfelt letter over sucking face in a restaurant any day of the week."

"A letter? I think the most I've ever written to a woman was a question on a sticky note. Does that count?"

She giggled, the melodic sound stealing my breath. "No, a sticky note doesn't count."

My gaze wandered back to her hair, following the silky spirals up from the curve of her breast to the shell of her ear. I really wanted to touch it. Would it be weird to touch it? *Yes.*

"Excuse me." The waitress pushed past me with another loaded tray.

"Sorry." I shuffled toward an empty high-top table so I was clear of the aisle. Poppy was so focused on her new boyfriend, she hadn't even noticed Molly's arrival. "I'm in no rush to get back to the kissing booth. Care to sit? You can educate me on all of the other old-fashioned customs missing in today's dating rituals."

"Like bundling. They should bring bundling back. And the pet name *darling*. Not darlin'," she drawled. "I hate darlin'. But *darling* is rather charming, don't you think?"

"It is." I grinned, pulling out her chair, then went to my own.

Molly glanced over her shoulder, dismissing Poppy and Jamie for the last time. When she turned to me and smiled, the whole restaurant disappeared. "Those two won't even know we're missing."

"What two?"

# one
## Molly

F *ifteen years later . . .*
        "Married, single or divorced?" the salesman asked, his finger poised above his mouse, ready to click the appropriate checkbox on the screen.

"Divorced." Even after six years that word still felt strange on my tongue.

Why did they even need to ask that question? Every loan application, PTA volunteer form and church questionnaire wanted to know your marital status. I was going to start checking the single box. What was the difference? I was buying this car. The fact that I had an ex-husband didn't make a bit of difference because me, myself and I had no intention of missing a payment.

"Address?"

I rattled off my address, phone number and social security number as requested, and after a hundred clicks, the salesman finally tore his eyes away from the screen.

"Okay, I think we're set. Let me get the finance guy in here and we can go over the terms."

"Great." I stayed in my seat as he left the office. When he was gone, I checked the clock on my phone.

I'd been here for two hours already, test-driving, then negotiating the price of the new Jeep Rubicon I was buying. I still had an hour and a half before I had to be home to meet the kids, but this had already taken longer than I'd hoped. I was anxious to get home with this surprise.

Kali and Max had no idea I was buying a new car and they were going to flip when they saw the Jeep in our minivan's parking spot.

Max hated the minivan because the backseat DVD player had quit a month ago. Like most eight-year-old boys, he thought any trip longer than twenty minutes was torture without something to watch. Not only did the soon-to-be-mine Jeep come outfitted with chrome rims and tinted windows, each of the kids would have their own entertainment consoles.

Kali didn't consider the TV a necessity like her younger brother, but she had just turned ten and was approaching the age where mean girls found their nasty streaks and anything and everything could cause debilitating embarrassment—like the minivan I was trading in today. Tomorrow I'd be rolling through the school drop-off line with new wheels, which were sure to earn me some cool-mom points.

I'd been running low on those lately. Their dad was the cool parent, not me. My areas of excellence were laundry, housekeeping and nagging until homework was done and vegetables were eaten. But at least now I'd have a trendy vehicle.

"Okay, Ms. Alcott." The salesman walked back into his office with a younger man following behind, a stack of papers in his hand. "We'll just go over the financing terms, sign a few papers and you'll be all set. I'm having the guys in the shop fill up the tank and do a quick clean. We'll have you out of here in thirty minutes."

I smiled. "Perfect."

An hour later, I slid into the black leather driver's seat and gripped the steering wheel, taking a deep breath of my new Jeep's smell. It wasn't a brand-new car. I was a divorcee with a mortgage and two kids who were constantly outgrowing their Nikes. I couldn't afford brand-new. But I could afford a shiny three-year-old model with low miles and eighteen months left on the bumper-to-bumper warranty.

"Oh my God, I love this car." With a happy squeal, I adjusted the seat and mirrors, then put it in drive and pulled off the lot. Excitement raced through my veins, and I fought to stay under the speed limit as I drove through town. The jitters didn't settle until I was parked in my driveway.

As I got out to inspect the gleaming black paint, I hid my smile with a hand. This Jeep wasn't just cool, it was badass, and so much better than the white minivan I'd left behind.

My gaze wandered to the garage where the minivan had lived and a pang of sadness hit. We'd nicknamed her Beluga and she'd been my trusty steed for years. She'd schlepped kids to soccer and me to work. She'd cared for hundreds of forgotten Cheerios and fruit snacks. She'd been there for me after the divorce, when I'd collapse into the steering wheel and let out rivers of tears before putting on a happy face to show the world.

I was going to miss Beluga. She'd been one of the last remaining artifacts from my married days.

Most of the relics from my failed marriage had been replaced over the last six years. The living room furniture Finn and I had bought together went first after Kali spilled grape juice on the upholstery and the stain had set. Next went the roof and siding of the house after a severe hailstorm. The beige home we'd bought was now white with black shutters and a charcoal tin roof. Pictures had been taken down. Memorabilia had been stowed in boxes and hidden in the attic.

And now Beluga was gone too.

*It was for the best.* That's what I'd been reminding myself these past six years. I was happier now than I'd been during the last year of my marriage. So was Finn. So were the kids.

It was for the best.

I smiled again at the Jeep, then took the sidewalk to the front porch. My lawn was lush and green and long. Ideally, it would get mowed today but I doubted I'd have the time, so the chore was added to my endless weekend to-do list. It was a good thing tomorrow was Friday so I couldn't tack on much more.

As soon as Kali turned twelve, Finn had promised to teach her how to mow lawns for extra cash. She was chomping at the bit. So was I. Mowing was one duty I couldn't wait to delegate to the kids. I'd gladly clean and cook and wash clothes for a hundred years if it meant never walking behind my red Craftsman again.

I'd done enough mowing for a lifetime.

After Finn had graduated from college, he'd gone to work at a local landscaping company, but his dream had always been to open his own. The year we married, he took the leap and started his business. *Our* business.

During Alcott Landscaping's first two seasons, I was the number-one lawn mower. While Finn did all things landscaping, from bids to design to the actual planting, sodding and whatever else that had to be done, I managed the mowing service. It was the side of the business that kept us in SpaghettiOs and corn dogs until Finn built up his reputation. Three college kids and I mowed hundreds of lawns, until finally I was able to step back from the mowing completely and run the office.

When we had Kali, I took a further step back and worked part-time. Once Max arrived, it made sense for me to stay home entirely. Finn took over all aspects of managing Alcott and I phased myself out.

The only lawn I mowed these days was my own. Even the smell of fresh-cut grass and the prospect of a tan couldn't get me excited for *that* chore.

I went inside and dropped my purse on the bench in the entryway. I walked around the corner into the kitchen, and as I looked out over the sink into the front yard, I sighed. I needed to mow tonight. It was unavoidable. Spring had been full of dewy mornings and sunny afternoons. If I didn't do it soon, I'd be facing a jungle.

Finn and I had bought this house the year Max was born. We'd wanted a nice spacious place in a friendly neighborhood. Alcott had become one of the biggest landscaping companies in the Gallatin Valley, so we'd splurged on a home with every upgrade and the best lot in the cul-de-sac.

Then Finn had gone crazy on our landscaping. This place had been his test site, the yard where he'd experiment with new shrubs or trees to see how they stood up before using them for clients. There was a fountain in the backyard. There were flower beds within flower beds. It was beautiful. The envy of all my neighbors.

And a maintenance nightmare.

Finn had created this intricate spectacle that required me to spend hours edging and trimming. I spent more time weeding than actually enjoying the flowers.

And I was too frugal to spend my single, working-mom income to hire a gardener or mowing crew. I hadn't even had professional help when I'd been married to Bozeman's king of lawn care.

"I hate my yard."

The doorbell rang, pulling me away from the window. I hurried to the front door. My neighbor Gavin waved through the glass.

"Hey." I opened the door with a smile.

"Howdy. I saw you pull up in your new rig. Had to come over and check it out."

"Isn't it fun?" I stepped outside, joining him on the wide, covered porch that wrapped around my entire house.

"Pretty snazzy car, Molly." Gavin tucked his hands in his cargo shorts as he walked down the porch steps and inspected the grass. "Want me to mow for you?"

I really wanted to say yes. "No, that's okay. Thanks though."

"You sure? I wouldn't mind."

"I'm sure. It's the only way I keep a tan."

Gavin had offered to mow my lawn a dozen times since he'd moved in next door two summers ago, but I'd never accepted. Mostly because it was such a chore. I wanted to stay in his good graces in case I ever needed a neighborly favor.

But the other reason I declined his help was because Gavin didn't have a knack for mowing. I grimaced at the bald spots cut into his grass and the random piles of mulch. Two years and he still hadn't figured out the right blade height settings.

I might not like mowing, but I was good at it. Better than most.

"Okay. Well, it's a standing offer." Gavin flashed me a grin and my heart sped up a beat.

He was handsome, with a trim goatee and silver flecks in his brown hair. He was a single dad who worked from home, five years older than my thirty-five. His office faced mine, and on the rare occasion I was sitting at my desk while he was at his, he'd wave.

We'd been spending more time with each other this spring. His twin girls were two years older than Kali, but even with the age difference, everyone got along. While the kids were playing together at the park or jumping on his trampoline, Gavin and I hung out. Our Friday-night pizza dinners were becoming a thing.

"How's work going today?" I asked as we strolled to my Jeep.

"Good. I'm taking a break for a few hours. My ex has the girls for the rest of the week and weekend. It's so quiet when they're gone that I'll probably work through dinner."

I knew exactly how lonely it was when your kids were at their other home. I opened my mouth to invite him over for dinner with us but stopped when a familiar navy truck came rolling down the street.

Max's window behind Finn's driver's seat was open. His head was sticking out, his mouth flapping open, as he stared at the Jeep.

Gavin chuckled. "Somebody's going to be excited."

"I'd better grab the keys. He's going to want to go for a ride."

I sprinted for the house with a huge smile, bursting through the honey-oak front door and swiping my purse from the bench. When I hurried outside, Finn was pulling into the driveway beside the Jeep, leaving space for me to back out.

"Mom!" Max screamed from the truck as he scrambled to get his seat belt undone. "What? Is that— What?"

I laughed, rejoining Gavin in the driveway.

Kali popped open her door and hopped out, her brown curls bouncing as she landed. "Mom, is this ours?"

"It is."

"No. Way." Her eyes were huge as she took a step for the Jeep. "I just—this—no way."

"Yes way. Surprise."

"Wow." She ran her fingers through her hair. It hung nearly to her waist these days, about six inches shorter than mine. I'd been trying to get her to trim it but she refused. She said her curls set her apart in a school where most girls were doing undercuts or dying their hair shades of blue or pink.

"Ahhh!" Max ran around Finn's truck, jumping up and down as he pointed at the Jeep. "This is so cool. Can we take it for a drive? Right now? Please? Let's go."

"In a sec." I waved at Finn, the last to emerge from his truck. "Hi."

"Nice wheels, Molly." He pushed his aviators into his thick, rust-colored hair as he rounded the hood of his truck. "No more Beluga, huh?"

"No more Beluga."

His blue eyes found mine, and they flashed with sadness for a moment.

I wasn't sure what to say. Somewhere on the road from our first cheeseburger to signing the divorce papers, we'd forgotten how to confide in one another.

It was all ancient history now. I was happily single. Finn had been dating other women for years. Like Beluga, some things weren't meant to last forever.

"Hey, Gavin." Finn walked up to us, his hand extended.

"Finn." Gavin returned the handshake, then looked over at me. "I'll get out of your hair. I'm around this weekend if you change your mind about the lawn."

"Thanks." I waved at him as he walked across my yard to his own.

"What about the lawn?" Finn asked when he was out of earshot.

"Oh, nothing. He just offered to mow it for me."

Finn frowned. "Not an option. Look at his yard. He can't figure out how to adjust his blades or walk in a straight line. You mow ten times better than that guy."

"At least he offered to save me the headache."

"Headache? I thought you liked mowing."

"Once upon a time." When my life had been a fairy tale. Before the glass slippers had splintered.

"Mom, let's go." Max was racing circles around the Jeep. His wide smile showed the two teeth he was missing at the moment. He needed a haircut because it was constantly falling in his eyes, but I hated cutting his hair. I had ever since he was a baby.

It was a mixture of Finn's and mine. Not quite red, but not my brown either. It wasn't as curly as Kali's—there was only a slight wave—and it had the same texture as Finn's thick, silky strands. Whenever I cut it, he looked so much older.

"I'm hungry," he shouted, still running.

"When is he not?" I muttered. "He's growing like a weed."

Finn nodded. "I was thinking the same thing the other day. He'll stay here a few nights and then I hardly recognize him when it's my turn."

Max was one of the tallest kids on his youth basketball team, and his frame actually filled out his peewee football pads. There was no doubt about it, he'd grow up to have Finn's broad shoulders and chest. He'd be tall like Finn too.

Max's only trait that was one hundred percent mine was his eyes. Both he and Kali had my brown eyes.

Finn's deep blue irises were his and his alone.

"Mom," Max huffed, opening the back door. "Let's go."

"Okay, okay. Let's unload your stuff from the truck first so Dad doesn't have to wait around for us."

"No, that's okay." Finn jerked his chin to the Jeep. "You guys go. I'll unload."

"All right. Thanks. I'll shoot you a text about drop-off on Monday."

"Sounds good."

I'd nodded good-bye and had taken three steps for the Jeep when Finn called, "Molly?"

I turned. "Yeah?"

He smiled. "You always wanted a Jeep. I'm glad you have one."

"Me too." I waved, not letting my gaze linger on my ex-husband for too long.

Finn was wearing his normal summer attire of a navy Alcott Landscaping polo, jeans and gray tennis shoes. His clothes used to be covered in grass stains, his hands marred with dirt. He'd come home to me smelling like sweat and sunshine and we'd go at one another without hesitation.

Those days were just memories now. Still, he was danger-ously handsome, standing with his legs planted wide under-neath the bright May sky. It was a good thing the kids and I were driving away. Too much time with Finn and my mind would start to replay those old scenes, the ones where his lips felt so soft against mine.

"Ready?" I focused on the kids, who were jumping into the car. When we were all loaded and the windows rolled down, I reversed out of the driveway, giving Finn one last wave before driving away.

I caught his wave in the mirror as he stood in the yard that had once been ours.

We'd been divorced for six years and three months, and damn it, Finn still looked like he belonged in that yard. Like Beluga, that house was an artifact that should probably have been buried too. I wouldn't move the kids, so it was one burial that would wait until they were in college.

"Well? What do you guys think?" I asked them.

"This is so much cooler than the van," Max yelled out his open window behind me.

I glanced over my shoulder to find Kali's smile waiting. "It's cool, Mom."

*Score.* "It sure is."

"Let's get pizza," Max yelled. The kid didn't know any other volume besides loud.

I laughed and yelled too. "Pizza, here we come."

Forty-five minutes later, the sound of a lawn mower preceded us as we turned into the cul-de-sac.

"Oh, great." I really hoped Gavin hadn't decided to do me a favor and mow my lawn. Sure enough, as we got closer, freshly cut swaths in my lawn greeted me. But it wasn't Gavin mowing.

"Dad's still here." Kali pointed to Finn's truck.

I blinked, certain I'd pulled onto the wrong street. Finn hadn't mowed that lawn in years, even when we'd been married. Back then, work had demanded his full attention and he'd get home past dark most nights in the summer.

The mowing duty had always fallen to me.

But here he was, pushing my red mower in diagonal stripes across the grass. The Weed Eater was propped up against the garage door next to a pile of extension cords.

"What's he doing?"

"Uh, mowing the lawn." Max laughed. "Duh."

I rolled my eyes. "Thanks for clarifying, Max."

"Ask a stupid question, get a stu—"

"Don't say stupid." I was glad he couldn't see my smile from behind me.

My son was a smart-ass. He dished out comebacks faster and wittier than most adults. Teasing Finn and me was one of his greatest pleasures. The only person he was gentle with was Kali.

She didn't have his thick skin. Maybe it was because she was getting into those difficult teen years. Maybe it was because the divorce had been so hard on her. Whatever the reason, Kali was more sensitive these days. And I'd always been grateful that Max loved his big sister so much that he went out of his way to protect her soft heart.

"Can you guys take the pizza inside?" I asked Max and Kali as I parked in the garage.

"Sure, Mom," my girl volunteered.

"Thanks." I had to find out what their father was still doing here.

As they carried the boxes inside, I walked out front to find Finn.

His shoes were coated with grass clippings, ruined for anything fancier than manual labor now. He spun the mower around, coming in my direction. When he reached the end of that row, he stopped the machine, the noise settling.

"What are—"

"Hey, Dad." Max appeared at my side, a stolen breadstick in one hand and a huge bite in his cheeks. Kali was right behind him.

"Hey, guys. How was the ride?"

Max swallowed. "Sweet. Kali and I have our own screens so we don't have to watch the same thing."

Finn chuckled. "Did you like it, Kali?"

"Oh, yeah. Mom has the coolest car of any of my friends now."

I smiled. *Mission accomplished.* "Will you guys go inside and set the table, please?"

Their feet stomped up the porch steps before they burst through the door, not bothering to shut it behind them.

"You didn't have to do this," I told Finn.

He shrugged. "No big deal."

Who was this stranger? Well, whoever the Finn imposter was, I at least owed him dinner. "We got pizza. You're welcome to stay."

"That'd be great. I'll finish up out here and hit the back. Then I'll be in. You guys go ahead. Don't wait for me."

"If you want to just do the front, I can handle the back. Really."

"Molly, it's fine." His voice was soft, smooth like the spring breeze. "I had nothing to do tonight but go home to an empty house."

"Okay." My shoulders relaxed. I wasn't putting him out, and his help was much appreciated.

I left him to it, walking over to the porch steps and glancing over my shoulder as Finn tugged the pull cord and brought the mower's engine to life.

He'd dropped the kids' backpacks inside the door. I carried them down the hallway, leaving them at the base of the stairs before ducking into the dining room positioned off the kitchen.

"Good job, guys." Max was setting out glasses while Kali placed napkins. They must have assumed Finn was staying, because there were four plates already set.

It was nice to see the dining room table full. Having it empty three or four nights a week when the kids stayed at Finn's house was depressing. So much so, I usually ate standing in the kitchen or sitting on the living room couch.

Anywhere but the dining room table, where the five empty seats made me feel alone.

"Oh, shoot." I'd forgotten all about Gavin eating alone and my earlier plan to invite him over.

"What?" Kali asked.

"Never mind." With Finn here, it would be too awkward to have Gavin come over. I could stop next door and invite him to a different meal later in the week after I'd caught up with the kids.

I opened pizza boxes and we each took our seats to dive in. When Max reached for his sixth piece, I swatted his hand away. "Save some for your dad. If he doesn't eat it all, you can have the rest."

"Okay." He patted his belly. "I'm kinda full anyway. Do I have to eat the crusts?"

"No." Though in an hour, he'd be hungry again.

"Can I go to my room?"

"Sure." I winked. "Please take your backpack with you and get it unpacked."

"Thanks, Mom." He stood from the table, taking his plate with him to the sink. Then he bolted for the stairs.

"That kid doesn't walk anywhere, does he?"

Kali giggled. "Can I go too?"

"Sure, sweetheart. Do you have any homework?"

She shook her head as she stood, also clearing her plate. "No."

I stayed in my chair, watching as she put her plate and Max's into the dishwasher. She'd always been my helper. I knew she helped at Finn's place too.

"I'm glad you're home."

"Me too." She smiled and came over for a tight hug, then she disappeared upstairs to her room.

I cleared my own plate just as the mower's noise outside stopped. Through the kitchen window, I watched Finn come around the side of the garage and go to his truck. He toed off his grass-stained shoes and tossed them into the back. Then he did the same with his socks, which were green around the ankles. He bent down and swatted at the hems of his jeans, clearing away grass clippings before cuffing them in a tall fold.

My eyes dropped to his ass. Habit, I guessed. It still looked as good as it had when we'd been married. Finn hadn't let age or sitting behind a desk compromise his muscled physique.

I was still staring when he stood and turned, his eyes finding mine through the kitchen window. I dropped my chin, hoping that by the time he walked inside the blush in my cheeks would be gone.

Finn came inside and straight to the kitchen. "Did Max save me anything but the crusts?"

"I guarded a few slices for you," I said as I got him a glass of water.

"Thanks." He washed his hands, then we both sat at the table, him on one side of a corner, me on the other. The silence stretched for a few awkward moments. "So, uh, how is work?"

"Good." I plucked at a hair tie on my wrist. "It's been busy. We're already starting to see the summer tourists."

I had the best job in all of Bozeman, working with my best friend, Poppy, at the restaurant she'd started nearly six years ago.

The Maysen Jar had always been her dream. When her husband Jamie had died in a tragic shooting ten years ago, she'd lost her footing. But that restaurant had helped her regain her balance. And not long afterward, she'd opened her heart to a new love. She'd married Cole Goodman, a man who lived up to his name.

Maybe it was time for me to find love again. Since the divorce, I'd focused on my career and the kids. But as they got older, as work got easier, I had more and more lonely moments.

Gavin had asked me out on two different occasions. Timing hadn't worked out for either because I'd already had plans. Maybe it was time to stop living this single life and take a risk.

Maybe when I purchased the Jeep's replacement down the road in seven or eight years, I'd check a different marital status box on the application.

Though the idea of dating anyone made me queasy.

Finn didn't have that problem. He'd moved on and had been dating on and off for years. He'd been with his most recent girlfriend for about a year. *Brenna*. I didn't know much about her, because I'd made it a point to know little about his relationships. I asked questions to be civil, these women were spending time with my children after all, but nothing beyond the surface.

With Brenna, things were getting serious. Whenever Finn didn't have the kids, she was attached to his side. She was even friends with Poppy. There was a picture hanging in the restaurant's office of her and Finn playing board games at Poppy and Cole's house.

When Poppy had asked me if I'd minded that photo, I'd lied and told her no. It was her restaurant. Finn was her brother. How she chose to decorate her office was her choice.

And when that photo had gone up six months ago, I'd started doing my office work out of the office.

I'd accepted divorced life. I had a way to go to accept Finn's love life.

"What's Brenna up to tonight?" If Finn was mowing my lawn, she must have had plans.

He swallowed his bite of pizza, chasing it down with some water. "I don't know. We broke up last weekend."

"Oh." That was surprising. Maybe I shouldn't have asked. "Sorry."

Finn shrugged. "Don't be."

I almost asked Finn how he was feeling about it, but discussing his feelings had been nearly impossible when we'd been married, let alone divorced.

Instead, I asked, "How were the kids?" He'd had them for the past three days.

"Good." He grinned as he chewed. "They're always good. Max can't wait for school to be out next week. Kali doesn't want it to end."

I smiled. "Max just wants to do basketball camp. Kali doesn't want to go the whole summer without seeing her friends."

"She asked me if we could figure out a way for her to take swimming lessons with Vanessa."

"Okay. I'll call Vanessa's mom and get schedule information. We'll see if we can fit it in between all their camps." Summers were always chaotic, running the kids from one summer camp to the next while still trying to work.

"Just let me know what I can do to help coordinate." Finn tossed his uneaten crust onto his plate. Like Max, he didn't eat the crust unless he was on the verge of starvation.

I, on the other hand, never turned down the carbs. I held out my hand, palm up. He chuckled and slid his plate over so I could take the crust. I ate it while he ate another piece of pizza.

"More?" He held up another crust.

I shook my head. "I'm full. Thanks again for doing the

lawn." It would save me from the chore this weekend and give me more time to take the kids out exploring in our new Jeep.

"No problem. What are you guys doing this weekend?"

"Nothing much. I was thinking of planning something fun to do with the kids. Maybe take them up to Hyalite Lake or something. You?"

He sighed. "I'll probably just catch up at work. I'm behind on a couple of bids."

No surprise there. Finn worked constantly when the kids were with me.

"Mom," Max hollered from upstairs. "Can we watch a movie?"

"Sure," I called back.

I stood from the table and cleared Finn's plate as footsteps pounded down the wooden stairs and the kids came running into the kitchen.

Max frowned when he saw the empty pizza box on the table. "Can we make popcorn?"

I laughed, walking toward the pantry. "Yes, we can have popcorn."

"Dad, do you want to stay and watch with us?" Kali asked.

My hand froze on the doorknob as I waited for his answer. She probably felt bad now that he was single again. No doubt he'd told the kids about his breakup with Brenna.

Did I want Finn to stay? Not really. He'd had the kids for three days and it was my turn. But for their sake, I'd never make him leave.

Finn and I made it a point to plan certain activities for the four of us. We'd have the occasional dinner or take the kids on a special adventure like skiing or hiking. It was important to us both that the kids saw us getting along.

But I spent *days* preparing for those times. I braced myself for how hard it would be to pretend we were a whole family, even for only a few hours.

"Maybe," Finn answered Kali. "I need to talk to your mom for a minute."

"You guys go pick the movie," I told the kids. "Together, please. No fighting."

When they were out of the room, I grabbed the popcorn from the pantry and put it in the microwave.

"Would you mind if I stayed?" he asked.

"Not at all." It wasn't a complete lie. After three glasses of wine, I wouldn't care a bit that he was on the opposite end of the couch.

The popcorn began popping and I went to my wine rack, pulling out a favorite red.

"I'll do it." Finn stepped closer and I dodged out of the way so we wouldn't bump into one another.

We didn't touch. There were no hugs or kisses on the cheek. We smiled. We waved. But we never touched.

I slid the bottle across the counter and took out the corkscrew from a drawer. While he opened the bottle, I found glasses. He poured for us both. I shook the popcorn into a bowl, and the two of us walked into the living room, the one we used to share, to watch a movie with our kids on *my* leather sectional.

This was for them.

The key to a successful divorce, I'd found, was establishing boundaries. Like touching Finn, there were things I didn't allow myself to do.

I refused to enjoy the sound of Finn's laugh. I didn't spare him a glance when Kali snuggled into his side, his arm curling around her tight. I didn't pay any attention to his blue eyes as they tracked me on my repeated trips into the kitchen to refill my wine glass.

No, I watched the movie on *my* TV from *my* couch in *my* living room. I focused on drinking *my* wine.

Boundaries, that was the key. And an armored tank wasn't getting across mine.

---

The alarm on my phone was always loud and shrill at five thirty in the morning. Today it seemed exponentially worse. I shot up from bed, sitting so straight the blankets and sheet went flying.

"Ugh." My stomach rolled. My head was splitting in two, and my naked skin felt sticky.

I'd had way too much wi—

*Why the hell am I naked?* I didn't sleep naked. Ever.

Not since . . .

I jumped from the bed, my eyes wide as they landed on the long, muscular arm curved around one of my white down pillows. A head of tousled red hair was resting on another. A leg, dusted with that same hair, was tucked outside a sheet.

"Oh my God," I gasped as it all came rushing back. The movie. Finn carrying the kids to bed. Standing too close in the hallway. The simple brush of our hands.

The kiss.

The sex.

No. *No no no no no.*

So much for my boundaries.

*Damn you, wine.*

*Darling Molly,*

*This is why people don't write letters anymore. I feel like a douche. But here I am, in all my douche glory, writing you a letter I am never going to send.*

*I'm glad my sister was too into Jamie to notice us. I'm glad you like burgers with extra cheese and extra bacon. I'm glad you gave me your phone number.*

*I'm not sorry I've already called you twice just to hear your voice.*

*So since you're never going to read this, I guess it's safe to tell you I had the best date of my life with you tonight. I don't know if you'd call it a date. But I'm calling it a date.*

*Watch out, Molly Todd. I just might have to marry you.*

*Yours,*
*Finn*

# two
## Molly

I was scrambling around the side of the bed, racing for the bathroom, when my feet got tangled in something on the floor. My knees crashed onto the rug. My hair flew into my face as my arms shot out to catch my fall.

"Sonofabitch," I whispered, pushing the hair out of my face to see what had tripped me.

*Panties.* My feet were tangled in the panties I'd pulled on yesterday morning and Finn had ripped off last night.

I kicked my feet free, then scooped up the gray cotton briefs, balling them up in a fist. If Finn woke up before I made it to the bathroom, there was no way I wanted him inspecting my comfortable, sexless underwear. With them hidden, I hurried—more carefully this time—for the bathroom, collecting discarded clothing as I shuffled along.

At the door, I risked a glance over my shoulder. Finn was still asleep. No surprise. The man had slept like the dead when we'd been together. When the kids were newborns, I'd have to kick him repeatedly to rouse him for his feedings.

I shut the door to the bathroom, leaned back against the white paneled wood and breathed a sigh.

*I slept with Finn.*

This was a disaster. What the damn hell had I been thinking? Finn and I had spent years getting to a place of friendship. I was happily single, I bought my own car, and I ran my own life. I'd even considered dating again. *Why? Why am I so stupid?*

I was shaking when I pushed off the door. I threw my clothes in the hamper, then turned on the shower. I spent a few extra seconds breathing in the steam and my rosemary and mint shampoo. Neither helped calm my trembling.

"So stupid," I told the spray. "I'm not doing this again."

I wasn't getting mixed up in Finn. I wasn't a casual sex woman and certainly not with the man who'd once been my entire world. What had happened to my boundaries? They were there for a good goddamn reason.

When Finn and I had broken up, it had destroyed me.

"I'm not doing this again."

No. No, I wasn't. With a sure nod, I shut off the water and stepped out of the shower. I dried my body with angry strokes then secured the towel around my chest. I twisted up my hair and marched out of the bathroom.

"Finn, get up." I shook his shoulder, then whipped the comforter off his back.

"Huh?" He sat up, dazed, blinking. Then he dropped his head back into the pillow. "Five more minutes."

"Finn," I snapped, pulling the comforter down even farther before poking his side. "Get up and get out. You need to leave before the kids wake up."

I was going to forget about last night the second the door closed behind him. The kids would never be the wiser.

They'd had a hard time with the divorce, Kali especially. It had taken her years to understand that her parents lived separate lives and were never getting back together. She didn't need to see her father naked in her mother's bed.

"Finn." I poked him again. God, why was he such a deep sleeper? "Wake up."

"Molly, five more minutes." He lifted his sleepy eyes and blinked. Then they widened. "Fuck."

He leapt out of bed, hissing a string of curses as he scanned the floor for his clothes. When he found his jeans, he dove for them so fast he'd have rug burns on his knees.

I rolled my eyes. I'd had a similar reaction, but he'd been asleep. He could have at least tried to hide his mortification from me.

"What happened?" he asked as he zipped up his fly.

I glared at his flat stomach. Those abs were to blame for this mess. They'd always been my weakness. Last night, I'd touched one of the six and, well . . . here we were. Divorced men in their late thirties weren't supposed to have that V along their hipbones. How was that fair?

Finn's hair was a mess thanks to my fingers. The matching scruff on his jaw was no less sexy than his half-naked body. He searched the floor for his shirt, going to the bed and throwing up the covers. He ducked down to see where it had gone.

"Where's my shirt?" He found it under the bed before I could help him search, then he put it on faster than a human being had ever donned a piece of cotton.

I ignored the sting of that too, along with the fact that he wouldn't look me in the face.

He picked up his watch from the floor and took a step for the door, but then stopped to look back. "Molly—"

"You need to go."

He still wouldn't look at me. "We should—"

"Go, Finn. I don't want the kids to see you here."

He sighed, then nodded and walked to the door. His bare feet made no noise as he snuck out of the house. The sun was beginning to shine through my bedroom window.

The front door opened and clicked shut. Thankfully, my bedroom was on the main floor and the kids were upstairs. Then I waited, listening for his truck to start up and rumble down the road. When it was silent again, I sank down on the edge of my bed.

He was gone. We weren't going to talk about last night. We weren't going to discuss the monumental mistake of sex with an ex-spouse. We were going to pretend it had never happened.

Once my disheveled bed was put to rights, I'd take a Magic Eraser to last night's memory and scrub with fury. Those damn things worked on everything. Surely one would work on my brain.

But instead of ripping the sheets from the mattress, I sat frozen, staring at the pillows.

I still hadn't gotten rid of Finn's pillow. He'd ordered it online because it was supposed to be good for stomach sleepers. I thought it was too firm and too thin, but I hadn't been able to toss it out. I washed its case weekly. I fluffed it each morning.

It had been there for him to sleep on last night.

When Finn had moved out, he'd taken my side-sleeper pillow by mistake. It had been one of the mix-ups in the *his* and *hers* shuffle. Instead of mentioning it and making a swap, I'd stayed quiet. I'd kept his pillow and bought a new one for myself.

Stupid pillow. I snagged it and threw it on the floor. *Stupid Molly.*

How could I have brought that man back into this room? Prior to last night, his memory had finally faded, but now I'd have to start the forgetting process all over again. I'd have to retrain myself that sleeping alone was better than sleeping with company because you got more leg room. I'd have to un-remember how his hands felt on my skin and the weight of his hips between my thighs. Or how it felt to tangle my legs with his before drifting off to sleep, draped over his back.

*Delete. Delete. Delete.* What I wouldn't give for a mental backspace button.

It was yet another mistake to survive.

Starting with making the bed.

I picked up Finn's pillow and straightened the twisted sheets. Laundry would have to wait until the weekend, meaning I'd have to live with his manly scent for one more night. Maybe I'd sleep on the couch until I could do the wash. I would have to vacuum too. A few blades of grass had hitch-hiked into my room on his jeans.

This weekend, I'd clean it all away.

But first, I had to get through my Friday.

I finished the bed and hurried through my morning routine, getting dressed in a pair of jeans and burgundy tennis shoes. Then I chose a fitted T-shirt, one of many from my closet. Today's was white. The restaurant's emblem was printed on the chest pocket.

I took the time to put on a full face of makeup. I tamed my curls, brushing them out before spraying a leave-in conditioner that would keep the frizz at bay. With three hair ties on my wrist, I went upstairs to get the kids ready for school.

The familiarity of the morning routine eased most of my nerves and irritation. There wasn't much headspace to fret about Finn when I was shouting at Max to brush his teeth and at Kali to remember her library book as I made them breakfast. We all ate. We all put our dishes away. And we all marched outside to the Jeep.

"Did we forget anything?" I asked as they buckled into their seats. I scanned to make sure they had their backpacks and I had my purse.

Kali smiled. "Nope. And I have my library book."

"I didn't brush my teeth," Max admitted.

I sighed. "Then do it twice tonight."

"Okay." He nodded. "It was fun having Dad stay last night."

My heart jumped into my throat. There was no way he could have known that Finn had stayed *all* night. Was there? I searched his cute face for any sign that he was talking about more than pizza and the movie, but as the seconds wore on, he just stared at me like I'd gone crazy.

Kali spoke up first. "Uh, Mom. We're going to be late."

"Right." I spun around to the wheel, turning on the car and reversing into the street. "I want to grab the mail, then we're outta here."

"Can I get it?" Max asked.

"Sure." I pulled forward, close enough to the curb that Max could roll down his window.

He had to unbuckle to reach out and open up the mailbox's hatch. He leaned out and came back with a stack of envelopes and a catalog.

"Thanks." I took it from him and tossed it all onto the passenger seat as he got resituated.

The drive to school didn't take long with the kids chatting the entire way. We waited in the drop-off line, and when it was our turn, I waved as the kids hopped out and ran toward school. Kali shot me one last smile as she pointed out the Jeep to her circle of friends.

I inched forward. The line to turn out of the parking lot was always slow.

"And now, we wait." I frowned at the line of cars ahead and a green sedan with its left blinker on.

Next year, Kali would be going to middle school. I wasn't sure how early we'd have to leave the house to get Max here, wait in this atrocious line, then deliver Kali to her school seven blocks away.

But we'd make it work. That was the life of a single mom. We made the impossible happen daily.

The line was especially slow today, so I reached over to the stack of mail and brought it to my lap, thumbing through it as I crept forward.

It was mostly junk mail. Everything would be tossed into the trash except for one bill from the power company.

And a letter.

I turned the white envelope over in my hand. There was no return address. There wasn't a stamp. The handwriting on the front wasn't familiar. I slid my finger into the corner to tear open the top but stopped when a horn beeped behind me.

"Sorry," I said to the car behind me and drove ahead, getting out of the school's loop. Then I set off across town toward the restaurant.

As I drove, I continued to glance at the letter in my lap. I so badly wanted to open it, but I also wanted to arrive at work alive, so I waited, resisting the urge to dive in at a stoplight. Instead, I took one of the hair ties from my wrist.

My hair was so full and thick, I quickly stretched out the elastic ribbon I preferred to wear, which meant I had to keep a backup or two handy. I gathered up my curls and was in the middle of tying them into a bun when the neon-green band snapped.

*No.* My stomach dropped.

My grandma had died of a heart attack the day a hair tie

had broken. My car, the one before Beluga, had been side-swiped in the grocery store parking lot after a hair tie had broken. And Finn and I had signed our divorce papers the day a hair tie had broken.

There were other, more minor examples, but these broken hair ties had become an omen. On the days they didn't just stretch but actually broke, bad found me. God, I hoped today was just a flat tire or a shitty time at work.

My eyes dropped to the letter. Was it the bad thing headed my way?

The sinking feeling continued all the way to work, and the second I had the Jeep parked, I tore into the envelope.

The envelope's handwriting was unfamiliar. But the script of the actual letter was unmistakable. Finn was the only one who drew the first peak of the *M* in *Molly* that way.

Even with the college-ruled paper firmly in my grip, I had to read the letter twice before my brain registered it as real. The letter was short, only taking up about half a page.

Finn had written this fifteen years ago. He'd written me a letter after our first date and never sent it.


*I just might have to marry you.*


Those words jumped out even as I read them for a third and fourth time.

He'd married me, all right. He'd divorced me too.

How long had it been since I'd seen the name Molly Todd? How long had he kept this letter to himself? And why would he give it to me now?

My fingers dove into my hair. What was happening?

In a flash, my phone was in my hand and I'd pulled Finn's

name up on the screen. But I couldn't bring myself to call.

I wanted answers. But I wasn't ready to talk to Finn yet. Not after last night.

Instead, I tucked the letter into my purse and got out of the Jeep, heading into the restaurant.

The rear entrance to the restaurant was for employees only and it led right past the office and into the kitchen. I set my purse inside the office and came into the kitchen. Poppy was at the large stainless steel table in the center.

"Morning." She smiled, her hands covered in flour as she rolled out a large oval of pie crust.

"Morning."

"So? Tell me about last night."

My jaw dropped. "What? How did you know?"

*Damn it, Finn.* Couldn't he have kept last night to himself? Or at least have given me a warning that he was going to tell his sister we had sex?

Poppy gave me the side-eye. "Because you told me."

"I did?" Maybe I was still drunk from last night. "When?"

"Yesterday." She nodded. "We were sitting in the restaurant. You had your computer. We were drinking coffee while you showed me pictures of the Jeep before you went to the dealership."

"Oh, the Jeep." I smacked a palm into my forehead. "Sorry. Not enough coffee this morning. Buying the Jeep went great. The kids love it."

"Good." She went back to her dough. "What did you think I was talking about?"

"Nothing," I said too quickly. "Nothing at all."

"You're acting weird this morning."

"I'm not acting weird. I'm just here at work. Nothing weird about that. It's the un-weird."

Poppy blinked and her hands stilled. "The un-weird?"

"I'm having an off morning. Let's just leave it at that."

"Okay. If you want to talk, I'm here."

"I'm fine. Really. But thank you." I smiled. "So how has the morning been going?"

"Good. The coffee rush was busy, but it's pretty much died down so I came back to start on some potpies for lunch. Mom has the front covered if you want to keep me company. There's fresh coffee."

"Bless you." I hurried over to the pot and filled up one of the ceramic mugs we kept in the kitchen. They were enormous and reserved for staff. After it was full, I leaned against the side of the table, taking slow sips until I started to feel more human.

My wine hangover had been temporarily chased away during the *kick Finn out of my bed* fiasco. But now that the adrenaline was gone, my headache came roaring to life. Living with it would be my penance.

"Want some help?" I asked as she started cutting circles in the dough.

"No, drink your coffee and hang out with me." She used the back of her wrist to push a lock of red hair off her cheek. The florescent lights of the kitchen always seemed to make her blue eyes even brighter.

Our restaurant T-shirts matched today, but she'd covered hers up with an apron that her kids had made her last Christmas. Tiny green and red handprints had been pressed into the cream canvas with *MacKenna* and *Brady* written beneath.

She smiled more when she wore that apron. Though, Poppy Goodman smiled almost constantly these days. She deserved every ounce of joy she'd found with Cole and their kids.

Poppy had endured enough heartbreak.

"I received a confirmation email from the newspaper

yesterday that they're going to do the feature for the anniversary celebration," I told her.

"Perfect. And that was the last item on your checklist, so we should be all set."

The Maysen Jar was turning six next month and we'd been planning our annual anniversary celebration for months.

It was hard to believe six years had passed since Poppy had turned this building into one of Bozeman's most popular cafés. Once an old mechanic's garage, this place was now widely known for delicious food served only in mason jars.

The Maysen Jar was named after her late husband, Jamie Maysen, who'd been murdered in a liquor store robbery eleven years ago. The anniversary of his death had been a couple weeks ago.

When he'd died, it had shattered us all.

I'd never known such darkness could take over a human being until I saw what Jamie's death did to Poppy. But she'd put her broken pieces back together by finishing Jamie's birthday list. To honor his memory, she'd done the things he'd wanted to do most. Along the way, she'd met Cole and he'd filled the cracks in her heart.

Poppy's last name wasn't Maysen anymore, but because of the sign on the front of this building, Jamie's name lived on. And every year, we celebrated the place where so much healing had begun.

For me, The Maysen Jar had been my life raft.

Finn and I divorced just months before the restaurant opened. In the weeks before we signed our papers, Poppy begged me to work with her as the café manager.

I clung to the job, and it kept me emotionally afloat as I adjusted to a new way of life.

Six years later, we were more profitable than I'd ever

imagined, and it would stay that way. For Poppy. For Jamie. For me.

This restaurant wasn't only a job. It was my safe place.

On the lonely nights when I didn't want to go home to an empty house because the kids were with Finn, I stayed here, visiting with customers or the part-time staff. On the days when I needed an extra hug, my best friend was right here with open arms. When I needed to give my brain a workout, there were always spreadsheets and graphs waiting with new challenges.

As manager, I oversaw every aspect of this business, and in six years, I'd created a well-oiled machine. Poppy took care of the menu and preparing the food, but I did all the ordering and budgeting for supplies. I was in charge of finances, marketing and social media. I hired, fired and supervised the employees. I was a waitress. A barista. A dishwasher. An administrator.

I did whatever had to be done so Poppy could focus on her passion: the food that brought people in the front door.

She'd even won an award for Bozeman's best restaurant last year.

In the beginning, the two of us had put in crazy hours, but we'd learned to delegate. She came in around six or six thirty weekday mornings to open by seven. Then she left to get her kids by three. Since Kali and Max were older and had after-school activities, I came in around eight and stayed until five. If the kids were with Finn, I'd stay and close down after eight.

Lunch was our busiest time, so Poppy and I made it a point to both be here. But we'd built a solid foundation to give us the flexibility to put our families first.

Our staff of two college kids and Poppy's mom, Rayna, covered the hours when we were home.

Rayna had been a chef in Alaska, where Finn and Poppy

had grown up. But eventually, the draw of grandchildren had been too much. She and David, her husband, had moved to Montana. She came into the restaurant most days to be with Poppy and because she simply loved to cook. She still made me my birthday cookies every year because she knew how much I loved them.

Even after the divorce, Rayna had kept me close. It was her nature to pull people into her circle and never let them go. And I think it was because she'd never really accepted that Finn and I were through.

But we were. We were through. So why had he given me that letter? Last night was fuzzy, but I did remember he'd been the first one to make a move. He'd started that kiss.

"Are you sure you're okay?" Poppy asked. "You're quiet this morning."

I looked over my shoulder and smiled. "I'm fine. Just tired and I have a headache. Unless you think they need me out front, I think I'll disappear into some spreadsheets in the office for a while."

"Go. Be with your precious numbers."

"Excel formulas are to me what fresh produce is to you." I gave her a smile and took my coffee into the office, closing the door behind me, because I wanted to read Finn's letter one more time.

I retrieved it from my purse and opened it carefully. Finn's handwriting hadn't changed much since college. My fingers skimmed the words written on the paper, touching them, as my eyes tracked from left to right.

That first date had been a whirlwind. We'd laughed for hours, talking about old dating customs. He'd teased me for wanting letters and being old-fashioned. Yet he'd gone home that night and written me one.

Why? Why hadn't he given it to me then? Why had he

sent it to me now?

Did I want those answers? Every cell in my being screamed *no*. Those answers terrified me. They'd rip open the scars that had finally healed.

If I could time travel, I'd reverse an hour and lump this letter in with the junk mail.

Because I hated this letter. I hated that I loved it. It was too strong a reminder of how good things had been. Maybe if we'd kept the happy memories closer to the surface, we wouldn't have sunk so deeply into the bad.

Somewhere along the way, Finn and I had lost that spark.

We'd lived together. We'd loved our children together. But we hadn't *been* together.

For a year, we'd fought constantly. We'd bickered endlessly. We'd tolerated each other, both of us waiting for the storm to pass. It hadn't. The thunderstorm had turned into a hurricane . . . and then we had the fight to end all others.

That fight started, ironically, with my lawn mower. I'd been outside cutting the lawn after putting the kids to bed. I'd had their monitors clipped to the waistband of my jeans. But I hadn't heard Kali sneak out of her bed.

After mowing the grass in near darkness, I went inside to find Kali in the kitchen, where she'd eaten an entire bag of chocolate chips. She puked for an hour.

Finn came home to find me holding back her hair as she wretched into the toilet. He blamed me for not being inside with the kids. I blamed him for not getting home from work in time to mow the lawn. Seething had turned into snapping. Snapping had turned into shouting.

After Kali finally went back to sleep, Finn and I had it out. We decided on a break. That night, he moved into the loft at his office.

I asked him to go to marriage counseling. He agreed but never showed up to a single session.

My life spiraled. I became a woman lost without her marriage as an anchor. And one night, when my hope in Finn and our relationship had been truly slaughtered, I drove the final nail into our coffin.

I made a mistake I'd always regret. I got drunk at a friend's bachelorette party.

I had sex with another man.

The next day, I told Finn the truth. I told him how I was at rock bottom. That I loved him and desperately wanted to revive our marriage. I begged him for forgiveness.

He told me to get a lawyer.

Honestly, I probably would have said the same. Some mistakes were unforgiveable. Some mistakes came with a regret that lived like a monster in your soul.

I shook myself into the present, shoving that monster way down deep. All of that drama was ancient history now. Finn and I were divorced. He was happier that way. So was I.

Except with his letter in my hand, it was hard not to question every day since. We'd had so much love. How did we get here? How did we get all the way from that letter to us now?

The rock in my gut told me there was only one thing to do.

The letter had to go. I tightened my grip, ready to crumple it into a tiny wad, but my fingers lost their strength.

"Fine." I refolded the letter and jammed it into my purse. I wouldn't throw it away, at least not yet. Instead, I'd return it to Finn.

I'd return it and remind him that our marriage was dead. Those happy times were dead.

And there was no use stirring up old ghosts.

# three
## Finn

Hours after I'd been kicked out of Molly's bed, I walked into The Maysen Jar, scanning the open room for her. But she must have been in the back with Poppy because it was just Mom at the espresso machine. I crossed the room to the black marble counter at the back.

"Hey, Mom."

"Finn." She smiled over her shoulder. "What a nice surprise. Give me one minute to finish up this latte."

"Take your time." As she went back to steaming milk, I slid into a stool next to Randall, one of the regulars at the restaurant. "Morning."

The old man jerked up his chin but didn't return my greeting. His cane was propped in the space between our stools. His gray driving cap rested on his knee.

"How are you?"

All I got was a one-shoulder shrug.

Randall didn't like me much. I didn't take it personally, because Randall James didn't like anybody much except for Poppy and Molly. He gave them a hard time constantly, griping that the background music was too loud or the lights were too bright. Any bullshit complaint he could dream up. He bitched and moaned because they limited the number of apple pies he could have in a day, but he loved them.

He'd been their first customer, barging into The Maysen Jar before it had even opened. And to my knowledge, he'd been here nearly every day since.

Randall sat in the same stool every day, one that Poppy and Molly had marked reserved so no one else would dare sit there. They didn't want customers to face his grumpy wrath. The seat on his right was also reserved, that one for Jimmy. He and Randall did everything together, including pretend they were archenemies.

"Morning, Finn," Jimmy greeted.

"Hi, Jimmy. How are you today?"

"Doing just fine. Be better if the Rockies could hire a damn pitcher."

Randall scoffed. "They don't need a pitcher. What they need are a couple of players who can hit the damn ball."

Jimmy rolled his eyes. "Do you know anything about baseball?"

"Clearly more than you if you think the Rockies have any hope of a winning season with their lineup."

Jimmy twisted in his seat, glaring at Randall as the two prepared for one of their daily showdowns.

Today's was baseball. Tomorrow would be the stock market. I'd been here a few weeks ago when the pair had shouted at one another about which smell better represented Montana: juniper bushes or sage brush.

Molly had been the one to break up that fight, threatening to revoke their second-dessert-free privilege if they didn't shut the hell up.

It was coincidence that had brought Jimmy and Randall

together. The two of them lived at The Rainbow, a local retirement home. When Randall had started coming to The
Maysen Jar, he hadn't known that his neighbor Jimmy was a
relative of its owner.

Jimmy was Poppy's grandfather-in-law. He'd been Jamie's
grandpa and had stayed close to Poppy after Jamie's death.
Since Jimmy didn't drive and Randall did, they came to the
restaurant together each morning. They'd drink coffee and
eat and bicker. My theory was they both lived to piss the
other off.

Poppy loved having them, not only because they were a
part of her family, but because they provided free entertainment for the restaurant's patrons.

Owning a restaurant had been Poppy's childhood dream
and The Maysen Jar was exactly her style. It wasn't big. She'd
bought an old, two-stall mechanic's garage and converted it
into a warm, open and thriving café.

The cement floors, which had been covered in oil
splotches, were hidden underneath a hickory herringbone
wood floor. The actual garage bay doors had been ripped out
and replaced with floor-to-ceiling black-paned windows. I
wasn't sure how many buckets of grime and grease she'd
cleaned away.

If I hadn't seen the original, I wouldn't have believed this
place was once a garage. She'd transformed it, only keeping
the original exposed red brick walls and leaving the tall,
industrial ceilings open. Black tables and chairs filled the
room. The counter at the back was the home base where
people could order coffee or meals from the display case.

It was trendy without being hip. It was classic without
being stuffy. It was Poppy mixed with an undercurrent of
Molly.

Molly's touch was everywhere, probably only noticed by

me. It was in the way the menu cards were stacked neatly by the register. How underneath this counter, the shelves were organized with bins and containers for silverware rolls or extra napkins. How the tables were arranged so the center aisle was wide enough to walk down with a bussing bin propped on a hip.

That was Molly. She put others first, and here, others meant Poppy, employees and customers.

She'd set up this business as best as possible to ensure Poppy's success. Molly had done the same for Alcott Landscaping when we'd started it together. Back when it had just been her, me and a couple of lawn mowers. She had an eye for efficiency and had helped our business take off.

Molly had a gift for keeping things organized, yet relaxed and fun. She infused love and family into everything she did. Alcott had lost a touch of that lately.

More than a touch, if I was being honest.

"Okay." Mom came back around the corner from delivering the finished latte. "What can I get for you?"

"I'd take a coffee."

"You got it." Without asking for specifics, Mom whipped me up my favorite caramel latte. I wouldn't tell Mom this, but Poppy's version was better. "So, what are you doing here? I thought you'd be at work."

"Just wanted to stop in and say hello. I had a slow morning."

I was lying through my teeth. My to-do list was growing faster than wet grass on a sunny day, but work was impossible for me at the moment.

After leaving Molly's, I'd gone home to shower and change. Then I'd gone into the office, hoping to get ahead for the day. I'd spent an hour staring at the screensaver on my computer while images of last night had run through my mind.

Her long hair on those white pillows. *My* white pillow. The smooth skin of her thighs caressing my hips. The tickle of her fingers as she ran them up and down my spine.

My cock twitched just thinking about sinking inside her again.

What the hell had we been thinking? It had been so long and fuck, I'd missed sex with Molly. It was so easy and natural. The years fell away as we drifted into that familiar dance.

I'd gotten lost in her last night.

No matter how many days or months or years went by, Molly was still unforgettable. The best I'd ever had. The way she felt beneath me, her fingernails digging into my shoulder blades as I rocked us into oblivion, was like nothing else in the world.

That meant something, didn't it? That we'd been just as good last night as we had all those years ago? It shouldn't mean anything. We were divorced. It was just damn good sex. That was all. Right?

Bottom line? Too much had happened to destroy our relationship. There were other things from the past that were unforgettable.

And unforgiveable.

"Finn." Mom waved her hand in front of my face.

I blinked. "What?"

"I asked if you wanted some breakfast to go with your latte."

"Oh, um, sure. Overnight oats, please."

"Are you all right?" She walked down to the refrigerated display case and took out the jar for me. "You look tired."

"I just got up early."

"You work too hard." Mom sighed. "When was the last time you took a vacation?"

"It's been a while."

Brenna had planned my last vacation. She'd begged me to spend a weekend skiing at Big Sky this past winter. The *maybe* I'd given her had been interpreted as a yes, and she'd taken it upon herself to plan the whole thing.

Brenna had booked a romantic weekend away for us at a local ski resort. Except somehow our wires had gotten crossed, because it had turned out to be my weekend with the kids. Our romantic weekend had turned into a weekend with *only* me and the kids because Brenna had pouted and gone back to Bozeman.

Max, Kali and I'd had a blast skiing and staying up late in the pool.

That had been the second time she'd gotten annoyed about me having the kids on a weekend. The third time had been last weekend, when she'd wanted to sleep over but I'd told her no because the kids were there.

She'd thrown a fit, so I'd called it off.

I didn't have a place in my life for a woman who didn't want to spend time with my kids. A woman who couldn't respect that I wasn't ready for certain things in our relationship. It wasn't entirely her fault but I'd made my position clear. She'd chosen to ignore me.

"Finn." Mom placed her hand over mine. "You are all over the place today. Take a vacation. Please. Work will always be there."

"I know. I'm cutting back."

She frowned. "Really?"

"I'm trying to cut back," I admitted.

"Try harder."

She'd said the same thing to me almost every week since she and Dad had moved to Bozeman. It was wonderful to have them closer, especially for the kids, but they had a lot more insight into my life.

And Mom—much like Jimmy and Randall, who were still arguing next to me—didn't hold back her opinions on my lifestyle. Dad didn't either.

They thought my business had caused a rift in my marriage that had eventually led to complete and utter destruction.

I didn't agree. Sure, I'd gotten busy, but I'd been providing for our family. Molly knew that too.

My phone buzzed in my pocket—a text from my land-scape designer, Bridget. She was having trouble figuring out a retaining wall for a property we were landscaping along the Gallatin River. I thumbed through the pictures she'd sent and texted back a couple ideas.

Then I dove into my breakfast and sipped my latte before it got cold. "Is Molly here?"

I hoped my question came across as casual, not the reason I'd come in here today. The last person who needed to know I'd had sex with Molly last night was my mother.

"I haven't seen her yet, but she's probably in the back with Poppy."

I swallowed the last drink of my latte and pushed up from my stool. "I'm going to head on back there then. I need to talk to her about something."

"Everything okay with the kids?" she asked.

My family knew that Molly and I didn't do much anymore but talk about the kids. Our once-epic relationship had been reduced to conversations about pickups, drop-offs and the kids' nights at her place versus mine.

"Kali and Max are great. I just need to visit with her about some schedule stuff."

It was worth the lie. The truth would send Mom into a tizzy. She'd get her hopes up that Molly and I might reconcile. Worse, she'd get Poppy's hopes up.

My sister had lived through enough heartache, so she didn't need to be on the roller coaster that was Molly and me.

That ride had ended.

I pushed through the swinging door that separated the kitchen from the restaurant and found Poppy at her workstation, pressing circles of pie crust into miniature glass jars.

"Hey."

"Hey." She looked up, her hands covered in flour. "What are you doing here?"

I shrugged, sticking with the same lie I'd told Mom. "I had a slow morning at work."

"Did you get breakfast?"

I nodded. "Mom fed me."

Since the divorce, everyone's top concern was my meals. Even though I'd taught myself how to cook—and pretty damn well—I was constantly given casseroles and frozen meals to reheat. It hadn't gone unnoticed that they showed up the night before the kids were with me.

But the kids and I loved Poppy's and Mom's cooking, so I hadn't put a stop to it.

"Is Molly here?" I asked.

"She's in the office."

"Thanks. I'm going to sneak back there." Leaving her to the pies, I went to the office, rapping my knuckles on the door before going inside.

Molly was at the desk behind a laptop. Her eyes widened as I walked inside. "What are you doing here?"

I closed the door behind me. "Well, you kicked me out before we could talk this morning, so —"

"There's nothing to discuss." She crossed her arms over her chest. "It was a one-time lapse in judgment."

"Yeah. I guess." She was completely right, but her words didn't settle with me.

I walked over to the wall Poppy had covered in corkboard squares so she could pin up a ton of pictures. I wasn't ready to turn tail and leave this conversation, but I also needed a few moments because I had no idea what else to say.

Most of the pictures on Poppy's wall were of her and Cole and their kids. There were some of me. Some of Molly. There were even a few from college, when Molly and I had been inseparable, when there hadn't been a party we all hadn't attended together.

When Jamie had been alive.

Damn, I missed that guy. I bet he'd tease the hell out of Molly and me for hooking up last night.

I wasn't sure how Poppy could come in here and see his picture. It gutted me every time I saw his face and remembered he was gone. I still remembered his mother's scream the night I'd called to tell his parents that their son had been murdered.

I forced my eyes away from a photo of Jamie sitting behind Poppy on a snowmobile. I scanned more photos, hoping Molly would be the one to break the silence.

I smiled at MacKenna's and Brady's faces. Even though she'd had a horrific few years, Poppy had made it through and was happier than ever with Cole by her side. With those two beautiful kids.

My smile dropped when I landed on a more recent photo. I hadn't been in here for months, but now I wished I'd stopped in the back more often. The picture was of Brenna and me playing board games at Poppy and Cole's place. It didn't belong on this board.

Why would Poppy put that up on her wall? She hadn't even liked Brenna that much. Maybe it was her way of telling me that she'd been trying to get to know my girlfriend.

It didn't matter now. I yanked on the bottom of the picture, tearing it free from its pin, then I crumpled it up in one hand and tossed it in the trash can next to the desk. When I looked at Molly, her brown eyes were waiting.

"I'm sorry about your breakup," she said gently.

"It's fine."

"Is that why you stayed for dinner last night? Because you were upset?"

"What? No. Things with Brenna haven't been going well for a while. Like I told you, it was time."

"You seem upset."

I ran my hand over my jaw. "I'm not upset."

"Well you just killed that picture. It seems like you're upset."

"I'm *not* upset."

"It's okay if you are."

*Fuck.* Would this woman ever listen to me? "I'm not upset!"

My voice bounced off the walls and I immediately regretted raising my voice.

Molly scowled, then turned back to her laptop. "Fine. I'm busy. I know you probably are too. Since there isn't anything else to discuss, you should probably get back to work."

"Kicking me out again?"

She pursed her lips, positioning her hands over the keyboard. "I'll have the kids call you before bedtime. Thanks again for mowing my lawn last night."

That fucking lawn. What a disaster it had turned out to be. I blamed it for getting us into this position.

"Molly." I sighed. "I'm sorry. I just . . . I'm not upset about Brenna. Really. I'm sorry I yelled."

"I don't want to fight, Finn."

"Neither do I." We'd done enough of that while we'd been married. "I'm off this morning. Last night was, well, I don't know."

"It was a mistake."

"Was it?"

Her eyes snapped to mine. "What do you mean?"

"Was it a mistake?" I'd been wrestling with that question for hours.

"We're *divorced*. Divorced people shouldn't be having sex with one another. It's too complicated."

"It didn't feel complicated."

She blinked at me, her mouth falling open. "What are you saying?"

"I don't know. I just know that last night was the best I've slept in years. And not just because I missed my pillow."

The corner of her mouth turned up. "I couldn't get rid of that pillow. I thought about it, but I just couldn't."

"I'm glad you didn't."

"Maybe you should take it with you. That way you'll have it at home."

*Home.*

The image that popped into my head at that word was *her* house, not mine. The place I'd lived for the past five and a half years had never felt like home. Taking my pillow wasn't going to change that feeling.

*Has another man slept on my pillow?* That thought hit me hard and fast, sinking like a rock in my stomach. The kids hadn't mentioned Molly dating anyone since our divorce.

Poppy certainly hadn't told me. But maybe Molly was hiding it. Maybe she'd had someone else in her life and I'd never even known.

Was it Gavin?

Had he mowed her lawn, then spent the night? I wouldn't let myself think of Molly with another man, her neighbor included. *The* other man, the only other one I knew about, was hard enough to live with. I'd spent years trying to block out visuals of another man's lips on her neck, his fingers in her hair.

If another guy had slept on that pillow, I sure as fuck didn't want it back.

"Keep the pillow."

"Okay." She dropped her gaze to her lap and picked at a fingernail. This was what Molly did when she was thinking her words through, so I braced. Normally this was when she said things I didn't want to hear. "I don't know what happened last night."

"You don't remember?" That was a blow to the ego. We'd both had quite a few glasses of wine, but she hadn't been blackout drunk, and I thought I'd done a pretty good job of making her toes curl.

"No. I remember what happened. I just don't know *why* it happened."

"I don't either." I walked to the desk and sat on the edge. "Were you lonely?"

"Yes," she admitted. "Were you?"

"Yes."

"Okay. Then I guess we were two lonely people having sex to feel a connection to another person." I hated the sound of that. It was not the right explanation.

Molly grimaced. "That sounds pathetic."

"I was thinking the same thing."

"Gah." Molly's fingers dove into her hair, pulling at the roots. It was her telltale sign a rant was coming. "What are we doing? We were finally figuring things out. Getting into a routine with the kids. Being around one another without fighting. Things have been so much easier lately. You even mowed my lawn. It's almost like we've been . . ."

"Friends."

Molly dropped her hands from her hair, which then fell over her chest as her shoulders collapsed forward. "Did we just undo six years and three months of hard work?"

*Six years and three months.* She'd been keeping track of how long it had been since the divorce. So had I.

"I don't have a good explanation for last night," I told her. "It happened. I'm not sorry for it. But I don't want things to be awkward between us."

"Me neither. I can't take it. Neither can the kids. I think the best thing is to forget it ever happened."

Forget? Not likely. At least not anytime soon. But for Molly, and for our kids, I could pretend it never happened. "Okay. If you think that's best."

"Well, don't you?"

"I, uh . . . yeah. Yeah, that's best."

Wasn't it? We were finished. So, yes. It was for the best.

My phone buzzed in my pocket again. The day at Alcott Landscaping was well underway. It was time for me to be a part of it. "I'd better let you get back to work."

"Yep." She nodded. "I'm sure you've got a lot happening too."

"See you Monday night?"

"I'll bring the kids over after I pick them up from school."

"Then chaos starts the following week."

She blew out a long breath. "This summer is going to be crazy."

The kids had one activity lined up after another to keep them busy so we could both work. Kali was registered for five weeklong camps over the three-month school break. Max had four. Only two of them overlapped on the same week, which meant Molly and I would be chauffeuring kids all over the county.

Meanwhile, it was the busiest time of year for Alcott Landscaping.

"I don't see a lot of sleep in my future."

It was a joke, but Molly didn't laugh. "I can keep the kids longer if you need to work. I know things are crazy in the summers."

"No, it's fine. I was joking."

"Were you?"

"Yes." No matter how much happened, my time with the kids was sacred. I'd work longer hours when they were at home with Molly.

"Okay. I know they'd hate to miss time with you."

"I'd miss them too." I already hated the nights we were apart. "So, see you Monday?"

"Monday."

I stood from the desk and walked to the door, waving good-bye as I opened it.

But before I could go back into the kitchen, Molly said, "Wait, Finn. There's something else."

I turned back. "Yeah?"

She opened her mouth to say something but stopped. Her eyes dropped to her purse as she studied it for a moment.

"Why did you leave that . . ."

I waited but she just kept staring at her purse. "Why did I leave what?"

Before she could answer, my sister's voice carried down the hallway. "Finn!"

"Yeah," I called back.

"Mom wants to know what she should send home with you tonight for dinner."

I rolled my eyes. "I don't need anything."

"If you don't choose, she will."

"Fine. Give me one minute." I turned back to Molly. "I know how to cook. I'm actually pretty decent."

She pulled in her lips, holding back a smile.

"What? I am. Ask the kids. Kali said the spaghetti I made for them this weekend was my best yet."

"I'm sure it was your best."

"Thanks." I turned for the door but backpedaled. "Wait. Do you know something? Do the kids not like my cooking?"

"I think they *like* it just fine. I think they *love* their aunt Poppy's chicken potpies and their grandma's tater tot casserole."

"Fair enough. I'll load up on their favorites for next week." I tried again to leave the office, but I stopped. "You were asking me something?"

"Was I?" She shrugged. "I guess I forgot."

"Are you sure?"

"I'm sure. Thanks for coming down today. It's nice to clear the air."

"You're welcome. Later."

She nodded. "Bye."

I walked out of the office, feeling better than when I'd come in. The air had been cleared. It was done. Molly and I would go back to the way things were.

Tonight, I'd be sleeping in my own bed with my own pillow.

Well, not exactly my own. It was Molly's. In a weak moment, I'd taken hers with me during the divorce, not wanting to forget the smell of her fancy shampoo.

My feet paused. *She kept my pillow. And I kept hers.*

Six years was a long time for a pillow.

What did *that* mean?

Nothing. It meant nothing. It meant we were both too lazy to buy new pillows.

Didn't it?

# four
## Molly

Poppy and I each took a stool at the stainless steel table in the kitchen. After Finn had left earlier, I'd finished my office work then gone to work at the counter. The restaurant's noon rush was over, and like we did most workdays, Poppy and I grabbed a salad from the fridge to eat together once things had died down.

Randall and Jimmy had left not long ago, heading back to The Rainbow for the rest of the day. I'd heard rumblings of a poker game with some of their other neighbors followed by a couple of hours enjoying Jimmy's HBO subscription.

Rayna had also gone for the day, handing over counter coverage to Dora, our newest employee, who worked part-time for us while she went to school at Montana State. She'd caught on fast, so Poppy and I were leaving her on her own more and more these days.

I poured my salad dressing into the jar of vegetables, rescrewed the lid then shook the hell out of it. This was the best part of eating salad, even though Poppy's were delicious. It was just that her macaroni and cheese was phenomenal. But I saved that for special occasions—and today was not one

—so I dumped my mixed salad onto my plate and lifted my fork.

"Is everything okay between you and Finn?" Poppy asked the question I'd been expecting all morning. "When he closed the door to the office, I was worried you were fighting."

"It's good. We had to work out a few things with the schedule." It wasn't entirely a lie. We had agreed that his schedule would never again include sleeping at my house. "He actually mowed my lawn yesterday."

"Who? Finn?" Her eyes widened. "That was, um, nice. Especially since he didn't do it when you were married."

I shoved a bite of salad into my mouth to hide a smirk. Poppy was possibly more irritated with Finn's behavior as a husband than I was. She'd held on to that resentment for longer too, whereas I'd let it go—mostly.

"It was great not to do it for a change," I told her. "It was either find the time or take Gavin up on his offer to do it for me."

"Gavin wants to mow your lawn?" Poppy smiled as she forked some greens and wagged her eyebrows. "You should let him."

"I'm blaming Cole's influence for all the innuendo you've been dropping lately. He's corrupted my sweet, demure friend," I teased.

"He has corrupted me." She smiled. "In the best possible way. Now I want someone to come along and corrupt you."

"Nope." I shook my head as I chewed. "I have a good life. I'm happy. No corruption needed, thank you very much."

"On the days you have the kids, you are. But on the days when they're with Finn . . ." She trailed off as she took another bite.

"I'm happy even on the days when the kids are with Finn." Happy. *Lonely.*

"Gavin seems like a nice guy."

"He is nice."

He'd come into the restaurant every now and then to say hello, and Poppy had been pulling for him since the beginning. She thought his goatee and tortoise-shell glasses were sexy.

"Why don't you give him a chance?" she asked.

"Maybe." Last night, I'd considered dating again, but then I'd had sex with Finn and remembered I didn't have time to deal with this kind of drama. Not that I could share that with Poppy. "Timing hasn't worked out with Gavin. We'll see how I feel if he asks me out again."

She rolled her eyes. "You can ask him out."

"No." I scoffed. "Never happening. The guy asks out the girl."

It was one of those things I'd been hung up on since I was a teenager. Maybe because of my parents' conservative upbringing, but I liked the idea of a man courting a woman. I liked it when the man took charge and went out on a limb to show the woman he was interested. When he jumped out of his comfort zone because she was worth the risk.

The letter in my purse popped into my mind.

I should have asked Finn about the letter. *Why didn't I?* It had been right on the tip of my tongue, but I'd chickened out and swallowed it back.

Ignorance was bliss, right? Knowing why he'd sent the letter now, why he hadn't sent it back then, was guaranteed to sting. The truth was, I didn't have the guts to bear that pain.

After we'd divorced, things between us were strained for months. Finn was so angry at me, rightly so, that he wasn't able to look at me. He spoke to me only when absolutely necessary. We moved around each other like magnets turned the wrong way, pushing instead of pulling.

Then one night he came over to talk.

It was right after Poppy had started dating Cole. My theory was that he'd finally stopped punishing me because she'd inspired him.

Poppy had found happiness after heartbreak, and Finn wanted that too. He admitted to being an asshole since the divorce and confessed he was tired of the animosity. *I'm ready to let it go*, he said.

I remember holding my breath as he spoke that night. I sat on the couch, stupidly thinking for a few blissful seconds that he wanted to get back together. That the next words out of his mouth would be he still loved me, *he forgave me*, and he wanted to put our family back together.

Nope. He wanted to date again. To move on, like Poppy had. She'd found love after Jamie had died. She'd found Cole.

He wanted new love too. If I'd had any oxygen left in my lungs, those words would have stolen the rest. The tiny shards of my broken heart had turned to dust, because he'd wanted closure.

Was the letter another piece of his quest for closure?

Finn would never forgive me for having a one-night stand with another man. He'd made it clear that he was looking for the next Mrs. Alcott, not at the former.

My guess was this letter was another mechanism for him to put things to rest. To dissolve everything Finn and Molly.

I didn't need or want Finn to spell it out for me, so along with last night, I was pretending that letter had never happened. If Finn had something to say, he could be the one to bring it up, not me.

"Will you make me a promise?" Poppy asked.

"I don't like the sound of this."

She giggled. "Please say yes if and when Gavin asks you out. Say yes if any guy asks you out. I want you to be happy, Molly-moo."

"Ooof. Pulling out the big guns." She must be really worried about me if she was using the nickname she'd given me our freshman year in college. "The last time you whipped out the Molly-moo was when you needed me to take the kids so you and Cole could disappear to go 'skiing' in Big Sky and not actually leave your hotel room."

She laughed. "That was a *really* good weekend. And I recall getting a Poppy-bear when I was hesitating to eat my first dinner with Cole."

"Remember that, do you?"

"Maybe Gavin isn't *the* guy. But he is *a* guy. And you haven't been on a single date since the divorce."

"I don't need to date to be happy. I love that you want me to find a relationship again, but I don't know if I've got the energy for one right now."

"You're lonely, Molly."

"I am not—"

"And before you lie to me, remember that I'm not just your best friend, I'm your sister. Divorced from Finn or not, you are my sister, so I notice things. I notice how you work here from open to close on the days when Finn has the kids. I notice how you go to movies alone. I notice that you haven't gone out for drinks since *that* night."

No, I didn't go to bars anymore. If it was unavoidable, then I drank water or soda. The only time I drank now was at home in my pajamas and ponytail, where there was no risk of a man saying sweet words and making kind gestures to get into my sweatpants.

Until Finn came over.

Maybe Poppy had a point. Maybe my willingness to jump

into bed with Finn last night was because I'd been desperate for some companionship. When we'd been talking in the office, he'd all but come to the same conclusion.

"Being lonely three or four days a week is no way to live."

"You're right," I told her. "I do get lonely. But I don't want to rush back into dating."

"Then—and I hate saying this—make some friends."

My face soured. "I have friends."

"I don't count. I'm family."

"I have—"

"Don't you dare say Randall and Jimmy."

*Damn it.* That meant I couldn't list Rayna either. "Okay, fine. I'll try to make some new friends."

"Thank you."

"When I invite my new girlfriends into the restaurant, you can't get all jealous. This was your idea."

She crossed her heart. "Promise."

"Okay. Let's talk about something else. Want to gossip about Finn?"

"Always."

I grinned. She was his sister, but like she'd said, she was mine too. And Poppy loved to gossip about her brother.

"He broke up with Brenna." If she'd known, she would have told me already. I wasn't sure why he hadn't told his family yet—it was bound to come out sometime—so I was simply fast-forwarding that announcement.

"What?" she gasped. "When?"

"Last weekend, I guess. After he mowed the lawn last night, the kids and I invited him in for pizza. I asked him if he had plans with Brenna and he said they broke up."

"Wow." Poppy sat back in her chair, shocked. Then she grinned. "Finally. I've been looking for an excuse to take down that photo in the office."

"What?" Now it was my time to be shocked. "I thought you liked Brenna."

"She's a nice woman and I got along with her okay. For Finn's sake, I tried. That's why I put up that picture, even though I knew you hated it in there."

"You did?"

"Like I said, I notice things. I should have taken it down but . . ." she trailed off.

"You were supporting your brother."

She nodded. "I mean it. I like Brenna. She's just not right for Finn."

*Because she isn't me.*

I pitied the women Finn introduced to Poppy. They had a brick wall to crash through if they wanted in her good graces. Because no matter what, they'd be compared to the ex-sister-in-law who was also the best-friend-sister. Even Brenna, someone who'd gone over to Poppy and Cole's many times in the year she'd dated Finn, hadn't come close to cracking that wall.

"Finn already beat you to it. The picture's in the office trash can."

"Uh-oh." She sighed. "Is he okay?"

"I think so. He told me they didn't have anything in common."

"She seemed nervous around the kids. And she hated hiking."

I winced. "That would do it."

Of course Finn wouldn't stay with a woman who wasn't good with Kali and Max. But on top of that, Finn loved hiking. Before the kids were born, our Sundays were spent exploring new mountain trails. After we had Kali, the hikes were shorter and smoother, but we still went with a baby strapped onto his back.

"I'm glad he started hiking again," I told Poppy.

"Me too." She gave me a sad smile.

Finn had stopped hiking after Jamie had been killed. Instead, he'd spent his free time at Poppy's house, coaxing her out of bed or into the shower. Even after she'd worked her way out of her depression, he hadn't hiked much. He'd worked.

It wasn't until we'd been divorced for a year that he got into it again. On the mornings when he didn't have the kids, he went hiking for an hour. The man would climb to the top of a ridge, then jog down. In the winter, he went snowshoeing instead because he loved to get outdoors.

"Do you think Finn's happy?" Poppy asked.

"I don't know," I answered honestly. "I hope so."

"I want you both to be happy. I don't—" She shook her head. "Never mind."

"What?"

Her blue eyes glistened with tears as she looked at me. "Sometimes I feel like if I had handled Jamie's death better, if I hadn't been such a wreck, you and Finn wouldn't have gotten divorced."

"Poppy," I whispered. "No."

She blinked a few times, clearing the tears. "May always makes me think."

*May.* There were too many anniversaries in May. It was the month she and Jamie had married. It was the month he'd been murdered, right before their one-year wedding anniversary. She'd spent five Mays wondering why he'd been taken. Wondering why his cold-blooded killer had gone free.

It wasn't until Cole came along and solved Jamie's murder that she was able to put those questions to rest.

Poppy hadn't been depressed, she'd been destroyed. Her

heart had been shattered, and she'd become a shell of a person, walking around like a corpse.

For months, Finn had gone to her house first thing in the morning. He made sure she was okay for work. He made sure she was alive. All those mornings, I kept my phone close, because I never knew what he'd find when he got there.

She'd been on the verge of dying from a broken heart.

"Please don't think that, Poppy. What happened with Finn and me doesn't have anything to do with you."

"I want to believe that. I really do. But the thing is, he held me together. You both did. Completely. If it wasn't for you two, I don't know if I would have survived."

"You would have been fine." Tears welled in my eyes. "I can't bear to think of this world without you."

"Those first few months are a blur." She folded her hands in her lap, looking down. "But I know how bad it was. I know the stress it put on Finn to watch out for me. And you."

"But that was years before we started having trouble."

She shrugged.

"Poppy, look at me," I ordered, waiting for her blue eyes to find mine. "You are not the reason we divorced. We fell apart because we forgot to watch out for one another. Not because we were watching out for you."

"Promise?"

I stole her gesture and crossed my heart. "On my life."

A tear dripped down her cheek and she brushed it away, then forced a smile. "Sorry. That got really heavy. But I've been thinking about it because—"

"It's May."

"Yeah." She nodded. "Cole knows it's been on my mind. He told me to ask you because you'd be honest. I love my brother, but I don't think he'd tell me the truth. He still thinks he has to protect my feelings."

Finn had always looked out for his younger sister, even before Jamie had died. But she was right. If Finn thought Jamie's death had impacted our marriage in any way, he'd never tell Poppy. "He loves you."

"I love him too." She stood up and took her salad jar to the industrial dishwasher, spraying it out and putting it in the rack.

I followed, doing the same with mine while she plucked her special apron off its hook and tied it around her waist.

"I'm going to work the counter for a while," I said, "roll some silverware for the dinner rush. Do you need anything?"

"No. I'm going to make a batch of banana bread. We went through a lot of those this morning."

Banana bread in a jar, sprinkled with chocolate chips. Behind her daily quiche, it was our number-one breakfast seller. It never ceased to amaze me the things Poppy came up with to make in a jar.

"Okay. Holler if you need me."

"Molly?" She stopped me before I pushed through the swinging door. "Love you."

I smiled. "Love you too."

I didn't care what she said. I didn't need new friends.

Not when I had her.

---

"What's Dad's truck doing here?" Max asked as we pulled into the cul-de-sac.

"Uh, I'm not sure."

I'd left the restaurant at four thirty to pick up the kids from their after-school program. Then we'd stopped by the grocery store to pick up a few items to make BLTs for dinner —it was Kali's choice tonight.

In all the hours since he'd left the restaurant this morning, I hadn't heard from him. So why was he back at my house?

I parked the Jeep in the garage, and the kids barreled out before I even shut it off. I hurried to catch up and was just stepping into the front yard when Finn rounded the far side of the house pushing a wheelbarrow and wearing different clothes than he'd had on at the restaurant this morning.

The front of his white T-shirt was streaked with dirt and his biceps strained against the hem of the short sleeves. His skin glistened with a light sheen of sweat.

He was wearing an old baseball cap, one I recognized from a decade ago. Its bright blue brim was frayed because whenever Finn took it off, he rolled it up and shoved it into the back pocket of work pants like the ones he was wearing now. They were tan except for the permanent smudges of dirt and grass on the knees and thighs.

I'd probably washed those pants a hundred times, but they seemed to fit Finn better with each wash. The curve of his perfect butt had imprinted on those pants. The canvas had been molded around his thick thighs.

A flush crept up my cheeks as I remembered all the times I'd stripped those pants from his body before joining him in the shower. A dull throb settled between my legs. I fought the urge to fan my face, taking a few deep breaths and chastising my traitorous body for such a reaction.

I mentally chastised Finn too. The sexy jerk. I'd gotten along quite well these last six years satisfying myself. At least I'd thought so. But then he'd reminded my body how it felt to have a decent orgasm.

How long was it going to take me to forget about that too?

"Dad." Kali reached him first.

"Hey, beautiful." He grinned, setting the wheelbarrow down to push up the black sunglasses from his face. Then he shucked off his leather gloves and bent to kiss her cheek before giving Max a high five.

"What are you doing?" Max asked, inspecting the empty wheelbarrow. "Can I help?"

Finn chuckled. "Sure. But you have to change out of your school clothes."

Without another word, both kids sprinted for the house. Max tore off his T-shirt as he ran.

"Hi." I waved and crossed the yard. "Did I miss a mention of you coming over again?"

"No. We said Monday. But then I got stuck on an idea." He spun his baseball hat backward, probably because he knew it would make me go weak in the knees and instantly forgive him for the massive hole in the front of my yard.

My brain caught up to my eyes. *There is a massive hole in the front of my yard.*

I'd been so distracted by Finn, I hadn't noticed the ruin that had once been the landscaped border that separated my yard from Gavin's.

I took a step closer to the wreckage. The hole was in the same place where a large bunch of Indian grass had been when I'd driven away this morning. Not only was the ornamental grass gone, but a long section of the curbing had been ripped out too. The landscaping bark that I'd spent hours replenishing this spring had been carted away.

"What. Is. Happening?"

Finn planted his hands on his hips. "This lawn is a fucking pain in the ass to mow."

"Tell me something I don't know."

"I'm fixing it."

"Say that again?"

He picked up the wheelbarrow's handles and wheeled it over to where he was working. "I know I should have asked you first. I'm sorry. I came over to look around a bit, one thing led to another, and I got carried away."

"You think?"

"Here's what I'm planning. I'm going to rip all of this out, grade it flat and seed it with grass. Then you won't have to use the edger over here at all." He turned and pointed to the opposite corner of the yard next to the driveway. "I'm going to leave that bed as it is, but I'm going to redo the edging into a wider curve so the mower can hit all of the grass. Same with the beds along the porch. What do you think?"

"What do I think? I, uh . . . okay?" It came out as a question. On the one hand, I hated mowing this yard. The prospect of not having to use my edger gave me nearly as much joy as one of the orgasms I'd had last night. But on the other hand, this was *my* yard. "You should have asked."

"You're right. I should have. If you want it all put back to how it was, I'll do it right now."

Did I really want that Indian grass? Not even a little bit. "No, it's fine."

"We can walk through the plans for the backyard too, but I wanted to start with the front. I can guarantee it'll get done in short order. The back might have to wait a bit. All my crews are slotted into my schedule for the summer and it's slammed."

"It's fine. If the front is easier to mow, that's good enough. Keep your crews where they're scheduled."

He shook his head. "That's not what I meant. I can't send a crew out, but I'll make time to do it myself. I'll probably have the front done in a couple weeks. I need to draw up a couple of ideas for the back, and I can get you a timeline on that."

*Timeline.* That word was always paired with another: budget.

"I can't afford a huge landscaping bill right now."

He frowned. "I'm not charging you. This yard is a pain in the ass because I was too busy experimenting to make it functional."

My jaw dropped. Who was this man and where had the real Finn Alcott gone? "Are you being serious? You're really fixing my yard?"

"I'd like the chance to try."

Before I could agree, the front door to the house burst open and the kids came rushing down the porch steps.

Max was wearing the garden gloves Finn had bought him last summer. He clapped his hands together twice as he smiled. "Okay. Where do I start?"

Finn chuckled. "How about we start by taking a walk through the backyard? I'd like to ask your mom how she wants it to look."

That statement sent my chin to the dirt. When Finn had done the landscaping here, he hadn't asked me what I wanted. Not once. I recovered from the shock quickly, knowing exactly what I wanted for my yard. "I'd like a lilac bush."

"What color?"

"Deep purple." I'd always wanted one so I could cut blooms in the spring and put them in the house to enjoy their smell. But with the other bushes and shrubs, there wasn't room. Lilacs expanded rapidly and there was enough trimming to do each year as it was.

"You got it." Finn led the way to the backyard, the kids skipping along at his side.

I trailed behind them.

Finn was fixing my yard. Personally. *What the hell is happening?*

He wasn't just tossing a side project to one of his foremen

to manage. He wasn't delegating this down the line to a crew of college kids who'd come over to my house and track dirt inside whenever they needed to use the bathroom.

He was putting in the effort to do this on his own.

The three of us walked around the perimeter of the backyard as Finn asked me questions about what I wanted to keep or ditch.

"What about the fountain?"

"I don't want it," I admitted. "It takes forever to clean and is always full of leaves."

He nodded. "Then it's gone."

If not for my heart swelling to three times its normal size, I wouldn't have believed this was real.

"We're having BLTs for dinner tonight," Kali said when we'd made the full loop of the yard. "Want to eat with us?"

He looked to me for permission. His blue eyes were bright in the sun. He smelled like the spring air and fresh grass. His square jaw was dusted in light scruff from the day. He looked so handsome, a small smile pulling at one side of his mouth, that I forgot all about my plans to ignore last night and keep my distance from Finn.

"Stay. Please."

His eyes flared at my words. I'd said the same thing last night when he'd had me pressed against the hallway wall outside my bedroom. His lips had been trailing down my neck. His hands had been cupping my breasts.

Dinner wouldn't just be dinner.

*Darling Molly,*

*I'm proposing to you tomorrow.*

*I'm so damn nervous I can't sleep. I'm not good at telling you how I feel. I get the words jumbled and nothing comes out right. I'm terrified I'm going to mess it all up and you'll say no. Maybe I'll keep this letter as my backup. If I start to say something stupid, I'll just hand this over. Not that you can even read it. My hands are shaking so bad I can barely write.*

*I love you, Molly.*

*I love that you, above all else, are honest. I love that you have an old soul and still bug me to write you letters. I love that you said no when I asked you to move in with me because you wanted to save that experience for married life.*

*I love that we have the same birthday. There isn't a person in the world that I'd want to share my cake with besides you. And tomorrow, when we blow out the candles, I'm wishing for you.*

*Please say yes.*

*Yours,*
*Finn*

# five
## Finn

"**F**inn, are you here?" Bridget called from her office.

"No."

She laughed as the wheels of her desk chair rolled over the wood floors. Gliding backward, she appeared in my doorway. "You snuck in while I was on the phone."

"There was no sneaking about it. You were shouting so loud you didn't hear me."

Bridget's lip curled up. "I was talking to that asshole, chauvinistic salesman from the nursery."

"You mean you were yelling at that asshole, chauvinistic salesman from the nursery. What did Chad do this time?"

"He screwed up my order. Again. He sent Colorado blue instead of Norway spruce and he knows how much I hate the blue with those sharp-ass needles. He didn't include our bulk discount, he sent two extra chokecherry bushes, and to correct his own mistakes, he said it will be another two weeks. My crew is ready to plant *tomorrow* on the Nelson project."

"Shit." I rubbed my forehead. "I'll call the owner."

"This is the third time. Chad always gets your orders

right. Always. He's batting zero on mine, and we both know it's because I'm a woman."

I wanted to argue and tell Bridget that Chad was just an idiot, but she was right. I'd been at the nursery the first time the two had met and when she'd gone to shake his hand, he'd blown her off.

"I'll call the owner. Either he puts a new salesman on our account, or we'll just use Cashman's."

And pay an extra five percent on every order. I'd been using this smaller nursery for the past year because their products were top-of-the-line and their prices were unbeatable. But I wasn't going to make Bridget deal with a prick.

"Thank you." She pushed her chair farther into my office, rolling right up to the edge of my desk. She smiled at the picture of Max and Kali on the corner. "Today is the last day of school, right?"

"Yep. It's hard to believe my Kali is going to be a middle schooler."

"It feels like yesterday that she came in here and played in the corner after preschool."

"The years are going by quicker and quicker." Not just the years. The days and weeks too. It felt like only hours ago I'd started on Molly's yard project, but it had already been a week.

"The summers are racing by," Bridget said. "We can't keep up."

I pushed my calendar over to her so she could scope out the lineup. "No, we can't."

I'd had to turn away three customers over the past week because we didn't have the capacity to bid their projects. Our mowing crew was maxed out and the waiting list was twenty-deep. Adding more staff wasn't possible until maybe next season—there simply wasn't enough trained labor in town.

The season was just starting and I was already behind on office work. Normally, I'd work late on the nights when Molly had the kids and catch up. But this week, I'd been leaving the office at five on the nose to go to her place and work on the yard. We'd have dinner and hang out with the kids. Then I'd spend the night, getting up early to leave before dawn.

I was sneaking around with my wife.

*Ex-wife.*

But damn the sex was good. Maybe better than it had ever been. The two of us were having a full-on affair in the house we'd once bought together. And I had no plans to stop, even if it was fucking stupid.

I had more energy now than I'd had in years. I caught myself smiling more throughout the day whenever I thought of her lips on my skin or my hands in her hair. Damn, but I loved her hair. When was the last time I'd gotten so caught up in a woman?

*Fifteen years ago.*

None of the girlfriends I'd had since Molly had ever given me such a thrill. I'd dated Brenna for a year, and for the last half of it, I'd spent more time avoiding dates than rushing toward them.

The three nights this past week when the kids had been at my place, I'd gone to bed grumpy, wishing it were Molly at my side, not my unopened laptop.

If there had been a way to sneak her over, I would have. Except my kids weren't stupid and they'd know something was up. I might have the excuse of landscaping to take me to Molly's. But she hadn't set foot in my home. Not once. Whenever she dropped off the kids, she said good-bye on the side-walk, staying back at least ten feet from the front door.

Why was that? I'd invited her in on more than one occasion, but in six years, she hadn't crossed the threshold. Not even when Max had invited her in to see his room. She'd made an excuse about being late and promised to see it another time—which had never happened.

These were all things we should have talked about instead of stripping one another naked like we had all weekend and last night too.

Sex was easier than talking. It always had been.

Molly and I had spent years communicating physically, learning and perfecting the way we silently came together. As soon as words were involved, things got dicey.

We'd agreed that first night was a mistake. I'd venture a guess she felt the same about the other three. But to hell with it, I was excited to go over there after work tonight.

The front yard was coming along, and it was a blast to have the kids help me out. Molly too. She'd joined us outside last night, wearing her own leather gloves and working for an hour before dinner.

For the first time, the four of us had worked on a project together. Like a family.

Max thought dirt was fascinating. Kali was going to have her own green thumb. And Molly had an eye for design I hadn't respected enough. The feeling of being next to them, hearing their ideas, had filled me with so much pride, I was tempted to stretch this project out for months because I didn't want it to end.

Except I couldn't afford to stretch the project out. I couldn't afford to spend all those nights at Molly's. I had to work. The only other option was to make some changes around Alcott.

Bridget was staring with wide eyes at my calendar. I had a separate schedule I used to track the mowing crews, the same system Molly had designed years ago. But this calendar was full of the major projects, the ones where either Bridget or I was assigned to oversee design and execution.

She had two crews who reported to her, each led by a foreman who was on-site and working each day. I had three reporting to me.

We used a color-coded system in the calendar to assign jobs. Her projects were yellow, mine blue.

The month of June was so full, if you squinted at the page, it all swirled green. Maybe it was time to admit we needed some help.

"It's only been the two of us designing and managing crews for a long time," I told her.

"It has." Her spine straightened. "Wait. Are you thinking of hiring someone else?"

"Maybe." I paused. "Actually, yes. I want to keep growing, but I need more staff."

Bridget's jaw tensed. "I can probably take on three more projects a month."

"I appreciate that, but I don't want you to get burned out."

"I'd rather work a little harder than throw someone in the middle of this who will just get in the way. Remember how unorganized things were when Jason worked here? Or that summer you hired She Who Will Not Be Named?"

"Athena."

She scowled. "What a bitch. She couldn't show up on time, and she stole ten customers on the mowing route when she left."

Ten customers I hadn't been sad to see go. Their homes were scattered all across the Gallatin Valley, and because they hadn't fit into our normal routes, I'd had to charge them a bit more to cover gas. Athena had gone to work for a competitor, taking them along with a promise of a lower price. It didn't bother me, but clearly Bridget was still hung up about it even though Athena had quit seven years ago.

And in Athena's defense, I didn't really set office hours. It had just always happened that Bridget and I arrived around the same time each morning.

"We haven't had another architect on staff for seven years," I told her.

"Because we don't need one."

Bridget had been the first architect I'd hired at Alcott Landscaping, so she'd been with me since the beginning, one of my first employees. I'd hired her as a college student to work on the mowing crew in the summers. She'd started as my design apprentice the day after she'd graduated from Montana State with a degree in landscape architecture.

We'd been together so long that our processes were perfectly in sync. Hell, she'd helped create most of them. And she was right. Every time we tried to bring on someone new, shit fell apart.

That didn't seem like enough reason to keep killing ourselves though. Surely there had to be someone out there who would actually contribute.

"I'm tired of turning clients away," I admitted. I was tired of always feeling behind. "I'd like to try, and I'd like your help. Maybe instead of hiring an experienced architect, it's time for you to have an apprentice."

The blockade she'd put up to the idea of another designer came down an inch. "I'm listening."

"We'll put an ad out. You can participate in the interviews. Or if any kids on the mowing crew show some promise, you could bring them in too. Think about it. Let me know. But it's time for both of us to cut back." I pointed to the framed picture of the kids. "Before long, Kali and Max will be leaving home to build their own lives. I don't want to miss the time I have."

"Okay." She blew out a long breath. "Message received. I'll get on board."

"Thank you."

She spun her chair around, pushing it backward out of my office and into her own. Then keys rattled as she appeared in my doorway again, this time standing. "I'm in the field the rest of the day."

"I'll call you once I hear back from the nursery."

Bridget waved then headed down the hallway to the front door. The moment it was quiet, I got on the phone and raised hell. Ten apologies, three half-price Norway spruce saplings and one new salesman staffed to our account later, I went back to my stack of unpaid bills and overflowing inbox.

I'd only managed to get logged into my online banking portal when the front door to the office chimed. I sighed as footsteps came my way. The bills would have to wait.

"Hey, uh, Finn?"

"Come on in." I waved Jeff in from where he was hovering outside my door.

He stepped into my office hesitantly, glancing at his muddy boots.

"You're not the first and you won't be the last guy to bring mud into my office. Have a seat."

"Thanks." He crossed the room, taking off the beanie from his head.

Jeff, my newest employee, had started at Alcott two weeks ago. Bridget, my foremen and a few of the others were kept on full-time year-round. They transitioned from landscaping to snow removal in the winters, except for Bridget who could do design work even after the snow flew. But since I needed more laborers in the summers than winters, I filled crews with guys needing seasonal work. April through October, we were fully staffed. Jeff had been a last-minute addition when one of the other new hires was a no-show.

"What can I do for you?" I asked Jeff.

"I, uh . . ." He dropped his head. "I was wondering if I could get a pay advance. I'm having some trouble with my ex-wife and she's taking me to court to get full custody of my daughter. I need to get a lawyer."

He seemed too young to have a kid and an ex-wife, but what the hell did I know. At his age, I'd been head over heels for my wife. If someone had told me I'd be divorced from Molly, I would have laughed and told them they were crazy.

Not many men stand at the altar and say *I do* to their wife thinking someday she'll be an ex. I certainly hadn't.

"I wish I could help you, Jeff. But I don't do pay advances." I'd done that once when I'd first started out. The guy had taken a thousand-dollar advance and never shown up at the shop again.

"I understand. I just . . . I'm not a deadbeat dad. That's what she's calling me. But my little girl is two and she's my entire world. My ex is a vicious bitch and she's using Katy to get back at me. I can't lose my daughter."

*Shit.* I liked Jeff and saw some potential there. He was on my best crew and had been pulling his weight, even as the new guy. He worked hard. According to Gerry, my most tenured foreman, Jeff was the first one at the shop each morning and never asked to leave early.

I felt for the guy. I couldn't imagine going through a nasty divorce.

Neither Molly nor I had gotten vindictive throughout our divorce. We hadn't squabbled over material things. I'd wanted her to have the house. She'd wanted me to keep Alcott Landscaping.

We'd both been completely dedicated to sharing custody of the kids.

Yeah, I'd been furious with her at the time. I'd been heartbroken over her one-night stand. In truth, I'd been an asshole. But I'd told my lawyer during our first meeting that this wasn't about revenge. I'd given him an order to treat her fairly. And he'd worked with her attorney to make that happen.

"I'm sorry," I told Jeff. "I really am. I got divorced a while back and I understand how stressful it is. Especially when you throw kids into the mix. But I have employee policies for a reason, and I can't give you an advance."

"All right. I knew you said during my orientation that you guys don't do overtime. If that changes, would you keep me in mind?"

"I will."

I wasn't going to tell Jeff, but I hadn't paid overtime in five years. Overtime wages were the fastest way to send Alcott's expenses through the roof. Instead, I managed the crews' hours and didn't commit to projects we couldn't fit into the schedule.

"Thanks, Finn. I'd better get out of here. The guys are waiting."

"Before you go." I held up a finger as he stood from his chair. I dove into my desk drawer, taking out a sticky note. I scribbled my lawyer's name on it and handed it over. "This was my lawyer when I got divorced. He's not cheap. But he's good. Really good. If you can swing it, try to get a meeting with him. He does some pro bono work too. Tell him you work for me."

"Thanks. I really appreciate it." Jeff nodded, tucking the note in his pocket.

"Anytime." I stood from my chair and followed him out of the office. One of our navy trucks, emblazoned with a white Alcott Landscaping logo on the door, was idling outside.

Jeff piled inside with two other guys and waved as they pulled away from the office. A quaking aspen was loaded on the flatbed along with some hostas.

As they drove away, I walked down the short gravel road to the shop. It was the heart of Alcott.

We were located on the outskirts of Bozeman on a three-acre plot. For the first couple years Alcott had been in business, Molly and I had rented a shop to store our equipment. We'd run the office from our dining room table at the small apartment we'd moved into after getting married.

But after we'd started to become more profitable, I'd found this property and we'd taken a gamble. It had paid off. We'd put up a small steel shop in the far corner of the property. After a year, we'd had to triple its size to hold the equipment and company trucks. The year after that, it was so crowded that Molly suggested we build an actual office so she could get out of the room we'd set up as an office slash storage locker.

At the entrance to the property, we'd put up a small, separate, two-story building. The offices and small conference room were on the first floor. At the rear, a staircase led to a small lounge on the second floor.

We'd planned to let the office staff use the lounge to relax or hold informal meetings. Molly had wanted a "soft" space for the kids to play whenever we were all there together, along with a bathroom.

Neither of us had planned that the lounge, with the couch

and kitchenette, would become my apartment when I moved out. Neither of us had planned that we wouldn't be working together at Alcott for years to come.

I stepped through one of the open bay doors of the shop and looked around. It was mostly cleared except for some of the larger equipment, like two skid steers that didn't go out every day. The mowing crews had left hours ago. The last landscaping crew was out in the yard, loading up a tree from yesterday's nursery delivery.

We used the yard as a staging ground, having all the supplies from our vendors dropped off here instead of individual job sites. There were trees and bushes in one corner. Along the far side of the property, we kept landscaping boulders and piles of pea gravel next to pallets of peat moss and manure.

"Hey, Finn." One of the guys came out of the shop bathroom, zipping up his pants.

"Hey. Heading out?"

"Yep. We're about loaded up. See ya." His footsteps echoed off the metal walls and ceiling before he stepped outside and into the sunshine.

I took a deep breath, savoring the smell of dirt and oil. I didn't get in here enough. I spent most of my days in the office. But this . . . this was the reason I'd started Alcott. I had to find a way to spend more days in the fresh summer air, not under the vents of my AC.

I spun in a slow circle, taking it all in.

We'd built so much. I wouldn't have even thought this was possible without Molly dreaming at my side. She'd supported me completely those early days. She'd stuck it out, working the long hours. It was only when we'd had Kali that she'd taken a step back.

As a breeze from outside rushed into the shop, a doubt came with it.

*Did I take this from her?* Did Molly feel like I'd shut her out of our business because I'd suggested she stay home with the kids?

I'd thought it would make life easier if she was at home and not working. But as I thought back, I couldn't remember *asking* her what she'd wanted. When she hadn't put up a fight, I'd assumed we wanted the same thing, much like the yard that I'd learned a decade too late she hated.

She loved Alcott—or she used to.

Molly hadn't been here in years. The last time I remembered seeing her on the property was before the divorce.

Was I missing something? Why hadn't Molly come inside my house? Why didn't she come out here?

Divorcees were allowed a reprieve from answering those types of questions. From opening up conversations that would probably only cause pain.

Until they started sleeping together.

Now those questions would be constantly on my mind. They were begging for answers I doubted I'd want to learn. I stepped outside, and for once, the fresh air didn't offer any kind of peace.

The last truck in the yard pulled out, two guys riding shotgun as Lena, another crew leader, drove away. She smiled as she passed me on the road.

God, I wanted to go with them. To run and hop into the back of that truck and get lost in June for a day. To forget the questions and doubts and just . . . work.

But the office summoned. The bills and schedules couldn't be ignored. So, I trudged inside, settling for an open window in my office as the only link to the work I actually loved.

I mentally added business manager to my list of potential employees.

Poppy had been brilliant to hire Molly to run the business side of the restaurant. It allowed my sister to be in the kitchen, doing what she loved. I needed a Molly to run Alcott. Except I'd had a Molly to run Alcott and then she'd left.

Or had I chased her away?

I managed to pay three bills before the front door chimed again. I dropped my head, blowing out a long breath. The chances of me getting out of here on time to get to Molly's were dwindling with each interruption.

The footsteps down the hallway were hesitant. It was probably a customer or potential customer coming in to visit. Hopefully they'd spend enough time looking at the photos in the hallway of our past projects to buy me another minute.

"Come on back," I called, barreling through one last bill.

I had just clicked the submit button when Molly appeared in the doorway. "Hi."

I did a double take. "Hey. What are you doing here? Is everything okay with the kids?"

"They're fine. Do you have a second?"

"Yeah." I stood as she crossed the room. "Want some water? Or coffee?"

"No, thanks." She took a seat in one of the chairs across from my desk and clutched her purse in her lap as she looked around the office. "It hasn't changed much in here."

I grinned and sat down. "No, I guess not. I was thinking earlier that you haven't been here in a long time."

Her eyes dropped to the edge of the desk. "It's been a while."

"Are you sure everything is okay?"

"Why did you send them?"

"Send what?"

She looked up. "The letters."

Letters? We sent out letters to customers in March reminding them that mowing season was right around the corner. Bridget had been ambitious last Christmas and sent out holiday cards. But besides those, I couldn't think of anything I might have sent Molly.

"What letters?"

She gritted her teeth and dove into her purse. Then she whipped out two white envelopes. "These letters."

I reached across the desk and took them from her hand. The handwriting on the envelopes wasn't mine. "These aren't from me."

Molly didn't say a word as I pulled out the folded paper from one. The minute the lined sheet was in my hand, an uneasy feeling settled in my stomach. There was something familiar about it. I peeled the ends apart and that sinking feeling turned to a lead rock.

"Where did you get this?" No one, especially Molly, was ever supposed to see this letter.

"It came last week."

"Last week?"

"The other one came today."

I tore into the other envelope like a madman, yanking out the paper and spreading it flat. It was the letter I'd written the night before proposing.

*Oh, fuck.* "How did you get these?"

"What do you mean, how did I get these?" Molly snapped. "*You* sent them to me. Why?"

"I didn't send these to you."

The word *liar* was written all over her face.

"Molly, I did not send these."

"But you wrote them?"

I nodded. "Yeah, I wrote them." *For me.* I'd never had any intention of giving Molly these letters.

"I don't understand." She sank deeper into the chair. "You wrote these but didn't send them? So how did they show up in my mailbox?"

"I don't know." I ran a hand over my face, rubbing my jaw. The letters were in my closet—or were supposed to be— in a box I hadn't opened in years. The last time had been after the divorce. I'd dumped my wedding ring in there, shoved it on the top shelf and pretended it didn't exist.

"It really wasn't you?" Molly asked.

"It really wasn't me."

"Oh." Something flashed across her face, but before I could make sense of it, she was out of her chair. With her hair swishing across her shoulders, she raced out of the office and down the hallway.

"Molly." I stood and chased after her, but it was too late. She'd already flown out the front door.

"I'm late for work," she hollered before getting into her Jeep and driving the hell off Alcott property.

"What the—" I dove for the phone in my pocket, pulling up her name. She couldn't just leave like that. We had to figure this out. We had to find out who was sending my letters.

My letters. She'd gotten two.

There were more.

*Many* more.

My knees buckled. Someone had found my letters. Someone was sending them to Molly.

I played it out, each and every letter.

"No. Oh, fuck. No."

I spun on a heel and sprinted for my office. I swiped the keys off the desk along with my sunglasses, then I bolted outside, locking up the office before running to my truck. I broke every speed limit on my race home.

I tore through my house, rushing to my closet and the box on the top shelf. It was in the exact same place as always. It didn't look like someone had gone through my house and stolen my most personal belongings.

"Please be here."

I took it down, tossing the top to the floor. Then fear turned to reality. It wasn't just those two letters missing. They were all gone. The only thing remaining was my silver wedding band and a photo of Molly and me kissing after the pastor had pronounced us man and wife.

The box fell from my grasp, landing with a soft thud on the carpet. The ring rolled out and got lost between a pair of tennis shoes.

All of the letters I'd written were gone. Letters I'd written over the snap of almost a decade. The two Molly had gotten were good ones, written in a time we were happy.

But there were more.

If someone was sending her my letters, it was just a matter of time before she received the ones I should have burned. The ones that were raw and angry. The ones I never should have written in the first place and sure as hell never should have kept.

"Fuck." I punched at the wall, then shuffled backward from the closet until my knees hit the bed and I collapsed on the edge.

I had to find out who was sending these letters and stop them.

Fast.

# six
## Molly

"What's wrong?" Randall asked me as I set down his dessert and a fresh spoon.

"Nothing," I lied.

He frowned. "That's my third berry crisp. You normally only let me have two before lunch."

"Maybe I'm feeling generous today."

"Maybe. But there's still something bothering you."

I leaned against the counter. "Maybe there is."

This morning had been a roller coaster. First, I'd woken up happy because Finn had been in my bed. He'd hurried out early so the kids wouldn't see him, like he'd done after all our nights together.

But this morning was different. He'd kissed me before he left. A long, slow kiss that stole my breath and put a dreamy smile on my face. I'd smiled while showering and dressing. I'd smiled while making the kids breakfast. I'd smiled while stopping at the mailbox.

Then I'd found the letter.

Good-bye, smile. Hello, tears.

It was a feat of sheer willpower to dry them up and hold

more at bay while I drove the kids to school. If not for their extreme excitement for the last day of school, they would have noticed my red-rimmed eyes and splotchy cheeks.

It wasn't just the words or the sudden appearance of his letter that had rocked me. It was reading the words and being thrown backward in time.

Finn had been so nervous that night. Once we'd discovered we shared a birthday, our celebrations had been spent together. Normally we planned a party with friends or a special dinner at a cool restaurant. We'd been together for two and a half years by that point so I hadn't expected our birthday celebration to be any different.

But Finn insisted we spend the evening alone. He cooked dinner, though I suspected Poppy had a hand in it. He fully admitted she was responsible for the birthday cake.

After we ate our lasagna, he brought out the double-layer, double-chocolate creation. Instead of a heap of candles for us both to blow out, there was only one. It was white. At its base sat a diamond ring.

Finn got down on one knee and asked me to marry him. I immediately said yes. He was so excited to see the ring on my finger, he slid it down, chocolate frosting and all.

We were married two months later.

We didn't live together before the ceremony because I wanted to save the shared bathroom, the shared closet and the shared space with my husband, so our engagement was short. I still had a month left of my senior year when we married in April in a small, simple ceremony—much to my mother's dismay. Poppy was my maid of honor. Jamie was Finn's best man.

I moved into his apartment, spent the next month finishing school, then donned my cap and gown for graduation before we took a weekend honeymoon camping. We barely left the tent.

Those had been some of the happiest days of my life. That was why the letter made me cry. Those tears? They were grief. Grief for a life that had long since passed.

"Are you going to tell me what's wrong or should I guess?" Randall asked.

"Don't guess." I walked around the counter and took Jimmy's empty stool. Jimmy hadn't come to The Maysen Jar this morning because he had a summer cold. He'd been avoiding everyone for three days, convinced he was contagious.

The restaurant was empty except for two people in opposite corners who had headphones on and were working on laptops. The only one working was me. Poppy was taking a day off to get the kids enrolled in summer swimming lessons and then spend a special day with them. Rayna had opened for us but had left shortly after I'd arrived. So, I was here alone until three, when Dora was coming in for the evening shift.

If I was going to confess, now was the time.

"This stays between us," I told Randall.

"That goes without saying."

"I'm sleeping with Finn." I set those words loose and a huge weight came off my shoulders. It was freeing, even though Randall wasn't pleased. He couldn't quite repress the tic in his jaw. "I know you don't like him much."

"The man's a fool for letting you go."

My heart. "That might be the nicest thing you've ever said to me."

"It's the truth. He's a fool. And so are you."

Okay. That wasn't quite as nice. "There's the Randall I know and love. I was worried you were going soft on me."

He didn't laugh at my joke. "What are you thinking?"

"I don't know that I am," I admitted. "It just sort of happened and we haven't talked about it. He's . . . Finn. He's the father of my children. I was in love with him for years. Those feelings didn't simply shut off the day we signed our divorce papers. There's history there."

Randall dug his spoon into his berry crisp, taking a large bite. "Did I ever tell you I was divorced?"

"Uh, no."

Randall didn't talk much about his life, not even after sitting on that stool for nearly six years. I knew that as a younger man he'd helped build this building. He was from Bozeman and had lived here his entire life, just like me.

He had chosen to sell his home years ago and move into The Rainbow because it was easier. He claimed it was for the food and on-site cleaning crew. I think he'd been lonely— something he'd never admit.

But I'd never known he'd been married.

"I was married for twenty-one years. My wife and I never had children, so it was just the two of us. Twenty-one years, and then one day we realized we were miserable together. But I never stopped loving her."

"Did she love you?"

"She did. I'd say she doesn't anymore. I talk to her a couple of times a month. She moved to Arizona because she hates the snow."

"What's her name?"

"Mary James."

*James.* She'd kept his last name. All I wanted to do was give this wonderful man a hug, but I kept my seat. I listened because there was a reason he was opening up.

"The thing about divorce is, there isn't always one mistake. One nuclear bomb dropped on a couple that destroys their marriage. Sometimes, it creeps up on you slowly. And one day, realization hits and all you know is that you don't want to be married anymore. Maybe a nuclear bomb would have been better than slowly burning to death. Maybe that wouldn't make you feel like such a failure. It kills you to give up, but you know it's the right decision. Because if you keep going, you'll hate each other. That's why Mary and I stopped. Because I didn't want to hate her. I didn't want her to hate me."

The air left my lungs. Randall sat here nearly every day and I hadn't known how close his story was to my own. Someone who really understood.

"I don't know what I'm doing with Finn," I whispered.

"If I had to guess, I'd say you two have more love than me and Mary ever did. You might even have some passion left in you. That's all good. But you got divorced for a reason. Probably more than one. Have those reasons gone away?"

"No." Those reasons were still there, floating under the surface. "He's been sending me letters." Well, someone was sending me his letters.

"What kind of letters?"

"There's only been two, but they're both from ages ago. The first one he wrote after our first date. The second was written the night before he proposed."

"And they're bringing up feelings," he guessed.

I nodded. "I was happy. *We* were happy."

"And you're not now."

"No, I'm happy. But it's not the same. It doesn't run as deep."

Randall took another bite, chewing as slowly as humanly possible. Then he did it again. I was sure there was a point to his silence, and he'd deliver it eventually, so I sat and waited.

Finally, he spoke. "That boy was terrible to you when I first started coming here."

"I know. But he was hurt."

"You always defend him," he grumbled. "The man was an asshole and you didn't deserve that."

No, I *did* deserve it. But I wasn't going to expand on the dirty details for Randall. Finn had been acting out of pain. The cold shoulders, the blank stares. I'd earned every single one.

"He hasn't acted like that in a long time," I said.

"He's still a fool."

"Thank you." I bumped his shoulder with mine. "I'm sorry about your wife."

He shrugged. "It's been a long time. And don't go gossiping about this. I don't need everyone putting their noses into my business. It's ancient history."

"Your secret is safe with me."

"It's not a secret," he muttered. "I just don't want to talk about it."

"Got it. Not a secret. But keep my mouth shut."

"Right."

Randall finished his dessert while I sat by his side. When he was done, he pulled on his driving cap and picked up his cane. "I'd better get home. Check on Jimmy. The big baby thinks he's got the damn plague instead of just a runny nose."

"Let me send some stuff with you." I hopped off my stool and hurried around the counter to fill a paper bag full of chicken noodle soup and some apple pies. "This is for Jimmy. You get one of these pies. He gets two. And I'm going to check that he receives them both."

"Fine." He scowled. Without another word, he took the bag and turned, shuffling his way to the door.

"Randall?" I called before he could leave. He paused but didn't turn back. "Thank you."

He lifted the cane in acknowledgement as he continued out the door.

I made a quick round of the restaurant, checking on the other two customers and making coffee for a woman who came in for a to-go order. Then I settled in at the counter, my purse beneath my feet.

Normally, I kept my purse in the office, but today I'd brought it out front because of the letter. Carefully, I fished it out to read again.

There were no tears this time. I felt more numb than sad. It was the same feeling I'd had walking into Alcott Landscaping. I hadn't set foot there in years, not since *that* night. It was eerie, like returning to the scene of a crime.

But I'd had to confront Finn. I'd worked up the courage because I needed to know why he'd sent the letters. One I could ignore. But two? Impossible.

Hope was a funny thing. I'd spent six years dousing it. Stomping it out so it was well and dead. But that second letter had flared my hopes to life.

Did he think there was a chance for us again? Did he want to try?

Randall was right. I was a fool.

Finn hadn't sent those letters. He'd hidden them away. He'd put his feelings down on paper not to share, but to live in a box or a folder or wherever the hell he'd kept them all these years.

I was mad at Finn for hiding them. More so, I was mad at myself for believing he wanted me again for more than a romp in his former bed.

I folded up the letter and tucked it away. The trash can next to my feet was tempting, but I couldn't throw it out. In those pages, written in blue ink, was happiness. Maybe one day Kali would want to read it. Maybe Max would want to know the kinds of things his father had felt about his mother. I'd save them, for the kids. I'd put the letters in a safe place and cross my fingers that these were the only two.

If Finn wasn't sending them, then who was putting them in my mailbox? My money was on Poppy. Maybe she thought it would bring us back together. Or Rayna. Tomorrow when we were all together, I'd ask. I'd make sure their hopes were as crushed as my own.

A customer came through the door, followed by another. The lunch rush was starting, saving me from my thoughts, and I worked with a smile, replaying Randall's story in my head one hundred times.

He'd given me a different perspective on the divorce. Finn and I had called it quits at the right time, before our anger and frustration with one another had turned to hate.

The last six years had been good for me. I'd found the me I'd lost when I'd given everything to Finn.

I'd worked for his business. I'd lived by his schedule. I'd gone on his hikes and mowed his lawn. I hadn't done enough for myself during our marriage. And at the time of our split, I'd been a stay-at-home mother who'd lost herself in the lives of those she loved.

Spending nights alone while Finn had the kids had given me plenty of hours to think. To reflect. And to change.

I'd worked on *me* over the last six years. I was a mom. A business manager. A lover of red wine. A hater of rice pilaf. I enjoyed going to movies alone, and I splurged on a pint of Häagen-Dazs cookie dough ice cream once a month. I only went places that made me happy. I stayed away from places that made me sad, like Alcott Landscaping and Finn's home.

I put up boundaries to keep out the ugly. I embraced the beautiful.

I found the Molly without the Finn.

This time around, I was holding on to her with a death grip. She was too important to lose again.

I worked through the afternoon, and when I left the restaurant in Dora's capable hands for the evening, I drove to get the kids with a lighter heart.

Max and Kali danced wildly, arms flailing with bright smiles as they ran to the Jeep. Not a second of silence occurred on the drive because both were so excited about their summer plans.

The moment they spotted Finn's truck, the excitement skyrocketed.

Mine tanked. I was in a better spot than I'd been this morning, but I could still use a break from Finn. I needed a few nights to put some walls up. To steel myself for those jitters that always came with seeing his handsome face.

*Damn you, jitters.*

"Dad!" Max yelled from the car window. "Are we working tonight?"

"If you're up for it."

Max clapped his hands once, then pointed to the garage. "I'll get my gloves."

I took it as my command to pull in and park. The kids got out, meeting Finn at the bumper.

"Hi, Dad." Kali smiled at him then followed Max to collect their gloves from a shelf on the garage wall.

Leaving Finn and me standing alone.

"Could you please text me or something before you come over?" That came out bitchier than I'd planned. *Oh, well.*

"Sorry." Finn hung his head. "I don't want to leave the yard a mess. I started all this. I need to finish it."

"Fine." I crossed my arms over my chest. "But a heads-up would be appreciated in case I have plans."

We both knew I didn't have plans, but I was scrambling to put him back in his place. We were divorced. Ex-husbands called before coming over. Ex-husbands didn't share dinners. Ex-husbands didn't sleep in the same bed as their former wives.

"Molly, we have to talk about the letters."

"Not right now."

The kids came running back, their smiles impossible to ignore. They loved having Finn here at night. They loved the attention from both parents.

Were we sending the wrong message? Did they think we were getting back together?

"You guys, you get a couple of hours to work with your dad, then he needs to get going."

Finn frowned and the smiles on the kids' faces disappeared.

"You can't stay for dinner tonight, Dad?" Max asked.

"I, uh . . ." Finn rubbed the back of his neck, stealing a glance my way.

"No, not tonight."

"Why?" Kali narrowed her gaze on her dad's face. "Do you have a date or something?"

"No date. I just have some stuff to do at home."

"What stuff?" The look on Kali's face was one I'd seen plenty of times before. My girl was stubborn, and until Finn gave her an answer she deemed acceptable, she'd wear him down with questions. She didn't do vague.

"Just stuff, Kali. So let's get after it." He turned and took a step but his answer hadn't passed muster.

Kali crossed her arms over her chest, mirroring my stance.

"It's the last day of school. We've had, like, the best day ever. You could hang out with us and not ruin it."

I rolled my eyes. "Let's tone down the drama."

She clenched her jaw and shot me a glare.

"Come on, Dad," Max begged. "We could order pizza again."

"It's your mom—" He stopped himself when my eyes widened. There was no way he was pinning this on me, not when he hadn't asked to come over in the first place. "Tell you what, guys. We need to haul that bark over in the corner, and then we can level out the ground for sod. How about you two start loading the bark into the wheelbarrow while I talk to your mom?"

Max nodded, immediately going to work. Kali kept her arms crossed over her chest as she walked across the lawn to join her brother.

"I won't stay for dinner," he said. "I'll make sure the kids know it's my choice, not yours."

"Thank you." I let my arms fall. "I need some space."

"Take it. The kids and I will work out here. You can disappear inside. When we're done, I'll go. But, Molly." Finn stepped closer, his fresh scent filling my nose as he dropped his voice to speak low. "Sooner rather than later, we have to talk about the letters."

"I agree, but not tonight."

"It's my weekend with the kids. What if you came over one night and we talked at my place?"

Not happening. "We can talk one day at the restaurant."

"Fine. We'll talk at the restaurant about everything. The letters. The sex. The reason why you won't set foot in my house."

I winced.

"Didn't think I noticed, did you?"

"No," I muttered. He'd never said anything before about my aversion to crossing his threshold.

"Dad, we're loaded," Max yelled.

Finn sighed and locked his eyes with mine. "We'll talk later."

By then, I'd better have a grip on my emotions. What Finn and I needed was an adult conversation, and with the way my heart was racing and my temper spiking, there was no way anything rational would come out of my mouth.

I retreated inside and spent thirty minutes tidying up. Every time I walked by a window, I'd steal a glance outside.

The kids were smiling. Finn was too. His was wide and bright, full of pride and encouragement as he taught the kids.

Those smiles weakened me. His put my temper on ice.

Finn caught me watching from a window and grinned. It was the same grin he'd flashed me on our first date, the one that was carefree and confident and so irritatingly forgivable.

That grin was the reason I walked over to the kitchen counter to dig my phone out of my purse.

And ordered pizza—enough for four.

---

"They're out." I joined Finn on the living room couch, making sure to leave plenty of room between us.

"Thanks for letting me stay for dinner and to hang out with the kids."

"You're welcome. Thanks for all the work you did in the yard."

He leaned forward on the couch, his forearms braced on his thighs. He'd worn jeans tonight, an old pair frayed at the hems. They'd gotten thin from so many washings and were threadbare at the knees. He'd taken off his shoes, lounging in the living room with bare feet like he lived here.

"I think you should go."

"I don't want to go."

"You can't stay."

"Why?"

I gaped at him. "Because we're divorced."

"Me staying doesn't change that fact."

"Then because it's foolish." Ever since Randall had said that word, it had been stuck in my head.

"Probably." Finn chuckled and stood from the couch. Then he held out his hand.

I shied away, sinking deeper into the couch.

He laughed again, then bent and swiped my hand off my lap so fast, I didn't even have time to blink before he'd hauled me off the couch.

"Finn." I tugged my hand, trying to get free, but he held it tight as he pulled me down the hall and to my bedroom.

When we were both inside, he let me go and closed the door.

I went to the end of the bed and sat. "This is not why I invited you to stay for dinner."

"I know that." He sat by my side. "And I'll go in a few minutes. But we need to talk about the letters."

"I don't want to talk about the letters."

"Why not?"

"Because . . . because you didn't send them."

His frame slumped, his broad shoulder leaning into mine. "I'm sorry, Molly."

"Why didn't you send them?" Above all else, I wanted to know why he'd chosen to hide those beautiful letters instead of giving them to me somewhere along the way.

"A lot of reasons. I wrote them to you, but they were more

for myself, if that makes sense. A way for me to get my thoughts together."

That made sense, especially given the actual letters. If he'd sent me that first one after our first date, I would have been creeped out. After one date, it was strange to know you wanted to marry someone. Wasn't it? Though it didn't feel strange. It felt . . . like us.

His explanation made sense for the proposal letter too. He hadn't said those words to me the night he'd proposed, but I could see why he'd want to have his thoughts down. Why he'd want to use the letter as a dry run before asking someone to become your wife.

"Are there more?" I asked.

"Yes."

"How many?"

He hesitated. "A few. Maybe six or seven. I don't remember."

If the person who'd sent the first two planned to continue, then I guess I'd find out eventually. "Do you know who could be sending them?"

"I have my suspicions," he grumbled.

"Me too."

We sat quietly for a few moments, his arm pressed against me. The heat from his skin melded with my own, warming me to the core. That heat was the reason we should have stayed on the couch.

"You'd better go," I whispered.

He nodded but didn't make a move to stand.

"Finn."

He looked down at me. "I don't want to go."

"You said you'd go in a few minutes."

"I lied."

I hated how good those two words felt. "What are we

doing?"

Finn raised his other hand and brought it to my face. He cupped my jaw, then slid his palm back until his fingers were threaded through my hair. "Being foolish."

Our lips collided as we both moved. Me, up into his arms. Him, backward, taking us higher up in the bed.

His tongue swept inside my mouth, exploring. My own twisted and tangled with his, tasting all that was Finn until he broke away to trail hot, wet kisses down my neck.

"I don't want to go." His fingers wrapped around the hem of my tee, pulling it up my ribs.

"Don't go," I panted, my own fingers reaching for the button on his jeans. The minute it was free, I slid down the zipper. Finn's erection throbbed inside his boxer briefs.

Before I could slip my hand inside, Finn brought my shirt up and over my head, forcing my arms away. With a flick of his wrist, the blue lace bra I'd put on this morning, the one I knew he'd like, was gone.

Finn sat up enough to strip off his own T-shirt, then smashed our lips together once more.

My nipples peaked against the firm plane of his chest, the dusting of dark red hair tickling them and sending a rush of desire to my core. And I forgot about the many rational reasons we shouldn't be doing this.

We simply stripped each other bare until Finn rolled me onto my back and settled himself between my thighs. My hips cradled his. My arms wound around his waist, holding us together as he eased inside me.

My eyes fell shut, my breath stolen by the sensation of him filling the voids I'd ignored for so, so long. Here, in this place, everything made sense. Nothing was careless. Here, together, it was like going backward in time. We traveled to the days when those letters were being penned. To when happiness radiated around us.

To when we got lost in one another, the rest of the world a blur.

Finn and I were so lost that neither of us noticed the person outside.

The person leaving another letter in my mailbox.

*Molly,*

*Tonight you told me you wanted to postpone the wedding. That was right before you asked me to leave your apartment so you could have some space. We're getting married next week and you need space. We're getting married next week and you want to postpone our wedding because your mother has convinced you that it's too soon. We've been dating for two and a half years, and it's too soon to get married? What the fuck?*

*I haven't said a thing about the wedding. I told you to do whatever you wanted, that all I cared about was that at the end of the day, you'd be my wife. But I've changed my mind. Now I want something. I want you to stop listening to the toxic words that spew out of your mother's mouth. I want you to stop letting her poison seep into our life. I want you to stop doubting me. Doubting us.*

*It's our life, Molly. Me and you. And every time you have one of your "sessions" with her, she twists you in knots. She says that I might not love you enough. She says that I may eventually look at other women behind your back. She says that our marriage could hold you back from your own dreams.*

*It's all bullshit. I know it. You know it. She knows it.*
*She knows you're the love of my life. She knows you're the only woman I see and ever will. But that woman fucking hates me. She has from day one. Nothing I do will ever be good enough because she thinks you can do better.*

*Fuck that. And fuck her.*

*You get twenty-four hours of space. That's it. There is no version of my future where you aren't by my side. So take your space. Sort it out in your head, just like I know you will. You always do. Then put it aside. Because we're getting married next week. And I can't wait to call you my wife.*

*I love you.*
*Yours,*
*Finn*

I opened the door to The Maysen Jar and stepped inside, scanning the room. The second I spotted her face, I spun back for the door.

*Did she see me?*

"Hello, Finn."

*Yep. Shit.*

I slowly turned around, wishing I had looked through the front windows more closely before coming inside. "Hello, Deb."

Molly's mother gritted her teeth. "Deborah."

"Right." I snapped my fingers. "Deborah."

For the first eight years I'd known her, she'd gone by Deb. Then she'd decided a woman of her age shouldn't go by shortened names. She hated Deb, so I only called her Deb. I took every opportunity to get my digs. She did the same. *Deborah* even bad-mouthed me to my own children.

"Leaving already?" she asked.

More like trying to escape. "Forgot my wallet in the truck."

Her eyes narrowed. "I'm sure my daughter and your sister rarely make you pay."

"Yes, but I do like to support the business."

Deborah gestured to the seat across from her, silently commanding me to sit. She looked like she always did, stiff and snobby in her black pantsuit. I'd never seen the woman in jeans. She had the same hair as Molly, but while her daughter let those dark curls run wild, Deb kept hers chopped short. It was just long enough to pull up into her fancy twists.

Her appearance screamed *I'm better, smarter and richer than you'll ever be.*

On a different day, I'd walk away from my former mother-in-law without another word. She could shove that chair up her ass for all I cared. But today, I was playing nice.

It had been a week since the latest letter had shown up in Molly's mailbox, the one I'd written in a moment of extreme frustration before the wedding. In that week, Molly had hardly spoken to me. If I pissed off Deb, no way would Molly be willing to talk today.

Her silence was killing me.

I'd apologized, but the damage had been done. Molly had pulled away over the last week. She'd gone quiet. Something I knew meant she was hurt.

I'd stayed away, giving her some space. I hadn't been to the house to work on the yard. I'd had the kids over the weekend and a few days this week. The nights when they were at home with her, I'd scheduled evening meetings with Bridget to review designs so I wouldn't be tempted to go over to Molly's.

But it was the weekend again and I wanted to work on the yard, which would be a hell of a lot easier if Molly wasn't dodging eye contact and running away from me.

So here I was, taking a seat across from my ex-mother-in-law to make sure I didn't further piss off my ex-wife.

"How are you today?" I asked Deb.

"I'm well. I was just down to see Molly. She's been so *busy.*"

I squirmed in my chair as her eyes looked me up and down. There was no way Molly had told Deb about us, was there? As far as I knew, Molly hadn't told anyone about our affair. The last person who would understand or have anything decent to say about it was her mother.

"Molly likes to be busy. She thrives on it." I studied Deb's reaction. If she did know about the affair, she wasn't giving it away.

"It's not mentally healthy to be so stressed."

*Ahh.* The busy comment wasn't about the affair. It was about Dr. Deborah Todd's constant need to pick apart every one of Molly's emotions.

In her mind, it wasn't right to have the normal gamut of emotions that came with life. Whenever Molly was worried or sad or angry, they'd have a session so Deborah could help delve into the root cause and diagnose a cure. If Molly wasn't in a constant state of tranquility, then there was something wrong with her.

"I don't think Molly is stressed." As if she'd heard my cue, Molly came out of the kitchen with a wide smile on her face. "See?"

Deb looked at her daughter but didn't seem to see the smile. "She looks tired."

"Oh-kay," I drawled. There was no point arguing with Deb. The woman would never concede a point. "Well, I'm going to go and say hello."

I stood from the chair and made it three steps away from the table when she stopped me again.

"Finn, I told Molly, but I'm telling you as well. You both need to watch Kali closely."

The hairs on the back of my neck stood on end as I turned. "What?"

"I'm concerned about Kali. The last three times I've seen her, she's been quiet and withdrawn. I think you and Molly need to consider putting her in counseling. I'm worried this behavior is a sign she may be depressed. The last thing we want is her acting out and doing something drastic as a call for help."

My hands balled into fists. "Kali is happy and healthy. There is nothing wrong with her."

"She's troubled."

"She's *not* troubled. She's a ten-year-old girl. Her moods swing all over the place depending on what's happening with her friends or her teachers or her brother. But she's a happy and healthy kid. And I am telling you right now, Deb. If you say anything different to her, if you plant these ideas in her head that she's unwell, you'll never see my daughter again. Are we clear?"

My chest heaved as Deb's jaw fell open. Dr. Deborah could diagnose her own daughter all she wanted but my child was off limits. I wouldn't have her twisting up Kali like she did with Molly.

"I'm simply looking out for Kali." She huffed.

"No, you're pulling your psychobabble bullshit. It stops. Now."

Deb's eyes widened as she stood. "I will not be threatened."

"This isn't a threat." I stepped closer, then I spoke loud and clear so there was no mistaking my position. "You will not talk to Kali about counseling. You will not talk to Kali about her moods. You will not talk to Kali about anything other than what Kali wants to talk about. If I find out otherwise, you won't see her again."

"Hey," Molly hissed, rushing over to my side. "What's going on? You two are making a scene."

"Finn is threat—"

"It's nothing," I barked. "Your mom and I were just coming to an understanding."

Molly looked back and forth between us. "Mom, is this about Kali? Did you tell Finn? I told you. She's. Fine."

"I disagree."

"She's—" Molly sucked in a calming breath. "You know what? I appreciate your concern, and I'll keep an eye out. We both will. Then *we'll* decide what's best for our daughter."

I opened my mouth to take them both on but stopped as Molly's words sunk in. Had she really just taken my side? Against her mom? I did my best to keep my expression neutral but it was a battle. I couldn't remember a time when Molly had taken my side in a battle of Finn versus Deb.

"In my professional opinion, you're making a mistake," she said.

Molly nodded. "So noted."

Deb frowned at Molly, waiting for a different response. When she didn't get one, she spun around and collected her purse from the table. "I've got to be going. We'll discuss this again at a later date, Molly."

I scoffed. "Just as long as you don't discuss it with Kali."

Molly shot me a look that said *shut up*, then she escorted Deb to the door. As her mom walked outside along the front windows, Molly scowled at me.

"What?" I held up my hands.

"Do you always have to argue with my mother?"

"Hey, I didn't start that."

She shook her head. "You never do. Mom is always the antagonist, isn't that right?"

"That's not—you know what? I'm not having this fight again. I came down here to talk to you."

"About?"

"The letter."

She shook her head, walking away from the door and through the restaurant to the counter. I followed, saying nothing as she led me into the kitchen.

"Hi." Poppy smiled from her side of the table as she mixed something in a large silver bowl. "Want some lunch?"

"Hi. I, uh . . . maybe in a minute." Molly was marching toward the office, so I held up a finger to Poppy and hurried to catch up.

Molly was waiting in the center of the room when I got there. She stayed tight-lipped until I closed the door.

"I'm sorry about the letter."

"It's fine." She shrugged. "It took me by surprise. But it's fine."

"*You're* not fine. You're pissed at me."

"Because you came into my workplace and picked a fight with my mother. Can't you just avoid her?"

I gritted my teeth. "I didn't pick a fight with your mother. I was trying to be civil but she crossed the line. If you want to swallow the shit advice she feeds you, that's your choice. But when it comes to Kali and Max, I won't have it."

"She gets paid a lot of money to give that 'shit advice.'"

My blood pressure ticked up a notch. I fucking hated air quotes. And this fight. We'd had it so many times but never come out on the same side. Molly always stood on her mother's, which left me standing alone, wondering how a woman with so much confidence and intelligence could let someone manipulate her.

"Tell me honestly. Do you think Kali is depressed?"

"No. Of course not."

"Well, your mom says Kali has been quiet and withdrawn. All the signs, she says, point to a depressed kid on the verge of acting out and making drastic calls for help."

Molly blew out a long breath. "Mom is overreacting. The last few times we went to see Mom, it was at her office. Kali gets bored there, so she plays a game on my phone. She got into it and shut out the rest of the world."

"Yeah, because she's a normal kid with a screen in front of her face. But the last thing I want is your mother convincing her that there's something wrong with her."

"Mom would never do that, Finn."

"Really?" I gaped at her. "Of course, she would. The woman has no limits. She tried to stop our wedding."

"Now who's overreacting?"

I crossed my arms over my chest. "Listen, that was a long time ago. But I remember, Molly. You wanted to cancel the wedding."

"No, postpone."

"Does it matter?" I shot back. "Cancel. Postpone. We were a week away from the wedding and you wanted to call it off because your mom had convinced you that we were rushing into it. Two months wasn't long enough to be engaged, and we were breaking one of her rules."

"She was just worried. We were both so young and the wedding planning was stressful."

"See? You always defend her."

"What's wrong with me defending her?" she asked. "She's my mom."

"Then maybe she could support you and your choices for once instead of always questioning them."

Molly was an incredible mother. Somehow she always

knew the right thing to say to Kali when she was upset. Or how to communicate with Max with just a single look. Because she was such a good mom, it baffled me that she didn't see how toxic her own mother's words could be.

"It doesn't matter anyway." Molly waved it off. "We worked it out."

Not fifteen minutes after I'd finishing writing that letter, Molly had knocked on my door. I'd apologized for getting so upset. She'd told me she didn't want to postpone the wedding, then we'd made love for hours, the fight forgotten.

Until that letter had shown up last week.

Now, thirteen years later, it was all coming back again.

The wedding lost some of its shine because of that argument. The week leading up to the ceremony, I was in a constant state of alert, waiting for Molly to change her mind.

I took over as much as I could to help reduce her stress, not just for Molly's sake but to keep Deb at bay. I became the liaison for the florist, caterer and photographer, making sure everyone knew when and where to show up. I packed up Molly's apartment and moved everything into mine so she could concentrate on the wedding and her classes. And I cleared my schedule, taking off more days from work than I'd planned so I was completely available to help if she needed it.

The day of the wedding, I stood at the altar in a panic that she'd changed her mind. When she appeared at the end of the aisle, I nearly cried. She was beautiful, my Molly. Full of joy and confidence. I would never forget how she looked that day in her white gown.

The strapless top was adorned with lace and a belt wrapped around her waist. It separated the lace from the billowing tulle skirt, one that had barely fit into the cab of my truck. We'd laughed about it, after we'd shared our vows and kissed. After we ran through a shower of birdseed to my truck—not a limo, because she hadn't wanted to share those first few moments after the ceremony with a driver.

It took us ten minutes to get her dress into the truck. The skirt filled up every available inch of room. We laughed the entire drive from the church to the hotel where we had the reception.

That laughter, it had erased the stress of the wedding. With Molly's ring on my finger, it was easy to forget the fight from the week before. The bad had simply been overshadowed by the good.

"We never talked about it," I said. "About that fight. We didn't really work it out, did we? We just went forward but never actually fixed the problem."

"You mean the problem of my mother?"

I nodded. "I wrote that letter because I had to get those feelings out. I'd been holding them in for so long. I know it was harsh but that was how I felt."

Molly walked to the desk and slumped down on the edge. Then she toyed with a green hair ribbon on her wrist. "I didn't like reading that letter."

"I know." I sat by her side.

"The other two letters were so special. There was love there. This one . . . it was so angry and raw. It took me right back, and I don't like being in that place again. It's been bothering me all week."

"Same here."

"It's made me think though. You were so . . . honest. Nothing in that letter was downplayed. You didn't sugarcoat anything."

I let out a dry laugh. "Because you weren't supposed to read it."

"I'm glad I did though. It made me see things from your perspective. And you were right. Mom has a way of making me question my decisions. I think she does it to challenge me and test my conviction. But because of the way she does it, I do end up doubting myself at times. I see that now."

*Halle-fucking-lujah.*

"Want to know the thing that's really been messing with me all week?" she asked. "I can't help but think Mom was onto something. Not about you. You were right, she's never liked you, and I'm honestly not sure why."

"Because I have a different opinion than her one hundred percent of the time," I muttered.

She smiled. "True."

"What was the great Dr. Deborah onto then?"

Molly looked to the floor. "That we've been doomed from the start."

Her words were like a knife to my heart. "Doomed? You really think that?"

"Well, we are divorced."

Yes, we were.

"I won't let Mom get inside Kali's head," she promised. "And I'll try to stop letting her get inside mine too."

"Good." At least one good thing would come from that letter. I bumped her shoulder. "I am sorry about the letter."

Her eyes came up to mine. "Thank you."

We kept our gazes locked and my heart trilled a beat faster. It would have been so easy to kiss her. I wanted to kiss her. Even divorced, there weren't many times when I didn't want to kiss Molly.

I leaned down an inch, her soft lips drawing me in.

She stayed perfectly still, her eyes holding steady as I came even closer. The minute my lips brushed against hers, her breath hitched. She didn't pull away.

I pressed against her, firmly running my tongue over the

small crease in the center of her full bottom lip. She opened for me, leaning in so I could get a deeper taste.

I sighed a moan as I wrapped my arms around her, bringing her even closer.

Molly relaxed into me, letting her tongue sweep into my mouth. Her fingers gripped my T-shirt, one hand in front and the other at the back, pulling it from where I'd tucked it into my jeans and belt.

My cock jerked behind my zipper, wanting the chance to lay Molly across this desk and take her hard and fast. But the clanging sound of metal bowls drove us apart, a reminder that Poppy was outside.

"What are we doing?" Molly whispered as she stood up. Her hand went to her lips, wiping them dry as she paced the office.

"It was just a kiss."

She stopped pacing. "Why are we kissing?"

Because I couldn't stop. Kissing her was as natural as breathing. "Do you want to stop?"

She shook her head but said, "Yes. We should."

I stood from the desk and rounded on her, framing her face with my hands. "We should."

My lips crashed down on hers again, this kiss hotter and harder than the first. When her lips were wet again and she'd yanked my T-shirt completely out of my jeans, we finally broke apart.

Molly smoothed out the hair around her temples that I'd ruffled. I tucked in my shirt, making sure my belt was straight and the bulge behind my jeans wasn't too noticeable.

"No more kissing me today," she ordered.

"I was going to come over tonight and work on the yard." And spend the night in her bed.

Her cheeks flushed. "Then no more kissing me until it's dark."

I chuckled. "Okay."

I'd gone years without sex, but this past week had been torture. Was this how addicts felt? Once they fell off the wagon, how did they get back on?

"I'd really like to know who's sending these letters," she said.

"Me too." Especially because then I could get them to stop. If Molly didn't like reading this letter, she was really going to hate some of the others. "What about one of the kids?"

She shook her head. "We have brilliant children, but that's giving them a lot of credit. Do you think it's Poppy?"

I took a step toward the door. "There's only one way to find out."

"Wait." Molly's hand shot out and caught my elbow. "We can't go out there. Look at us. She'll know exactly what we were doing in here."

A part of me wanted to walk out there and proudly show off the lip gloss I'd stolen from Molly. But it would only make things more complicated. "I have to leave at some point."

"Here." She hurried around the desk, grabbing a napkin from a drawer. She tossed it at me while she went to her purse for a compact mirror. "Ugh. My lips are all swollen."

I hid my smile in the napkin as I wiped my lips clean. "Five minutes and they'll be back to normal. Let's just hang out for a few."

"Okay. So how do you want to do this with Poppy?"

"Let's just ask her."

She gave me a flat look. "If it is her, she's not just going to come out and admit it. She's gone to a lot of trouble to hide this."

"It's her. I know it's her." There was only one person more devastated by the divorce than the kids, Molly or me, and that was my sister. "She's at my house on a regular basis. She probably stumbled on the box where I was keeping them and thought . . . well, I'm not exactly sure what she thought."

"Probably that the letters might get us back together." Molly sighed. "I don't want to get her hopes up. The letters might force us to deal with some old wounds, but we're not getting back together."

"Right," I agreed, but something about her declaration didn't sit well. We *weren't* getting back together. So why did her words sound so wrong?

"How are my lips?" Molly asked as she applied some lip gloss. "Does it look like we were kissing?"

"No, you're fine. Let's go." I shook off the strange feeling and led the way out of the office and into the kitchen.

Poppy was right where I'd left her, standing at the table with a smile on her face as she filled small jars with cornbread mixture.

"Hey, you got a sec?" I asked her.

"Sure. What's up?"

I looked at Molly. She gave me a nod to go ahead. "We need to talk to you about the letters."

"Letters?" Poppy's forehead furrowed. "What letters?"

"The ones you've been putting in my mailbox," Molly said. "The ones from Finn."

"Uh . . ." She shook her head, clearly not tracking with us. "I have no idea what you're talking about."

"Come on, Poppy. Just fess up so we can talk about it."

"I'd love to 'fess up,'" she said, adding the air quotes, not happy that I'd all but called her a liar. "But I swear I have no idea what you are talking about."

"Really?" Molly asked.

"Yes." Poppy crossed her heart. "Promise."

She was telling the truth. Poppy wasn't only my sister, she was my best friend. She'd done that heart-crossing thing since we were kids. It was sacred to her, meaning she was telling the truth.

"What kind of letters?" Poppy asked.

I ignored my sister and looked at Molly. "If she's not behind the letters . . ."

"Then who is?"

*Darling Molly,*

*I need you to tell me what to say. Jamie's funeral is tomorrow and I'm supposed to speak. But I don't know what to say. Here's my problem. Well, one of them. I don't want to ask you for help. I don't want to put this on you. It's hard enough to carry myself, so let's pretend, okay? Let's pretend you'll read this and help me decide what to say.*

*Jamie's been gone eight days. You keep saying how it doesn't feel real. Maybe I'll say that tomorrow. I'm sure everyone will relate. Except here's the thing. It does feel real.*

*He's gone. I had to call his parents and tell them. I'll never get his mom's scream out of my head. I'll never forget the sound of his dad crying into the phone. I'll never forget the look on Poppy's face that night when I got to their house. Her light was gone. How is she going to survive this? I honestly don't know if she will. But I can't say any of that tomorrow, not when his family is expecting me to keep my shit together. Everything is different now.*

*I can't do this. I can't do this, Molly. I don't want to tell funny stories about my best friend. I don't want to talk about how much he loved my sister. Mostly, I'm scared I won't know where to look when I'm standing in front of everyone. I guess to you. I'll always look to you.*

*It doesn't feel like I can do this right now, but I'll look to you. And the right words will come.*

*Yours,*
*Finn*

# eight
## Finn

"Hey," I answered Molly's call. "What's up?"

She sniffled. "I got another letter."

My heart stopped. She was crying, which meant the letter was not a good one. *Fuck*. Me and my fucking letters. I couldn't remember them all exactly word for word. I remembered their moods. About half had been written with a full heart. The other half, a broken one.

One of them was catastrophic. I knew Molly well enough to know that if she'd gotten that one, I wouldn't be getting a phone call. She'd just never talk to me again. I'd thought about asking her not to open them, but it would be like telling a kid not to touch a bright, shiny toy placed right in front of them. Curiosity would get the better of her. Besides, I didn't have that kind of pull with Molly. Not anymore.

She didn't have to listen to me. She didn't have to do me favors or trust me because I was her husband. That time had passed.

Which meant I really needed to find out who was sending them. In the past week, since we'd confronted Poppy, I'd studied the handwriting on the envelope for hours trying to place it but had come up empty. They were coming in order, and as long as that continued, I had a little time.

The last letter had shown up in Molly's mailbox over two weeks ago. With every day that went by without another, I started to breathe easier, thinking maybe that was it. That maybe the person who'd stolen my most personal thoughts had reconsidered their actions.

But I'd used up my luck years ago, the day I'd found Molly.

"What did it say?" I stood from my office chair, already collecting my keys and wallet. I'd come in early today, hoping to get some office work done before noon. Then I was spending the day on field visits, reviewing a project bid with one client and meeting with another to get their signoff on the project we'd completed yesterday.

But depending on the letter, those meetings might have to be rescheduled.

"It was the letter you wrote after Jamie . . ."

*Died.*

My knees weakened, and I sank into the chair.

Of all the letters I'd written, that one I remembered the clearest. It was also the one I'd never opened after the day I'd folded it in thirds.

I found the strength to stand again. "I'm coming over."

"You don't have to," she said. "I'm sure you're busy."

"I don't want to talk about this over the phone. Are you home?"

"Yeah."

"See you in a few." I hung up and rushed out of my office door.

"Finn," Bridget called as I walked past her open door.

"What's up?" I stepped back, not going inside.

"Are you leaving? I thought we were going to go through those applications before lunch."

"Shit." I checked my watch. "Sorry. Something came up."

She frowned. "A lot has been coming up lately. What's going on with you?"

"Just some personal stuff."

My relationship with Molly had never been Bridget's business. That didn't stop her from inserting herself. When we'd been going through the divorce, Bridget had sided with me. She was one of the few. I'd made the mistake of telling Bridget about Molly's one-night stand. Bridget had labeled Molly a cheater and said nothing nice about her since.

It wasn't often, but occasionally Bridget would make some comment running Molly down. Molly hadn't understood the business. Or Molly hadn't understood the commitment and hours it took for me to run Alcott.

Bridget was wrong but it wasn't worth the drama to tell her so.

The two women had never gotten along, even when Molly had worked at Alcott and Bridget had been one of her employees.

But I had enough to deal with. I didn't need to hear Bridget's opinion on the added time I was spending with Molly. Ultimately, it was none of her damn business.

"Well, are you coming back?" she asked.

"I'm not sure. I don't know how long this is going to take."

"Fine." She scowled. "I guess we can go through them after your client visits tonight. We can get some food delivered and work in the loft. Like old times."

"Actually, I can't stay late. I've got plans." I'd moved on to the backyard at Molly's and tonight I was taking out the fountain. The kids had asked me if I'd grill cheeseburgers for us all once we were done working.

Bridget didn't like that answer either. "So when?"

"How about this? You go through them all, pick your favorites, then I'll review them with you in the morning. Maybe we could meet early?"

"I can't tomorrow. I've got client meetings back-to-back starting at eight."

"Meet you at seven? I'll bring your favorite coffee."

She fought a smile. "My favorite coffee is the kind I make here every morning."

"Exactly. I'll deliver it personally, all the way from the coffee pot to your office. I'll even make sure to use our cleanest mug."

"Go." She waved me away. "I'll see you tomorrow."

"You're the best," I called as I walked down the hallway to the front door.

My phone was dinging with emails in my pocket and the list of things I needed to do was enormous, but all I could think about on the drive to Molly's was that letter.

God, I'd been heartbroken. Jamie's death had destroyed us all.

The trip to Molly's took longer now than it had years ago. Bozeman had grown too fast for the existing infrastructure, so streets were constantly busy. Even now, with the college kids gone for the summer, the influx of tourists to our popular town made traffic slow.

Finally, I turned off the main roads onto less crowded side streets. Kids rode their bikes, enjoying the summer sunshine. Sprinklers were whirling, keeping yards a lush green, and the sun was streaming through my window.

It all screamed happy. It normally would have made me smile. But my mind wasn't on this beautiful June day. It was on a day in May, years ago, that had been black as night.

I pulled into the driveway at Molly's, jumping out and running for the door. Gavin was outside and he waved from his spot on the porch. His phone was pressed to his ear as he sat outside, his computer on his lap.

I waved back then dismissed him. I didn't bother knocking on the door. I opened it and raced down the entryway. I found Molly at the dining room table, the letter on the wood next to a box of tissues.

"Hey." Her eyes were red. "You didn't need to come here."

I went right to her side, took her hand and pulled her from the chair.

The moment my arms were wrapped around her, the tears came again, soaking the front of my shirt. This was how we'd gotten through those days after Jamie had died. We'd held on to one another, mourning the death of our brother and friend.

"I hate this," she whispered.

"So do I."

"I feel like every time I go to the mailbox, I'm going to get blasted back into the past. I already cried these tears. I don't want to do it again."

I kissed the top of her hair. "I'm sorry."

"It's not your fault."

"It is. I wrote them. And I should have gotten rid of them years ago."

"No." Molly shook her head as she went back to her seat. "I'm glad you didn't. This one . . . I needed to read this one."

"Why?" I took the chair by her side, toying with the side of the letter.

I didn't want to open it again. I didn't want to read it and remember. Because it wasn't fair that she'd had to relive it and I hadn't, I slid the paper across the table and opened the folds, reading the words I'd written in agony years ago.

I swallowed the lump in my throat and closed the letter, hoping the emotions would stay on the page and in the past where they belonged.

"I need to tell you something." Molly blew out a long breath. "Poppy and I were talking the other day. She wondered if Jamie's death was the reason we split up. She thought if she'd handled it better, we might still be together."

"Damn it." I raked a hand through my hair. "I hate that she feels that way. She wasn't the reason we split up."

"That's what I told her too. But ever since, I've been thinking. All these letters . . ." She pointed to the paper. "They've made me think. For so many years, I've tried to pinpoint it."

"Pinpoint what?"

She paused. "The beginning of the end of us."

I rocked back in my chair. "You think this was it?"

"I don't know. I didn't. But now that I've read this letter, yes. I do."

How could this letter make her think this was what had caused our split? "I'm not following you. We had some good years after this. We had Kali then Max after this."

"You said it in your letter. Everything changed. After Jamie died, everything changed."

"His death wasn't the reason we split up."

"Then what was? We were different after his death."

I opened my mouth to answer but shut it when the words didn't come. What *had* caused our divorce? What had taken us from a place where all I needed to get through one of the hardest moments of my life was one glance at her?

"I don't know."

"It wasn't just one thing," she said. "But after this, the bad days started."

"What bad days?"

"*The* bad days. We conceived Kali during makeup sex. We'd both been so tired and exhausted. You were spending nearly every second with Poppy, making sure she was . . . well, you know."

*Alive.*

My parents had gone back to Alaska after the funeral. They'd each had to work because . . . life went on. Except for Poppy, it hadn't. She'd spent months nearly comatose.

Poppy had slipped so far into a depression, nothing had helped. Nothing I said would make her smile. Nothing I did made her open up and talk. She didn't even cry.

Without Jamie, she'd lost her heart. So I'd fought. I'd fought hard for her. I'd called her constantly. When she didn't answer, I went to check on her. I stayed late at her house, lying next to her on the couch until her brain would shut down and she finally fell asleep. Then I carried her to bed. Day after day. Week after week. I spent every minute of the day fearing for my sister's life.

Everything else was shut out, Molly especially. She took over a lot at Alcott and covered when I needed to be with Poppy. She made sure my laundry was done and the lawn was mowed. She ran our lives.

In return, I came home from Poppy's house miserable. I snapped at Molly, taking out my frustrations about Jamie's death on the one person I loved the most.

"What did we fight about that night?" I asked. "I can't remember."

She grinned. "The price of Swedish aspen."

"That's right. For the Bexter project. God, he was an asshole."

"He sure was. That was the first and only time a client made me cry."

Alan Bexter was a guy who'd moved to Bozeman on a whim, a trust-fund kid who'd thought paying full price was beneath him. It was a big project and worth it for Alcott to tackle, even after giving the guy a discount. I'd made a verbal agreement with Alan for a reduced price on the trees he'd wanted to line his driveway.

I'd been in the middle of that project when Jamie was murdered.

By the time we'd wrapped it up, weeks had passed. Molly was doing all the billing for Alcott and she'd sent Bexter his final invoice. All fifty-six Swedish aspen had been itemized at full price.

Bexter had called Molly, ripping her up one side and down the other. Then he'd called me, giving me an ass-chewing before recommending I fire my bookkeeper. The idiot hadn't put two and two together to realize he'd been talking about my wife.

"I swear I told you about the price change," I said.

"And I swear you didn't." The truth was a mystery. Not that it mattered now.

"Damn, that was one hell of a fight."

She grinned. "I don't remember who started throwing the food first."

"You." I chuckled. "I was shocked when you threw those noodles in my face."

"Oh, lord." She dropped her face into her hands. "Not my finest moment."

"No." I reached out and took her hands away, keeping hold of one. "It was perfect. That was the first time I'd laughed in weeks."

That food fight had reminded me of Jamie. He would have done that, started a food fight to defuse a situation. Maybe that was why I'd joined right in, tossing a bowl of

Caesar salad in her face at the same time she'd swatted at me with the loaf of French bread.

We'd collapsed together in the kitchen, laughing hysterically, Bexter and his towering trees forgotten. Then we'd made love on the floor, surrounded by our discarded clothes and uneaten dinner.

That was the night we'd made our Kali.

"Things were better after that." We'd talked all night, and we'd started doing things together again, rather than dividing things up. And we'd gotten real with Poppy.

We flew my parents down to see her again. They'd been calling every day, but on the phone, they hadn't seen how bad things had gotten. Then we all sat her down and told her how worried we were. Poppy felt awful. She felt guilty. Mom and Dad asked her to move home to Alaska and she thought about it.

But then we told them we were pregnant. It was early, but we were too excited not to share the news.

"It was Kali," Molly said. "I think she would have gone to Alaska with your parents if not for Kali. She wanted to be a good aunt. It gave her something to smile about."

"It was the turning point."

So how had things gotten so bad again? How had we found ourselves in more fights? More arguments?

We both stared at the letter again, the quiet settling around us like a heavy cloak. Was she onto something? Had Jamie's death been the beginning of our end?

I refused to believe it. I wouldn't pin this on him.

That funeral had been one of the hardest days in my life. But I made it through. I stood at the podium at the church so full of people there was barely room to stand in the aisles, and I talked about Jamie. I told a room crowded with his friends and family how the two of us had bonded over our shared love of cold beer and greasy cheeseburgers. I talked about the time we'd gone skiing together and had to be rescued by the ski patrol, because we'd convinced one another that the out-of-bounds markers had been put up wrong.

I talked about how he'd been a goof on the outside—how his ability to lighten a room had been unparalleled—and that on the inside, he'd had a heart of gold. That he'd loved nothing more than making the women in his life smile. His mother. And his wife.

I stood in front of hundreds but spoke to only one.

To Molly.

Because, like I'd known in that letter, the only way I could make it through that day was by keeping my eyes on her.

Jamie's death wasn't what had started our downward spiral. I refused to believe it.

"I'm not blaming Jamie for the end of our marriage."

"Finn," Molly said gently. "That's not what I'm saying. We broke. Things got hard and we didn't stick together. And I know this seems strange, but I needed this letter. I needed a reason."

A reason why we'd ended.

"He wasn't the reason," I said firmly.

She closed her eyes. "That's not what I'm saying. I loved Jamie. I miss Jamie. But you can't tell me things didn't change."

No, I couldn't.

"We need to figure out who's sending these letters." I stood from the chair, pacing the length of the table as I changed topics.

"Did you talk to your mom?"

I nodded. "It's not her or Dad."

I'd gone over last week and sat down with them both.

Then I'd begged them for the truth. My parents didn't lie to me, so when they said it wasn't them, I believed them.

It hadn't been easy to tell them about the letters. Or Poppy, for that matter. I didn't want to explain why I'd written them, let alone kept them. But my desire to stop the letters from coming to Molly's mailbox was more than the desire to hide my vulnerability where she was concerned.

Thankfully, my family hadn't prodded. They'd let me get away with a vague explanation and then promised they weren't involved.

"It's not Poppy. It's not your parents. It can't be the kids." Molly sighed. "So we're back to square one."

I nodded. "Who else could it be? Who else would have found them in my closet?"

"Cole?"

"I don't think he's ever been in my bedroom." I ran a hand over my face. "I'm out of guesses."

"I might need to start staking out my mailbox."

I stopped pacing. "That's not a bad idea."

"I was joking."

"Why?" I went back to the table, sitting by her side. "The kids go to Alaska next week with my parents. They'll be gone for two weeks, so I don't need to be sneaking around. Let's stake out the mailbox."

My desperation was showing, but I didn't care. I knew what was coming. If Molly did too, she'd be as anxious as I was to stop it.

"Let's start with Cole," she said. "Then we can evolve to night-vision goggles and watch in shifts."

"Deal."

Molly stood and went into the kitchen for a glass of water. "Sorry to pull you from work."

"It's no problem."

She gave me a skeptical look. "Finn. It's summer. I know how busy you are. I'm good. I appreciate you coming over so we could talk. But you don't need to stay. And while the kids are gone, you can forget my yard."

Was she kicking me out? "You don't want me over here?"

"No, it's not that. But you've been here a lot. I'm sure you're swamped."

"I am."

"Then take the time. Get caught up when you don't have to do extra laundry or cook or run the kids around."

"I don't know how you do it all," I admitted. "How you work at the restaurant and manage to keep everything so clean." I stood up and leaned against the counter. "My place is a wreck most of the time, and I feel like laundry piles up while I'm asleep."

She giggled. "Welcome to the life of a mom."

"I don't say it enough. Thanks for all you do. I know you do most of the laundry for the kids so I don't have to. I know you make sure they've got their stuff for school. I appreciate it."

"Thanks." Her cheeks flushed before she shrugged it off. "They're my kids."

It was more than that. Even after the divorce, when I'd been an asshole to her, she'd always done her best so I wouldn't struggle on the nights when I had the kids alone. It had taken me a lot of years to develop a better routine. To figure out how to do dinnertime, bath time and bedtime without one or both kids having a meltdown. Or without wanting to pull my hair out.

Everything suffered for a while, my business and sanity mostly. For years, it had been a shit show. But I'd gained respect for Molly. I'd always thought things were easier for her because she'd been staying at home while I worked. She'd never complained.

I had no idea how hard it was.

"I took you for granted."

She blinked up at me. "What?"

"You. I took you for granted. I'm sorry for that."

"Oh, um . . . thank you."

"I should have said it sooner."

She dropped her gaze to her water glass, blinking quickly.

My phone rang in my pocket, breaking the moment. There was more to talk about with Molly. I still needed to get to the bottom of why she didn't come to Alcott and my house. If she'd resented me when she'd stayed at home with the kids.

But she was right. I was fucking busy and needed to get back to work.

"I'm planning on coming over tonight to work on the yard."

"You don't have to."

"I want to," I said. "I want to spend time with the kids before they leave. And you."

She nodded, following me to the door. I waved at her as I opened it, but she stopped me. "Finn?"

"Yeah?" I turned over my shoulder.

"Do you think we would have made it if Jamie hadn't been killed?"

My shoulders fell. "I don't know. I really don't know. Do you?"

"Yes." She didn't hesitate. "But it doesn't matter now."

"No, I guess not."

We were broken.

Because everything had changed.

# nine
## Molly

"So, are you still . . ." Randall's eyebrows shot up as he trailed off.

"Being foolish?" I asked and he nodded. The kids were in Alaska and Finn hadn't spent a night in his own bed all week. "Yes."

His frown made me feel worse than the time I'd gotten a speeding ticket in high school with my mom sitting in the passenger seat.

Randall was as close to a grandparent as I'd ever had. Mom's parents lived on the East Coast, both too old to travel. I hadn't been close to them as a child and wasn't as an adult. They'd never even met my kids.

My father's parents had lived in Bozeman, but they'd both passed when I was young. My father was twelve years older than my mother. In a lot of ways, he'd been more like a grandparent than a father. He'd spoiled me with treats behind her back. He'd let me stay up past my bedtime when she was away. I couldn't remember a time when he'd punished me. But we weren't close either. He was a retired professor at

Montana State. He'd always been more interested in spending time with his grad students than with his daughter. I think Mom had wanted a child and had given Dad an ultimatum. He never argued with Mom. He did what she wanted then disappeared to his library before she could ask for something else.

I saw him every couple of months when Mom would force him to visit the kids, but I'd given up on building a close father-daughter relationship with him years ago. I didn't interest Dad, and we didn't have anything in common.

It made me wonder how life would have been if Randall had been a parent. Or my parent. Maybe I would have had someone's shoulder to cry on during the divorce. Instead, I'd kept my tears hidden, not wanting to burden Poppy with them. She'd been swamped trying to get the restaurant open, and given how close she was to both Finn and me, both of us had fought hard not to make her choose a side.

Mom had smiled like a Cheshire cat when I'd told her about our separation, so I didn't share my tears with her either.

Maybe if I'd had a Randall, I wouldn't have made such a horrible mistake. I wouldn't have slept with that other man.

"Be careful," Randall warned.

"I am."

It was nice to have his warning. And I was being careful. Even though this affair had come out of nowhere, I was keeping up my guard. I didn't need Finn's affections to bolster my confidence anymore. I could end this at any time.

I could end it today if I wanted.

I didn't want to, but I could.

"What's going on?" Jimmy asked, his cheeks puffing out with a bite of cornbread and chili.

"None of your damn business," Randall muttered before I could dodge the question.

"Fine." Jimmy finished chewing and swallowed. "You two always have your inside jokes and hushed conversations. It's damn annoying. And kind of rude. But it gives me and Poppy something to talk about behind your backs."

"What?" My eyes bulged, a smile tugging at my lips. "You do not."

He nodded. "We do. We talk about you two all the time. How you two can't keep up with our jokes. That's probably what you're talking about. We figured you've been explaining them to Randall here for years."

Randall's face turned magenta as he scowled.

Jimmy met my eyes, his own twinkling as he fought a smile by shoving another bite of chili in his mouth. He didn't care a bit if Randall and I had our own language. We'd had it for years. He and Poppy had their own too. But any excuse to rile up Randall and Jimmy would hit those buttons faster than a kid playing whack-a-mole.

"Your jokes are so damn simple, Brady could understand them," Randall snapped.

"Brady might only be one, but he's brilliant. Sure, he could understand them. He's my great-grandson, so he's got superior genes."

Randall ripped his cap off his knee and tugged it on his head. It was the end of June and plenty warm outside, but not a day went by when he didn't wear that cap. With it secured and his cane in hand, he stood from his stool.

"Hey." Jimmy had just shoved another bite in his mouth and with his shout, little crumbs went spraying. "Where are you going?"

"Find your own ride home. Maybe Brady can drive you on his plastic tractor."

I giggled, quickly covering my mouth with my hand. My laughing would only make it worse.

"Get back here," Jimmy ordered. "Poppy made fresh apple pie this morning and I'm not missing it."

"I'll leave if I damn well want. And you're not getting rides from me anymore."

In six years, that was the 729th time he'd made that threat. Poppy and I had a running tally beneath the cash register. I bent down, slowly grabbing the pencil on the notepad and crossing out the old number to add in the new.

Poppy poked her head through the swinging door from the kitchen. "What's going on out here?"

"I'm leaving," Randall barked, shuffling closer toward the door. "I don't need to deal with this harassment every day."

"Oh, okay. Bye." She smiled at Jimmy. "I was just experimenting with the chocolate mousse. I made a raspberry compote to spoon on top. Want to try one?"

Randall's body stilled, his ears perking up. He didn't just have a sweet tooth. Every bone in his body was addicted to sugar. Mention chocolate and the man practically vibrated.

"I'll have one," I told Poppy. "If there's any extra."

"I just made a small batch. Only four jars until I know that people like the recipe."

"What are you waiting for?" Randall spun back around, his sight set on his stool. "Get those jars."

Poppy disappeared into the kitchen, I went to get four spoons, and Jimmy polished off his lunch while we waited for the mousse. Randall was on his stool, today's bickering forgotten as quickly as it had started.

Four chocolate mousses later, we all agreed that Poppy's raspberry concoction would be a hit.

"I think I'll go whip up some more before I forget what I

did. Then we can freeze it and have it for the anniversary celebration next week."

"Want some company in the kitchen?"

"Sure. Dora just clocked in so she can take over out here."

We left Randall and Jimmy at their stools and went into the back. Dora was at the sink, washing her hands to begin her shift. I said hello, then chatted with her about her classes before she left Poppy and me alone in the kitchen.

"Any more letters?" Poppy asked, measuring sugar into a bowl.

"Nope. Nothing." I hadn't told her much about the letter Finn had written for Jamie's funeral. I'd simply left it that I'd received another letter and it had made Finn and I talk about some things.

"And you still have no idea who's sending them?"

"It's not you."

"It's not me," she promised.

"It's not your parents. Do you think it could be Cole?"

She shook her head. "I asked him about it when you guys first asked me. He was just as confused as I was."

"Damn. Then I'm at a loss."

"What about Kali?"

I laughed. "Finn thought it could be her too. But I don't know. The handwriting on the envelope isn't hers. It looks too adult."

"And you're sure it isn't Finn?"

"Finn?" I hadn't even thought to question it. He'd told me it wasn't him, and I'd believed him. "He was so shocked when I told him about the first two, I don't think he could have been making it up."

"I can't believe he kept them all this time."

I sighed. "Me too. I wish . . . I wish he had sent me those letters after he wrote them. They've been good for us."

"How so?"

"They've made us talk through some old arguments. Relive some good moments. I think it's healed a lot of the wounds we inflicted on one another. That and—" *The sex.*

It wasn't the first time I'd almost blurted out that Finn and I were sleeping together. Keeping secrets from Poppy was completely foreign to me. I hadn't kept something like this from her during our entire relationship, and I couldn't think of a time when she wasn't the first person, besides Finn, I ran to with good news. The same was true with the bad.

Was it good news or bad news that Finn and I were having sex daily?

Good news. It had to be good news. The way Finn made me feel, the way his hands made my body come alive couldn't be bad.

"That and, what?" she asked, taking a huge box of raspberries out of the fridge.

"I love that you do that."

"Do what?"

"You always start something new with a sample. You get so worried that it won't be good. But deep down, you already know it's going to be amazing because you've already bought the ingredients in bulk."

She shrugged, but a smile ghosted her lips. "We could have used the raspberries in the salads. And don't change the subject. We were talking about you and Finn."

*We're sleeping together.* The words were right there, ready to spill onto the table next to the cartons of fruit.

"I, uh, me and Finn." My throat closed. I wanted to tell her so badly, but would it do her harm? When Jamie was alive, I would have told Poppy without a moment's hesitation. But I'd seen her broken and at her lowest. It was hard not to want to protect her, even though she'd built herself up.

Maybe this would help her understand and believe that she wasn't the reason we'd divorced. Maybe telling her about Finn would actually ease some of the doubts in her mind.

Poppy looked at me, waiting.

"It's more than just the letters. We've been . . . seeing each other."

Her eyebrows came together. "Like dating?"

"No, not really. He's been coming over and we've been, uh, sleeping together."

A mixture of emotions flashed across her face. Excitement. Hope. Fear. "W-what does this mean? Are you getting back together?"

"No," I said immediately. "No. I don't want you to get your hopes up, because we are absolutely not getting back together."

"How did this happen?" She blinked twice. "Was it the letters?"

"Yes and no. Remember the night he mowed my lawn? He stayed to watch a movie with me and the kids. We had a lot of wine. One thing led to another and we had sex."

"It's been weeks. And you didn't tell me?"

I winced. "I'm sorry. I didn't know what to say. I was so surprised. I wasn't sure what was happening. Honestly, I still don't."

"So you're having sex but not getting back together?"

"Right." I gave her a definite nod. "We are *not* getting back together."

"Are you going to keep sleeping together?" she asked, coming around my side of the table, the raspberries forgotten.

"I guess? I don't know that either. I mean, it's got to end at some point. Right?"

"Molly, what are you doing?"

"I don't know. It's Finn."

"You're going to get your heart broken again."

"Not this time. It's different now."

"How?"

"I'm not in love with Finn."

She flinched. "Oh."

And that was why I'd kept this to myself. Poppy believed I was in love with Finn. That he was in love with me. Yes, there was love there. I loved him as the father of my children. I loved him as my first love. But I wasn't *in love* with Finn. Not anymore.

I wasn't sure if my heart was capable of being in love with anyone again.

"Okay," she finally said.

I was glad the secret was out in the open, but I didn't like the judgment on her face. She wouldn't come out and say it like Randall. She wasn't a blunt person. But I knew her well and I knew that stern look. She thought this affair was foolish too.

She wasn't wrong.

The door to the kitchen swung open and Cole walked inside.

Poppy's face lit up like twinkle lights on a black night, her irritation with Finn and me forgotten. "Hey. What are you doing here?"

"Hoping to snag a late lunch." Cole walked straight to his wife for a long kiss on the mouth.

He was wearing his signature jeans and black Bozeman Police Department polo. His holstered gun and shiny badge were clipped on his leather belt. His hair was pushed back away from his forehead by the aviator sunglasses he was never without.

Cole Goodman had hot cop perfected. With those light-green eyes and a body toned to steel, he was the detective every woman wanted on the Bozeman Police Department's annual calendar. However, much to the female population's disappointment, they'd been doing local scenery, cutting themselves short on fundraising opportunities.

I loved him for Poppy. She was his life, along with their kids, and I hoped he used his handcuffs on her regularly.

"Get a room," I teased when their kiss dragged on.

Cole just grinned against Poppy's mouth. When they eventually broke apart, he threw an arm around her shoulders and surveyed the table. "What are you making?"

"Raspberry compote for the chocolate mousse. I was experimenting earlier, and it turned out all right."

"More than all right." I rolled my eyes at her modesty. "It's amazing. So good it made the menu for the anniversary celebration."

"Have any more?"

She frowned. "No, I only made four. If I had known you were coming, I would have saved mine for you."

"It's okay, beautiful. It's never a hardship eating the apple pie."

"What do you want for lunch?"

He shrugged, letting her go. "Surprise me."

Poppy grinned and went to the fridge, pulling out a tomato, lettuce and some leftover bacon. Then she grabbed some sourdough from the pantry shelf.

"Had I known you'd be willing to make one of your famous BLTs, I would have skipped the mousse too," I said.

Her BLTs were my favorite. Poppy wasn't satisfied with mayonnaise on the sandwich. She'd mix in a bunch of spices that took the simple sandwich to the next level. But like a lot of her recipes, the spice mixture was impromptu. It was never the same, though always delicious.

"Want one?" she asked.

I was full, but these sandwiches were not to miss. "Would you go halvsies?"

Before she could answer, the door swung open again.

My heart skipped as Finn walked inside. With his natural swagger and sexy grin, which let a few of his straight white teeth show, the man's presence had always sent zings through my body.

"Hey, guys." He waved and walked over to shake Cole's hand. "What's going on?"

"Just came down for lunch. You?"

"Same."

"I was just making BLTs," Poppy told him. "Want one?"

He rubbed his hands together, practically drooling. "Hell, yeah. I'm starving. I missed breakfast today."

I dropped my gaze to my feet, hoping to hide my flushed cheeks. With the kids gone, he didn't have to rush out of the house before dawn, so I'd been making him breakfast every morning. I'd been just about to crack some eggs this morning when he'd come into the kitchen and kissed my neck. That kiss had led to another, then another, until we were horizontal on the kitchen floor, Finn's mouth between my legs.

Technically, he'd had me for breakfast.

And coffee. I was a generous hostess. I'd sent him on his way with a travel mug of coffee after he'd filled me with his own release.

"Hey." Finn came to stand on my side of the table.

The magnetic pull was there, the urge to stand close enough that our arms would touch. But we fought it, standing stiffly, twelve inches apart to maintain distance. His fresh, outdoorsy scent was even more appealing than Poppy's cooking. It was impossible not to stare a moment too long at his bright-blue eyes as they glinted with mischief.

He was definitely thinking about his *breakfast*.

My cheeks hurt as I forced myself not to smile.

"What are you guys up to tonight?" Cole asked.

"Nothing," I answered too fast.

"Probably having sex," Poppy muttered.

"What?" Finn's mouth hung open as Cole muttered, "Huh?"

"Poppy," I hissed.

She turned from the flattop, spatula in hand, and waved it in a circle. "As soon as you both left, I was going to tell Cole anyway."

"So much for keeping it to ourselves," Finn grumbled.

"Sorry. It just sort of came out."

"It's okay." He ran a hand through his hair, the red strands sticking up funny. "You two don't have secrets."

I smiled. He understood my friendship with his sister so well.

"Are you guys getting back together?" Cole asked.

"No," we answered in unison.

"It's, uh . . ." Finn trailed off. "Complicated."

Well, at least I wasn't the only one who didn't know how to explain our affair.

Cole left the explanation at that, maybe because as a detective, he knew when he'd hit a dead end in a line of questioning.

"What were you going to ask about for tonight?" Finn asked.

"Oh." Cole picked up a raspberry and plopped it in his mouth. "My parents want to take the kids for the night. Since we're all kid-less, I thought we could go out and get a beer or something."

"Or I could cook?" Poppy offered.

Cole shook his head. "You're taking a break tonight."

"I'd be up for that new Thai place," I suggested. "I've been wanting to try it but the kids won't eat it."

While I loved hitting the movie theater solo, eating at a restaurant alone was not my thing. I admired women who could do it.

"I have a better idea." Poppy brought over the toast and warmed bacon to the table, starting to assemble the sandwiches. "How about we order takeout from the Thai place and have a game night?"

A game night. I hadn't gone to a game night in a decade.

Poppy loved playing board games, something we all used to do together during and after college. After Jamie died, Poppy hadn't played a board game until Cole came into her life.

Now the two had built quite the collection of games and hosted game nights every so often. *Ugh.* Finn used to take Brenna.

"I'm in," Finn said and took the sandwich Poppy slid across the table.

"Nice." Poppy handed Cole his sandwich next. He grinned at her then shoved a huge bite in his mouth.

Game night. I'd worked so hard to be happy about Poppy and Cole doing things with Finn and whichever woman he was dating. It was strange to be in that place. The other woman's place. Strange yet . . . comfortable.

Excitement bubbled. "Sounds great."

We all stood around the table, eating our BLTs, too consumed with food to talk. Until Finn broke the silence.

"So, Cole. What are the chances you'd be willing to fingerprint a few letters for us?"

Cole chuckled. "About as good as me agreeing to let MacKenna date before she's thirty."

"Hmm." Finn frowned. "Then I'd like to report a crime. Someone broke into my house, stole some old letters and snuck them into Molly's mailbox."

"Still can't run the fingerprints."

"Damn." Finn looked to me. "We're back to square one again."

"Mailbox stakeout?"

He grinned. "I'll bring the night-vision goggles."

---

"Bye." I waved at Poppy and Cole as they stood on the porch of their house. My sides hurt from laughing so hard all night. "I love game night."

Finn chuckled. "Me too. Especially when we dominate."

"Did they win anything?"

"Nope." Finn held up his hand for a high five. "Team Alcott cleaned up."

I smacked my hand against his. *Team Alcott.*

It was like we'd gone back in time. Tonight had been so much fun, laughing and teasing one another as we'd played game after game. It was hard to remember the downward spiral that had happened between this game night and the last one we'd played in college.

Death and divorce.

"Cole is a good sport," I told Finn as we walked down the sidewalk toward his truck.

Jamie had been so competitive, there'd been a few game nights in college where things had turned from fun to fight. But not Cole. He was competitive enough to present a challenge, but when he lost, which they had a lot tonight, he didn't get angry.

"Yeah, he is." Finn opened the door for me and helped me inside.

He'd picked me up tonight from home so we could ride here together. We both just assumed he'd be coming home with me. While I strapped on my seat belt, he closed the door and went around to his side, climbing in and getting us on the road.

My head was light from all the wine and even a little dizzy. Tomorrow morning might be miserable, but it had been worth it.

"What do you say we go to my place instead?"

My face whipped to Finn's profile. "What?"

"I'd like to stay at my place for a change."

"Oh, uh . . ." I scrambled for an excuse. "I don't have any of my stuff."

"What stuff?"

"My toothbrush. Pajamas. Extra hair ties." I only had one on my wrist, so I needed to go home for a second.

"I've got an extra toothbrush. Kali has a pile of hair ties in the bathroom." He met my gaze. "And you won't need pajamas."

I didn't have another excuse other than the truth. We'd had such a fun night, and I didn't want to dive into this conversation.

"Why won't you come inside my house?" he asked gently.

"Do we really have to talk about this tonight?"

We approached a stop sign on Main Street. Taking a right led to my house. A left to his.

He answered my question by turning left.

My shoulders sagged. "It's your home."

"Exactly. What's wrong with my home? The kids live there fifty percent of the time."

"No." I shook my head. "You don't understand. It's *your* home."

"What are you saying?"

"I'm saying, it's your home. A home you created without me. We've broken so many boundaries these past few weeks. This one, I need this one, Finn. It's your home. Your place. Not mine."

This line was one I would not cross. Because if I walked into his house and fell in love with the rooms he'd set up for the kids, or the way it felt to sleep beneath his sheets, it would be even harder to shore up that boundary when this was over.

Finn drove in silence for a few more blocks. My heart was in my throat, wondering if the end was closer than I'd thought this morning. But then he flipped his turn signal, taking us around a block until we were stopped at another intersection.

This time, he turned right.

Toward *my* house.

"Thank you," I whispered.

Maybe it was the wine. Maybe it was the fact that he hadn't argued but had listened to me and heard what I was saying, but tears flooded my eyes. In the quiet and dark cab, one dripped down my cheek.

If Finn saw it fall, he didn't say a word. But he did stretch his arm across the empty seat between us, beckoning me closer.

I took the invitation, unbuckling and flipping up the console to slide over into his side. Finn always insisted that all Alcott trucks have a center seat because more often than not, a crew of workers would pile inside. One bench seat saved a six-person crew from taking two vehicles.

I was glad for it. I curled into his side and his arm wound

around my shoulders. And I murmured another, "Thank you."

"What was I thinking? We have a mailbox to stake out."

"True."

Though at the moment, I didn't want the letters to stop, because I had a sinking feeling that once they did, Finn and I would stop too.

*Darling Molly,*

*It's four o'clock in the morning. I haven't slept for more than two hours in a row for five days. You're passed out right now in bed and I should be next to you. But before I can sleep, I have to get this out.*

*You're the most amazing woman I've ever met. I didn't think I could love you more, but then I watched you bring Kali into this world. Nineteen hours. No drugs. And you didn't scream, not once. Amazing. The pain on your face looked unbearable, but you held tight because you didn't want the first sound our daughter heard to be your cries. It was the most amazing thing I've ever seen. And you're so amazing with her. Breastfeeding hasn't been going well. She isn't sleeping. I can tell you're sore because you wince every time you walk. But you haven't dropped your amazing smile. How do you do that?*

*You're amazing. I'm exhausted and can't think of any other word right now for it. For you. But you're amazing. I love you.*

*Yours,*
*Finn*

# ten
## Finn

"Do you like it?" Kali asked me as I chewed a bite of my taco.

I nodded, swallowing before I smiled. "They're great, sweetie. Nice job."

"Great? Or *amazing*," Molly teased. "I think they're *amazing*."

I shot her a glare as I took another bite.

I was never going to live down that last goddamn letter. I'd written it in a state of delirium. It was the one letter I'd fully intended to give to Molly as I'd scribbled the words. After I'd folded it up and left it on the office desk, I'd gone to bed that night with a stupid smile on my face.

Everything I'd written was true. Molly was amazing and I'd never forget those first two sleep-deprived weeks after Kali was born.

The next day, I woke up and went to get the letter to give to Molly, but then I reread it. *Amazing* had been in almost every damn sentence, so I didn't give her the letter. I hurried to stow it away with the others so she'd never find it. Instead, I *told* her how amazing she was.

I told her while she was in the rocking chair in Kali's room. They'd both been relaxed and sleepy, but awake, staring into one another's eyes.

I sat on the floor by the chair, took Molly's free hand and told her how brave she was. How selfless. How strong. The words I hadn't been able to come up with the night before were much easier after a few hours of sleep.

But ever since the letter had shown up in her mailbox yesterday, she'd been teasing me relentlessly with the word *amazing*.

"These are really good, Kali," Max told her, his cheeks bulging with his own bite.

She blushed, holding her own taco. "Thanks."

While Max and I had worked in the yard tonight, Molly and Kali had made the tacos. Molly had given Kali credit for the meal.

*My kids are amazing.*

That thought crossed my mind at least once a day. I might overuse *amazing*, but it was accurate in this case. They awed me. They left me wondering how in the hell they'd turned out so good when half of each week they were left with me.

It was Molly. Her goodness had seeped into them from the beginning.

"I'm glad you guys are back," Molly said. "It's too quiet around here without you."

The kids had flown in on Friday night with my parents, just in time for the anniversary celebration at the restaurant yesterday. The celebration had been a raging success, like the parties from each year before. And since Poppy and Molly had both worked for nearly twenty hours straight to make sure it went off without a hitch, they'd each taken today off before returning on Monday.

I'd spent my Sunday morning at home, working on my

laptop at the dining room table while Molly was home with the kids. Then when I couldn't stand the idea of being alone any longer, I'd driven over, not caring if she had plans or wanted time with only the kids. I'd come under the guise of working on her yard, when really, I'd missed Kali and Max.

And Molly.

After two weeks of sleeping in her bed each night, I'd been tossing and turning in my own bed because I hadn't had my pillow.

"What did you do while we were gone?" Max asked.

"Don't talk with your mouth full," I told him quietly.

He nodded and chewed faster before repeating his question. "What did you do while we were with Grandma and Grandpa?"

What did we do while they were gone? *Each other.*

"Oh, not too much." Molly's eyes flicked to mine.

We'd spent the last week on mailbox stakeout duty, which was really nothing more than occasionally looking at it from the window or spending our evenings on the front porch instead of inside.

We were awful at surveillance, probably because we'd get antsy sitting on the porch, mere inches away from one another. The tension would grow thick, the air hot, and we'd retreat to the comfort of Molly's cool bedroom sheets.

Which was how the last letter had come and we still had no clue who'd dropped it off.

"We actually went and had a game night with Aunt Poppy and Uncle Cole," I told the kids.

"Who won?" Kali asked. My sweet girl had a competitive streak.

I chuckled. "We did. Duh."

Max grinned and high-fived me. "Nice."

We spent the rest of the meal hearing more about the kids'

trip to Alaska, then we all went outside to toss a Frisbee around in the yard before they had to go to bed.

Not once throughout the night did they ask me when I was going home. They didn't ask what I was doing over at their house.

"Thanks for dinner," I told Molly as we loaded the remaining dishes into the dishwasher. After dinner, we'd left them in the sink so we could spend the evening outside before the sun set.

"No problem. I'm glad we could both see the kids tonight. I missed them."

"Me too." I put the last glass into the top rack and closed the door. "Should I go?"

She glanced in the direction of the stairs. "I don't know. They start camp tomorrow, and they're both excited. I doubt they'll wake up too early, but I don't want to push our luck."

"Yeah," I muttered. "I don't want to leave."

Molly came to lean against the counter at my side, speaking in a hushed voice. "I don't want you to leave. But . . ."

"I know. The kids can't know I've been sleeping in their mother's bed."

We could tell them until we were blue in the face that we weren't getting back together, but if they caught us, it would send a completely different message.

"Should we just end this now?" she asked.

I stiffened. The immediate answer was no. Hell no. I didn't want to give this up. But logic began to creep in, like a fog dulling the sunlight.

This was going to end at some point. Molly and I weren't getting back together, so this fling would eventually expire.

"I don't want to," I whispered. "I'm not ready yet. Are you?"

She didn't hesitate. "Not even close."

Our eyes locked, holding one another captive. Hers were so expressive and hungry. There was something beneath the lust, something familiar, but I couldn't place it.

Once, years ago, Molly and I could carry on entire conversations with our eyes alone. But that was before we'd learned to hide things from one another—before I started keeping my problems from her, and she started hiding her true feelings from me.

I didn't try to solve that look. This wasn't about Molly and me working things out as a married couple. It was about sex.

Only sex.

I leaned closer to her, dropping my chin so my cheek brushed against her hair. It was pulled up into a messy knot, but some of the tendrils had escaped since dinner, dangling loose toward her neck.

Molly drifted my way, her breaths coming faster. The air in the kitchen crackled with anticipation.

"Kiss me."

She gave me a slight nod, rising up on her toes.

I dipped, my breath coasting down her cheek, but then I remembered where we were. "Wait. Not here."

She huffed when I pulled away, taking a few deep breaths as I took her hand and dragged her down the hallway to her bedroom. The second we were away from the stairs—with the door closed and out of danger that one of the kids would walk in on us—I framed her face with my hands and slammed my lips down on hers. I swallowed her gasp and let my hands roam from her face and down her shoulders. I pulled her closer, needing to feel her against me.

Her hands went for my fly, tugging the button on my jeans open to dive inside. The feel of her grip, those long fingers wrapped around my shaft, was so incredible I nearly blacked out.

How was it possible for us to go so wrong? We were good together. So. Fucking. Good.

"Finn," she moaned into my mouth, her tongue sliding along the seam of my bottom lip. Her fist wrapped around my shaft tighter, stroking the velvet flesh inside my jeans. "More."

I pulled her closer, my hands everywhere. Under her shirt. In her hair. Palming her ass. I couldn't find the right spot. The right grip so I wouldn't lose her.

"I can't . . . I need . . ." She let go of my cock and her fingers fumbled for the zipper. She got it down and then shoved at the hem of my shirt. "Closer. Get closer."

I reached behind my head and jerked off my shirt. Before my skin could even register the cool air, her hands were on me, leaving a hot trail as they traveled up and down my chest and stomach.

Next came her shirt in a swish of cotton sailing toward the hardwood floor. Only then did I get closer. I wrapped my arms around her body, letting my hands dive underneath her panties.

Molly hissed as the rough tips of my fingers bit into her soft curves. But she gave as good as she got, her nails scratching up my spine as I walked us backward toward the bed.

Jeans were lost along the way, hands only breaking contact for split seconds to rip and tug ourselves bare.

When the backs of my knees hit the bed, I hoisted us both onto the mattress, scooting myself toward the headboard.

Molly followed on her knees, her breasts heavy, her nipples peaked and tight. Then she gave me a wicked grin that went straight to my balls. "I want to ride you."

"Climb on up, darling."

*Darling.* I'd let that slip, but she didn't seem to notice. With her knees bracketing my hips, she fisted my cock again, dragging it through her slit.

"Fuck, you're soaked."

"Hmm." Her head lulled to the side as she took my tip and rolled it against her clit. The shudder that ran through her body shook the bed. She did it again, using my cock to work herself up.

As much as I wanted to watch her get herself off on me, I was losing control. Her scent surrounded me. The heady smell of sex was in the air, and I needed her pussy. I sat up straight, taking her hips in my grip. Her eyes popped open, dark and dizzy. Drunk.

With one thrust of my hips, I filled her.

"Oh, fuck." I fell backward, letting her tight heat squeeze me as she cried out my name.

I held her in place, her entire body tense as she waited to adjust around my size. When she was ready, she opened her eyes.

"Good?"

Her eyes twinkled. "Amazing."

My deep chuckle filled the room, then she dropped her hands to my shoulders and *moved*.

I held on to her hips with a light grip, ready to help if she got tired, but she was in control. She set the pace. And she rode me until we were both glistening and breathless.

Every muscle in my body was strained—my balls were tight, ready to empty into Molly's luscious body. But as she closed her eyes, a furrow between her eyebrows, I knew there was something going on in her head. Something was keeping her from letting go.

With one hand, I latched on to a nipple. With the other, I strummed her clit with the pad of my thumb.

Her eyes shot open. They locked on mine.

"Finn," she whimpered.

"Come. Come with me."

That was all it took. A gravelly order and she exploded, her head falling back, that gorgeous hair spilling from its loose tie. It cascaded down her back, rubbing against my thighs.

And as she clenched around me, pulse after pulse, I stopped fighting my own release. I poured myself into her, shooting long and hard until I was wrecked and limp.

Molly fell on top of me, that hair draping around us like a blanket. My hands wound into the spirals, each finger claiming a few strands of its own to twirl.

*Where did we go wrong?*

The question rushed into my mind, taking the spotlight away from anything else. Where had we gone wrong? How could we be this good and lose it all? How could we throw this away?

The fights. The missed dinners. The nights we went to bed, our backs turned on one another.

The other man.

Just the thought of her with another man made me queasy. I rolled her to the side, sliding out to sit and swing my legs over the bed.

"Is everything okay?"

I glanced over my shoulder, Molly's flushed face and tousled hair a sight I'd once thought was mine and mine alone. She'd shared that with one other man. Were there more? My stomach rolled again.

"Finn?"

I blinked out of my stupor. "I'll get a washcloth. Hang tight."

She fell into the pillows as I stood and walked to the bathroom on shaking legs.

I hadn't let myself think of the other man in years. Each time I did I felt sick. The night she'd told me about it, I'd puked for an hour when she'd finally left me alone. But that was years ago. It wasn't supposed to still shock me this much. It wasn't supposed to still hurt.

I splashed some cold water on my face in the bathroom, waiting a few minutes until the ache in my chest went away. I stared at my face in the mirror and remembered what this fling was about.

Sex.

I was having sex with Molly. We didn't need to dig up everything from the past. I didn't need to think about the past.

When it was all blocked off, secured away in the dark corner of my mind that I refused to visit, I ran warm water on a washcloth for Molly. Then I went back into the bedroom and handed it over to my wife.

*Ex-wife.*

---

"No."

Molly's gasp woke me up.

"Mom?"

Kali's voice sent me flying out of the bed.

"Ew."

Max's groan sent me back into the bed when I remembered I was buck-ass naked.

*Fuck.* The sunrise cast a faint glow on the window's

shades and I glanced at the clock. Five in the morning. It was too early for the kids to be awake during summer break. Fifteen more minutes and my alarm would be blaring. I'd have been dressed and halfway out the door.

"What are you guys doing up?" Molly asked, holding the sheets to cover herself. Her hair was everywhere, her cheeks crimson red.

"I don't feel good." Max held his stomach as he came to the bed, not caring that his parents were in it together. Naked.

"He threw up," Kali said. "I heard him in the bathroom."

"You're sick? Oh, no." Molly stretched for the throw blanket she kept at the foot of the bed. She yanked it up, replacing it as a cover for her chest as she slid out of bed. Then she wrapped it around herself like she did with her towel after showering.

I took the sheet with me as I stood, winding it around my hips and holding it up with a hand.

Molly rushed to Max, her hands going right for his forehead and cheeks. "You're hot."

He leaned his face into her palms. "Can I still go to camp today?"

"Sorry, honey. I don't think so. Not if you're sick."

"Ah." His face crumpled, his eyes welling with tears. "I really want to go."

"I know." She pulled him into her arms as he collapsed against her chest. "Let's rest today and hopefully you'll feel up for it tomorrow."

He sniffled and nodded, his eyes drifting shut.

I walked over and knelt down, ruffling Max's hair. "Want to come and hang out with me today? You can rest on the couch in my office and watch the iPad."

Molly looked up. "I can stay home. Poppy can cover the restaurant today."

"It's up to you. If it's easier for me to take him along, I can."

She stroked Max's hair. In just moments, he was practically asleep on her shoulder. "I'll stay home with him."

"Okay. Then I'll take Kali to camp and pick her up tonight."

Kali stood back from the three of us. Her eyes were full of confusion as they darted between me and Molly.

An invisible fist closed around my heart, making each beat hurt. The disbelief in her gaze. The hope. We were going to crush it.

*Fuck. What have we done?*

"You stayed here?" she whispered.

"I did." I wasn't sure what to say but the truth couldn't hurt. Much.

"B-but—"

"Come on." Molly stood up, cutting Kali off. She hoisted Max up with an oomph, his legs circling around her waist. He was too big for her to carry but her strength never ceased to surprise me. "Let's go to the living room. Then we can talk."

Kali spun around slowly then hesitantly led the way.

"I'll carry him." Though I wasn't sure how, since I needed one hand to hold up my sheet.

"I've got him." Molly shook her head. "You get dressed."

But instead of finding my clothes, I followed her out into the living room.

Kali was perched on the edge of the couch with her arms wrapped around her stomach.

Max was in a daze as Molly laid him down next to his sister.

She kissed his forehead. "Be right back."

Molly and I both rushed to her bedroom. She went right

for the bathroom, grabbing a red silk Kimono robe she hadn't had when we'd been married.

I scrambled to find my clothes strewn on the floor and pulled them on. "What are we going to tell them?"

She came out, tying her hair up as she walked. "The truth."

We'd always been honest with Kali and Max, even when they were little. I don't think either of them had really understood what it meant when we'd told them about the divorce. Max had only been two and Kali four. But they'd learned over time. When we'd had Mommy nights and Daddy nights, when *good nights* were done via FaceTime, they'd learned.

Molly and I shared a worried glance as we headed for the living room. The kids may have adjusted to our divorced lifestyle, but that didn't mean finding their parents in bed wouldn't have an impact. *Goddamn it.* This conversation was going to be miserable.

When we reached the living room, my heart sank. The distraught look on Kali's face was the reason we shouldn't have started up this affair. I hated that I put it there.

Molly sat in between the kids, taking Kali's hand from her lap to hold it on her own.

I went to Max, picking him up so he could lean against my side. "Wake up for a second, big guy."

He nodded, cracking his eyes open. Then I looked to Molly, hoping she knew where to start because I didn't have a damn clue.

"Dad slept here last night. With me." She cut right to the chase.

"Are you getting back together?" Kali asked.

"No," Molly said gently. "No, we're not."

My daughter's frame shrank, confusion becoming devastation.

"We love you both so much. I'm sorry if this is confusing."

Kali didn't say a word. Neither did Max.

Molly's worried gaze met mine as we waited for the kids to say something. Anything. But as the minutes wore on, I realized there wasn't anything more to say.

"If you guys want to talk about it, we're here," I told them. "Always."

Kali stood and looked to Molly. "Can I stay home today too?"

"Sure, sweetheart. You guys can get snuggled on the couch. I'll turn on a movie."

I stood up to let Max lie down. Kali took the corner where Molly had been sitting. When they were both covered with blankets and the television was on quietly, I followed Molly back to the bedroom, closing the door behind us.

"We can't do this to them, Finn. Not again."

"I know." I rubbed my jaw. "Ready or not, we have to stop."

She sat on the edge of the bed, leaving a space for me to sit too. With our thighs touching, I put a hand between us, palm up. She instantly put hers palm down, threading our fingers together.

"It was always going to end, wasn't it?"

She nodded. "Yeah. It was."

"I'm not sorry."

"Neither am I," she whispered. "Maybe this was the ending we should have had all along. The one we missed because we were too busy being angry and bitter and hurt. I like this ending much better."

"So do I."

We sat together, hands clasped, until it was time to break apart. When she attempted to pry her fingers loose from mine, I didn't let go at first. But she wiggled them again and I had no choice. When she stood and walked to the bathroom, I felt it again.

The hole.

It had been gone for the last month, temporarily filled.

I stood from the bed and went to the bathroom door to say good-bye. I pushed it open a crack. In the shower, Molly's shoulders were hunched forward, shaking.

She was crying.

Fuck, but I wanted to hold her. I wanted to promise that it would be okay. We'd figure it out together.

But we'd tried that once. I'd made those promises when we'd been married and hadn't kept a single one.

So I backed away, closing the door to just a crack so she wouldn't think I'd been watching.

"I'm going to take off," I called.

"O-okay."

"Bye." I closed the door and sagged against the frame. Then I did what I should have done last night. I left.

Everything about it felt wrong. I was leaving Molly in tears. Max was sick on the couch. Kali had retreated into her own world, barely saying a word as I kissed her good-bye.

I didn't drive home but to work instead, wearing yesterday's clothes. If I went home, I'd shower. I didn't want to shower, not when Molly's scent lingered on my skin.

I was the first to arrive at Alcott. My truck was parked alone in front of the office, like it had been many, many mornings. Before I got out to go inside, a memory hit me hard.

When Max was one, he'd gotten sick with a summer cold. Molly got it too. She was miserable and asked if I could stay home for the day to entertain Kali. I left for work instead, leaving her to handle the kids alone. I parked alone that morning too. What I should have done all those years ago was turn around. Or better yet, not left in the first place.

"Goddamn it," I cursed at the steering wheel.

I was making the same mistakes over again, except today was different. I couldn't go back to Molly's and fix this. If I went back, I would just make it worse and confuse the kids even more.

So I went inside the office and turned on my computer. I worked unfocused and angry, wondering how many other mistakes I'd made, knowing there had been many.

I stared at design plans for a project, the lines and words blurring together. Work, my constant companion, wasn't such good company today. This wasn't my refuge anymore. I couldn't solve this problem by working harder.

I'd always thought that if Alcott was successful, it would give me more freedom to help at home. It would ensure that Molly and the kids would be fine if anything ever happened to me. If I died, they'd be set for life.

Goal attained. Alcott was successful, whether I was at the helm or not.

And it had cost me everything. It had cost me my wife.

Something I'd realized a bachelorette party and one-night stand too late.

# eleven
## Molly

Finn and I kept our distance from one another the week after the kids found us together. We retreated to our post-divorce routine, where the kids were at his house or mine and with only one parent present. Our only time spent together was when we were making the switch.

The universe must have known I couldn't handle another letter because I hadn't gotten one all week. I didn't have the energy to relive the past or the courage to talk about the way things had been.

It was better this way, the single way.

It was better to focus on the now. Finn and I were not in love. That love was history.

The kids had been in off moods all week—no surprise there. Max had recovered quickly from his twenty-four-hour stomach bug and had spent the rest of the week at camp. He'd been quiet all week, his smiles rare. Kali's had been nonexistent. She'd been so excited for camp, but because she was angry and confused, she went each day with a bad attitude. I felt awful for the counselors.

Because it was all my fault.

I'd gotten lost in memories. I'd let those letters cloud the reality of my situation. I'd gotten swept up, for the second time in my life, by Finn.

I wouldn't think of my affair with Finn as wrong. It had felt so good to be touched, caressed, kissed . . . wanted. But I would think of it as reckless.

Having the kids catch us had been sobering. Mostly, I didn't want Kali to think less of me. I didn't want my daughter to grow up thinking I was at her father's disposal. That wasn't how Finn treated me. *I* knew that. But did she?

The morning was quiet as I sat at the kitchen table, eating my breakfast alone. I'd gotten up early, unable to sleep, and made myself some oatmeal. It was Finn's favorite, which was not why I'd made it. It was my favorite too.

With the bowl empty, I stared at my fingers. You could barely see the indentation from my wedding rings now. It had taken a long time to fade, or maybe it only seemed like a long time because my finger looked naked without my wedding and engagement rings.

They were upstairs in a small box in my dresser. I'd taken them off three days after the divorce. I probably would have kept them on longer but I hadn't wanted Finn to see them. He'd taken his off the day before we'd signed the papers. I'd waited until it was official.

For a year, I'd slip them on occasionally. Usually on nights when I was alone and missed him terribly. But I hadn't had that urge for ages. Why did I want to this morning?

I shoved that temptation from my mind and got up to rinse my bowl and leave for work. I'd be early this morning and that was fine by me.

I went out the front door instead of the garage, wanting to check the mail before leaving. I walked down the porch steps, but instead of heading to the mailbox on the street, I paused and looked the other direction.

Gavin's lights were on. The blinds were open to his office and he was already sitting at his desk, his eyes glued to a computer screen.

*Forget the mailbox.* I walked across my lawn, crossing the invisible boundary onto his, and marched up to his front door, not letting myself hesitate a second before knocking. I shifted from one foot to the other as his footsteps approached from inside.

When he opened the door, I forced a breathless smile. "Hey."

"Hey." His eyebrows came together as he glanced over at my house. "Is everything okay?"

"Yeah," I said too loud. My heart was racing. "It's good. Great. I was, um . . ." I took a deep breath. "I was just wondering if you'd like to go out to dinner with me. On a date."

"Oh." Surprise flashed across his face. "A date?"

"A date."

"I, uh . . . yeah." He adjusted his glasses on his face. "I'd like that. But I have to be honest. I've noticed your ex's truck in the driveway. A lot."

"He's been working on the yard."

"I noticed that too. Not exactly what I'm talking about though."

Damn it. No doubt Gavin had noticed Finn's truck—and Finn missing from the yard—because he'd been in my bed.

"The truth is, Finn and I were together for a long time. We didn't exactly end on the best of terms. I think we both had some unfinished feelings to work through. But it's over now."

"You're sure? Because, Molly, I like you. I've liked you since the day I moved in next door."

"Thank you." A blush crawled up my cheeks. How long had it been since a man had said he liked me? A guy who was kind and sweet. And handsome too.

"But."

"Uh-oh," I groaned. "Had to throw that in there, didn't you?"

"But . . ." Gavin chuckled. "I don't want to step into the middle of something that's unfinished."

"I get that. But it's finished. For good."

Saying those words stung, more than they should have. But it was time to move forward, painful or not. It was time to take enough steps forward that I'd stop looking backward.

"Okay." Gavin grinned. It was a little lopsided and completely cute. "Then I'd love to go to dinner. On a date."

"Really?" I'd just asked a guy on a date and he'd said yes. I smiled as my confidence soared.

"Really. What day?"

"Good question." I thought through my schedule. "I don't have the kids tomorrow. That's kind of short notice though."

"I could do tomorrow."

"Then it's a date. Seven?"

"Seven." The phone rang inside and Gavin hooked his thumb over his shoulder. "That's my first morning conference call."

"I'll let you get to it. See you."

"See you." His smile stretched wider. "Tomorrow."

I skipped down the porch steps. The adrenaline rushing through my veins made me want to run over to my house, but I forced my feet to walk.

*I have a date.*

Poppy was going to be so proud.

I decided to skip the mail. If one of Finn's letters was in there, it would have to wait. I wasn't going to let it taint this feeling. Because this morning was about me, not Finn, so I hurried inside and grabbed my things then drove to work.

Poppy was sitting at the counter when I got there, a steaming latte in front of her and a jar with her delicious spinach and onion quiche. "Hey. You're here early."

"I was up." I shrugged, going to the coffee pot. A few tables were occupied by happy customers, so before the morning rush hit, I took the few moments alone with my best friend to talk. "So, I have a date tomorrow."

She stopped chewing, her eyes blinking twice like she hadn't heard me right. "A date?"

"Yes. With Gavin."

A flicker of disappointment hit her eyes, but it was gone fast, vanishing with her wide smile. "I like Gavin."

"Me too."

"I'm glad he finally had the guts to ask you out."

"Actually," I splashed some cream in my coffee and took it over to the counter, "I asked him out."

"You did? That's so . . . bold and modern. I'm impressed."

"Thanks." I smiled. "It was time."

"Yes, it was. I'm happy for you, and in my opinion, it's exactly what you need."

I'd come into the restaurant last week to tell Poppy that my fling with Finn was over. I'd expected some disappointment, maybe some shock. Except she hadn't been surprised because Finn had already told her about the kids finding us in bed. The day it had happened, they'd had one of their lunches together and he'd confessed everything.

It was how she'd heard about the divorce too. Finn seemed to know the conversations I didn't want to have with Poppy and had them for me.

He saved me from having to cry in front of her.

Crying in front of people, even my best friend, was something I tried my hardest to avoid. My mother had people crying to her all day long. When I was a kid, I remembered her coming home on more than one occasion and saying how happy she was to not have anyone cry to her for a few hours.

Mom loved her job. She loved helping people, but I could see how having everyone else's burdens and tears unloaded on you would be draining. So I spared her mine. And over the years, it had become a habit.

I'd cried more over the letters this past month than I had in years. It was another reason ending my affair with Finn had been the smart choice.

"So what's the plan for today?" I asked Poppy after making my own latte.

"Well, I think I'm finally caught up from the celebration. The fridges are stocked again. Dora was a champ and wrapped a ton of silverware last night on her shift. She even deep cleaned the bathrooms."

"I love her. I wish we weren't going to lose her so soon."

"Me too. Stupid college. Stupid dreams."

I giggled. "Right? Why would she want to go be a successful lawyer when she could keep working here for the rest of her life? It's selfish really."

"Completely." Poppy laughed. "We should ask her if she has any younger friends who want to take her spot."

"Way ahead of you. She's already asking around."

"I should have known." Poppy went back to her quiche. "You're always ahead. I'm not actually sure how Finn managed Alcott without you."

My smile faded. "He figured it out."

He hadn't really needed me there, after all.

Poppy's phone rang and she picked it up, smiling as she answered, "Hi, Dad."

The joy on her face disappeared two seconds later. The

color drained from her cheeks, the light in her blue eyes went out.

*Cole.*

*No.* No, the universe wasn't this cruel. It wouldn't take one of Poppy's loves and then steal the other too.

I went around the counter, rushing to her side as David's voice relayed information rapid-fire. Except it wasn't Cole's name I kept hearing through the phone's speaker.

It was Finn's.

The world tilted under my feet, and I stumbled sideways, gripping the counter for balance. My free hand dove into my pocket, searching for my phone, but came out empty. *My purse.* My phone was in my purse.

I kept one hand on the counter as I went around to the other side, dropping to my knees as I dumped out lip gloss and sunglasses and two of Max's Hot Wheels onto the floor, searching for my phone.

I'd missed three calls from a number I didn't recognize. There was a voicemail, but before I could listen, Poppy caught my attention.

"Okay, Dad. We'll be right there."

"What?" I shot to my feet. "What happened?"

"Finn was in an accident."

---

"Any news?" Bridget asked as she came back into the waiting room with a cup of coffee.

I shook my head, my eyes staring unfocused at the wall across from me. Max was in the chair to my right. Kali my left. We'd been at the hospital for six hours, waiting to hear news about Finn.

The first hour went by in a flash. Poppy and I left the

restaurant in a dazed panic. As politely as possible, we asked the customers to get the hell out, taped a sign to the front door, locked everything down and raced in different directions.

Poppy came straight to the hospital where they'd brought Finn.

I went to Alcott to get my kids.

Max and Kali didn't have a summer camp this week. It was one of the few weeks over summer vacation where they didn't have anything planned, so they were hanging out with us at work. They preferred going to Alcott, because the loft above Finn's office was basically play central.

It had a large television and a wide variety of movies the kids enjoyed. There was also an Xbox. When they came with me to the restaurant, they got bored. I gave them easy tasks to help out, and they did love eating there more than at Finn's, but I couldn't compete with video games. Even when they had to get up extra early to go in with Finn, they didn't care. They'd fall asleep on his couch and then wake up to play.

So we'd arranged for them to spend this week at Alcott.

They'd been there for the accident. I *hated* that.

One of the regular crew members had called in sick, so Finn had asked them to stay inside while he went out to the yard to help load up materials for a job site.

Max and Kali had been in the office while Finn was loading up a bucketful of large landscaping rocks in a skid steer. They heard the shouts when a rock toppled out of the raised bucket and landed in the path of the machine's wheels. They heard the screams when the loader hit the rock, lurched forward and threw Finn to the ground when the seat belt latch malfunctioned.

Even though everyone hurried to get Finn free of the equipment, his body had been crushed under its front wheels.

And Max and Kali watched as the ambulance sped away, their father loaded into the back.

When I arrived, Alcott was in chaos. All of the crew members were in the yard. Five of the men had blood staining their pants.

I took one glance at them and nearly retched, but I pushed it aside to focus on finding my kids.

Most of the people were rushing around, putting things away, but a few were grouped together with shocked and stunned looks on their faces.

Bridget was there, talking with two police officers. Gerry, Finn's favorite foreman, who'd worked at Alcott since the early years, was on the phone, pacing near the skid steer that was still in the yard.

I didn't spare any of them more than a glance. I parked, hopped out of the Jeep and ran.

Max and Kali were standing outside, holding one another. Only one man was bothering to help with the kids. I didn't know him, but apparently he'd been standing by Max and Kali, watching over them until I arrived.

The second they saw me, Kali and Max sprinted my way, tears running down their precious faces.

After a tight hug, I loaded them up and raced across town to the hospital to join Finn's parents, Poppy, and Cole. He took Kali and Max to the cafeteria while the doctor explained the severity of Finn's accident.

Then we all sat in the waiting room and . . . waited.

Finn had been stabilized and taken immediately into surgery to repair the damage done to his internal organs. They'd been at it for over five hours.

He had injuries trailing down the right side of his body. Broken arm. Broken ribs. Broken pelvis. Broken leg. From the initial intake assessment, the doctors suspected one, if not both of his lungs had been punctured and his liver lacerated. Half of his body was broken. Had he been tossed one foot in the other direction, the skid steer would have crushed his skull and he would have died instantly.

The chances he still wouldn't survive this accident were staggering.

After that first hour in the waiting room, time slowed to a near stop. Every second was torture as we sat in a crowded room full of people I didn't know. Full of people I didn't want to see.

My hair felt heavy on my neck and shoulders, so I slipped my arms free of the kids and plucked a hair tie from my wrist. It was black. I piled my hair on top of my head, ready to wind it up, but when I stretched the hair tie wide, it broke.

I nearly fell off my chair. No. No, this wasn't happening. We'd had the worst today. Hadn't we? This could *not* get worse. We couldn't lose Finn.

I took a deep breath, then another. I threw the broken band away and let my hair fall. I wouldn't tempt fate by trying to put it up again. Then I distracted my thoughts from the worst by studying the people in the room.

Gerry and each of the other foremen from Alcott had come to the hospital, a slew of crew members filtering in after them. Bridget was here too, sitting across from the kids and me, drinking her coffee and grimacing after each sip.

"You don't need to stay." It was the nicest way I'd come up with in the last five hours to tell her to leave.

She met my gaze, her own narrowing. "Yes, I do."

"Why?"

She wasn't family. She wasn't a friend here. She was Finn's employee and I hated her. I hated her blond pixie cut. I hated how she wore tank tops that fit her toned body perfectly. I hated that she made a men's style of work pant look cute. I was woman enough to admit there'd been jealousy there at one point. She was this tiny ball of muscle with a cute face and a bright smile, and she was at Finn's side every single day.

But that wasn't why I hated her. I hated her because she thought it was her duty to judge me. Bridget thought she was above me, better. That despite being on the outside, she knew more about my marriage than me. I hated that Finn had told her about my one-night stand. I hated that he'd trusted her with that information, and she'd used it against me.

The last time I'd been to Alcott, right before the divorce, she'd called me a whore to my face.

I hadn't seen Bridget since then. She looked exactly the same, though with a few more fine lines on her face. Working in the sun all the time was taking its toll.

"I'm staying. Finn is important to me," she snapped. "So are his kids."

*My kids.*

I clamped my mouth shut and went back to staring at the wall. Nothing good would come from me fighting with Bridget today. Not when I had more important things to worry about.

Like how I was going to survive if Finn didn't. Or how I was going to keep our children afloat if their father died.

My stomach rolled, saliva filled my mouth, and I swallowed hard, forcing myself not to puke. I had to be strong. For Kali and Max, I couldn't give in to the dread and doubt that was slowly taking over.

Why was this surgery taking so long? Was it because the doctors were struggling to fix him?

*Don't take him. Please.*

The three of us were on a small loveseat. Normally, there'd barely be enough room for Kali, Max and me to fit.

But since they were both lying on my lap, their bodies squished to mine as tightly as they could, there was room to spare.

*Please don't take him.*

I hadn't had a chance to pray for Jamie. He'd been stolen from us before we'd had the chance. But for Finn, I prayed. I'd been praying for hours. Praying for a miracle.

"Can I get you anything, Molly?" one of Finn's employees asked. He was the guy who'd been standing next to the kids. He'd come to the hospital after we'd left, along with a bunch of other guys and the foremen.

"I'm sorry. What is your name?"

"Jeff, ma'am."

"No, thank you, Jeff."

Kali had told me after we'd arrived at the hospital that the three calls I'd missed had been from her. Jeff had let her use his phone.

He pointed to the kids, mouthing, "Anything for them?"

I shook my head.

Kali and Max both had their eyes closed. Max was asleep. The emotional stress from the day had worn him down completely. Kali wasn't though. She looked like she was asleep, but every few minutes, her body tensed.

Each time, I held her closer.

*Please don't take him from us.*

In the other corner of the room, David and Rayna sat in chairs closest to the hallway. I'd always thought David looked so young for his age. He was handsome, much like Finn. But today, he looked haggard. The white around his temples was more pronounced. The fear in his heart was seeping through his skin, turning it an ash gray.

Rayna, always beautiful like Poppy, was sitting stoically by his side. Her chin was held high. Her shoulders pinned back like she expected nothing other than her beloved son to come walking out in a few minutes and joke about how he *had* been wearing his seat belt.

She was trying hard, like I was, to keep the worst hidden. But her eyes betrayed her. They were full of terror because she'd heard the doctor's warning too.

The chance of Finn surviving so much trauma was slim at best. Five percent. That's what he'd told us the chance of him surviving surgery was. Five percent.

We were all praying for that five percent. For a miracle.

David had gotten the call first. Bridget had called him after the first responders had arrived and taken over the situation. He'd called Cole, then Poppy, because David knew that after the initial shock faded, after it sunk in, Poppy was going to get hit and hard.

It happened about three hours ago.

We'd all been sitting in the quiet waiting room—the only sounds from people shifting in their chairs and the hospital staff working in the background—when a sob escaped Poppy's mouth.

She'd broken down, collapsing into Cole as she cried uncontrollably. He'd picked her up and carried her out of the room without a word. They hadn't been back since.

But I wasn't worried about her. Cole would take care of her. He'd pull her through this, no matter what happened to Finn.

I didn't have a Cole to lean on.

Finn was my Cole.

A sharp sting hit my nose. The tears welled. I sniffled and Kali's body flinched. The arm I had wrapped around her tightened.

Her arms were wound around my thigh and she hugged it even tighter as she whimpered, her shoulders shaking.

I bent and whispered into her hair, "Deep breaths."

She nodded, sucking in some air. "I'm scared."

"Me too, sweetheart. Me too."

If I cried, she would break. So even though my throat was on fire, I forced myself to hold tight. I'd have my moment later, when I was home and alone and could drown out the sound in a hot shower.

A doctor cleared his throat as he walked into the waiting room wearing teal scrubs and matching booties over his tennis shoes. "Mr. Alcott?"

The room sprang to life, suddenly noisy and bustling with movement, even though it had been still and silent just moments ago.

Kali shot off the loveseat as I carefully set Max aside, making sure he wouldn't fall when I stood.

I grabbed her arm before she could run to the doctor. "Kali, wait. Stay with Max."

"Mom—"

"Please. In case he wakes up." And in case the doctor didn't have good news.

She would not hear it from a fifty-something-year-old doctor with a mole on his chin. If there was bad coming, my daughter would hear it from me.

Her shoulders dropped. "Fine."

I kissed the top of her hair, then rushed across the room.

The doctor had called Finn's dad's name, yet everyone here had converged on him. Bridget, of course, was front and center. "Is he okay?"

"Excuse me." I shoved past her, joining David and Rayna as they stood beside the doctor.

"Mr. Alcott." The doctor gestured for David to follow him into the hallway. Rayna grabbed my hand, pulling me along as she followed David.

Kali and Max waited at the waiting room entrance, peering down the hallway as we eased out of earshot. Kali had probably woken him up the second I'd stepped away.

"My kids are right there," I told the doctor. "Would you mind turning your back to them?"

He nodded once, pivoting so they wouldn't be able to read his lips or see the expression on his face. "Finn is out of surgery and in recovery. He's had a lot of internal damage. Right now, we're worried about infection and swelling. But if he makes it through the next twenty-four hours, his chances improve drastically."

"But he's alive?" I croaked out.

The doctor nodded. "He's alive."

*Thank you, God.*

Rayna's hand came to her mouth as she wept tears of relief. David pulled her into his side, holding her tight and turning her sideways so the kids wouldn't see.

I wrapped my arms around myself, physically holding the emotions inside. "Can we see him?"

"I can let you in there for just a few minutes, but he's not awake. We're keeping him sedated for the time being."

"You guys go," I told Rayna and David. "I'll tell the kids."

"No," Rayna said. "You should go."

"But—"

"Molly." David touched my arm. "Go."

"Kali and Max—"

"We've got them," he said. "Go."

"Okay." I nodded and followed the doctor down a series of white hallways until we stepped into the ICU. When we entered Finn's room, my thundering heartbeat drowned out the sound of his monitors.

My hand flew to my mouth, my eyes squeezed shut. A

tear dripped down my cheek as I took three breaths to get myself together.

Finn, my Finn, was barely visible beneath white mounds of gauze and bandages. It was hard to see more than the tubes and wires connected to his still body.

"I'll give you a minute." The doctor touched my shoulder then left the room.

My shoes shuffled along the floor, the rubber soles squeaking because I didn't have the strength to lift my feet.

Finn's hand was cold when I took it in mine. A hundred things to say ran through my mind. Pleas for him to fight, to survive for our children. Sarcastic jokes about his inability to operate heavy machinery. Questions about why he'd kept me as his emergency medical contact after all our years apart.

But if Finn could hear me, if he didn't make it through the next day, then there was really only one thing to say.

"I love you. I love you so much, Finn. I'll always love you."

# twelve
## Molly

"Hey." I smiled at Gavin as I stepped up to his porch. He leaned against one of the posts, a glass of iced tea in his hands. "Hey."

I bent down to pick up the glass he'd set on the top step for me. "I love your sun tea."

Gavin chuckled and sat next to me on the stair. "This is the last batch."

"What?" I stared at him in horror. "Why can't you make more?"

"I ran out of tea bags."

"I can pick some up at the grocery store later." I was dedicated to Gavin's tea. It had been one of my favorite things during the past six weeks. Sitting on the steps with him had become my little time-out from reality.

"I have some coming but it's back-ordered."

"I'm going to tell you a little secret." I leaned in closer to whisper. "This company called Lipton is fairly famous for their tea. They actually carry it at the grocery store. Here. In this town."

He chuckled. "I can't do Lipton."

"Too good for Lipton, huh? I had no idea you were such a tea snob. I feel like I don't even know you."

"It's my mom's fault. When I was growing up, my family took an annual vacation to the desert. My mom stumbled on this little café outside Flagstaff, and it became our place. They had the best sun tea. Over the years, she became good friends with the owner and found out the brand of tea she used. Mom ordered it and never looked back. She has early-onset Alzheimer's, and we had to put her in a home a couple of years ago. There are days when she doesn't remember me or my sister or my dad. But she's never forgotten that tea."

"And you make sure to order it too."

"Always."

I smiled, taking a healthy pull from my drink. "Thank you for sharing it with me."

"The pleasure is all mine. You are my favorite neighbor."

"Don't tell that to Mrs. Jarrit." I nodded to the house at the end of the cul-de-sac. "I think she has a crush on you."

"There's just something about me that seventy-year-old single women can't resist. I think it's my glasses."

I giggled, finishing my tea. I swallowed the last drop as a black van turned onto our street. My shoulders fell, the exhaustion from the last six weeks hitting me full force.

"Today's the big move day?"

I sighed. "Yeah."

"How's everyone doing?"

I stared at the van as it crept toward my driveway, not sure how best to answer that question. "I don't know. It's been hard. I know I told you this yesterday, but I really appreciate everything you've done to help out. From mowing the lawn, to sending over the girls to play with Kali and Max, to bringing pizza over. And the tea."

These five-minute breaks on Gavin's porch had become a

highlight of each day, mostly because we didn't talk about all the bad things. He told me anecdotes from his childhood or about his job. We joked about the other neighbors. But for five minutes, I didn't need to think about the kids or the changes coming.

I didn't have to think about Finn.

"I'm always happy to help. Just let me know what the girls and I can do."

"Thank you."

He clapped me on the knee as the van pulled into the driveway.

Poppy waved at me from the passenger seat. Cole shut off the van, and the big door on the side slid open. Kali and Max barreled out.

"Hey, Mom." Max waved. "Hi, Gavin."

We both waved back and I stood from the steps. "Thanks again."

"Anytime. See you around."

Today was my last tea break with Gavin. After today's move, I wasn't sure when I'd have time to come here again.

I set off across the grass, jogging to the van to give Poppy a hug. "How did it go?"

"Good." She nodded. "We're good."

Kali and Max joined us, and we all stood away from the van as Cole fiddled with the wheelchair ramp.

Getting Finn in and out of the van was going to take us all some practice.

Six weeks after the accident, he had finally left the hospital.

The first few days after his initial surgery had been a struggle for all of us. I never wanted to set foot in a hospital again. Max had said the same this morning.

Finn had been extremely lucky to get through his surgeries without infection, but the damage to his body was so severe, it had been hard for me to think about that without feeling sick.

He'd had three surgeries since the day of the accident, and with each one, I'd spent the hours praying he'd make it out alive.

His leg had been broken in four places, and after the last surgery, it was more pincushion than appendage. The same was true with his arm. Both his leg and his arm were frozen in thick, white casts. Finn's pelvis had been broken as well, and because of it, we were looking at another month of this wheelchair.

But the internal injuries had healed. They'd been the life-threatening ones. Now what he needed was time, rest and rehab.

"Hi." Finn smiled at me as the wheelchair rolled off the van's ramp.

"Hi." My heart melted at his smile.

He was hiding the pain. He was frustrated and pissed off that he was confined to a wheelchair. But he was alive. He was smiling. For me. For the kids. For Poppy, who'd had a harder time than the rest of us.

He was smiling because today was the first day in six weeks he wasn't stuck in a hospital bed.

It was gorgeous, that smile more soothing than a deep breath of fresh air after a summer rain.

"Are you sure you want to do this?" he asked. "I can wheel myself right back into the van."

"You're not going anywhere." I rolled my eyes and went around to the handlebars of his chair. "Welcome home."

He looked up at me over his shoulder, his eyes warm. "It's good to be here."

I winked at him, then nodded to the kids. "Lead the way."

Kali and Max giggled as they raced for the ramp that Finn's employees had constructed for him.

When the doctors had given us the details of Finn's recovery plan, it had been clear he wouldn't be going to his own home. Well, it had been clear to me and everyone else in the room that day. Everyone except Finn.

He spent an hour explaining to me, Poppy and his parents how he'd be fine at his house. His chair had an automatic option, so he could motor himself around with the control stick. He had one working arm and could eat sandwiches for a few months. He'd pee into a bottle and could manage a one-handed sponge bath.

When he was done explaining his ludicrous plan, I pulled out my phone in front of him and called Gerry at Alcott. I told him I needed a wheelchair ramp to my front door. When I arrived home that night, his entire crew was there along with a trailer full of lumber.

They built it in two days.

"Want me to push?" Cole offered.

"No, I've got him."

Cole pulled Poppy into his side, and the pair followed the kids up the ramp and into the house.

I held back, wanting a few moments with Finn. "How's the pain?"

His shoulders sagged. "It's been a lot of moving around today. I'm feeling it."

"I've got your prescription inside. Have you eaten?"

"No. I couldn't stomach one more hospital meal."

"Okay. Food. Pills. Nap." I pushed the chair forward slowly.

"Molly, I . . ." He ran his hand over his face. He'd grown quite the beard in his time at the hospital. I'd offered to shave him a few times—so had a couple of overeager nurses I

wouldn't miss—but he'd declined. He liked the low maintenance of the beard.

"What?" I slowed us to a stop.

"Thank you." His blue eyes lifted up to mine. "You didn't
have to do this. I could go home. Hire a nurse. Mom said
she'd stay with me for a while. This is a huge burden on your
life."

I walked around the chair and knelt so we were eye level.
"Finn, you're not going anywhere. Until you're healed, this is
your home. The kids need to see you. They need to see that
you're getting better." *So do I.*

"I need to see them too." He stretched his good hand over
the arm of the wheelchair and cupped my cheek. "And you."

I gave him a small smile. "We'll be okay."

David and Rayna would have done anything to help. The
same was true of Poppy and Cole. But none had made the
offer to bring Finn into their homes. Why? Because I made the
decision to bring him here before they even had the chance.

He was here. At home.

Where we all needed him to be.

I pushed him up the ramp, his chair heavier than I remembered, but not unmanageable. When we reached the porch, I
waved to Gavin, who was still standing outside.

He waved back before we disappeared inside.

"Tell Gavin thanks for mowing the lawn," Finn said.

"I did."

"No, tell him from me."

"All right."

I still felt awful for standing Gavin up for our date. He'd
called the night we were supposed to have dinner, but I'd
been at the hospital. Finn had just been taken off his sedatives
and we'd all been waiting anxiously for him to wake up.

I hadn't even realized what time it was. What day it was.

Hours had blurred together, and when Gavin called, I went to a quiet corner. He asked me where I was. I crumpled into a heap of tears.

I cried hard, finally letting it go. Gavin stayed on the phone the entire time. When I pulled myself together, I told him about Finn's accident. He listened and promised to be there if I needed help.

He didn't ask to reschedule our date. I didn't offer. We both knew there would be no date.

I'd learned something since the accident.

My love for Finn wasn't going to stop. I could tell myself and others I wasn't in love with Finn. It was all lies. I'd buried that love deep, shoving it down whenever it threatened to appear, but it was still there.

It had always been there.

Until I figured out how to deal with it, there was no room for another man in my heart.

"Dad." Max came careening down the stairs as I pushed Finn into the living room. There was a stack of books under his arm. "Check this out."

"What?" Finn forced the pain and exhaustion from his face. He had been trying his hardest since the accident to hide it from the kids.

"Grandma Deborah gave me all these books yesterday. You have to find Waldo."

"That was nice of her."

Max nodded. "Grandma has some of these in her office but some other kid circled all the Waldos already. These ones are different and waaay harder."

I smiled, pushing Finn next to an end table so Max could set the books down and they could hunt for Waldo together. "I'm going to make some lunch. Max, help out your dad if he needs something."

Finn gave me a smile before turning his attention to the first page Max had opened. "We'll be fine."

Mom had stepped up these past six weeks. She'd never been one to volunteer to babysit, especially when the kids were still in diapers. But when I'd spent my free hours at the hospital, taking shifts with Poppy and David and Rayna so Finn wasn't alone, Mom had spent more time with the kids than she had in the past few years combined.

I wish I could say it was for Finn. But I knew Mom. She was doing it for me, and at the moment, I'd take it.

I went into the kitchen and found Poppy, Cole and Kali already making lunch. Bread and cold cuts were laid out on the counter. Kali was slicing up a block of cheese. Cole was setting the table for six.

"I was just going to do this. You guys don't need to make lunch."

"I'm happy to." Poppy smiled from where she was assembling sandwiches. "You don't have to do everything yourself."

Except for so long, it had been just me. Even before the divorce, I'd done everything in this house. Laundry. Cooking. Cleaning. Yard work. It felt strange to watch other people work, so I got drinks out for everyone.

"We brought over enough clothes from Finn's for a while, along with his toiletries. But there might be some other stuff he wants." Cole set a stack of napkins on the table for us. "Just let me know and I'll bring it over."

I nodded, grateful I wouldn't need to go into Finn's house and search through his home for personal belongings. "Thanks. I'm going to run out to Alcott and pick up his computer and calendar. He's going to try and work on the laptop a little bit each day and get into the swing of things."

"Want me to go over?"

"No, I can do it. But thanks." I glanced over my shoulder. Poppy and Kali were laughing about something by the sink. They were in their own world, and we were far enough away that I could ask Cole the question that had been on my mind often lately. "Is she okay?"

Cole looked at his wife, his eyes softening. "She's the strongest woman I've ever met."

"Yes, she is."

"She's okay. She just got scared."

"We all did," I whispered.

"What she needs right now is to help. She needs to be there for Finn. He pulled her through after Jamie died. You both did."

"I was there, but Finn was the one who got through to her. He was there at rock-bottom."

"She wants to be there for him. I know you can do this on your own, Molly." Cole met my gaze, his light-green eyes pleading. "But don't. Drop a couple of balls for once in your life and let her pick them up. She needs to balance the scales. She needs to have a chance to be there for Finn like he was for her."

I nodded, my throat too tight to speak.

I didn't want to give up control of the juggling act. I didn't want to hand over something to Poppy. Truthfully, if I handed over one ball, I was afraid all the others would fall. But I'd risk it for her.

"Lunch is ready," Kali announced, shouting for Finn and Max as she carried over two plates to the table.

"Thanks for cooking," I told Poppy as she walked to the table.

"It's just sandwiches. Technically, no cooking involved."

"It's still appreciated."

"I was thinking of making double of everything I do at

home," she said, setting down the plates and taking a seat as Finn and Max came into the room.

Cole lifted the chair at the head of the table and put it in the corner so Finn could wheel his chair up.

Poppy's happy face faded when she looked at her brother. She saw what I saw. Finn was struggling. He was going to keep struggling because this road to recovery was going to be long and hard. He was a man who loved to work with his hands and be outside, yet he was confined to that chair.

Once he was out of the wheelchair, there'd be intense physical therapy. He wasn't going to jump out of that chair and say *Ta-da, let's go plant some trees*. The doctors said he might have lasting effects from the accident.

"Anyway," Poppy cleared her throat. "I was thinking of making double everything I do at home. Then you won't have to cook."

I opened my mouth to tell her I could manage but stopped before the automatic response came out. "That would be great."

This next month would be brutal.

Work at the restaurant was as busy as ever. I couldn't wait for school to start back up again, because as much as I loved summers with the kids, this summer needed to be over. They were bored and irritable. They'd spent more hours in the hospital than I'd ever wanted.

School was going to be my saving grace. Maybe then I'd tell Poppy she could back off the meals. But if cooking made her feel useful, I'd take it.

Finn thought he'd be able to dive right back into work, but I knew it wasn't going to be quite so easy. He was going to need a chauffeur to get to job sites and inspect work done. He would need someone to pick up the slack in the office because his energy waned so quickly. That would all fall to me.

And Bridget. As much as I hated her, I was grateful for Bridget's undying loyalty to Finn. While he'd been at the hospital, she'd taken over everything on his projects, running them along with her own. She'd visited him every other day to keep him apprised of business.

Gerry and the other foremen had stepped up too. They'd come to the hospital once a week to relay progress. They'd kept Finn in the loop, and it had saved Finn's sanity.

Part of his sanity. We hadn't let him have his laptop while he'd been in the hospital, worried it would cause him too much stress. But Finn was anxious to know how much had been overlooked in the office. Bridget might have the design side of the business covered, but she didn't pay the bills or work with vendors.

What he didn't know was that I'd taken over the office work.

On the mornings his parents took the kids or they were at camp, I spent a few hours at Alcott, relearning the things I had once known inside and out. Then I went back after my workday at the restaurant was over.

I paid the bills. I returned messages from vendors. I turned down prospective clients, putting them on next year's wait list. I thrust myself back into a world I'd once helped create, enjoying the bittersweet familiarity.

"What's the plan for the rest of the day?" Kali asked. Her eyes looked longingly outside.

"Nothing." I shook my head. "We're just going to relax."

Well, they could relax. I was going to do some cleaning that hadn't been done in too long. I was going to unpack some of Finn's things and make sure he was set up in the guest bedroom. And then I was going to mow the lawn.

But Kali and Max were free.

"Can we ride our bikes?" Max asked.

"Sure."

The kids shared a smile. Poppy and Cole shared a look filled with silent *I love you*s. And my eyes turned to Finn.

His were waiting, a smile toying with the corners of his mouth.

*Finn.* My Finn. Alive.

And for the time being, home.

***

The improvements Finn had made to the front yard made mowing a dream. But the backyard was a nightmare. Not only did I have the normal embellishments to work around, but I now had piles of dirt and a hole where the fountain had been too. I pushed the mower onto the grass, dreading how long it would take for me to get it done.

Probably two hours. Maybe three. While Gavin had kept it from turning into a jungle, he hadn't done the edging quite clean enough for my liking.

After lunch, Cole and Poppy left to get their kids from Cole's parents' house. Max and Kali had spent the time it had taken me to mow the front yard riding their bikes around the neighborhood. But they'd retreated inside about five minutes ago to play in their rooms.

Max went back to *Where's Waldo?* while Kali wanted to tackle the jigsaw puzzle Mom had bought for her.

And Finn was taking a nap.

I'd set him up in the guest bedroom so he had plenty of space. Even though it would be completely sex-free for him to sleep in my bed, I tended to sprawl or cuddle and didn't want to accidently roll into him in my sleep and risk bumping his broken leg or jostling his hips. So he was in the guest bedroom because it was the only other room on the main floor.

His entire right side was extremely tender. The bruises had lasted longer than I'd ever expected, turning half his body a dark purple before fading to lime green. I grimaced just thinking about how he'd looked that first week, all puffy and blue.

I took a deep breath, bending for the cord to get the mower going, but stopped when a car door slammed shut. Then another.

I left the mower in its place and walked along the side of the house toward the front as three guys were piling out of a navy Alcott truck parked along the street. Behind it was a mowing trailer.

"Hi." I waved as I walked their way, getting their attention. All three guys waved back, though I only recognized one of them. They were probably here to see Finn, but I didn't want them waking him up. "Finn is taking a na—"

"Hey, guys."

My head whipped to the side. Finn was in his wheelchair on the front porch.

"Hey, boss." One man grinned as he hooked a thumb at the van. "New ride? It's sexy."

Finn chuckled. "Thanks for coming over so soon."

"Not soon enough." He surveyed my freshly mowed grass. "Sorry."

"The back needs to be done," Finn told them. "You can hit it today. And then put it on the rotation for every Friday."

All three men nodded, turned and went for their equipment.

I watched with my mouth hanging open as one of them

backed a riding mower off the trailer, another unloaded a push mower and the third grabbed an edger.

"Can I get to the backyard this way?" one of them asked.

I nodded, sliding out of the way as they went toward the fence. Each of them smiled as they passed me.

When the machines started up, I went to the porch. I stopped two steps from the top so I was eye level with Finn. "What are you doing?"

"Something I should have done a hell of a long time ago. Alcott has the lawn from now on."

How many times had I mowed this lawn, wondering why Finn didn't have his crew here to do it for us? I'd always assumed he wanted to save the money. Or that he didn't have time in the rotation to fit it in. When we got divorced, I figured it would be strange to have a crew mow his ex-wife's lawn. But here they were.

A small gesture. But one that touched my heart. "Thank you."

"Don't thank me. I'm sorry I didn't do it sooner." His eyes were full of remorse as he stared at me. His frame, though broken, was poised in determination to make it right.

Kali came outside, interrupting the moment. She leaned against Finn's chair, something that had become her new kind of hug. "Dad, do you want to help me with my puzzle?"

"I'd love to, sweetie."

She smiled at him, kissed his cheek and darted inside. Finn shot me a grin, then steered his chair back inside too.

I stayed on that step for a few long minutes, marveling at how much had changed in such a short amount of time. How my feelings were so different now.

The power of fear was terribly magnificent.

I turned on the step, descending to the sidewalk, then

walked to the mailbox as the sounds of whirling blades snipping grass buzzed in the distance.

I was lost in the sunshine and the way my stomach wasn't in knots for the first time in weeks. Having Finn home was a relief I hadn't let myself hope for, at least not in the beginning. Those first few days in the hospital, I'd prepared myself for the worst.

Enjoying that relief, savoring that we were out of the woods, I didn't pay much attention to the mail. Finn's old letters had stopped.

Finn had asked me last week if there had been more, and I'd told him no. We were both glad to be done with them. We had enough to deal with, and the past, well . . . it needed to stay there. I thumbed through the stack, sorting junk into one hand and bills in the other.

But then a familiar curve of handwriting caught my attention.

We weren't done with the letters after all.

*Darling Molly,*

*I'm failing you. I know I'm failing you, but I'm not sure how to fix it. Max is six days old, and maybe because I've been home, it hit me that I haven't been doing enough. I disappear to work and leave you here. You handle it all. The house. The kids. You greet me with a smile when I get home.*

*But I see it now. I see that I'm not doing enough. You're exhausted. You cried in the shower this morning. I fucking hate that. I hate that I'm letting you down.*

*What should I do? I don't know how to even ask you that question. I'm scared that your answer will be nothing. That no matter what I do, it won't be enough. That you know I'm failing you and you've given up on me.*

*I think I need to push harder. Work harder. I can work harder. Once things at Alcott are set and I know that no matter what, you and the kids will be okay if something happens to me, we'll be better.*

*You fell asleep on the chair across from me. I'd planned to sit down and talk to you, but by the time I got Kali to bed, you were already asleep. Max is perfect. He's sleeping in your arms. I don't want to move him.*

*But you're breaking right in front of me. Life is too heavy right now. I'm taking another week off to help. I hope I can help. I want more than anything to give you this letter. To talk to you. But I'm scared. I'm scared it will just add to your burdens.*

*I need to figure this out. I will figure this out. I promise. I'll do better. I'll do better for you and Kali and Max. I love you. You're the center of my world. Just hold tight for a little bit longer.*

*Yours,*
*Finn*

# thirteen
## Finn

I hung up the phone and dropped my head into my good hand, rubbing my forehead, hoping the headache building would hold off for another hour. I needed to finish up a design for a client, and if this ache turned into the same blinding throb I'd had for the last few days, it would never get done.

Sitting at the dining room table, I focused on the computer screen, willing the throb to go away. My leg was sore. My hips hurt. My neck had a kink in it from only using one arm and stretching at odd angles all day. And I was sick to death of being in this *fucking* wheelchair.

What I really wanted was a pain pill and a nap. To pass the day in bed while I waited for the kids to get home with Molly. But I didn't have time for a nap, and as of this morning, I'd stopped taking pain pills. I had enough problems. The last thing I needed was a drug addiction.

They put me in a haze and I didn't want to be fuzzy while I was here with all of us living under one roof. This living situation was the only good thing to come from the accident.

The rest of my life was in fucking shambles.

I took a deep breath, blocked out the pain, and focused on the one thing that had gotten me through most of the shit times in my life: work.

Alcott was a mess at the moment. Everyone had done their best to keep projects moving while I'd been in the hospital. Bridget and each of the foremen had stepped up. But it hadn't been enough. I did the work of three designers. Bridget, though she tried, was out of her league. She'd attempted to chew what was on my plate, but it was no more than little nibbles here and there. What we needed to get caught up were bites. Big, stuff-your-mouth, cheeks-bulging bites.

The only part of the business that wasn't in complete and total disarray was my books.

All employees had been paid. Deposits had been taken to the bank. Bills had been sent and paid.

Because of Molly.

Somehow in the weeks that I'd been in the hospital, the weeks when she'd run out to "do a few things," she'd actually been at Alcott, making sure my business was churning. She'd stepped in like she'd been there all along.

More efficiently than I ever could too.

She hadn't said a thing. She had to have been going there when the kids were with my parents. Or maybe at night. I wasn't sure. Without a word, without expecting any kind of gratitude or praise, Molly had been my savior.

Thanks to her work, I'd been able to focus on the projects that would wrap up the summer and fall rather than digging myself out from under the office work. This design I needed to finish today was the last. After I cranked it out, every project would be officially kicked off, and then we just had to see them through to the end.

For a right-handed guy, working with a full right-arm cast was extremely frustrating. I'd been gritting my teeth for hours, probably the reason for the headache. Using only my left hand, everything took three times longer than normal. But after two hours, I was nearly done.

Then the front door opened.

"Shit," I cursed quietly. I was so goddamn sick of visitors I could scream.

My parents stopped by daily to fuss over me. If Bridget wasn't calling me, she was coming over in a frantic blur, rattling off question after question, barely pausing to listen to my answers. And the crews had clearly been assigned shifts. In the two weeks since coming to Molly's house, I'd figured out the pattern of who would be stopping by "because they were in the neighborhood."

What I needed was for everyone to leave me the hell alone so I could work.

"Finn?" Poppy's voice carried down the hallway from the front door.

I relaxed. My sister was the one person whose visits never got on my nerves. "At the table."

She came through the kitchen and into the dining room with a smile on her face and a paper bag from the restaurant in her hand. "Hi."

"Please tell me there are cookies or pies or something with sugar in that bag."

She scrunched up her nose as she set it on the table. "It's, uh, some kale salad."

"Fucking kale," I muttered.

"You know what the doctors said. Leafy greens will help you recover quickly."

"Once I get out of this chair, I'm never having kale or romaine or spinach or cabbage or goddamn Swiss chard again."

Poppy laughed. "Please. It's not that bad."

"Really? And what did you have for lunch? Was it this delicious *kale salad*?"

"Okay." She held up her hands. "Point made."

She'd probably had some of her macaroni and cheese. The kind with crispy crumbles on the top and loads of gooey cheese that made me want to eat until I was miserable.

"How are you?" she asked, taking the seat next to me.

"Fine." I slid my laptop out of the way and reached for the bag.

But Poppy grabbed it before me. "I'll get it."

"Thanks." I let her. Since the accident, I'd given up pretending I could do everything for myself.

I'd come to Molly's thinking I could hang out, and she'd be around if I needed some help. I figured the nurses at the hospital had been picky, not wanting me to do anything for myself. They poured me water and helped me in the bathroom because it was their job.

No, they'd just known what I hadn't: I couldn't do shit for myself.

Literally. I couldn't shit by myself. I couldn't get myself out of the chair and onto a toilet without someone to help me keep my balance.

I figured that out the first night I was here. Then the next morning, I learned I couldn't shower on my own or brush my teeth on my own. The only thing I was really capable of was wheeling myself around. Oh, and I could eat cold cereal because it was easy to "make" with one hand.

I would have been fine eating Rice Chex and Honey Bunches of Oats for a few months, but the women in my life wouldn't let me skip these *delicious leafy greens*. They were trying to turn me into a rabbit.

Poppy mixed my salad with the dressing, a generous amount, thank God for that, and then grabbed a fork from the kitchen. With it all plated, I dove in, grimacing at the first few bites.

Fucking kale.

At least the dressing was Poppy's signature ranch, my favorite. She'd brought enough that the salad was edible.

"Are you working today?" I asked.

"Yeah. Molly is covering the lunch hour so I could stop by and say hello."

"I'm glad you did."

She touched the tip of my fingers sticking out of my cast. "So am I."

I set down my fork, wanting to give her my full attention. I'd actually been waiting for one of these quiet moments with her. There were things I hadn't had a chance to say at the hospital or here because there were always too many people around.

"I'm sorry."

"For what?" she asked.

"For scaring you. For the accident. I know it brought up a lot of old memories."

"Oh." Her eyes dropped to the table. "It wasn't your fault."

"I'm still sorry."

Her eyes flooded with tears, but she blinked them dry, forcing a smile. "I'm okay. It scared us all. I don't want to lose you too."

"I'm not going anywhere," I promised.

"Good. How are you feeling?"

My first response was to tell her I was great. That things would be fine and set back to rights in no time at all. But I was so tired, I didn't have the energy to lie.

I met her gaze. "I'm struggling."

"With the pain?"

"Yes. No." I blew out a long breath. "With the fact that I almost died two months ago. I almost left Kali and Max without a dad. And Molly . . ."

My throat closed just thinking about it. I'd worked so hard for so many years to prepare for this kind of accident. To make sure that if something happened to me, they'd be covered.

I'd been blind to what really mattered.

We'd gotten another letter two weeks ago. Molly and I had both read it and then put it aside. There hadn't been much to talk about. I *had* been failing her. I'd known it. I'd *written* it. But I hadn't done a damn thing to change it.

"You know what's really messed up?" I asked Poppy. "I'm glad."

"That you lived?" she teased. "Yeah, we are too."

"No, that it happened. I had a lot of time to think in the hospital. I had a lot of time to realize . . . I ruined my life, Poppy."

"What? No. You didn't. Once you get out of this chair and start physical therapy, you'll be walking in no time. Your arm won't be in the cast forever. You didn't ruin your life."

"No, I don't mean the accident. After Jamie." I swallowed hard, knowing this conversation would be difficult to have with Poppy, but she was the only person who might understand. "I ruined my life after Jamie died. I sabotaged it."

"What do you mean?" When I didn't answer, Poppy thought about it for a moment. Then she got it. "Oh. With Molly."

"Not on purpose. Molly told me a while ago that you talked to her about the divorce. She told me you were worried that you were the reason we broke up."

The color drained from Poppy's face. "I was, wasn't I?"

"No. Not you. It was me. Jamie's death spooked me. I

started working so hard. I wanted Molly and the kids to be set if something happened to me. And it just snowballed. I knew I wasn't doing my best as a father and husband. But I was so focused on Alcott, on making sure I could . . . die."

"Oh, Finn." Poppy's eyes filled with tears.

"I lost her. And I think . . . I think I pushed her away."

"Not just because you were scared you would die."

I nodded, wanting her to speak the thought I couldn't. The thought that had plagued me as I spent days staring at the ceiling of my hospital room.

"You pushed her away because you were scared *she* would die."

I dropped my head, my vision blurred with tears. "I ruined my life. Because I was scared that I'd end up—"

"Like me." Poppy wiped a stray tear from her eye then took my hand. "You were scared you'd end up like me."

"What the hell did I do?" I whispered.

Molly had tried so hard. She'd kept reaching out to pull me back to her. But I'd kept turning away, toward work. She'd pulled. I'd pushed.

*Far too hard.*

What had I pushed Molly to do?

"You have to fix it, Finn."

"I know."

"How?" Poppy asked. "What are you going to do?"

"Well, first, I need to get Alcott sorted. Then I—"

"Finn." She rolled her eyes. "What's it going to take for you to realize that Alcott isn't your answer here? It's been your demise."

I gaped at her. "What? What do you mean?"

"You want a life with Molly?"

"Yes." Admitting it out loud sent a jolt of electricity

through my veins. I wanted a life with Molly *and* my kids. I wanted my family back.

"Then Alcott has to go."

*Never.* "I'm not giving up my business." It was my livelihood. It was the security that my family would be safe. It was also my passion. "There has to be a way to have both."

Poppy thought about it for a moment. "You know what I never understood? How you and Molly could work together. When you guys started Alcott, I couldn't believe you could work with each other all day and then go home together at night."

"Well, we didn't work together all day. She did the mowing at first then covered the office. I was doing the landscape jobs, so we weren't together *all* day."

"Yeah, but it was everything, to both of you."

"Okay," I drawled, wondering where she was going with this. But she didn't give me anything more. "So?"

"It's just an observation." She shrugged. "How's the accident investigation?"

"Fine. It'll be fine."

"Please, don't do that. Don't sugarcoat it like you do everything else. Tell me."

"I don't sugarcoat stuff."

She laughed. "Oh, my dear brother. You are the king of downplaying your own stresses because you think you're shielding the rest of us. When in reality, you just shut us out."

No, I didn't. Did I? I opened my mouth to argue, but Poppy shot me a look. Okay, maybe I did shut people out. "I don't mean to."

"I know. So let's try this again. How is the investigation going?"

I frowned. "I just got off the phone with my lawyer before you got here. It's going to be a goddamn mess."

"It'll get sorted."

"Yeah, but it might take years. I'm just glad it was me. The thought of one of my employees getting thrown makes me sick."

"It shouldn't have happened to anyone. That seat belt shouldn't have malfunctioned."

"You're right. But it was a fluke deal."

According to my lawyer, the manufacturing company of that skid steer was dedicated to making it right. They'd arranged for me to have the new wheelchair-accessible van until I was walking again. They'd paid for a motorized wheelchair when my insurance would only cover a manual one. And they were covering a large portion of my medical expenses that my insurance wouldn't pay. They were doing everything in their power so I wouldn't sue.

Even if they hadn't offered to help, I had no intention of suing. Accidents happened. Life was unfair. I knew that. Sometimes people were in the wrong place at the wrong time, like Jamie. And the last thing I wanted was to drag my family through a long and expensive legal battle.

One thing was for certain: I'd never gripe about paying my insurance premiums again. It was damn expensive for small businesses to provide insurance for their employees. I'd taken it for granted because in all the years I'd been in business, I'd never had a major claim. One guy got his hand gashed by a utility knife when he was opening a bag of mulch. Another broke his toe when a pallet of sod landed on his boot. Besides those minor injuries, we'd been extremely lucky.

Until now.

"Well, I'd better get back to work." Poppy stood and kissed my cheek. I'd finally decided to shave my beard this morning and her kiss felt cold. "Call me if you need anything, okay? Or if you want to talk?"

"Thank you. And thanks for lunch."

"You're going to eat cereal as soon as I leave, aren't you?"

"Yep. I'm tossing out this salad as soon as I hear the door close."

Poppy laughed. "I'll see you later."

"Bye."

She turned and walked toward the kitchen to leave, but before she disappeared down the hall, she paused and turned back. "I love you."

"I love you too."

"Do me a favor. You said you ruined your life?"

I nodded. "Yeah."

"Ruin it again."

*Ruin my life.* The one where I spent most nights alone. The one where I didn't get to see my kids every single day. The life where work was great but being at home was sad and lonely.

It was definitely time to ruin that life.

---

"What exactly are you doing?" I asked, rolling up behind Molly.

She dropped the binoculars from her eyes and smiled over her shoulder. "Mailbox stakeout."

The mailbox was yards away, not miles. She'd brought those binoculars out here as a joke during the last mailbox stakeout, the one before the accident. I guess she'd kept them close.

She was seated on the top step of the porch. It was twilight, the last lingering rays of sunshine fighting to hold on to the day for a few more minutes. She looked beautiful, sitting there with her hair down, the wisps around her temples blowing with the warm breeze.

A sudden jolt made my heart skip. Had I still been hooked up to a monitor, the jump would have brought the whole nurses' station rushing to my bedside. As it was, I was glad the fading light hid the color on my face.

God, I was nervous. Not just nervous, I was terrified. My free hand was strangling the control stick of the wheelchair. My palm beneath the cast was clammy. Even my toes were shaking.

The last time I'd felt this anxious around Molly had been during our first date. But here we were again, at the beginning.

How was I going to do this? I'd spent the better part of my day after Poppy left thinking about our conversation and how I was going to go about this with Molly. My conclusion? I had no earthly clue what I was doing. Molly might not even want me back.

She had every right to tell me to shove it. I hadn't been the man she deserved. I hadn't been the husband I'd promised to be. I'd let her down more times than I could remember.

None of those reasons were going to stop me from trying.

"I was wondering if you wanted to take a small woll around the block with me."

"A woll?" she asked.

"Yeah. You walk. I roll. We woll."

She giggled and stood, setting the binoculars aside. "Then let's woll."

I rolled forward a few inches but stopped when she came behind the chair, pushing it instead of letting me use the controls. "I can drive."

"I don't mind." She didn't rush as we set off down the ramp and onto the sidewalk. "It's nice out tonight."

In the distance, the laughter and shouting from the kids filled the air. "Sounds like the kids are having fun at the park."

"I'm glad. They could use some days of fun before school starts. This summer's been . . . something else."

"How are you?" I asked.

"I'm good."

"How about the real answer? Not the one you automatically give." I looked over my shoulder. I wasn't the only Alcott who sugarcoated their feelings. "How are you?"

"Sometimes I forget how well you know me."

"Better than anyone, so don't dodge my question."

She walked us down five cement squares before answering. "I'm kind of tired. I haven't been sleeping."

"Why not?"

"Because of you."

"Me?" The pain medications knocked me on my ass. Combined with the physical therapy I'd been doing and a heavy mental-stress load, when I was out, I was out. "I've been sleeping like the dead."

"Bad joke, Finn."

I winced. "Sorry. But seriously, why me?"

"I keep having this dream that I wake up and you're gone. The only way I can go back to sleep is if I go in and check on you."

*Fuck.* "I'm sorry."

"It's not your fault. It might take me some time, but I'll get past it."

"Do you want me to sleep in your bed? So you don't have to get up and check on me?"

"No." She laughed. "The last thing we need is the temptation to jump into a physical relationship again."

"Darling, in case you hadn't noticed, I'm not jumping anywhere."

She laughed. "True. But, no. I'll be fine. Did you get your design layout done today?"

"Yep. After Poppy left, I knocked it out."

"That's good. She told me you guys had a nice talk. What was it about?"

"You."

She slowed her pace. "Me?"

"We were talking about Alcott and how things used to be there. She said she was always so surprised that we could work together and live together."

A slow smile spread across her face. Her eyes were aimed down the street as we walked, like she was staring into the past. "It was fun, wasn't it? We were so poor and there was so much work. But there were some good days."

"Some of the best." I nodded. "Can we talk about the last letter for a minute?"

"I don't know if there's anything more to say. Like I told you the night I got it, I think you were too hard on yourself. I wish I had known how you were feeling about Jamie. I didn't realize that was why you were working so hard."

"I didn't want you guys to be in a bad spot without me."

"I see that now, and it helps to know that you were thinking of us. For a long time, I thought . . . never mind."

"Thought what?"

"That you went to work to avoid me and escape."

I hung my head. "Can you stop for a minute?"

"Sure." She slowed my chair to a stop, clamping on the brake. Then she came around the front. "Are you okay? Is something hurting?"

"The truth?" I extended my left hand, waiting until she placed hers in my palm. Then I threaded our fingers together, turning our hands over and back, loving the way her slim fingers wound between mine. "I was avoiding you."

She flinched but didn't speak.

"Not intentionally. I think, after talking to Poppy today, a part of me was running away from you. Jamie's death scared me more than I let on. I ran because I was afraid I'd lose you. And it would have killed me."

"Oh." She stared at our hands, letting my words sink in. "I, um . . . oh."

"I let my own fears drive me away. I isolated myself. And for that, I'll always be sorry." I kept a firm grip on her hand, not wanting her to pull away. "I'm sorry, Molly."

"I get it," she whispered. "It hurts. But I get it. It makes me wish that we had talked more."

"Me too."

"None of us really did. Me. You. Poppy. We lost Jamie and life went on. But we didn't heal. We buried our pain and our fears because it was too hard to talk about."

"I was a coward."

"You were just doing the best you could. We all were." She gave my fingers a squeeze, then unlaced our hands to go behind the chair again. She pushed me farther down the sidewalk, until the light was nearly gone and it was time to go home.

It felt like there was more to say. That one apology wasn't enough.

So I'd give her others, every day until the heaviness in my heart was unloaded.

The house came into view and I looked over my shoulder again. "Thank you for all the work you did while I was in the hospital."

"Like I told you the last four times you thanked me, it was nothing."

Fuck, I hated this goddamn chair. I hated that she was behind me. That I couldn't stand and look her in the eyes so she knew how sincere I was.

"It wasn't nothing. It saved me."

She smiled. "It's a good thing you still keep all of your passwords written down on a sticky note in your desk drawer. I would have been lost without that. Also, you shouldn't write down your passwords."

"I'll remember that for next time." I chuckled. "One last question before we get to the house?"

"You sure are full of questions tonight. That must have been some talk with Poppy."

It had been. It had been the conversation I'd needed to have for years. "Do you feel like I took Alcott from you? It was ours. And then it was just . . . mine."

The wheels of my chair slowed. Then stopped.

I waited for her answer, my heart thundering.

"Yes." It was no louder than the breath of wind whispering across my cheek.

I hung my head. "I'm sorry."

"I loved that place. I don't think I realized just how much I've resented you for pushing me out."

"I didn't do it intentionally. I swear."

"It's in the past." She started us forward again, our leisurely pace gone as she rushed home. "We'd better call for the kids, otherwise they'll stay at the playground all night."

And with that, the door to the past slammed shut. *Damn*.

The kids were already inside when we got home. They were jumping around the living room wildly, excited to have spent some time with their neighborhood friends. Hours passed before they went to bed. Molly let them stay up later than usual since there was no agenda for the next day, though I suspected it was really because she didn't want to talk to me.

It was after midnight and we were both spent by the time she helped me use the bathroom and get into bed.

"Molly?" I called before she could slip out of the room.

"I'm tired, Finn. I can't take any more talking tonight."

I sighed, nodding. "Okay."

It wasn't okay.

I wanted to hold her. To tell her that she was the most incredible woman I'd ever known. To ask her if she thought we might have the energy to give us another go. To promise I'd never stop loving her, that she'd owned my heart since the day we'd met.

Instead, I simply said, "Sweet dreams."

Molly,

Is this really what you want? Me, living in the loft at the office? You, home alone with the kids? Because what the actual fuck just happened?

I came home Friday. We got in a fight that lasted two days. I was tired of arguing. I was tired of you saying you needed space, so I packed a bag to spend a night at the office. You told me to pack enough for a week.

Fuck this. Fuck all of it. How can you be okay with me leaving? For a week? Do you even care?

I don't think you love me anymore. How the fuck did that happen? So I'll just sit here, alone in my office, writing another one of my fucking letters that don't do a fucking thing but let me get some of this out. If I told you any of this, we'd just get in another damn fight.

You hurt me. You fucking hurt me. Maybe I should have packed enough stuff for two weeks.

Finn

# fourteen
## Molly

"Today's the day." Finn's physical therapist, Ashley, smiled at him. "Ready to get out of that chair?"

"More than ready."

She clapped her hands together. "Then let's do this."

"I'll wait over there," I told Finn, thumbing at the chairs along the far wall. "Good luck."

He grinned. "Thanks."

It had been ten weeks since Finn's accident. A few days ago, he'd gotten a new, shorter cast on his arm, giving him mobility from his shoulder to his elbow. He'd also had his leg cast removed. In its place was a special boot to give his bones some stability as they finished mending. His pelvic bone had fused together. The damage to his internal organs was a distant nightmare now. He was recovering, better and faster than the doctors had expected.

For weeks, Finn had been working hard to build the strength for walking with exercise bands and light weights. Today was the test. If he did well enough in physical therapy, he'd get rid of the chair and graduate to crutches.

I smiled as he stood from his wheelchair. Over the last two

weeks, he'd started to stand on his own. He'd gained some freedom from the chair that was driving him crazy.

He was healing.

We all were.

I walked over to the blue pleather chairs and took my usual seat, second from the end. It gave me the best view of where Finn and Ashley were working. Then I pulled out my laptop from my purse and got it going.

Finn's physical therapy appointments had been a demanding obligation for all of us. He had to have a ride, which defaulted to me. Since I wouldn't let myself get behind at the restaurant, I'd gotten really good at working from this tiny screen perched on my legs. Anything that had to be done on the computer, I saved for these two-hour sessions. That way when I got back to the restaurant, I could cover the floor for Poppy.

It had been an adjustment, but we were making it work. School was back in session and the kids were into a normal routine. We were finding normal again, something I yearned for and dreaded at the same time.

Normalcy meant life before the accident. To the time when Finn lived at his home with the kids three or four days a week. And I was all alone.

I wasn't ready to be alone again.

Since Finn had moved in, it had been easy to fall into thinking we were a family. That my home housed four, not three. When he left, I'd get used to it. I'd adjust.

But I wasn't the only one who'd fallen in love with this living situation.

Kali was so happy to have Finn around every day. She talked to him more than she talked to me. She'd tell him about her friends, about what she was looking forward to in her classes. She'd come home one night last week in a horrible mood. No matter how many times I'd asked her what was wrong, she'd insisted it was nothing.

Finn had asked once. *Kali. Sweetie, what's wrong?*

Cue the waterworks. Apparently, there was a girl at her middle school who'd been teasing Kali about her body during recess. Kali hadn't started to develop breasts yet, and this other girl had teased her for being flat chested. All the other girls were in training bras.

As I'd listened in on Kali telling Finn all about it, I'd fought the urge to track down this little brat's mother and chew her up one side and down the other. But I'd stayed quiet. I wasn't sure why Kali hadn't told me, maybe because Max had been in the car with us. I knew my daughter and she would have opened up to me eventually, but she and Finn had this connection. Even when talking about bras and breasts and getting older, she trusted him completely.

He didn't have to coax things from her. He was her confidant. Her safe zone.

Max loved having Finn around too. He was as carefree and jovial as always. I swear that kid had the strongest cheek muscles in the world because he could smile for hours. But with Finn home, it was more. Max's light was set to high beam.

Soon, that would end.

Across the room, Finn took a pair of crutches from Ashley and fitted them under his arms. Determination was written all over his face. He was leaving the chair behind today. He wouldn't need my help for much longer. He couldn't drive yet, but that would happen before long too. His leaving was only a matter of time.

We needed to prepare the kids.

He shot me a smile as he took one step, then another. Ashley loomed close, touching his arm.

My eyes narrowed on her hand.

She always touched him. No, she *felt* him. It had rubbed me the wrong way from the beginning. It was too intimate, not the way therapists should touch their patients. It reminded me of how the head cheerleader at my high school had always found ways to touch the football team's quarterback.

Besides, wasn't she supposed to be helping him walk? On. His. Own?

I turned my attention to the computer screen, refusing to look up, because I knew the expression on my face wasn't pretty. My skin was probably turning green.

Ashley's irritating giggle sailed across the room. I should have brought my earbuds to wear so I could listen to music and block her out. But I was stupid and had forgotten them today in the bag I'd packed for the gym.

Packing and unpacking that bag had become part of my routine these last few weeks. I was determined to take advantage of having Finn around in the mornings. I could go to the gym before the kids woke up because he was home if they needed something. So I packed my bag each night, set my alarm for four and fell asleep. I woke to the beeping and reset it for five thirty, and before drifting off again, I promised that backpack tomorrow would be the day.

Tomorrow was never the day.

But I still packed that bag.

Ashley laughed again, snagging my attention, and I clenched my jaw. It wasn't just her laughter that grated on my nerves. It was the way she purred his name, adding an unnecessary number of *n*s. And it was how he always laughed back. He always smiled around her.

Of course he did. She was beautiful. She was fit underneath her navy scrub pants and simple white tee. She probably made it to the gym each morning at four. I bet she was the perky one who smiled as she ran or climbed a mountain of never-ending stairs. Her and her sleek brown ponytail.

*Whatever.* My hair was never going to be sleek and shiny. I was never going to grow the motivation to go to the gym at four in the morning. And I was never going to be okay watching another woman flirt with Finn.

"You did it!" Ashley squealed, clapping and jumping up and down. The ponytail swung wildly.

Finn had just crossed the room using his crutches. Usually it took him longer to go that distance, but he was motivated today. He wanted out of that chair and nothing was going to stop him.

His smile was blinding, so beautiful it stole my air. He flashed it at Ashley and her cheeks flushed.

My heart plummeted. *No.* Finn and I had built such an easy relationship lately. It had been easy to pretend the past had been forgiven. That he didn't want to find a new woman for his life, because I was that woman.

But here we were. I had a sinking feeling that I would be stuck with Ashley.

He'd get through this physical therapy and start driving on his own. I bet after a few appointments where his ex-wife wasn't in the room, he'd ask her out to dinner.

I was going to get stuck with that ponytail as Finn's new girlfriend.

The happiness I'd felt for Finn seconds ago fell away. Because if it wasn't Ashley, it would be someone else. I focused on my laptop for a few moments, taking a break from the soon-to-be couple.

"Thank you." Finn's deep voice was nothing more than a whisper but it carried across the room. It almost sounded like it was meant for me, not her. I looked up just in time to see Ashley rush to his side and touch his shoulder.

"I'm so proud of you." Her hand traveled up and down his arm.

I was expecting him to knock her off her feet with another sexy smile. But instead of looking at her, he turned to me.

I got the smile.

"Thank you," he mouthed.

A single nod was all I managed in response.

"So, um . . ." Ashley muttered. "Let's go back to the other side. We'll do some stretches and see how your pelvis is feeling."

*Pelvis*. She was always saying pelvis. She always touched his hip when she did.

I hated that Finn didn't seem to mind.

I concentrated on work, doing my best to block out her giggles. But whenever I looked up from my computer, Finn seemed to be glancing my way.

He probably wanted me to disappear, go get coffee or something. Maybe he was waiting for a moment alone to ask her out.

Unable to focus on the financial projections I'd been working on all week, I shut my laptop and stowed it in my bag. Then I left the room, striding down the long hallway that led outside the physical therapy office.

I sent Finn a text that I was outside before wandering down the sidewalk, the sunshine warm on my shoulders. I found a small garden in front of the building, bordered by a thick cement ledge.

The garden was peaceful. All the plants circled a small rock fountain. The varying shades of the leaves and flowers made a spiral that burst with color. I sat on the ledge, mesmerized by the swirl of yellows fading into oranges and then reds. White flowers on emerald vines wound around the border.

It was a new discovery in an old town that was changing by the minute.

Bozeman wasn't the quaint Montana town it had been when I'd been a child. It was now one of the fastest-growing cities in the country.

The sunrises over the mountains were too beautiful. The lush, green fields of the valley were too breathtaking. The winters, when the trees were blanketed with snow that glittered beneath the sun, were too majestic.

Everyone wanted to live here.

Except me.

If not for the kids, I would have considered moving after the divorce. But I didn't want to take them away from Finn. There was no way he'd move away from Alcott.

Bozeman's growth was part of the reason Alcott had been so successful. In the early years, when Bozeman was expanding faster than laborers could keep up, his services had been in high demand. He could have worked twenty-four hours a day, seven days a week and it still wouldn't have been enough to keep up.

Maybe that was why I resented Bozeman's growth so much. Not just because the town I'd loved as a child was gone forever, but because that growth had played a part in ripping my marriage to pieces.

"Hey."

I jumped at Finn's voice. "Oh, hey. I didn't hear you come out."

"It's fine. Are you okay?"

I nodded and hopped down from the ledge. "Just thinking."

"About?"

"Bozeman. None of this was here when I was a kid." I waved my hand to the new building across the street from a new subdivision and new community park.

"Did you know I did this?" He pointed to the garden where I'd been sitting.

"You did?"

"Yep. Two or three years ago. I can't remember. The years are blurring together."

"It's stunning." Maybe that was why I'd been able to tune out the world so quickly and actually think for a change. Finn's work created serenity.

I took one last look at the garden then turned to Finn.

Finn, on crutches.

"No more chair?"

He grinned. "Nope. Ashley is going to take care of returning it to the hospital. I get to use the crutches for a few weeks and then we'll see if we can get rid of them and the boot altogether."

"I'm glad. I know you were sick of the chair."

"The only thing I'm going to miss are our nightly wolls."

"Me too." I smiled. "Ready to go?"

"Lead the way."

We walked slowly back to the van. Without the wheelchair, Finn could actually sit up front with me, and it was so nice not feeling like his chauffeur.

"So, Ashley was pretty excited today." I glanced over at Finn in the passenger seat to gauge his reaction to her name. There wasn't much, no shy smile or gleam in his eyes.

"She thinks I'll make a full recovery. She's been hesitant to say anything, but she told me that today. Even my ankle."

"Really? That's great."

The doctors had been worried that Finn's leg wouldn't heal correctly because of the severity of the breaks. They'd also cautioned that he could have lifelong problems with his knee. They knew he'd be able to walk again, but they were worried he'd develop a limp. He hadn't said anything to me, but I knew Finn had been worried it could impact his work and ability to go hiking.

His relief was palpable in the confines of the van.

"You know the first thing I'm going to do when this boot and cast come off?"

"Take a shower without Saran wrap?"

"Smart-ass." He chuckled. "I'm going to take you and the kids to Fairy Lake."

It was an easy hike. Not really a hike at all other than descending some stairs made out of railroad ties. But Fairy Lake had been a regular picnic spot for us when the kids were tiny.

That was when Finn hadn't worked every weekend.

When we'd been a family and acted like one too.

"Finn." I sighed, my worries from earlier plaguing my mind again. "We need to start preparing the kids."

"For what?"

My grip tightened on the steering wheel. "For when you go home."

"Oh." He turned to look out his window. "Right. Okay."

We drove the rest of the way home in silence. When we pulled into the driveway, Finn got out without needing help. But before he closed the door, he paused. "Do you want to keep the van any longer?"

"No." I was ready to drive my Jeep.

"I'll have someone come pick it up."

"All right."

He slammed the door and walked to the house, using his crutches like he'd had them for days, not less than an hour.

When the front door closed behind him, I dropped my forehead to the steering wheel.

What was he mad about? He had to have known this was coming.

I shook it off and took a hair tie from my wrist. I went to pull my hair up, tying it around the curls, but it snapped.

"Damn it."

Another broken hair tie. My heart sped up. My shoulders dropped.

*It's just a hair tie, Molly.*

Maybe my broken hair ties weren't a bad omen. Maybe this was a good thing. The last time one had broken had been at the hospital, and we'd gotten good news that day. Finn was alive.

I pulled my backup tie from my wrist, glad when it held strong. When my curls were secured in a mess on top of my head, I picked up everything that was mine from the van.

There wasn't much. My purse and a water bottle. Max had dropped a candy bar wrapper on the floor next to where Finn's chair had been. I grabbed it and the keys then got out. With my purse slung over my shoulder, I made my way to the mailbox.

It was empty, except for one unstamped letter.

*Damn it. Not today.*

The letters had stopped while Finn had been in the hospital. Whoever was sending them had to have known we weren't equipped to deal with them during those weeks. I still wasn't, but I didn't have a choice.

There was no energy left for a letter today. And that broken hair tie was a sign this one wouldn't be gushing about my amazingness.

I opened the letter cautiously, glancing around the street to make sure I was alone, then I read Finn's words.

His angry, bitter words.

*You hurt me. You fucking hurt me. Maybe I should have packed enough stuff for two weeks.*

My hand came up to my chest, rubbing the ache behind my sternum as I read those words scribbled before his name.

In the end, he should have packed enough for forever. Finn hadn't come home after that.

I stared at the page, shocked by its severity. The harshness. The letters before had been painful. They'd hurt.

This was the first one where I got angry.

How dare he say *I* hurt *him*? He'd broken me. He'd shattered me to pieces the day he walked out our front door with his weeks' worth of clothes.

*Fuck him.* Finn didn't get to write this letter. He didn't get to send his words into the universe in a way that gave me no chance to defend myself. He certainly didn't get to say this was entirely on me.

I stomped into the house, throwing my purse on the floor as I went in search of Finn. I found him on the couch, his laptop open and ready.

"Are you heading back to work now?" he asked.

"No." I threw the letter at him. The envelope went sailing. The paper floated to the seat.

"Why—oh."

I crossed my arms over my heaving chest, waiting for him to read the words. He had the decency to look apologetic after he reached the end.

"Fuck, Molly." He hung his head and set the letter aside. "I'm sorry. I was angry."

"So was I!" I shouted. The lid on my temper blew like a rocket, straight through the roof and into outer space. "You have no right to blame this on me."

"It was a long time ago."

"That's no excuse," I hissed. "That day was not my fault."

"I didn't mean it." Finn huffed and grabbed a crutch propped next to him on the couch to help him stand. Then he tucked it under his arm to use it for balance on his bad side. "Can we talk about this without shouting?"

"No."

"Molly—"

I held up my hand, silencing his protest. "Do you even remember what we were fighting about?"

"Kali ate those chocolate chips and got sick while you were outside."

"Yes, I was outside. I was taking care of the house and the lawn. I was busy cooking dinners that you missed."

"It was just a few dinners."

"A few? You missed dinner ten nights in a row. Ten," I spat. "And the month before those ten, you were hit or miss half the time. You were too busy taking Bridget out to dinner because you needed to catch her up on some designs."

Even when he had come home, his laptop had been on constantly. I'd gotten used to falling asleep to the sound of him working in bed while I was curled up on my side. Alone.

I'd told him all of this. I'd shouted and screamed, hoping he'd listen. That for once, he'd put his wife before his job. Instead, he'd told me I wasn't being supportive. He was doing this for us, after all. Building a legacy.

Three days. Friday. Saturday. Sunday. We fought for three days, barely able to look at one another. Finally, I told him maybe we needed to take a break. Our argument was just running laps. Every few hours, we circled back to the beginning and started all over again.

He left.

I put a smile on my face for the kids.

And that night, I cried until I was so exhausted, I eventually passed out.

My anger surged one last time before it morphed to pain. I blinked rapidly, not letting myself cry. But I felt the tears burn. They were the frustrated, uncontrollable tears of the heartbroken woman I'd been all those years ago.

"I'm sorry," Finn whispered. He reached for my arm, but I took a step away.

"Why would you write that?" My voice shook.

"I was so angry."

"How could you be angry at me? I just wanted you home for dinner."

"It wasn't you." He shook his head. "I was angry. I didn't know it at the time, but I was angry at myself. It was easier to take it out on you than to admit I was the problem. That you were right all along."

"I—what?"

He shuffled closer, leading with his good leg. "You were right."

I slapped a hand over my mouth, holding in a cry. Those words were so welcome. And much, much too late. My hand fell away, my chin dropped. "I don't want these letters anymore."

"I'm sorry." Finn stepped closer.

The moment his hand touched my arm, I lost it. After weeks of doing everything for everyone, of stretching myself to the thinnest to keep him and the kids together, I broke.

The tears came. The sobs escaped. My shoulders shook.

I broke.

But for the first time in over six years, I didn't break alone. Finn wrapped me in his arms and I cried. For the first time in years, I shared my tears with another person.

And when I was all cried out, I let Finn hold me.

"Please, Molly. I'm begging you. Don't read them. Please, stop reading them."

I stiffened. "How many more are there?"

"Promise me you won't read them."

I pushed him away and looked into his eyes. "Are they like this one?"

He didn't answer. He didn't need to. The remorse in his gaze told me everything I needed to know.

They weren't like this letter.

They were worse.

# fifteen
## Finn

"You're doing so well." Ashley clapped. "I'm so impressed."

"Thanks, Ashley." I grinned at her then finished the set of bicep curls I was doing with an elastic exercise band.

The name of our game at the moment was Muscle Mass. My right arm looked like a limp noodle compared to my left. Both of my legs had slimmed down and my thighs didn't fill out my jeans anymore. Instead, they draped down my legs, covering the toothpicks that had become my calves, so I'd been working hard to replace the muscle I'd lost after the accident.

I'd never been vain about my body. I wasn't a gym rat or obsessive about my diet. I had a physical job and loved hiking in the mountains, both of which kept me in shape. But after months of being trapped in a bed or chair, I was not happy with the reflection in the mirror. I looked like a string bean.

When Ashley gave me the go-ahead to start bulking up, I dove in, doubling up on protein and throwing myself into these sessions. My arms were getting stronger. So were my legs. I'd even begun to gain back some definition in my abs.

It wasn't lost on me how much Molly loved my flat stomach. Her nails had always lingered in the dips of my washboard abs. If I had the chance to get her into bed, to win her trust and heart once more, I wanted every bit of stamina I'd once had to make her toes curl.

"Done." I breathed heavily after finishing the last rep. "What's next?"

Ashley smiled. "I think that's it for today. Don't overdo it."

"I don't want to back off."

"You're doing great, Finn. That's plenty for today." Her hand rested on my shoulder. "Though, if you want to hang out with me, you're my last patient for the day. I was thinking of going downtown and grabbing a drink after work."

"Uh . . ." A rush of panic hit as I scrambled for what to say. Ashley was nice. She was beautiful and the hints she'd been dropping hadn't been missed. But I'd hoped she'd picked up on the fact that I only had eyes for Molly. Besides, wasn't there some rule about not dating patients? I wasn't sure how that worked for physical therapists.

"Sorry," a voice called behind me. "He's already got a date."

My head whipped around as Cole walked up. He'd taken the afternoon off and brought me here today because Molly and Poppy were both busy at the restaurant. I'd planned to buy him a beer for shuttling me here. Now I'd buy him two for coming to my rescue.

"Bummer." Ashley pouted. "Maybe another time."

"I don't think so," I told her, watching her face fall. "Sorry, Ashley."

She shrugged and put on a fake smile. "It's cool. See you next session."

"All done?" Cole asked.

"All done." I nodded, then looked at Ashley. "Thanks again."

"Bye, Finn."

I grabbed my crutch and followed Cole out the door. I'd decided last week, after about two days of dealing with both crutches, that it was more of a pain in the ass than it was worth. I'd given Max one crutch that he'd been pretending was a laser gun.

"Thanks for that," I said as we walked outside.

Cole laughed. "You were white as a sheet. I'm guessing there's no interest in dating Ashley."

"None." My heart was already taken.

We got into his truck without much delay, then he turned it on and rolled down our windows. Fall in Montana was a short season, warm during the day and cool at night. Soon, we'd be dealing with snow and ice, but for now, there wasn't a better way to travel through town than with the windows down.

This weather always made me long for the outdoors. I loved working in the field this time of year. Normally, I adjusted my schedule so I could be out with the crews, planting trees or laying sod. There was just something about working with the warm sun on my back, sweat dripping down my body, that made me feel at peace. Made me feel like I was where I needed to be.

"Damn, I want to get back to work."

Cole chuckled. "Soon enough. What did the doctors say?"

"A week or two longer with the crutch and boot, then I can drive again. If PT keeps going well, I should be able to ease into work at the end of the month."

Work would be dwindling by then, but anything was better than nothing.

"Nice. Are you still up for grabbing a beer?"

"Absolutely."

Cole and I tried to meet up for beers once a month. In the fall, we spent our Saturdays watching Montana State football games together. Since he'd come into Poppy's life, the two of us had become fast friends.

Besides Poppy, I considered him my best friend. He was so solid, so levelheaded. Whenever I needed advice, about a girlfriend or a problem at work, Cole was there.

Maybe if I'd known him when Molly and I were going through our divorce, he could have saved me from myself. He could have slapped some sense into me when I'd started pushing Molly away.

We drove downtown, searching for a rare parking spot. College kids were back in town and Bozeman was bustling. After a few laps around the block, we found a space and headed for our favorite bar. Cole and I settled into an outdoor seat and ordered, and the waitress brought over a local beer soon after.

"I miss beer." I sighed after that first sip. "Molly only ever has wine." She used to keep beer in the house. When I lived there.

"How's it going with you two? I bet it's not easy having to live with your ex-wife. Ready to kill each other yet?"

"No, actually, it's going good. I, uh . . ." I took another drink, not sure exactly how to word this. "I'm going to try and win her back."

Cole's glass, which had been halfway to his mouth, froze in midair. "Win her back?"

"I love her. Always have. Always will."

He set his glass down, studying me for a few long

moments. As a detective for the Bozeman Police Department, his stare was always unnerving. It was like he could look right into my mind and pluck out my thoughts.

It was strange that Poppy hadn't told him about our conversation and her advice to ruin my existing life. Maybe she didn't think I'd go through with it. Maybe she didn't believe I'd win.

Finally, after I'd begun to sweat under Cole's scrutiny, he picked up his beer and took a healthy chug. "What's your plan?"

The tension left my shoulders. "Take it slow. Try and forget about all the shit in the past and start fresh." Which would be easier if those fucking letters would stop.

"Forget, huh? Don't you think you guys need to hash that history out?"

I shook my head. "Nothing good is going to come from us digging up old skeletons. I mean, we kind of already have. Those letters have forced us to talk about some things we should have when we were married. But trust me, the other stuff is just better forgotten."

I could get past Molly having a one-night stand during our separation if I just didn't think about it. There was no reason to talk about it. No reason for us to both go through that time again and relive it.

Forgetting was better. And since she'd promised not to read any more letters, I didn't have to worry about it coming up.

"Speaking of letters, did you guys ever figure out who was leaving them?" Cole asked.

"No damn clue. I've spent so much time thinking about who could have found them that I'm more confused than ever. Honestly, I still think it's Poppy or my mom."

"Poppy would never lie to you. That's not her," he said,

leaping to his wife's defense. "Do you really think your mom would either?"

"No," I admitted. "I just can't think of anyone who would care. Or who'd had access to my closet."

"What about Brenna?"

"Brenna?"

Cole shrugged. "You dated for a year. I'm guessing she spent plenty of time in your bedroom."

No, she hadn't, which was why we'd broken up.

But she had been in my bedroom. Could Brenna have found the letters? "Why would she send them?"

"Maybe she was threatened by Molly. Maybe she thought it would be a way to turn Molly against you. I mean, you said you guys have had some fights over the letters."

"Then why drop them off instead of stamp and mail them? Why would she leave the nice letters? Trust me when I say that if she wanted Molly to hate me, all she needed to do was send a few."

Like the ones Molly hadn't gotten yet.

"I'm just tossing out ideas." Cole shrugged. "Sometimes when we're stuck on a case, we throw out random ideas to shoot them down. It helps broaden our focus."

"Well, I guess it doesn't really matter anyway. From what I remember, there are only a few letters left and Molly promised not to open them."

"Really? Why?"

"Because I asked her not to. The letters . . . they aren't good. I wrote them when I was pissed and hurt. They aren't how I really feel."

"Hmm." Cole took another pull from his pint glass. "You really think you guys will get back together?"

"She's the love of my life. The accident . . . it's been an eye-opener. All I could think about when I was in that hospital bed was how I wanted to go home. And home wasn't my house. It was with her and the kids. She's the best thing that ever happened to me and I fucked it up."

"I wish you luck. I don't think it will be easy, but I'm pulling for you guys."

"Thanks." I took another drink. It felt good to admit to Cole that I wanted Molly back. It was nice to know I had his support, but I also didn't want to jinx myself. Molly and I hadn't even talked about reconciling.

She might laugh. She might tell me she was happier divorced than she'd ever been married.

"I need to run an idea by you." Cole propped his forearms on the table, leaning closer. "I want to take Poppy to Italy. I'm thinking next May because she hates May. I thought it might be something fun for a change. And if I can swing it, I'd like the trip to be a surprise."

"Oh." I shook my head. "My sister does not like surprises."

Cole chuckled. "She'll like this one. I found this villa outside Rome for the two of us to stay a week. They've got a pool and a spa. They have an on-site chef who does private cooking lessons. It's the dream vacation she doesn't even know she wants yet."

"Sounds awesome. What do you need from me?"

Cole launched into his plan to make it a surprise, from booking the tickets on my credit card to arranging for his parents and mine to watch the kids. The more he talked, the more excited I was for the trip and I wasn't even going. And Cole was right, Poppy would love this trip.

We finished our beers and made our way back to Cole's truck.

"Home or Alcott?" he asked.

"Home." As much work as there was to do, I didn't want

to be in the office. I wanted to be outside, and the deck over-looking Molly's backyard was becoming my favorite place to set up shop and work on the laptop.

Earlier in the week, Bridget had come to collect me. She'd driven me all over so I could check on my project sites as well as hers. Most were in a good spot, though they were also a week or so behind schedule. But since I couldn't jump in and help lay sod or plant trees, there wasn't much I could do other than office work, which I could do from home.

"I appreciate you driving me today," I told Cole as he parked in the driveway.

"No problem."

I opened the door and lifted out my crutch but paused before getting out. "Poppy is going to love the surprise. And I think May is a good time. It will make her smile."

"There's nothing I won't do to make my wife happy." Even spending a good portion of his paycheck to take her to Italy in May, hoping it would make the month easier to bear.

Cole Goodman was a godsend. He loved Poppy uncondi-tionally. He brought so much light into her life, it was hard to even remember the dark days.

I wanted that for Molly. She deserved to have the man of her dreams, a partner who supported her and whose purpose in life was to make her happy. I hadn't been that man.

I'd failed her.

I wouldn't fail her again.

Waving good-bye to Cole, I made my way into the house then stopped inside the front door. The lights were on in the kitchen, but I'd shut them off when I'd left.

"Molly?" I called without an answer.

I walked down the hallway, checking the kitchen then her bedroom. Other than the lights, there was no sign of her. Could she be at Gavin's house? I went to the garage, finding her Jeep parked inside, so I poked my head outside the door leading to the backyard.

And there she was.

Her hair was piled up in a huge mess. A couple of loose curls were poking out, trying to make their escape. Molly was on her knees next to a bed of flowers, yanking weeds with an unbridled fury. Dirt flew. Leaves shredded. She'd piled heaps in various spots along the edge of the yard.

I leaned against the doorframe, watching her work. Due to the accident, I hadn't had the time or ability to finish the changes here, though there wasn't much left to do. A few edges needed to be squared up and the beds prepped with weed block before I laid down fresh mulch. It was easy stuff I could have had a crew come out and finish. But while I'd given them the mowing, I hadn't wanted to hand over this yard.

It was *my* yard. Our place. I wanted to be the one to finish it. And I wanted to be the one to plant Molly's lilac bush.

"You little—" Molly grunted, her hand wrapped around a stubborn dandelion, pulling with all her might. But the weed didn't budge. Instead, her hand slipped and she fell back on her ass. "Bastard."

I laughed, loud enough that she spun around, clutching her heart.

"You scared me." She scowled.

"Sorry." I grinned and made my way across the yard. Then I tossed my crutch aside and eased myself to the grass at her side. The dandelion she'd been trying to pull was huge. Its leaves were stripped and the stalk exposed, but it had broken an inch above the soil, meaning it would be back.

I stretched past Molly and grabbed the hand trowel in the dirt. With a hard stab, I felt the root break beneath the surface. I yanked it out by the stub and tossed it into her pile. "There."

She rolled her eyes. "It's more satisfying if you use your hands."

"There are a lot of things more satisfying when you use your hands."

"Oh my God." She nudged my shoulder, her cheeks flushing. "You're such a teenager."

"I couldn't resist. That was too easy."

She giggled, wiping a bead of sweat from her brow with the back of her hand. "How was PT with *Ashley*?"

"*Ashley*," I mimicked. "If I didn't know better, I'd think you were jealous."

"I'm not jealous," she muttered, her hands diving for another weed and ripping it from the ground. "But I think she's been testing the limits of professionalism."

I opened my mouth to tell her that Ashley had asked me out today but decided it was better to keep that to myself. Her flare of jealousy was enough to make me grin, because Molly wouldn't be jealous if there weren't something between us.

"I don't want Ashley," I told her.

"Oh. Whatever. It's not my business."

I didn't miss the small smile tugging at her supple mouth.

Scooting over a foot, I started on another patch of weeds, adding to Molly's pile.

"I let it get out of control back here." She shook her head, scolding herself.

"You were busy."

"I know. But I hate weeds."

"I can get you on the rotation with the flower crew." I had a team solely responsible for flowers. They traveled around the valley, tending to clients' flower beds and flowerpots so there was never any weeding or trimming necessary. It was an elite service, mostly requested by my wealthier customers.

"No, but thank you," she said. "I don't mind. When it's not so far behind, it's actually kind of a stress reliever."

"You're home early today. I thought you'd be at the restaurant until six."

"Me too. But it was really slow. It happens when the weather gets like this. People get in their sunshine while they can. Poppy and I flipped a coin for who had to stay and work. I won."

We continued to weed along the flower bed until we reached the end. My good hand was smudged, my cuticles stained brown. "Damn, but I missed dirt."

Molly laughed and scooted closer, pulling off her gloves. Her fingers were much cleaner, but her face had a few smudges. "It's weird to see your hands clean. They just don't look right unless there's some dirt under your fingernails."

"And I've always thought you were sexy when you got a little messy." I brought my hand to her face, using my thumb to rub a streak of dirt from her cheek.

Our eyes caught. Hers flashed darker. A rush of color spread across her face as I let my hand drift across her cheek, the tips of my fingers skimming up and over the shell of her ear.

"You're beautiful."

Her breath hitched and her lips parted.

The warmth from the sun was replaced by the scorching heat between us. I leaned in, letting her draw me closer.

Molly didn't lean back. She stayed there on her knees, her hands at her sides as I brushed my lips across hers. "Finn," she whispered.

"Molly."

"What are you doing?" Her breath caressed my mouth.

"Kissing you."

She stayed still as I repeated the movement, this time

letting my tongue dart out and trace the seam of her lips. She tasted like mint and sunshine. She smelled like heaven and earth.

"Kiss me," I ordered.

"I don't—"

"Kiss me. Kiss me like I know you want to."

She let out a small moan of protest.

*Fuck.* I'd pushed too hard. I was certain she'd pull away any second, but then her arms lifted, hesitantly looping around my shoulders. Her chest pressed into mine.

It was all the agreement I needed.

I crushed my lips to hers, slipping my tongue past her teeth. I wrapped my arm around her back, pulling her tight as I immersed myself in the sweetness of her lips.

A rush of blood pulsed in my cock. The familiar twitch was so goddamn welcome. Thank God, it still worked. I hadn't asked the doctors if sex was on the table. I didn't care. I'd reinjure myself every day of the week if it meant getting another shot with Molly.

I shifted closer, wanting to press my arousal into her belly, but my boot caught on the lawn as I shifted and sent a sharp sting up my leg.

"Ah." I winced, pulling away from Molly's mouth.

"What?" She was off me in a flash, her eyes scanning me from head to toe. "What happened?"

"Nothing." I waved her back into my arms, but she was already gone.

She stood, wiping the loose tendrils of her hair out of her face, then she ran a hand over her mouth.

So close. I hung my head, taking a few breaths to get my dick under control. I silently cursed the boot.

"I think you need to go home."

"What?" My eyes whipped up to Molly. Home? I was home. "What do you mean?"

"I think you need to go home. It's too confusing." Her arms were closed around herself. She took another step away.

I used my good side to stand, careful to avoid too much weight on my bad leg. "There's nothing confusing about this, Molly. I'm here. I want to be here. And not just until I can drive or until I'm completely mobile. I want to be here. With you."

Her mouth fell open a bit, her lower lip still puffy from our kiss.

I took her momentary shock and shuffled closer. "What if we took this slow? I'll court you. You can remind me of all those old-fashioned rituals you love so much."

"Finn—"

"Think about it. Don't answer now. I'm going to go inside and take a shower. A *cold* shower. Then we can have dinner together when the kids get home. We can watch a movie and if you want, you can hold my hand. Then tomorrow, we'll do it again. Until the day you realize I'm here. I want to be here. With you."

Molly studied my face, her eyes narrowing like she didn't believe a word I said. "There's so much history."

"Then we forget it. Erase it completely. We start with a blank slate."

"Forget it?" A flash of irritation crossed her face. "I can't forget. I *won't* forget."

Before I could grapple with what I'd said to piss her off so quickly, she stormed past me and into the garage.

I took a step to chase her, but the fucking boot slowed me down. So I hopped over to my crutch. Then I chased.

When I found her, she'd shut herself into her bedroom. I

listened at the door and heard the water running in the shower.

"Well, shit."

*What did I say?* Why wouldn't she want to forget about the pain we'd caused one another?

I tested the knob. It was unlocked, so I opened the door a crack, peeking inside to make sure she wasn't in the bedroom. She wasn't. I let myself inside and walked to the bathroom door.

I left that one shut, resting my forehead on its face. I spoke to the wood, hoping she could hear me over the running water.

"What did I say, Molly?"

Footsteps stomped my way. The water turned off one second before the bathroom door flew open.

"I don't want to forget," she snapped. "I don't want to forget all the times you said you loved me. Or how it felt to be a family. I don't want to forget the times we laughed together. Or the times you made love to me. Those memories, they've kept me going for six years. Six. Years. I don't want to forget them. Not when I've cherished them."

"That's not what I meant."

"Whatever." Molly tried to shove past me, but I caught her by the elbow.

"That's not what I meant," I repeated. "I'll never forget the way you used to steal pencils from my backpack because you kept giving yours to the kid in Econ who never had one. I'll never forget the way you smiled at me when you were in labor with Max, even though you were in so much pain, because you wanted me to stop worrying. I'll never forget the way you used to whisper you loved me right before you fell asleep. I don't want to forget those times. I want to forget the bad times. The fights. The divorce. The—"

"Other guy?"

My entire body jerked. Pain seared down my spine at the reminder.

"That's just it, Finn." She dropped her chin. "We can't forget. It's not possible. The good turned bad. If we forget that, it will only happen again. And I don't have it in me to go through it again. It almost broke me once. I can't risk it. So please, go home."

My arm dropped away from her elbow.

She hurried out of the room, leaving me alone as her words sank in.

She didn't want to forget. Okay, then what did she want? That kiss in the yard said she still wanted me, at least.

I turned to follow her because I wasn't letting this go. I wasn't leaving either. But as I took a step away from the bathroom, my eyes caught on an envelope on her nightstand. I didn't need to see the handwriting to know what it was. Another letter had come and she'd hidden it from me.

I grabbed it then relaxed when I found it unopened.

She'd kept her word.

I took it to the kitchen where Molly was at the sink, scrubbing furiously with a bleach cleaner.

"Were you going to open this?"

Her hands stilled. "No. Maybe."

"I asked you not to."

She tossed the sponge into the sink and hung her head. Then she rinsed her hands and dried them before spinning to meet my gaze. "I wasn't going to. It came today and I told myself I wasn't going to read it. But then . . ."

"Then what?"

She crossed the distance between us, lifting the letter out of my grip. "I have to know."

"Nothing good will be in that envelope. Rip it up. Please."

"And forget?" She stared at the envelope for a few long moments.

I held my breath, hoping the next sound I'd hear was that of crumpled paper, because if she opened that letter, we wouldn't have a future. "Please, Molly."

She looked up at me with tears swimming in her eyes. "I have to."

*How could you?*

*You are my wife.*
*You are MY wife.*
*You are my WIFE.*

*I hate you for this. I hate you for letting another man inside you. I hate you for throwing away everything we ever had. You broke my fucking heart.*

*We're done.*

# sixteen
## Molly

It didn't take long to read the letter. The first time through, a stab of pain pierced my heart so deeply I nearly collapsed. But my knees held strong. They locked tight, enough for me to read it again.

Then again.

By the fourth time, the pain faded away.

I was numb.

Maybe Finn had been right. Maybe I should have ripped this one to shreds. But he'd told me at the beginning these letters were his way of expressing his feelings. They were raw and real.

And since he'd hidden the raw and real from me, kept it back, these letters were the only way to see into his soul.

The gushing wound was there, laid out with blue ink on white paper. It was devastating. I'd destroyed him.

I'd destroyed us both.

There'd be no tears for this letter. I didn't get to cry. We'd had problems in our marriage, but the person who'd torn it apart was me. I deserved every single lick of his pain. I deserved to read this letter every day.

What I didn't deserve was Finn.

"Okay," I whispered, folding the letter back up and sliding it into the envelope with shaking hands.

"Okay?"

I nodded and handed Finn back the letter. "Okay."

He took it, staring at me like he was waiting for an explosion. There wasn't one. I went to the sink and resumed my cleaning.

"That's it?" he asked.

"That's it."

Finn stalked close and slammed the letter on the counter. The paper didn't make much noise. His palm did. "That's it? You make a big show of opening this letter, and that's it? Why?"

"I had to."

"Why?"

"Because." I whirled on him. "You don't trust me enough to tell me how you feel. You kept things from me for years, choosing to write things in letters you never sent. You escaped our problems by running to work. You kept me in the dark. After all this time, after everything we've been through, I have a right to know how you really felt."

"I kept them from you because it was for your own good." He swiped the letter up, shaking it in his fist, the paper crackling. "Did you really want me to leave this lying around?"

"At least it would have made us talk."

"There's nothing to talk about."

I clenched my jaw. "You can't forget it happened."

"I can sure as fuck try."

"And that's why we're never going to work," I shot back. "I had sex with another man."

He grimaced, the pain on his face rolling over his entire body. "Don't."

"Don't what? Don't say it out loud? It happened. I made the biggest mistake of my life and this letter is the first time you've actually admitted out loud that I hurt you."

"That's not true."

"Yes. Yes, it is. I told you the truth. I came to you the next day and owned my mistake. And instead of yelling or crying or showing me any kind of emotion, all you said was, 'Get a lawyer.' You were indifferent. You were done with me. I got the cold shoulder for months, to the point where I didn't know if you had *ever* cared. I hurt you and you dismissed me. You shut down."

"You broke me. That wasn't a secret."

"And I'm sorry. I'm so sorry. I've lost count of the times I've apologized. I'll always regret it."

"Just . . . don't." Finn ran his hands through his hair. "Please, I don't want to talk about it. I can't."

"Fine." I sighed. "Listen, I've got a bunch of stuff to do before the kids get home. Maybe you should pack. I think Poppy and your parents can get you to and from work and PT for the next couple of weeks."

He staggered back a step. "You're really kicking me out?"

"Yes." I nodded. "I meant what I said outside. This is too confusing. I can't do this with you again. My heart can't take another ending with you."

"Molly," he said gently. "It doesn't have to end."

"But it will." I lowered my voice. "It will. You want to pretend like we didn't slaughter each other. This." I picked up the letter. "This is a problem. It will resurface, maybe not tomorrow or the next day. But eventually, it will come up again and rip us apart. We can't ignore it."

"You really want to talk about it?" His jaw ticked. There was fire in his eyes. "You want to know how I feel?"

I braced. "Yes."

"I feel the same way I did when I wrote that letter. I hate you for it."

A punch to the gut would have felt better. "You hate me?"

"I hate what you did. I hate that another man was inside of you."

"So do I." My chin fell as shame washed over my shoulders.

"How? Why, Molly? Were things really that bad and I didn't see it? Why didn't you talk to me?"

Talk to him? The pain eased as my temper flared.

"I tried to talk to you," I snapped, poking a finger into his chest. "I tried to talk to you every day. Yes, things were that bad. But you didn't want to talk. You moved out. And every time I tried to talk to you or offer up a solution, you shut me out. You didn't even bother showing up to a single counseling session."

"I was busy."

"Right," I muttered. "Too busy. That was always the excuse. You were too busy to try and save our marriage. All I asked for was a few hours of your time to talk to a counselor."

"You know how I felt about that counselor."

"No. I don't. Because you never told me. You just didn't show up."

"There was no way I was going to talk about our marriage to one of your mother's fucking friends. The last thing we needed was Dr. Deborah knowing all about the shit going on in our life."

"Seriously? That's your excuse?"

"It's not an excuse."

"Why didn't you tell me?" My arms flailed in the air. "I would have picked another counselor. I would have gone to anyone. But instead, you just didn't show."

"I told you from the beginning I didn't want to see that counselor. You made the appointments anyway."

"Because I wanted to save our marriage. We were drowning." *I'd* been drowning. I hadn't tried to hide it either. I'd worn my exhaustion on my face. The slump of my shoulders. The way I'd curl into a ball and sleep huddled into myself at night. They'd been there. All of the signs. "And you didn't seem to care."

"That's bullshit."

I steeled my spine and challenged, "Is it?"

He opened his mouth but clamped it shut with a snap.

"Everything that happened. All of it. I thought you were done. I thought you didn't care. I thought we were over."

And instead of telling me, or showing me that he cared, he'd turned to blank pages. He'd given the pen and the ink his feelings.

He hadn't trusted them to his wife.

"We weren't over, Molly. We were still married. You were still my wife."

"You're right. You're absolutely right." My agreement caught him off guard. I guess he'd been expecting me to argue, but I *had* still been his wife. And I'd betrayed him.

We'd betrayed each other.

"I don't say this because I am making an excuse," I said. "But, Finn, that might have broken you. But you crushed me that night."

"What night?" he asked.

"*The* night. The night of Lanie's bachelorette party."

His forehead furrowed. "What are you talking about?"

"I came to Alcott that night. Before the party. I was all dressed up in that black dress you always loved. I thought, I had a babysitter, you were alone, and maybe what we needed was a night to ourselves. No distractions. Just you and me remembering that we loved each other."

I'd spent an hour on my hair, taming the curls. I'd watched three YouTube videos to learn how to get that smoky-eye look with some charcoal eyeliner.

Finn shook his head, trying to remember. "You never came there."

"I did. You weren't alone."

"Who . . ." His face fell as he answered his own question. "Bridget."

"She was there. Cuddled up to your side as you watched a movie in the loft."

Bridget and her tight little body. She'd fit well into Finn's side. Maybe that was why I hated her so much. She fit with Finn.

And I . . . I was just a woman who'd spent hours getting ready to impress a man whose gaze had already wandered.

"Molly." He held up his hands. "There has never been anything between Bridget and me. I swear."

Was he lying? I searched his face, every crease. Every angle. He was telling the truth. "You swear?"

"On Jamie's grave," he said with a sure nod. "I have never touched Bridget in that way."

The relief made my knees weak. I'd always wondered . . . but the way Finn had reacted after my one-night stand convinced me he'd never done anything with Bridget. He wasn't the kind of man who'd punish me for a mistake he'd already made himself.

But then there were the years after the divorce. They worked late together. They were close. I'd convinced myself years ago that they'd had something going on at one point or another.

The image of them cuddled together that night was one I'd never forget.

"I came up the stairs. Quietly, I guess. Or else the TV was too loud because you didn't hear me. I froze when I saw you both together."

"She kept me company. That was all."

"Kept you company? She was there, inches away from you, ripping me to shreds. Your wife. And you just sat there."

"What? No." Finn shook his head. "I wouldn't let her run you down."

I fumed. Wasn't this conversation about honesty?

"I was there. You two were sitting together, eating from the same bowl of popcorn, like *we'd* done time and time again. She asked you if you were going home. You said, 'No.' She asked you if we were getting divorced. You said, 'Yes.' Then she proceeded to go on a rant about how I wasn't good enough for you. That I wasn't the wife you needed because I didn't support you. She called me a bitch for kicking you out of the house and separating you from the kids. And what did you say? Nothing."

Finn opened his mouth but no words came out.

"We were only separated. We hadn't decided to get a divorce. Or at least, I thought we were still trying to fix our marriage. But you'd already decided we were done. And instead of telling me you wanted a divorce, you told your employee, the woman who called me a bitch to your face and you . . . You. Said. Nothing."

"Molly," Finn said, hanging his head. "I don't know what to say. Hand to God, I don't remember her saying that."

"I'm not making it up."

"I didn't say that." He held up his hands. "I'm not calling you a liar. If the TV was on, if I was tired . . . I don't remember. Are you sure I was even awake?"

"Yes." Maybe. Was he awake? I'd been so focused on Bridget's profile, the way her body had leaned into his side. I hadn't really noticed much of Finn's face. He'd been sitting with his arms thrown over the back of the couch. His face had been aimed at the TV, not hanging loose or lulled to the side. But I couldn't remember if his eyes had been open. *Oh my God.* Could he have been asleep?

Bridget had been talking to him like he'd been awake. But could he have nodded off?

The idea that I could have misread the entire thing, that he might not have even heard her words, made me want to curl into a ball and cry. A strangled sound came from my throat.

"Why didn't you confront me about it?" he asked.

"Because." I blinked, the doubts fogging my mind. "Because it was too late. I left Alcott, thinking we were done. I met up with Lanie at her party. Poppy wasn't there because she was having a hard night, so I was alone. I drank too much. I listened to the girls tell me how I deserved better. How you were probably fucking Bridget anyway."

"I wasn't fucking Bridget," Finn gritted out.

"She's been in love with you since day one. It was easy to believe you were into her too."

"What?" His entire body jerked. "Bridget is not in love with me."

"Then you're blind," I huffed.

Bridget looked at Finn like he was a rock god on stage, surrounded by a mass of people, singing only to her.

"Whatever." Finn waved it off. "You should have confronted me."

"While you were snuggled up with Bridget?" I shot back. She'd been wearing shorts. They'd ridden so far up that her entire bare thigh had been pressed against his jeans.

"What about the next day? You could have confronted me the next day."

"It was too late. After . . . after it was done, when I came to tell you the truth, I tried to tell you everything. I tried to tell you that I'd been blitzed out of my mind. That there was this group of guys following us from bar to bar. That one of them was flirting with me. But you didn't want to hear it."

"I didn't then. I don't now. So, stop. Just stop."

"No!" I yelled. "You don't get to pick and choose parts of the story to hear. The guy who was flirting with me was sweet. He called me beautiful. He gave me water when I was getting too drunk. He walked me outside to wait for my cab so I wouldn't be alone."

"Stop!" Finn yelled, backing away from me.

"He kissed me. It was dark. I can't remember if there were other people around, but I remember him kissing me."

"Molly," Finn pleaded, taking a step away. "Stop. Please."

"The next thing I remember was being backed up against a wall. He pulled up my dress and—"

"Shut up!" Finn roared. He threw his crutch, sending it flying across the kitchen and crashing onto the floor. It skidded to a stop by the dining room table.

I flinched. I'd gone too far. I hadn't meant to share the details with Finn, but the dam had been opened. I'd never told a soul about what had happened that night, not even Poppy. I'd told them I'd had sex with another man and let everyone assume the details.

"It lasted a whole five seconds until I realized what was happening. I pushed him away. I told him I was sorry and then I ran. He wasn't you, and I knew I'd made a horrible mistake. But it was too late."

The air in the kitchen stilled. Finn's chest heaved. His eyes were blank.

I shook from head to toe. I'd finally gotten it all out. Finally relived that night, not only for Finn, but for myself. He wasn't the only one who'd blocked it out for years. But now there'd be no forgetting. There'd be no ignoring this and pretending we could be that loving couple again.

The dream of Finn and Molly was over.

"Why are you telling me this?" Finn's voice was flat as he spoke.

"You had your letters. I had nothing. The person I talked to, the person I turned to when my life was upside down, was you. It was always you. And you weren't there."

"That's not a good enough reason to fuck another man."

"No, it isn't. And I'm sorry." My chin quivered uncontrollably. "I'm so sorry I hurt you. I'm so sorry I betrayed you in that way. It's something I'll regret until the end of my life. But it happened. It happened, Finn. It all happened. Just like you being with other women happened. I hate thinking about you with Brenna or any of the others. But it's there. We have to live with the wounds we've inflicted on one another."

"There weren't any others," Finn said so quietly I almost missed it.

"No. I haven't been with anyone since the divorce. Except you."

"That's not what I meant." Finn looked up, his blank stare gone. "There weren't any others. Since you, there weren't any others."

There weren't any others? *What?* "I don't understand."

"Women. There weren't any other women."

I blinked at him, replaying his words. "You've been dating for years."

"Yes, I have. And not once have I taken another woman to bed."

My knees had held out until that point, but with that

blow, they didn't have any strength left. I stumbled sideways, my hip crashing into the side of the counter so hard it would bruise.

"No." I closed my eyes, my hands coming to my face. "No, no, no."

There were supposed to be other women. They were supposed to even the score. I'd become celibate and Finn had become the town's most eligible playboy.

But the scales tipped again, right back in his favor.

"What about Brenna?"

He scoffed. "Brenna got tired of waiting around. She gave me an ultimatum. Intimacy or we were done. That was the week before I started sleeping with you."

My head was spinning and the only thing I could think to say was, "Why?"

"Why? I've been in love with you since I was twenty-one years old. I might not wear the ring, but that doesn't mean I don't feel it there."

All this time, he'd been free.

And he'd held on to me.

The air in the kitchen was suffocating. I couldn't fill my lungs. I couldn't clear the fog, so I bolted past Finn and ran down the hallway toward the front door.

The moment I flung it open and the summer air hit my face, the tears spilled down my cheeks. But I didn't make it one more step.

"Do not run from me."

I froze in the doorway at Finn's booming voice. Behind me, he shuffled to catch up, then his heat was at my back.

"I need air," I choked out.

"Then we'll sit on the porch. Together. But don't you run from me, Molly. Not again. You wanted to open all of this up. It's open. And we're not leaving it undone. Not again. So don't you dare run from me. I'll break my leg all over again chasing you. And make no mistake, I will chase you."

I didn't doubt him for a second.

I turned, the tears making his stern face blurry. "I'm so sorry, Finn."

"I know." He took my elbow and escorted us outside. When we were both seated on the front step, he pulled me into his side. "I know."

"I'd take it back."

"I know."

"Do you?"

He hesitated, long enough that I knew his answer would be honest. "I know."

We sat there in silence for a long time. The birds chirped as they flew between the trees. The slight breeze rustled the leaves. The world was bright and beautiful.

Everywhere but on this step.

The gloom hovered over our heads. The weight of all that had happened sat on our shoulders.

"It's too heavy," I said, breaking the quiet.

"What's too heavy?"

"The past. It's too heavy to forget." It was too heavy to forgive.

But that was what needed to happen. We had to forgive. Each other. Ourselves.

How many times had I wished to go back in time and change my actions? How many hours had I spent loathing myself? I'd been living with so much regret. So much guilt.

Until I forgave myself for being human and flawed and impulsive, the past would haunt me.

It would haunt us.

"Can you forgive me?" I asked Finn.

He leaned back to look in my face. His eyes gave me the answer before his mouth. "I don't know."

"Fair enough."

The silence returned, the only noises on the porch coming from the neighborhood. A kid was playing basketball on the next block over and the thud of the ball's dribbling echoed off the homes. A plane flew overhead, the buzz fading as it ascended into the clouds. The world went on around us without a care as Finn and I sat frozen on the porch, reeling from the truth.

Things might have been so different . . . if only.

*If only.*

Finn cleared his throat. "My doctor said with my PT going so well, I could get into a different boot or maybe no boot at all in two weeks. Regardless, I should be able to drive by the end of the month. Would you mind if I stayed until then? I'd like a little more time with the kids."

"Okay."

As hard as it would be to have him here, it was the right thing to do. I wanted to ease Kali and Max into the fact that we were all splitting up again.

It was for the best.

"I'm sorry, Molly."

I leaned into his side and rested my head on his shoulder. "I'm sorry, Finn."

"I love you."

I closed my eyes. "I love you too."

It felt good to say those words. To let them float into the wind and fade with the sunshine.

It felt good to say those words.

One last time.

*I never thought this would be us. I never imagined we'd be here, getting a divorce.*

*I feel like I'm going to wake up tomorrow morning in our bed and this will all have been a nightmare. But it's real.*

*I'm ashamed of you. I'm ashamed of myself.*

*You quit me.*

*And I quit you.*

# seventeen
## Finn

"I'm done." Max rushed over from his corner of the yard.

"Awesome. Let me check." I pushed up off the grass and slowly made my way to the other side of the yard. My boot had been removed yesterday and the doctor said I'd be fine to walk with only my crutch. But that thing was a pain in the ass, so I'd ditched it in an empty hallway at the hospital and I was taking it slow instead.

Max beat me across the yard and was jumping up and down next to the patch he'd been smoothing out with mulch. "See?"

I grinned. "Looks perfect, son."

His chest swelled with pride. "What's next?"

I spun in a slow circle, taking in the yard. Over the last two weeks, I'd spent most of my free time out here. With things being tense and awkward with Molly, I'd escaped to the yard to finish the project I'd started at the beginning of summer.

The odd angles and sharp corners had been removed. The trees and shrubs Molly hadn't liked—the ones I'd planted as experiments—had been removed. All that remained was to plant her lilac bush.

Kali was on her hands and knees in the opposite corner of the yard, tending to the hole we'd dug. Because lilacs had a tendency to get so large, I wanted this one to have plenty of room to grow and bloom. Even with the distance, the fragrant blossoms would carry across the yard to the back deck. If Molly left the screen open, she'd catch whiffs of the scent all spring.

"Run inside and get your mom," I told Max.

He nodded and took off while I ambled toward Kali.

"I poured the water in the bottom, just like you said." She smiled up at me. "What's next?"

"We'll take the burlap off the roots and get it set." I pulled a utility knife from my pocket and bent down, cutting away the cloth from the bush's roots.

"Dad, I . . ." Kali hesitated, her eyes aimed at the hole.

"What?" I asked gently.

She gave me those sad eyes, the ones that melted my heart. "I wish you didn't have to go to your house."

I tossed the knife aside and put my hand on her shoulder. "Me too. But that's where I live."

"Do you . . . never mind." She dropped her gaze to the dirt, spreading some beneath her fingers.

I gave her time, letting her work up the courage to talk. That was the way with Kali. She'd always open up if I didn't rush her. She was like me in that way. She pondered things before she spoke. She kept more inside than I wished she would.

"This sucks," she mumbled.

"Yeah, sweetie. It does."

She looked up at me, her bottom lip worried between her

teeth. "Do you think you and Mom might ever get together again?"

My shoulders sank. More than anything, I wanted to tell her yes. To tell her that we'd be a family again. "No. I don't think so."

"Oh. Okay."

"I love your mom."

"You do?"

I nodded. "I'll always love your mom. She's the best person I've ever met. And she gave me you and Max."

"Then I don't understand. I know Mom loves you too. So why can't you be together? Don't you like living here with us?"

"More than anything." I gave her a sad smile. "I know it's hard to understand. We love each other, but we have to be able to make each other happy too. And right now, we don't. Does that make sense?"

She shrugged. "Sorta."

That was a no. It didn't make sense. I was struggling to comprehend it all myself. And I was dreading the end of this day.

After our fight two weeks ago, Molly and I had been avoiding one another. It had given me plenty of time to ponder our situation. To dig deep and decide if I could truly forgive Molly for what had happened that night.

Fourteen days, and I wasn't any closer to the answer.

So today, after the yard was finished, I was going home.

Alone.

"What's up?" Molly asked as she stepped through the patio door, following Max as he raced toward me and Kali.

"We're ready to plant the lilac bush."

She smiled, doing a sweep of the yard. "It looks so wonderful out here."

"Yeah, it does." The best yard on earth. Not because of the landscaping, but because of her and the kids. Because we'd built it together.

Molly came over and knelt down next to me and Kali. Max hovered around us, bouncing from one foot to the next as I lifted the bush above the hole.

"Need help?" Molly asked, her hands reaching out.

"I've got it." With the bush placed in the hole, I gave the nod to start pushing in dirt. "Okay, guys. Fill it in."

Four pairs of hands dove into the dirt, shoving and packing it around the roots.

"That's it?" Max asked when the hole was filled.

Molly laughed. "That's it. What were you expecting?"

"I don't know. I think I like tearing stuff out better than planting."

I clapped him on the shoulder. "The next time I need an extra hand on a demolition job, you're my guy."

"Yes." He fist-pumped. "Mom, can I go to the park?"

"As long as your sister goes too."

Max's eyes snapped to Kali. "Pleeease come with me."

"Sure." She smiled and stood, brushing dirt off her bare knees.

Molly tapped the watch on her wrist. "Don't stay too long. It's almost dinnertime."

"Okay, Mom." Kali nodded before she and Max took off for the gate in the fence.

"Hold up," I called, pushing off the ground. Then I caught up to them before they disappeared down the neighborhood trail system that led to a playground. "I'm heading home soon."

"Oh." Max's frame slumped. Kali wouldn't make eye contact with me.

"How about a hug?"

They both rushed me, latching their arms around my waist like they were drowning. I put a hand on each of their heads. "Love you, guys."

"Love you, Dad," Kali whispered.

Max just hugged me tighter.

Behind us, Molly stood with her arms snaked around her waist and her gaze pointed anywhere but at us.

We'd talked last night about how this would go. Molly didn't want to make a big deal about it. She said we'd treat it like any normal day. I wanted to work in the yard. She needed to do some house cleaning. Then when the day was over, I'd go home.

Normal. Routine. *Miserable.*

"See you guys in a couple days."

Max nodded against my hip.

Kali pulled away and ducked her head as she swiped at her eyes. "Come on, Max."

He squeezed me one last time then let go and bolted for the fence.

I watched as they sprinted down the path, their tennis shoes pounding on the packed gravel as they ran. It was a punishing run, like they were both taking their frustration with their parents out on the gravel.

I waited until they were out of sight, then I turned and walked toward the house.

Molly met me on the way and I held the patio door open for her to go inside. The house smelled of bleach and lemon. My cleaning service used the same products as Molly, per my request, but they didn't smell the same.

*This* smelled like home.

"Can I help you pack?" she asked, toying with the hair ties on her wrist. Today's were coral and yellow. Neither went with her outfit, but that was what I loved about them. They were always bright.

"No, I'm good. I just need to clear out the stuff from the bathroom and I'll be set."

She nodded toward the kitchen. "I'll just finish in there. Say good-bye before you go?"

"I will." I went to the guest bathroom and packed up my leather toiletry case. The sound of running water came from the kitchen.

*Fuck.*

This was harder than it should be. I had a home, a life to get back to. A single life. A life I'd been living for six years. A life I'd told my sister I wanted to ruin, but here I was, rushing back into it.

The past two weeks had been strange. With school in full swing, we'd spent most of our nights helping kids with homework. We'd had dinner together, watched TV if there was time or played a game. And through it all, Molly and I had existed in peace.

Something unexpected had happened since that last fight. It had been calm. Quiet. Like the angry ghost had curled up in its grave to finally rest.

We'd gotten along after the divorce, but this was different. This wasn't simply a sense of civility or friendship. This week had been . . . easy. It was all out there. The wounds were exposed to the air and they were closing up.

Years too late.

"Finn?" Molly called.

"Yeah?"

"I'm going to grab the mail."

I hung my head. "All right."

There was one more letter. One I'd written at the time of

the divorce. I'd been walking on eggshells, expecting it to come.

I hoped it would be today. That when I left, we'd be done with them for good.

I quickly finished packing my stuff then went into the guest bedroom and zipped it all into my suitcase. With it loaded and a bulging backpack slung over my shoulder, I made my way to the living room and put them both next to the couch.

Then I waited for Molly to come back inside, holding a stack of envelopes in one hand, a single envelope in the other.

"It came?"

"It did." She crossed the room and extended the letter. "Here."

"Go ahead."

"No, it's okay."

I took the envelope from her hand. "I thought you wanted to read them."

"I did. I don't need to anymore."

"Why?"

She gave me a sad smile. "Because you finally told me how you felt."

If nothing else, that had made writing these letters worth it.

I tore into the envelope, pulling out the single sheet of paper. A sharp sting hit my chest as I remembered how I'd felt that day. Six years later and it was still hard to believe we'd quit each other.

"Here." I held out the letter, but Molly shied away. "It's raw. But . . . it's real."

"Okay." She took it and read it over. "Wow."

"I'm sorry."

"Don't be. I feel the same way. We gave up on each other."

"How?" I asked. "How did that happen?"

"I don't know. The days got so hard. We stopped fighting for each other and fought for ourselves instead. In the end, I think it—us—got to be too much and we gave up. I'm sorry."

I hated hearing those words from her mouth. It seemed like she'd said them so damn much. "Can you do something for me?"

"Sure."

"Don't apologize to me anymore."

"Huh?"

I took the letter and crumpled it into a tight ball. "This letter is bullshit. Well, half of it. You didn't quit me. I quit you. I haven't said this enough, but *I'm* sorry. I'm so damn sorry, Molly."

She stared at me for a few seconds, then she closed her eyes. "I think we've apologized plenty. Maybe we could both stop."

"Not quite yet." I stepped closer and took both her hands in mine. "I'm sorry. For pushing you away after Jamie died. For putting Alcott above our marriage and using work as an excuse to hide from my feelings. For being such a fucking asshole to you after we got divorced. For all these letters. You didn't deserve how I treated you."

Molly rocked back on her heels, the shock of hearing my statement written all over her face.

Which meant this apology wasn't just necessary, it was long overdue.

I'd blamed her for our divorce. I'd given her the cold shoulder for months in the hopes of making her pay for how hurt I'd been. I'd been in so much pain it had physically hurt me to look at her.

"It wasn't fair for me to put it all on you," I told her.

Tears welled in her eyes. "You had a good reason."

"No, I didn't." I framed her face with my hands. "I'm sorry."

A tear fell. "Thank you for saying that."

The distance between us was only inches but I pulled her into my chest and wrapped her up tight. I breathed in the rosemary and mint scent of her hair as she wrapped her arms behind my back.

Our embrace didn't last long. Much too soon, Molly pushed me away. "That's the last letter, right?"

I nodded. "That's it."

"Phew." She smiled, blinking her eyes dry. "I'm glad. I can't take all this crying. I'm getting dehydrated."

I chuckled. "You think we'll ever figure out who was sending them?"

"Since we've interrogated every person we know, I'm thinking it's a mystery for the ages."

"We didn't ask the kids."

Molly blew out a long breath. "I don't think it's them."

"Kali asked me earlier if we were ever going to get together again. It could have been her."

"I don't think so." Molly shook her head. "You know your daughter, Finn. She shows everything she feels. Some of those letters were devastating to read. I don't think she would have been able to read them and hide it from us."

"Yeah," I muttered. "You're probably right. Okay . . . a mystery for the ages."

"I'm actually glad I don't know who."

"You are?"

"I don't want to know someone else's motives for doing this to us. I'm just glad they did. We left too much unsaid. Now it's all out there. Now we can finally breathe."

I went to the couch and picked up my backpack, slinging it over my shoulder. "I agree."

"I'll walk you out." She went for my suitcase, rolling it down the hallway behind me. "Take care of yourself."

"I will. Same to you." I bent to kiss her at the front door, going for her lips, but she turned her head so I got her cheek instead. I lingered there for a moment too long. It never did feel right kissing her on the cheek, not when I knew how good it felt to have her lips instead.

"I'll bring the kids over tomorrow," she said, taking a step away.

"Great. See ya."

And that was it. Back to two homes. Two schedules. Two separate lives.

I took the suitcase from her hand and left. The ramp the Alcott guys had built for my chair had been removed this past week. Without another good-bye, I walked down the stairs to my truck. I'd driven it over the day my boot had been removed.

"Finn," Molly called.

"Yeah." I sighed, wishing she hadn't called me back. I needed to go while I still could. Every step away from the house was forced. Had leaving the first time been this hard?

"Thank you for the letters." In her hand, she'd uncrumpled the last one.

I nodded once then turned again and loaded up the truck.

She stayed on the porch, waiting for my driver's side door to close, then she disappeared inside the house.

My heart felt like it was being ripped from my chest as I backed out of the driveway. The pain got worse as I drove across town. When I arrived at my house, it looked the same as it had when I'd left. Clean. Expensive. *Lonely.*

Homes in this neighborhood rarely went on sale and when they did, they were sold for asking price or above. This was the neighborhood where everyone wanted a house.

Everyone except me.

Too much had changed.

I pulled into the garage, parked, then went inside. Mom had promised the place was clean. Poppy had stocked the fridge for me. I walked through the laundry room, taking my bags to my bedroom and setting them on the comforter.

"I forgot my pillow," I grumbled.

I'd left it at Molly's because it was Molly's. Except it was mine.

I took a slow tour of the rest of the place. The kids' rooms were spotless, their beds made and ready for them to come over tomorrow for the weekend. There was a small fern on the kitchen counter—something new Mom had probably found at the grocery store. All the other houseplants were watered and thriving, and the refrigerator was indeed stocked with my favorite dishes.

Mom and Poppy must have spent an entire day cooking. It was good the kids were coming over because otherwise, I'd never get through it all by myself.

The quiet was unnerving so I went to the living room and switched on the television. I found a baseball game and sat in my recliner. It wasn't as comfortable as I remembered.

Only one inning went by before I lost all interest in the game, so I pulled my phone from my pocket to call Poppy.

"Hey," she answered. "Are you at home?"

"Yes, thanks for the food."

"Sure. How are you feeling?"

"Fantastic," I deadpanned.

"Uh-oh." In the background, the kids were laughing and playing with some sort of toy musical instruments. "Hold on one second. Let me go to a quiet room."

I waited, muting the TV as she maneuvered through her house.

"Okay, what's wrong?"

"I'm not in the right place."

"And the right place is . . ."

I rolled my eyes. "You know the answer to that."

"*I* do. But do you? What happened to ruining your life?"

"That plan kind of fell apart when Molly and I got in a fight over one of the letters." I rubbed my jaw. "It was bad. It was about her and that other guy."

"Oh." Poppy's voice fell.

"She asked me if I could forgive her. I said I didn't know."

The other end of the line went silent. It lasted so long, I was sure I'd dropped the call. "Poppy?"

"I'm here."

"You don't have anything to say?"

"You don't want to hear what I have to say."

"No, I really do."

"You have no right to hold that night against Molly. And shame on you if you do."

I winced. Poppy's sharp tone was one I hadn't heard in, well, ever. "Ouch."

"I'm not done." She. Was. Pissed. "It's time to pull your head out of your ass. Be with Molly, or for God's sake, let her go. Please, let her go. She deserves to be happy. You both do. Be the man she needs or walk away. Because we both know she'll love you until you tell her to stop."

I loved her too. And I'd been telling myself to stop for years.

"Mommy," a little voice yelled in the background.

"I'm in here, Brady," Poppy yelled back. "Finn, I need to go and get dinner started before Cole gets home."

"Okay," I croaked.

"Love you. I'll call you later. And . . . sorry. I've been holding that in for a while."

"Yeah." I had whiplash. She disconnected the call, but her words were still echoing through my quiet house.

She was right. On all points. I had no right to hold that night against Molly, not when she wasn't holding so many of my mistakes against me.

So why was it so hard to forgive? To let it go?

I stood from the chair and went to the windows that lined the far wall of the room. Outside, one of my neighbors was teaching his son how to swing a baseball bat. I'd done the same out there with Max. I'd spent hours playing with my kids on the wrong fucking lawn.

*Forgive.* That's all I had to do. I had to forgive Molly for the other man.

I closed my eyes, replaying that night in my head. I thought about her standing on the stairs to the loft, listening to Bridget run her down. She must have been devastated to see me sitting there, on the couch with another woman, not saying a thing.

I imagined her slipping down the stairs, silently retreating to her car. I bet she had fought hard not to cry because she'd been all dressed up and had her makeup done. That first shot probably went down too easy. She probably welcomed that numb feeling.

Because I'd broken her. Not just that night, but all the ones before. I'd abandoned her. I'd wrapped myself in a cocoon called work. I'd let her sit alone with a marriage counselor while I stared at the clock, knowing I was supposed to be at her side.

I'd let her down.

Me.

And in that moment, as I opened my eyes and the boy outside swung his bat too hard, missing the ball, I knew I didn't need to forgive Molly.

I had already, years ago.

I didn't want her to suffer or feel guilty for her actions. I wanted her life to be full of joy. Of laughter. I wasn't harboring this load of resentment.

Molly shouldn't be begging for my forgiveness. It was the other way around.

I needed hers.

This was all on me.

*Be the man she needs or walk away.*

Poppy, bless her soul, was so right. There'd be no more walking away. It was time to fix the mistakes I'd made all those years ago.

And I knew how to start.

I abandoned the window, walking straight down the hallway for my office. I sat in the chair, rifling through a drawer until I found a half-used legal pad. Then I got out a pen.

The first two words of my letter brought a smile to my face and hope to my heart.

*Darling Molly*

*Darling Molly,*

*I would be honored if you'd join me for dinner this Saturday night.*

*Yours,*
*Finn*

# eighteen
## Molly

"You guys are going to make yourselves sick." I rolled my eyes at Jimmy and Randall.

Poppy stood by my side with her arms crossed over her chest. "I am not cleaning up puke. I love you both, but there are lines I will not cross."

"I'm not going to puke," Jimmy mumbled. The words were barely audible since his mouth was bulging with food.

Randall just shot us both a glare as he chewed. His mouth was so full, he couldn't even close his lips all the way.

"Seriously, you are grown men. Seniors. Have some self-respect." I handed Randall a napkin so he could wipe up the drool on his chin.

The pair didn't listen to a thing we said. They hadn't for the last twenty minutes. They just kept shoveling.

The counter was littered with partially empty jars. Chili. Cornbread. Cinnamon rolls. Macaroni and cheese. Apple pie. Chocolate mousse. Banana bread. Why? Because they were having an eating contest.

"If you stop this right now, I'll name an item on the menu after both of you," Poppy said. She'd been trying to bribe them since before this disaster had even begun. First, she'd offered to give them an extra dessert—on the house. Then she'd offered two desserts. Normally, sugar incentives were all it took to get these two in line.

But today, they were on a mission to one-up the other. I wasn't sure exactly what had sparked this particular battle, but I'd overheard some grumblings and the name Nan more than once. Nan was probably a new resident at The Rainbow who'd snagged Jimmy's and Randall's attention, and this contest was some manly show to determine who would get to pursue Nan's affections.

"And to think when I dropped the kids off at school this morning, I thought how nice it would be to spend my day with *adults*."

Jimmy snapped his fingers in the air, pointing to his empty jar of chili.

"That is not how we order food in this restaurant," Poppy snapped.

He sent her a pleading stare, glancing at Randall's collection of jars. He was winning by one chili and a triple-berry crisp.

"No." Poppy crossed her arms over her chest.

"I got you, Jimmy." Cole went to the refrigerated display case at our sides and grabbed a chili from the top shelf. "Hot?"

Jimmy shook his head and waved Cole over.

"You are not helping, Detective." Poppy glared at her husband.

His shoulders shook with silent laughter. "It's too late now. We might as well see which one of them gives up first."

Cole was the reason Jimmy and Randall had gotten the idea to start this whole ordeal. He'd come down to eat lunch at The Maysen Jar with Poppy. Apparently, they'd had some physical testing thing at the police department today, and he'd been cutting back carbs for a couple weeks to prepare. With the test complete, and reveling in his dietary freedom, Cole had inhaled two jars of mac 'n' cheese like a kid who'd been given permission to devour his pillowcase of Halloween candy.

Seeing Cole eat so fast had triggered Jimmy's and Randall's animal instincts.

*I could eat a jar faster than that.*

*I could eat two jars faster than you could eat one.*

Then Cole had chimed in with the brilliant idea to have a contest.

One jar had led to two, then three.

When Poppy and I had both adamantly refused to serve them another jar of anything, Cole had come behind the counter and assumed the role of supplier.

"I can't watch." Poppy turned her back to the counter.

I did the same. We could still hear silver spoons scraping glass jars, but at least this way we didn't have to see the idiots make themselves sick.

"Do you guys have any plans this weekend?" I asked Poppy. "I was thinking about kidnapping MacKenna and Brady on Saturday night. With everything that happened this summer, I feel like I didn't get to spend much time with them. Max and Kali will be with Finn so if you and Cole want a date night, I volunteer as babysitter."

She didn't hesitate. "Done. We'll bring them over around six."

"Perfect." I smiled. It would be nice to spoil them rotten—and have them so I wasn't home alone.

Max and Kali had been at Finn's place two nights this past week and it had been torture. With them gone a few nights each week and back in school, my house was too quiet.

Though Randall and Jimmy's antics had gone beyond the spectrum of crazy today, I'd needed it. I'd needed a good day at work and to remember the life I'd built post-divorce.

"What else is on the docket for today?" I asked Poppy.

She glanced over her shoulder then rolled her eyes. "I hadn't planned to restock macaroni and cheese until tomorrow, but I'd better do it today instead."

"Chili too," Cole added. When she shot him a glare, he held up his hands. "What? It's almost gone. Jimmy's on three. Randall only two. I do feel sorry for the residents on their floor tonight. That's going to stink."

I coughed to cover up a laugh.

Poppy pulled her lips in to hide a smile.

*This is exactly what I need today.*

"Okay, I'm going to walk away from this." I tossed a thumb over my shoulder. "I'm going to do a quick sweep of the tables then grab the laptop and get caught up on some emails."

"I'm going to head back to the kitchen," Poppy said then looked at Cole. "Are you heading back to work?"

He nodded. "As soon as we declare a winner here, I'm taking off."

"Okay. Come say good-bye before you go." She walked over and kissed him, melting against his chest as he slanted his head and deepened it.

They were adorable. And lucky. So damn lucky.

I left them all and went through the swinging door to the kitchen. The morning had been busy, the restaurant filled with college students. Half the tables were occupied with textbooks and laptops as kids studied, so I hadn't spent much time in the office, sticking out front to help.

I settled in behind the desk, opting to sort through mail first to snag any bills. Mostly, the stack was junk. Poppy's favorite kitchen supply company had sent her a new catalog that she'd be drooling over later.

My hands paused on a letter toward the bottom of the pile. It wasn't addressed to the restaurant but to me. And it was in Finn's handwriting.

"What is this?" I grumbled. Weren't we done with the letters? Seriously, I needed to be done with the letters.

The other mail was tossed to the side as I tore open the envelope's seam and pulled out the single piece of paper.

My jaw fell open as I took it in.

Dinner? I turned the page over, but the back was blank. Then I read it again. Why would he want me to go to dinner? And why would he invite me with a letter?

I stood from the desk and hurried out of the office, letter in hand.

Poppy hadn't made it to the kitchen yet. She was laughing with Cole as Randall lifted his hands in victory.

Jimmy was breathing hard, his face a shade of green as he clutched his stomach. "Nan is a sweetheart, but no woman is worth this kind of pain. I'm already gassy."

Randall chuckled.

"Some women are worth it all," Cole said, pulling Poppy into his side.

I opened my mouth to pull Poppy aside but stopped short. Everyone was in such a good mood, despite the foul odor creeping into the air. This letter, though not bad, would take the spotlight.

Randall slid from his chair, his arms still raised and started dancing around the floor.

"For a guy who uses a cane, you sure are nimble," I teased.

His response was a smirk and to gyrate his hips.

"That Nan, she's a lucky woman," Poppy teased.

Cole let out a catcall before belly laughing as he got out his phone to record the show.

I folded up the letter, joining in the laughter, determined not to let it bother me today. I wasn't sure what Finn was playing at, but today was one of the first normal days I'd had in a while.

I needed normal, not more letters to confuse my emotions.

With the letter folded in half and shoved in my back pocket, I turned to go back to the office but stopped when Mom's voice carried through the restaurant. "Molly."

"Hi, Mom." I abandoned the kitchen door with a smile and met Mom in the middle of the restaurant for a hug. "What a surprise. What brings you here today?"

She smiled. "I hadn't been in for lunch in a while, and I had a client cancel their session. I thought I'd come and say hello."

"Wonderful. I'll sit with you. What would you like?"

"A salad, please. Whichever you'd recommend."

"Okay. Pick a seat and I'll bring it over."

She nodded, eyeing Jimmy—still groaning—and Randall —still dancing—along with their piles of jars.

I hurried to get her some lunch, a spinach salad with an incredible champagne vinaigrette Poppy had mixed up this morning.

"How are you?" I asked after sitting down across from her.

"Fine." She went through prepping the salad. "Just fine."

"And Dad?"

"Fine as well. He's been editing a colleague's book this week, so I've hardly seen him."

And for Mom, that was probably preferred. Dad too. They liked their lives separate, something I'd never been able to understand since Finn and I had merged every single piece of our marriage. Relationship. Business. At the beginning, we'd been virtually inseparable.

Finn and I might not have worked out, but I wouldn't have traded those days for anything. Mom and Dad, they'd never had that. They'd never had the passion or the love for one another that burned brighter than a star.

Even though our star went dark, it had been worth it.

"I got an interesting call this morning," Mom said before taking another bite. "This is delicious."

"Poppy's a culinary genius."

"That she is. So anyway. The call. It was from Lauren Trussel."

"Oh?" I straightened in my chair.

Lauren Trussel was the marriage counselor I'd gone to see before the divorce. After those sessions with her alone, with me making excuses for why Finn hadn't bothered to show up, I'd finally given up. How many sessions did it take before Lauren wrote us off as a destined-for-divorce case? One? Maybe two?

"And what did she say?" I asked.

"She said she got a strange call yesterday from Finn. He wanted to schedule some time to visit with her."

I blinked. "Finn? My Finn?"

"Well, he's not *your* Finn anymore. You *are* divorced. And now that he's finally out of your house and back in his own, you can move on with your life."

"That's not . . ." I trailed off, not wanting to get into a discussion about her fears that I had an unhealthy attachment to my ex-husband. She didn't know that Finn and I had been sleeping together before his accident. She didn't know about the letters. She wasn't going to find out either.

"Why would Finn want to see Lauren?" I asked. "And why would she tell you about it?"

"We've always kept in touch. She keeps me privy to things I need to know."

"Things you need to know? And that includes Finn? What about doctor-patient confidentiality?"

"Well, Finn isn't technically a client. At least not yet."

The hairs on the back of my neck stood up. There was something more here. Something Mom was keeping to herself.

"Mom," I said gently. "Did Lauren keep you privy to the sessions I had with her?"

Another shrug as she finished a bite of salad. "I knew at a high level what was happening."

"Define 'high level' for me, please."

"She gave me an assessment of your mental and emotional state on a scale of one to ten. She felt it important that I know when you were close to a breakdown so I could be there to support you, since Finn never bothered to show up for your sessions."

And there it was. All this time, Finn had been right. If Lauren was comfortable telling Mom about how I'd been feeling, she would have been just as comfortable giving high-level details of the sessions had Finn showed up.

He'd been worried that Mom would learn about us. And he'd been right.

*Damn it.*

"That's not okay." My hands were balled, the muscles furious as I spoke. "She had no right to share that with you."

"Don't get all flustered about it, Molly. There aren't many therapists in town. We all keep in touch in case we run into a difficult case and need input."

"I'm not a difficult case. I'm your daughter."

"A daughter who let her partner rule her life for far too long."

Rule my life? That was ridiculous. Mom made Finn out to be this controlling, egomaniacal villain. "You never liked Finn. I don't understand why."

"You're a different person when he's around."

"A different person? What do you mean?"

"You're more worried about his feelings than you are your own. You give him too much power."

"Power over what? I've always made my own decisions. I've always lived my life. Taking his feelings into account isn't a bad thing, Mom. That's what you do when you love someone."

"You never moved to New York after college. You gave up that dream."

I rolled my eyes. "That was my dream for about a month when I was sixteen, when I thought I wanted to work on Wall Street. I mentioned it to you once and you never let it go. My dreams changed."

"And what about his business? You started that business together and once it was established, he all but shoved you out the door."

"I stayed home with our children. But you are right, that was hard for me to accept." I'd give her that one.

"Does this really matter?" she asked between bites. "I came to have a nice lunch with you and to let you know Finn is seeking counseling. Maybe it's because of the accident, but you should know. He could be on the verge of an emotional crisis. It might not be safe for him to be alone with Kali and Max."

*What the hell?*

"Do you hear yourself?" I shook my head. "Finn would never do anything to harm our children. He isn't having an emotional crisis. He went through an incredible trauma. You of all people should applaud him for wanting to talk through any issues that may have caused."

Though it would have been nice to know he was struggling. After all the letters, after all the air we'd cleared these past few months, he still didn't trust me with his feelings.

"I have your best interests at heart."

I'd heard that statement from Mom a thousand times, always when I didn't agree with her. "I'm not doing this anymore."

"Doing what?"

"Playing both sides. I love Finn. I will always love Finn, whether we are together or not. He's the father of my children and a *good* man. You can judge my failed marriage all you want, but it's time you learn to keep those opinions to yourself. Do not come here or to my home and belittle him."

Mom looked at me like I'd gone crazy. "What is wrong with you?"

"Nothing." I stood from the table. "I'm just making my position perfectly clear. In the choice of you versus Finn, he will always be the winner. Call that unhealthy. Call me a pushover. Call me whatever you want. That's your decision. But I've made my choice. I hope you can respect that. Please enjoy the rest of your meal. It's on me."

Without another word, I left my mother sitting slack-jawed at the table. I crossed through the restaurant, my heart racing. I passed Randall and Jimmy as they sat nearly comatose on their stools. Cole must have snuck out the back door. I managed to keep my chin up and shoulders pinned until I made it into the kitchen, then I blew out the breath I'd been holding and let my hands shake.

Poppy was at the table working. She abandoned whatever she was mixing when she saw my pale face. "What happened? Are you okay? You're as pale as a ghost."

"I'm okay." I took three deep breaths. "I'm okay."

"Are you sure?"

I nodded. "I need you to tell me something as my best friend and not as Finn's sister."

"Okay."

"Is it crazy that I love Finn?"

"Maybe," she answered. "But I'd rather be crazy in love than just crazy."

I giggled, my shoulders relaxing away from my ears. Leave it to Poppy to make me smile. I walked to the table, dropping my elbows to the top and resting my face in my hands. "I don't think I'll have the mother-daughter relationship I've always wanted."

"Sure you will. With Kali."

My heart swelled as I pictured Kali's face from this morning, her smile wide and bright as she walked away from the Jeep to start her school day. "God, you're so right. I feel like I've been trying for years to build this easy dialogue with my mom and it's just . . . not easy. It never has been."

Mom lectured. I listened. I placated her because it was too exhausting to debate with her. I'd learned that at an early age. Mom had an answer for everything. Rarely was it *You're right, Molly.*

"I'm tired of trying," I admitted.

The door swung open with a squeak, and I braced, expecting Mom to storm through with some choice words.

Instead, Finn strolled inside. "Hey."

"Hey." I stood up from the table. "Was my mom still out there when you came in?"

"Yes."

"Did you talk to her?"

"Yes."

I gave him the side-eye. "What did you say?"

"I started with hello, then I told her that shade of navy looked good on her but hustled in here before she could say something to piss me off."

"Thanks for that. It's probably best that only one of us fights with her today."

He blinked at me twice. "You got into a fight with your mom? Like a real fight?"

"I don't know if it was really a fight," I told Finn. "But she made me mad, and I drew a line in the sand."

"I'm going to head out front and keep an eye on things. Let you guys talk." Poppy wiped her hands on her apron, then she squeezed Finn's arm as she passed by and out of the kitchen.

"Let's go to the office."

He followed me down the hallway, taking the seat across from me at the desk, leaning his elbows on his knees to give me his full attention. "What happened?"

"Mom doesn't like you."

Finn chuckled. "Tell me something I don't know."

"I guess I thought that someday she would. But I see now she won't. I made it clear that she can keep those opinions to herself because they aren't welcome in my presence, that I'm on your side and she needs to be respectful."

"You stuck up for me with your mom?"

"I did." I nodded. "I'm sorry I didn't do it sooner."

"Wow." He sat back in the chair. "I, um . . . thanks."

"You're welcome. I'm sorry that you're struggling right now. If there is anything I can do to help, even if it's just to listen, I'm here."

"Uh, I'm struggling?" Finn's eyebrows came together. "What are you talking about?"

"Mom. You were right about the counseling. She would have known all about our sessions with Lauren Trussel. She came in for lunch today and told me that Lauren had called her and said you'd scheduled some time to talk with her."

"Annnd I'll be canceling that appointment."

"It's not fair. You should be safe to talk about the accident if it's causing you stress. I can do some digging to find a therapist in town who doesn't associate with Mom."

"I'm not stressed about the accident. It's over. I'm fine. I feel lucky and really fucking happy to be alive. I wanted to meet with Lauren because *you* met with Lauren."

"I'm confused."

He stood and came around the desk, sitting on the edge. "The counseling appointment wasn't for me. It was for us."

"Huh?"

"I had planned to bring you along. For marriage counseling."

"We're not married."

Finn shrugged. "Did you get my letter?"

"Don't change the subject. You want to go to marriage counseling with your ex-wife?"

"Better late than never."

My head was spinning, and it took me a moment to let it all sink in. Finn wanted to go to marriage counseling with me. That was . . . odd. And incredibly sweet. "You want to go to counseling?"

"I thought maybe we had some things to talk about, but it doesn't matter now because I'm not going to meet with Lauren. I'd hoped I was wrong and paranoid about her being one of your mom's spies. Guess I was right."

"Yes, you were. But that aside, thank you. The gesture of the counseling . . . I appreciate it."

"You didn't answer my question. Did you get my letter?"

I shifted in my seat so I could pull it out from my pocket. "This letter?"

"That's the one." Finn grinned. "What do you say? Have dinner with me Saturday? My parents already agreed to watch the kids."

"I have plans. Sorry." I stood from the chair and walked past him toward the door. I wasn't sure what was happening, with the counseling thing and the letter asking me out, but we'd already decided to go our separate ways. More than once.

"Hold up." Finn rushed to catch up as I walked through the kitchen. "What plans?"

"I'm babysitting MacKenna and Brady so Poppy and Cole can have a date."

"Oh," he grumbled. "Then how about Sunday?"

"It's a school night."

"Last time I checked, you're not in school."

"We have two kids who are. They should be at home, getting ready for the week."

"My mom can come over and watch them there. They'll be in bed by nine, just like every other night."

I went through the swinging door and behind the counter. "I'll take over out here."

"Okay." Poppy smiled and disappeared back into the kitchen.

Finn was standing at the end of the counter, his legs planted wide and his arms crossed over his chest. "I'll pick you up on Sunday at six."

"No."

"Why not?"

"Because," I hissed, walking closer to him so Randall and Jimmy wouldn't hear. "We're not doing this again."

Did he think I'd jump back into the affair we'd had before the accident?

"I'll repeat, why not?"

"We've been down this path. Too many times. We agreed it was better this way, so . . . there."

"I changed my mind," he declared. "I'll change yours too."

Before I could come up with a retort, Randall interrupted us from his chair. "What are you two whispering about?"

"Nothing," I answered.

"I asked Molly on a date."

"Finn," I snapped, smacking him on the arm.

"What? They're going to find out anyway."

"And why is that?"

He grinned. "Because after our date on Sunday night, you'll be all smiles come Monday morning."

# nineteen
## Finn

"You're taking me to Burger Bob's?" Molly asked as we walked down the sidewalk along Main Street.

I grinned and dropped my hand to the small of her back. "You still like burgers with extra cheese and extra bacon, don't you?"

"Duh."

"Then Burger Bob's it is." My smile widened as I opened the door for her. We both took in the restaurant, standing in the threshold for a long moment. I steered Molly to a high-top table along the far wall, one that would give us privacy to talk.

It hadn't been easy to convince Molly to come out tonight. She'd declined five more times the day she'd gotten my letter at the restaurant. But I'd stood behind the counter, asking over and over with my feet bolted to the floor, refusing to leave until she'd agreed to a date tonight.

Finally, she'd huffed and said yes. Jimmy had clapped for us. Randall had glared.

I'd picked up Molly twenty minutes ago. Mom had arrived early at my place to hang with the kids. She'd promised three times to adhere to their normal bedtime—but we all knew Kali and Max would get to stay up late on a school night.

I'd knocked on the door with two bouquets of lilies in hand: one for Molly's bedroom and another for the kitchen.

She loved lilies. She said they made the house smell like a fairy garden. As I'd handed over my credit card to the florist, I'd realized it had been much too long since I'd bought her flowers. Molly deserved them weekly, and if this worked, if I won her back, she'd have them.

Maybe by bringing her here to Burger Bob's, to the place where we'd met, she'd remember that excitement. She'd relax and enjoy an evening out. As it was, she'd been tense on the ride over. She'd been quiet. But the greasy smell in the air, promising a good meal, would loosen her up. I was sure of it.

I wasn't planning on talking about anything serious tonight. This meal was all about spending time with each other. I wasn't going to tell Molly that I was in love with her. I wasn't going to tell her I wanted to move home and sell my place. I wasn't going to tell her that we didn't need to forget our past because I forgave her. I was working on forgiving myself.

I wasn't going to beg her to pardon me for all of the wrong I'd done in our marriage.

Those declarations would come.

Tonight, I wanted to soak up her smile and savor her laughter.

Molly sat at the table first, tucking her purse underneath. She was wearing a pair of skinny jeans that showcased the gorgeous curve of her hips. Her hair was down, falling across her bare arms and the thin straps of the gray satin and lace tank top she'd chosen—thank you, Mother Nature, for the unseasonably warm Montana October.

Molly looked sexy as hell. It had been hard not to take her into my arms on her doorstep, but I'd resisted, biding my time for a good-night kiss later tonight when I dropped her at home.

"You know what I love most about this place?" Her eyes roamed over the high ceilings, the wooden tables—years of scratches on their surfaces—and the plethora of frames with photos of Bozeman memorabilia adorning the walls. "It never changes. It always smells the same and feels the same. Since college, it's never changed."

I stretched my hand across the table to cover hers. "Thank you for coming here tonight."

"You're welcome." She flipped her hand over so we were palm to palm. The hair ties on her wrist tickled my skin. "Why did you ask me on a date?"

"You know the reason."

"I don't."

"Yes, you do."

"Why'd you pick Burger Bob's?"

"To remember. And to start again." I wrapped my fingers around her hand. "There are other things in this room that haven't changed since college."

"Like the grease coating the floor?"

"No." I chuckled then locked my eyes with hers. "Like when you're in the room, you're all I see."

Her cheeks flushed, her eyes darting to our hands. If she was going to say something, it got lost when two plastic menus were set down on the table.

"Welcome, guys. What can I get you to drink?" the waitress asked.

Molly and I each ordered a beer. As the waitress left to get them, I released Molly's hand to scoop up both menus. "May I order for you?"

"Yes, but I reserve the right to interject if you get it wrong."

"Wrong." I scoffed. I'd memorized Molly's cheeseburger order the night I'd met her. And I knew it hadn't changed in fifteen years.

The waitress appeared with our beers. "What are we having?"

"Two burgers, medium well. Both with extra cheese and extra bacon. Fries with each. Side of ranch with hers. I'm good with ketchup."

My eyes flicked to Molly. Her chin dropped as she tried to hide a smile. *Nailed it.*

"Okay." The waitress collected the menus. "I'll get this going."

"Cheers." Molly raised her beer glass.

I nodded, clinking the rim of mine to hers before taking a drink. "What are you doing next Saturday night?"

"Uh, nothing. Hanging out with the kids. Why?"

"I was wondering if I could take you to a movie."

"Trying to lock in another date already?" she teased. "That's risky. What if this one turns into a disaster?"

"As long as I get to spend time with you, it'll never be a disaster."

She blushed again and added an eye roll. "Laying it on awfully thick tonight."

"Isn't courting all about the man doling out these gushing compliments to woo his woman?"

Her eyebrows came together as she studied me for a moment. "You're courting me?"

"I'm trying."

"I, um . . ." She swallowed hard. "Oh."

We sat in silence for a few moments, sipping our beers, until she said, "Yes. I'd love to go to a movie."

"Darling, the pleasure will be all mine."

"I'll ask Poppy if they can take the kids."

"Already did. She's in."

Molly fought a smile then glanced over at the corner booth on the opposite side of the room. "I haven't been here in years. Not since . . ."

Not since Jamie had been killed.

"Me neither." There were quite a few places in Bozeman that I'd stopped going to simply because the memories with Jamie were imprinted into the walls. Burger Bob's was one of them. It had been a favorite hangout for all of us in college. We often found ourselves here for a late-night burger and some laughs.

But it was time to put those ghosts to rest too. It was another reason I'd chosen this place for our date. I wanted Molly to see that his death wasn't going to plague me. Not anymore.

"It's not as hard as I thought it would be," she said. "It's bittersweet. I'll always miss Jamie. But I can't imagine a life without Cole."

"I feel the same. I think it took a long time for me to realize it wasn't this or that. It's *and*. We had Jamie. *And* we have Cole."

"Cole." Molly frowned. "I got a parking ticket the other day when my meter ran out, and he wouldn't fix it for me. Asshole."

We both laughed and conversation turned easy. For hours. We didn't talk about the kids or work. We just talked about life. What TV shows I'd been watching. Molly told me about a book she'd recently read. When our dinners came, we ate, chewing fast so we could talk some more.

"I'm so full." Molly sighed. Her plate had the last few

remains of her burger and a few uneaten fries. "That was delicious."

"Would you like dessert?"

She shook her head. "No, thanks. I have no room."

"Okay." I glanced over my shoulder, getting the waitress's attention for the check. The restaurant was busy, even for a Sunday.

"I'm going to use the restroom before we go," Molly said then ventured to the back of the room as the waitress came over to take my credit card and to clear away the dishes.

I studied the table, its dents and dings, smiling at how the evening had gone. It was the best date we'd had, with the exception of the first. And I wanted more. A lot more. A lifetime of more.

"Finn?" I looked up from the table, surprised to hear Bridget's voice. "Hey."

"Hey." I smiled. "What are you up to?"

"Raylene and I were just grabbing some dinner." She held up a finger to her friend, who went in search for a table while Bridget came over to mine. "Are you just getting here? You can join us."

"About to head out, actually."

"I didn't know you were going to eat alone. You should have called me. I would have met you for dinner."

"Oh, no." I shook my head. "I'm not alone."

Bridget's smile fell and the slightest wince pulled at her cheeks. Her eyes darted away too.

A reaction that made my cheeseburger churn.

When we'd had our big blowup, Molly had said Bridget was in love with me. I hadn't thought much about it since because emotions had been running high that day. There had been many more important things in that fight to focus on than my employee.

But had Molly been right? Was Bridget in love with me?

My mind raced as I thought back to all the times the two women had been together. Even in the beginning, Bridget had never really warmed to Molly. Not that they'd worked together much. I'd taken Bridget under my wing, and in those early days, we'd been together from clock-in to clock-out.

There'd been times in more recent years when a girlfriend of mine would stop by Alcott. Brenna used to come down and bring lunch on occasion. I couldn't recall if Bridget had even said hello.

*Oh, fuck.*

Molly was right. I'd been blind.

"Finn?" Bridget touched my arm. "Are you okay?"

"Excuse me." Molly cleared her throat.

I jumped, twisting in my seat. The movement knocked Bridget's hand off my arm. The frown on Molly's face was as unwelcome as the realization that my most trusted and loyal employee had feelings for me.

Bridget looked between the two of us, putting the pieces together. Then she looked at me, her eyes wide and full of judgment. "*She* is your date?"

"Would you mind?" Bridget was blocking Molly's chair. She took a step forward in an attempt to make Bridget back off. "I need to get my purse."

Bridget didn't budge. And I knew her well enough to know she'd dug her heels in. She'd make Molly walk all the way around to get her purse.

God, I was such a fucking moron. Did all men miss shit like this with women? Or was I especially clueless? I saw it now though. It was lit up brighter than the neon Bud Light sign in the restaurant's front window.

I stood from the table, inserting myself between the

women. It forced Bridget back two steps, giving me enough room so I could duck under the table and retrieve Molly's purse and pass it over.

She slung it on a shoulder then crossed her arms. Even with them wrapped tight across her chest, her shoulders trembled. Not in fear, but anger. Her eyes were cold as she looked at Bridget.

Molly didn't hate. Ever. She didn't antagonize. She didn't make enemies, which meant for her to look at Bridget like she was ready to wrap her hands around Bridget's neck, Bridget had pushed much too far.

My protégé—my friend—had been awful to my wife.

It had happened right under my nose, and I'd been oblivious.

"We'd better get going." I took Molly's elbow, prying her arms apart. She fought me for a moment then gave in. With her arms hanging by her sides, I captured her hand and held it tightly.

Bridget scowled at our clasped hands, then she looked at me, her eyes full of disbelief. "Really, Finn? *Her*?"

What the fuck? Who was this stranger? Because she certainly wasn't the Bridget I'd known for years.

Molly tried to pull her hand away, but I tightened my grip.

"Yes, her. It's always her." I pushed past Bridget, tugging Molly along. "See you tomorrow. Enjoy your dinner."

The fresh evening air was impossible to enjoy as Molly and I walked to my truck. With every step, she retreated away from me, even though our hands stayed locked.

All of the progress we'd made, the good time, had been ruined.

I took some deep breaths as we walked, hoping to calm

down. But my anger only burned hotter. We were ten feet from the truck, but I couldn't take another step.

My feet ground to a halt. "What did she do?"

Molly tried to keep walking. I didn't loosen my grip. "Let's just go, Finn."

"What did she do?"

"It's nothing."

"Molly," I whispered. "Please. Tell me."

She met my gaze. "You work with her. I don't want to cause problems with that."

"There are problems. No matter what you tell me tonight, we've got big problems. And I'd really like to hear it. From you."

Her chin fell as she nodded. "I think she thought I was a joke when she started at Alcott. That I was just your silly wife, pretending to manage a business. She was curt. Polite, but curt. Then we got divorced. The polite stopped."

My molars ground together as I forced myself to stay quiet and let Molly continue.

"She took your side. I understood that. But she was nasty, always glaring and muttering things behind my back. Then there was that night, the one where I went to Alcott and she called me a bitch while you were watching TV."

"I swear I didn't hear it." I wouldn't have let that go. Fuck, I hated myself for that night.

She nodded. "I believe you."

"What else happened?"

"Well, you told her about me. About . . ."

"The other guy." I closed my eyes. "Fuck. I'm such a fucking idiot. I never should have told her. What did she do?"

"She stopped muttering things behind my back and told me right to my face that I was a whore."

*What. The. Fuck.* My vision turned red. "You're not a whore."

"No." She locked my eyes, her spine straightening. "No, I'm not."

"Anything else?"

"She's been her usual bitchy self ever since. I've avoided her at all costs."

"Is that why you stopped coming to Alcott?"

I shrugged. "It's part of it. Mostly I stopped coming because it was yours, not ours anymore."

"I'm sorry. I want you to know I'm going to make this right."

"Don't stress over it." She squeezed my hand once then nodded toward the truck. "I don't need that woman's approval to be happy."

No, she didn't. But she did need to know that I had her back.

And tomorrow morning, Bridget and I were having a discussion.

The drive to Molly's house was quick and quiet. It was hard to block out the incident with Bridget, but I was determined to get this date back on track. So I drove with one hand, the other holding tight to Molly's so she knew I was there. I wasn't letting her pull away.

"Thank you," I said as I pulled into the driveway.

"You're welcome. I had a nice time. See you later." She wiggled her hand free.

"Wait." I stopped her as she reached for the door handle. "I'll get it."

"It's—"

"Please. Let me open your door."

"All right."

I hustled out of the truck and to the other side. With her

hand in mine as I helped her down, I sent a silent prayer up to the twilight sky. *One kiss. Give me one kiss.* If I could get an opening for one kiss, I might have a shot at turning this night around.

"Can I escort you to the door?"

"If you insist." She nodded and let me lead the way. "It's strange without the ramp. It didn't take long but I got used to it."

"I can have them build it again. I know Max would love to have it for his skateboard."

She laughed. "I'll get used to the steps again and the way things were."

We reached the door and she looked up at me. Her hand didn't go for the knob.

*Yes.* Someone upstairs still liked me.

Without a word, I cupped Molly's cheeks in my palms, then I put my lips on hers, swallowing her gasp of surprise.

Her hands came to my chest, tentatively resting on the starched cotton of my button-up. As I coaxed her mouth open and slipped my tongue past the seam, her hands pressed against my chest, her fingers fisting the material as I slanted her head and dove in deeper.

She moaned. I moaned. We surged against one another, my hardness pushing against her hip. Her breasts smashing into my chest.

We kissed hot and wet, each of us panting when I finally pulled away.

"I . . ." She gulped. "Wow."

"I want to come in." I took one step away. Then another. "But I'm going to head home."

"Okay." Her cheeks were flushed, her lips swollen. She touched one, the corner of her mouth turning up. "That's probably smart."

"Thank you for dinner."

"That's my line."

"I'm sorry about Bridget."

"It's fine." She waved it off. "It's not your fault."

"It is. I'll fix it." First thing tomorrow morning. I stretched between us, scooping up her hand, and brought her knuckles to my lips for a soft kiss. "Good night, Molly darling."

"Good night."

She stood on the porch, leaning against a post as I jogged to my truck and pulled away from the house. *She kissed me back.* Despite Bridget's untimely appearance, Molly had kissed me back. The smile on my face stayed in place all the way home.

"Looks like you had a nice time," Mom said from my couch as I walked inside and tossed my keys on the kitchen counter.

"I did. The kids asleep?"

"Max is. But I told Kali she could read for a while in her bed."

"Okay. I'm going to go in and say good night."

Mom pushed up from the couch and came over for a kiss on my cheek. "I'm heading home."

"Thanks for babysitting."

"Anytime. And I do mean that. Whatever it takes for you to win Molly over again, I'm here to help. We've missed her."

"You work with her. Daily. You see her more than I do."

"It's not the same. She's missing from our family."

Christmases. Thanksgivings. The random barbeques we'd had since Mom and Dad had moved home from Alaska. Mom was right. Molly had been missing from our family.

But I'd get her back, and we'd fill that void. And it would never be empty again.

"Drive safe." I hugged Mom then went down the hallway,

toward the golden glow underneath Kali's door. I eased my way inside, in case she'd fallen asleep. But there she was, her curls still damp from her shower, reading a book propped up on her knees. "Hi, sweetie."

"Hi, Daddy." She closed the book. "How did it go?"

I grinned and crossed the room, bending to kiss her forehead. "Good."

"Did she say yes to the movie? Or are we going with Plan B?"

I wasn't even a little bit ashamed to enlist my daughter in my plan to win back her mother. Kali was on deck as my backup for the movie date. If Molly had said no, Kali was going to ask Molly to have a sleepover at a friend's house. We'd already brainstormed an excuse to get Max over to Mom's. And that would free me up to take Molly on a surprise movie date.

"She said yes. You guys can stay at Aunt Poppy and Uncle Cole's house."

Kali fist-pumped. "Yes."

"Okay, you'd better get some rest. School tomorrow." I kissed her forehead again. "I'll see you in the morning. I love you."

"Love you too." She snuggled in as I flipped off her lamp. "Night."

"Dad?" She called to me before I reached the doorway. "I know you can make Mom happy."

I smiled. "Me too."

---

"Morning," Bridget muttered, her sunglasses still on as she walked into her office.

I sighed, draining the last swallow of my coffee. I'd been

dreading this conversation all morning. Once I'd dropped the kids off at school, I'd come to Alcott expecting her to be here already.

Bridget was normally in before eight to help get the crews loaded up in the yard. But the clock on the wall read nine.

She was probably pissed at me, yet I didn't fucking care. She'd crossed a line. She should have known better.

Molly was off-limits.

I stood and went to her office door. She was pulling a bottle of pain pills from her desk drawer. "I need to talk with you this morning."

"Can it wait? I have a nasty headache, and I'm leaving in thirty to check on the Morrison project."

"No, it can't. I'll give you a few. Come in when you're ready."

"Fine," she bit out.

I returned to my office, mentally running through the things I wanted to say then pulled out my phone to send Molly a text.

*Me: So? Have you been smiling all morning?*

I hit send and immediately three dots appeared.

*Molly: You'll never know.*

That was a yes. I chuckled at the screen as Bridget came into the office, a plastic water bottle in hand. "What's up?"

I put my phone down, leaning my elbows on the desk. "We need to talk about Molly."

She rolled her eyes.

"That." I pointed to her face. "That's the last time. You *will* treat her with respect."

"Or what?"

"Or you're fired."

"What?" Her eyes bugged out. "You can't fire me."

"Have you forgotten whose name is on the sign out front?"

"You need me. This place would collapse without me."

"Bridget, you are talented and hardworking. You bring a lot of skill and experience. You know our systems inside and out and working with you is easy. But I will not, under any circumstances, allow you to run Molly down. She's the most important woman in my life and always has been. She helped create this business from the dirt up. I'm asking you as your colleague to show her respect. I'm telling you as your employer you will."

"You're giving me an ultimatum? I have to play nice with a woman who didn't support you or this business? A woman who cheated on you or I'm out of a job?"

"That's right."

She sneered. "You'll drown without me."

"Everyone is replaceable. Everyone. Including you."

I didn't want to fire her. We'd been working together for so long—she had so much on her plate—and I'd have a hell of a mess on my hands. But I'd figure it out. The season was almost over and I'd have things put back to rights before next spring.

"Then you better have a decent lawyer. There's no law that says I have to be nice to my boss's ex-wife. If you fire me, expect a lawsuit."

A threat. Now it wasn't a matter of *if* I fired her. Now it was a matter of when. Bridget had no intention of respecting Molly, and that wasn't going to work for me.

"Do you know that Molly owns ten percent of Alcott?"

Bridget's face paled. "No."

Not many people did. Molly hadn't wanted Alcott in the divorce. She'd wanted the house instead. But the value of the business compared to the home was such that she was on the losing end of the deal. So I'd offered to give her a lump sum. We went round after round trying to settle on a figure.

In the end, we'd agreed she could keep ten percent ownership as an investment. According to my corporation's bylaws, the ten percent meant nothing. She had no control, no say in the business-making decisions. But if Alcott ever sold, she'd get a return.

She'd protested the ten, saying five was enough. But I'd insisted. She'd earned that much and more. My original proposal had been for fifteen.

"Molly is an investor in this company," I told Bridget. "Consider her one of your bosses. Treat her like you do me and we'll all be fine."

The room went silent. She stared at me like she couldn't believe this was happening, that my request was completely unreasonable, until finally she said, "Then I quit."

I closed my eyes. It hurt to hear those words. It pissed me off too. She had no right to hate Molly so much. Certainly not enough to give up her career here instead of growing up and acting like a damn professional. But I wasn't going to budge.

"I'm sorry that it's come to this." I stood from my desk. "I'll escort you out."

"My things—"

"I'll have them packed and couriered over to you tonight."

"You're treating me like I'm a criminal!" she shrieked, flying out of her chair.

"This is policy when someone is terminated or quits," I reminded her. Hell, she'd been the one to pack up a locker or two.

I'd never taken someone's two-week notice. If they were gone, they were gone. And I didn't want soon-to-be ex-employees packing up their stuff—or any of mine—so we packed for them and had personal belongings delivered.

This was the policy. I stuck to policy.

She stared at me for another long moment, then stormed across the room. She went right into her office, swept up her purse, keys and sunglasses before marching to the front door.

I followed, standing outside as she went to her car. I was sure she'd leave without a word and never look back, but as she opened her door, she spun around to face me.

"I could have been, we could have . . ." She shook her head. "You've always been a fool over her."

"Always. And I wouldn't have it any other way."

*Darling Molly,*

*I've missed you. I've missed seeing your smile and hearing your voice. Saturday can't come soon enough. Dinner with you at Burger Bob's was one of the best nights I've had in months. Years, actually. I want to make it a regular thing for us, sharing a meal that you don't have to cook. One where we can laugh and talk and just enjoy each other's company. I hope you want that too.*
*Tell me you want that too. That you want us.*

*I'm not giving up this time. No more excuses. No more obstacles. I'm not letting anything keep us from being together. Even if it's just one date, one week at a time.*

*Yours,*
*Finn*

# twenty
## Molly

"Are you sure about this?" I asked Finn as we walked down the hallway at the theater.

My arms were loaded with a medium popcorn, a box of Mike and Ikes, chocolate-covered raisins and a large soda. Finn had a similar haul in his arms, except he'd opted for nachos with his popcorn and only one box of candy.

"We can handle it."

"The last time I made movie snacks a full meal was in college."

"I remember." He chuckled. "Those were some of the most expensive dates we had."

"But some of the best too. They were the special ones."

It had cost Finn a small fortune to pay for the movie tickets and snacks we bought in lieu of a real dinner. He'd always insisted on paying, much like he had tonight. So even though going to the movies had been one of my most favorite dates, I'd always been careful not to suggest it too often.

"Have you been to any movies lately?" Finn asked.

"No. There wasn't much time this summer."

"Yeah. This summer was something else."

"I used to go to the movies a lot," I told Finn. "It was my treat whenever you had the kids on the weekends."

"Who did you go with? Friends?"

"No. I came alone."

Finn slowed our pace. "Really?"

The look on his face. The pitifully guilty droop of his mouth was comical. "By choice. I like going to the movies alone."

"I don't like you going alone." He frowned. "But I guess it doesn't matter anymore. I'm your movie date from now on."

A warm tingle spread across my skin. The way he said it, the way he'd approached this rekindling of our relationship with so much surety and determination, it wasn't really a rekindling at all. It was more like a new beginning. And though it made me nervous, Finn's absolute confidence in where we were headed together was thrilling.

He'd sent me a letter this past week. I'd gotten it at the restaurant again, and I'd smiled like a loon as I'd read it over and over again.

*No more excuses. No more obstacles.*

Reading those words, I hadn't really believed them. I hadn't really thought Finn would change. But then Poppy came to tell me about Bridget. That Finn had sat down with her and demanded she treat me with respect, and that when she'd refused and quit, he'd walked her out the door.

It gave me hope. *He* gave me hope.

Hope wasn't an eraser for my fears. We'd started brilliantly once before and we'd ended in ashes.

There was something different about this though. The difference was Finn.

Mom had always said he was a closed-off man. I wouldn't tell her she'd been right, but the accident, the letters, they'd both forced him to open up.

Maybe this time, we'd get it right.

Like I'd done before our dinner date at Burger Bob's, I'd pushed my fears and doubts aside and climbed into Finn's truck for this movie date with an open mind.

Finn and I found our seats in the theater. We crammed snacks into our drink holders. Tubs rested on our laps. And as the previews started, we scarfed our irresponsible, unhealthy and delicious meal.

When the popcorn cartons were resting by our feet, I kept my eyes on the screen but my attention was on Finn's hand, waiting for it to take mine.

On our first movie date, it had taken him halfway through the film to finally touch me.

Tonight, it took minutes. As soon as he finished his last nacho, my hand was in his. He kept it until the lights turned on and the credits played.

"What did you think?" Finn asked as we strolled outside. It was dark now. The evening light from when we'd gone in had long disappeared.

"It was okay."

"Okay." He scoffed. "You hated it."

I grinned. "No, it was all right."

"Molly, I could hear your eyes rolling."

It was arguably one of the worst movies I'd ever seen. The plot was predictable. The acting was barely passable. The male lead's character was too stupid to live—the only bright spot of the movie was at the end when they killed him off.

"The movie wasn't the best," I admitted. "But I still had a good time."

"Me too." He swung our hands between us, like we were two kids young and in love with stars in our eyes. "Feel like grabbing a drink?"

"Sure." The kids were at Poppy and Cole's for the night. I

didn't have anything to hurry home to other than an empty bed.

When we pulled out of the parking lot, I expected Finn to turn toward the downtown bars. Instead, he went the opposite way.

"Where are we going?"

He leaned over and put his hand on my knee. "My place."

My entire body tensed, the muscles seizing.

Finn felt it. He didn't take his hand away but drew circles on my jeans with his thumb. "It's just my house. You said you didn't want to go there because you needed to keep the boundaries erect. But they have to come down, Molly. All of them."

He was right. And his house had become less intimidating now that I knew he'd never had a woman in his bed.

"Okay," I breathed. If we were going to date, this was inevitable.

My stomach was in knots by the time we pulled into his garage. I hadn't gone crazy tonight. I'd eaten just enough to feel full but not enough to get sick. So much for my restraint. The popcorn-candy combination was whirling around my insides like a rainbow tornado.

Finn opened my door for me, taking my hand as he led me into his house.

My aversion to Finn's home was stupid. I knew it. But it still took me a few moments to breathe.

The smell hit me first as we went inside. It was clean with a hint of lemon. And underneath that was Finn's manly scent. The garage opened to a laundry room. He had a nicer washer and dryer than I did, and the tile floors were spotless. There wasn't a small pile of lost socks on top of the dryer like I'd had on top of mine for the past three years.

From the laundry room, the house opened into an open-concept space. I stopped just shy of the living room and took it all in. The dark beams in the vaulted ceiling were exposed. The doors and trim were all stained a rich brown to match. The walls were sparse with a few Montana landscapes here and there. The cornerstone of Finn's decor theme was—no surprise—plants.

There was a Boston fern in the dining room on a pedestal, its soft green leaves draping nearly to the floor next to one leg of the oval mahogany table. A hoya in a large sage-green ceramic pot was in one corner of the living room. A weeping fig in another.

The kitchen had a tray of succulents. There was an African violet on a coffee table, its velvety leaves begging to be touched. It reminded me of the one he'd brought me once as a random gift. I had placed it on the ledge of our bedroom window until it died.

There used to be plants all over my house. Finn's clients had often gifted him houseplants when a job was complete. He'd left them behind when he moved out. And slowly, heartbreakingly, they'd all died. Even the violet.

Finn had been the one to care for them. I'd neglected them, often forgetting to water one until the soil was cracked and the leaves crispy. Each time I'd thrown one into the garbage can, I'd been heartbroken.

"What do you think?" he asked.

"You have a beautiful home. Really. It's lovely. I can see why the kids like it."

In a lot of ways, it reminded me of my house. He'd created a home similar to the one we'd shared, whether he'd meant to or not.

Finn tugged me farther into the room. "What would you like to drink?"

"I'm not picky."

"I've got a growler with the latest amber from Bozeman Brewing."

"That sounds perfect."

His grip tightened for a second, then he let my hand go so he could head into the kitchen.

As the refrigerator door opened, I made my way over to the fireplace mantel to inspect the framed pictures. Max's school picture was in one. Kali's was in another, smiling brightly in her volleyball uniform. There was a selfie of the three of them crouched together on a gravel hiking trail.

I stepped down to the other end of the fireplace, expecting more pictures of the kids. I blinked twice as my own face smiled back at me.

One frame held a family picture of the four of us. It was from years ago when Poppy had been working to finish Jamie's birthday list. She'd organized a paint fight, one of Jamie's items. We'd all met in a park to throw paint-filled water balloons at one another. Jimmy and Randall had been there, and she'd even invited Cole.

It hadn't been long after our divorce, and that paint fight was the first time Finn had stopped being so cold and callous toward me. In the photo, a four-year-old Kali was covered in pink paint. Max was only two and his cheeks were streaked with yellow. Finn and I were covered in a kaleidoscope of colors.

We'd been happy that day. Not long after the paint fight, Finn had come over to eat dinner with us. We'd sat down and talked after the kids had been put to bed. We'd promised each other we'd do better, that we'd get along, for them.

He'd also told me that night that he wanted to date.

That was the day a piece of me had shut down. The day the boundaries had fallen into place. I hadn't come into his house after he'd bought it. I'd avoided Alcott completely.

Even when we'd been having sex, I'd refused to let myself have feelings for Finn. I'd reminded myself that it was only sex.

I'd held up those guards for years.

They all came crashing down when I stared at the last picture.

It was of Finn and me at my college graduation. I was wearing a black cap and gown. His parents had come to celebrate with Poppy and me, and Rayna had asked Finn and me to pose for a picture. But instead of taking a pose, Finn had wrapped his arms around my waist, trapped me against his chest and tickled my ribs until I'd laughed so hard I cried.

Rayna had scolded him for nearly ruining my mascara. The photo she'd taken in that moment had become my favorite. It was us.

I'd framed it for Finn's office when we'd started Alcott. While Finn had been in the hospital and I'd gone to Alcott, I'd wondered where that photo had gone.

It had been on his mantel the whole time.

"Here you go." He came into the living room and set two frosty mugs on the coffee table.

I pointed to our picture. "How long have you had this here?"

"A while."

"Define a while."

He gave me a small smile. "Since I moved in."

"The whole time?" I whispered.

"The whole time."

"But . . ." My words died as my mind raced. He'd had this photo of us, just us, on his mantel for years. He'd kept it there when he could have put it in a drawer and hidden it away. He could have thrown it out. But he hadn't. He'd left it out on display for the kids to see. For his parents and Poppy and

Cole. For any visitor who'd come here. He'd left it on display, along with a family picture, for his girlfriends to see any time they came to his place. "Why?"

He sighed. "At first, I was trying to make this place a home for the kids. I thought having pictures of you and all four of us would make them feel like this was their home too."

"That was six years ago. They're plenty well-adjusted now."

"I know. But I couldn't take it down. Every time I tried, my hand didn't have the strength to lift it off the mantel. I needed to see your face every day. I needed you here. In my house."

Tears flooded my eyes. "We were divorced. You were dating other women."

He stepped closer, his hands skimming up my cheeks, his fingers disappearing into my hair. "And you stayed on this pedestal the whole time. Now you know why I've been dumped consistently over the last six years."

I laughed, dropping my gaze. Finn wasn't the type of man who'd take pleasure in hurting those other women. Still. "You deserved to be dumped."

"Yeah. I was the worst boyfriend ever." His grin fell. "And husband."

"No." I pressed closer, my breasts brushing against his chest. "Not the worst. We just failed a test, but that doesn't mean we haven't learned."

His free hand banded around my back, pulling me forward until I was flush against his torso. "Let's try again, Molly. Please. I know we won't fail a second time. I won't let us."

"On one condition."

He held his breath. "What?"

"Kiss me."

His lips came down on mine so fast, I gasped. Finn's tongue dove inside, twirling against my own as his lips consumed mine.

I let out a moan, which was met by one of his. We were a mess of wet lips and grappling fingers and shuffling feet as we made our way down the hallway.

Finn walked me backward, his arm never once leaving my back. His hand was firmly tangled in my hair, holding my head at whichever angle suited his tongue best.

Patience had disappeared the second his lips touched mine. As I tugged at his shirt, we crashed into the wall, my hip ricocheting hard enough to tangle up my feet. Finn held tight, steadying me. But instead of continuing our walk, he pressed me against the wall.

One of his hands moved to my breast. The other moved from my hair down to my ass. He squeezed both, the bite of his fingertips sending a rush of pleasure to my center.

I was throbbing, aching for more. I met his darkened and hungry gaze then circled my hips forward, wanting to feel his erection beneath his jeans. It felt like years since we'd been together, not months. And tonight was more than sex.

This was the turning point.

Finn was claiming me. We both knew that after this, we'd never go back. We were all in, taking this journey together. Taking another chance on one another.

There would be people who'd call us reckless for getting together when we'd already tried once, crashed and epically burned. I didn't care what people thought. No one knew about Finn and me. No one except us.

Finn pulled me away from the wall, his hand on my ass holding tight. The hand on my breast lifted so he could snake it around my back, then he rushed down the hall. At the doorway to his bedroom, we stumbled again, his shoulder smashing into the doorframe.

We were like a pinball, bouncing off every surface until we finally found the bed. We broke apart and I hopped onto the mattress, still bouncing as I ripped my shirt over my head. Finn kicked off his shoes and toed off his socks. He undid just enough buttons on his shirt to reach behind his head and pull it away.

By the time he was unzipping his jeans, I was naked but for my thong. The moment his eyes landed on the scrap of fabric, he let out a long curse that filled the room. "Fuck."

"I'd love to." I smirked. "Lose the pants."

His devilish grin made me shiver. The pulsing in my core was like a bass drum as he unzipped his jeans and ripped them down his legs along with his boxer briefs. His cock sprang free, thick and hard and weeping for attention.

I licked my lips as he settled between my legs. As he leaned down, my nipples skimmed against his hard chest, making me desperate.

Finn kissed at my neck, moving his way down my collarbone to the valley between my breasts. Then he dipped lower, his tongue snaking its way across the curve of my belly.

"Finn." His name was a whisper as he sank to his knees and stroked his tongue through my folds. I was so primed, so needy, I arched off the bed when he placed a soft kiss on my clit. My fingers dove into his hair, the rusty locks smooth and silky between my fingers.

He stroked and lapped, bringing me close to an orgasm in seconds. Then, when my legs were shaking and my heart racing, he pulled away. My head flew up off the mattress, my eyes wide. Finn's cocky grin was waiting as he wiped his bottom lip.

One of his hands slid down his flat stomach, bringing my gaze along with it. He fisted his shaft and stroked twice.

"God, I never thought I'd get to see this."

"What?" I whispered.

"You. Naked on my bed. More beautiful than the day we met."

My heart. I held a hand over my bare chest to keep it from flying away.

Finn came to me, his eyes locked on mine as he lowered his weight onto me. He dragged the tip of his cock through my center once and thrust forward, stealing my breath as he brought us together.

I was lost in the feel of him inside me as he began to move. Just like we had for years, he made me tremble. He brought us to the edge in a way that made me forget everything but Finn.

We came together in a rush, the build so strong and consuming I opened my mouth in a silent scream. Finn's entire body quaked as he poured into me, the aftershocks leaving us both a loose-limbed heap on the bed.

When we'd regained our breaths and the white spots had cleared from my vision, I smiled against his stubbled cheek. "I like your bed."

"Good." He chuckled. "Because you're sleeping in it tonight."

With a quick kiss on the neck, he pushed off the bed and went into the attached bathroom, flipping on a light. The sound of running water echoed into the bedroom and I smiled. He knew I liked to clean myself, and he was making sure the water would be warm when I went into the bathroom.

I pushed off the bed and wandered around the room, my legs jelly and my steps unsure. My eyes darted into the dark closet as I passed the opening. Was that where he'd kept the letters he'd sent me? The question came out of nowhere, but I wanted to know.

"Did you keep the letters in this closet?" I asked Finn.

He nodded. "Yeah. In a box in the top. Why?"

"Just curious." I stepped into the bathroom, squinting as my eyes adjusted to the bright lights bouncing off the white stone tile on the floors and the spacious shower. The marble counter had two bowl sinks resting on top. Finn was at one. The water ran for me in the other and a washcloth had been laid out along with a new toothbrush.

Finn finished brushing his teeth then dropped a kiss to my bare shoulder as he left the room. It didn't take me long to join him in the bedroom, crawling under the corner of the sheets he'd turned down. The moment I was horizontal, Finn rolled on top of me, pinning me down for a slow, lazy kiss.

"I had fun tonight," he said after tucking me into his side.

"Me too." I rested on the pillow, but an odd, familiar feeling hit me. It was . . . I shot upright. "Is this my pillow?"

He chuckled as I fluffed it and skimmed my hands over the case. "Maybe."

"It is. You stole my pillow."

He laughed harder. "So? You kept mine."

"I thought you'd left it behind."

"Only because I needed to make a clean getaway with yours. I didn't want them both to go missing."

I closed my eyes and wrapped an arm around his waist. "We wasted so many years."

"Then we'll make this year and all those to come count double."

I nuzzled closer, taking a deep inhale of Finn's earthy and clean scent.

"I love you." Finn kissed my hair. "In case that wasn't

perfectly clear. I love you, my darling Molly. For the rest of my days."

"I love you too." And no matter what happened, I'd tell him every day. It didn't take long for my body to relax. I was on the verge of sleep when another question popped into my mind. "Finn?"

"Hmm." He was already half asleep.

"Where did you keep those letters when we were married?"

"In a box in the closet," he answered.

"Did you take it with you when you moved into the loft at Alcott?"

He shifted to look down at me. "No. Why?"

"Well, the last letter was written right before the divorce. Did you put it in the same box?"

"Yeah. I came home to see the kids. Put them to bed. Wrote it before you got home."

Those were the limbo nights before he'd found this house. He'd come to my house in the evenings to see the kids. I'd leave for a few hours to help Poppy as she set up the restaurant. I'd get home, the kids would be asleep, and Finn would leave for the loft at Alcott.

"Why do you ask?"

"I'm trying to—" The timeline of our divorce ran through my mind as I tried to recall exactly when he'd left and when that box should have been taken. "You packed up the week after the divorce."

"Yeah. So?"

"So . . . are you sure the letters went with you? Or could they have been taken from my house instead?"

*Darling Molly,*

*You're asleep in my bed. If I get my way, this will be the only time you wake up in this house. If I get my way, we'll sit down and tell the kids I'm coming home tonight. If I get my way, I'll never spend another night without you in my arms.*

*We're going to make mistakes. But I promise, if you let me get my way, from here on out my letters will be yours.*

*You should really let me get my way.*

*Yours,*
*Finn*

# twenty-one
## Finn

"I don't want to get out," Kali said from the backseat of Molly's Jeep. Her eyes were aimed out the window, locked on the yard at Alcott. Locked on the spot where I'd been nearly crushed under a skid steer. "Do I have to?"

"No." I reached back and put my hand on her knee. "You can stay in the car."

"Can I stay too?" Max asked. He was staring at his lap, refusing to look up.

"Yeah, son. You can stay. We won't be long."

Molly and I shared a glance as she turned off the ignition. We got out and, hand in hand, walked into Alcott.

Once we were inside the office, I glanced over my shoulder. "They'll never like coming here again."

"It's just hard right now. It will pass."

I didn't agree. It had been months since the accident, and the few times I'd brought the kids here, they'd both refused to set foot on Alcott soil. They wouldn't even come into the office.

It was another reason the decision I'd made last week was the right one.

"Come on." I pulled Molly down the hallway toward my office.

She followed, her gaze roaming over the quiet and empty office that had belonged to Bridget.

It had been over two weeks since Bridget quit. The first week had been chaos. I'd rushed around constantly putting out fires but then things had settled. I found a groove and got through it. I delegated more. I hadn't missed listening to whatever drama Bridget created. I hadn't even noticed until she was gone how much drama she caused.

It was refreshing to work hard during the day so I could leave each night on time. Whatever got missed, well, it was there the next morning.

The never-ending tasks didn't rank as important as they had once.

Molly and I had been inseparable this past week—as inseparable as two adults with two children and two full-time jobs could be. But whenever possible, ever since the morning after our movie date, we'd been together. I'd left my latest letter next to the coffee pot. She'd opened it, read it once and burst out laughing.

Then she'd let me have my way.

That night, we'd sat the kids down and explained we were dating. And by dating I meant I'd be living in their house and sleeping in their mom's bed indefinitely.

Molly and I had both thought it would be a big deal. That they'd have questions, maybe some concerns. Max's exact words were, "Cool. Will you go play catch with me?" Kali smiled, gave me a high five then went to her room to draw.

That was it. Then I went to my place to pack up some stuff while Molly cooked dinner. On the way, I called a property management company and started the process of renting out my house.

In seven days, my personal belongings had all been moved home. The kids' beds had been donated to charity. And today, a guy who'd just relocated to Bozeman was renting my former house with the remaining furniture.

Molly hadn't said a thing about how quickly we were moving. Her mother had called and warned Molly it was too fast. I'd been standing in the kitchen, listening to the call on speaker. Molly's response? *Not fast enough.*

This was our first weekend together as a family. The first weekend we didn't have to think about kid swaps or separate schedules. We were taking the kids on an easy hike, something I hadn't done since the accident.

But first, I had to make one last change.

I'd told Molly that I needed to stop by Alcott and pick up some things. It wasn't a lie. I needed to pick up some paperwork—after she signed it.

We reached my office and my heart was nearly beating out of my chest. My hands were clammy. Sweat beaded at my temples because today I was going to ruin my life.

In the best possible way.

"Okay." I blew out a long breath and stopped in the middle of the room. "We're not just here to pick something up. First, I need you to sign some papers."

"What papers?" she asked, her gaze wary.

"I'm selling Alcott."

She blinked, shook her head, then blinked again. "You're what?"

"I'm selling Alcott. Since you own ten percent, I need you to sign the buy-sell agreement so I can get it back to my lawyer."

"What?" She brought her hands to her cheeks as she paced around the room. "You can't sell Alcott. Why? What? Why? No."

"It's gotta go, Molly."

"But why? You love Alcott. This is your job. Your passion. Think of all the time and energy you've put in here. The blood and sweat you've put into this place. You can't just sell it."

"It's sold."

"You already did it? Are you crazy?" she yelled. "To who?"

I chuckled. "About a year ago, this guy from California called me. He'd had a huge landscaping company in Sacramento and had sold it. He moved to Bozeman to retire but turns out, retirement didn't suit him. He didn't feel like starting from the ground up, so he asked me if I'd ever sell. At the time, I said hell no. Then things changed. I called him on Monday. We've been negotiating the price all week. Landed on one yesterday. Now all I have to do is sign the papers. So do you."

"But, Finn." Molly's eyes flooded with tears. "This . . . this was everything."

"It was. When we did it together. But Alcott Landscaping hasn't been Alcott Landscaping for a long time. Since before the divorce. When you stopped working here, a lot of the heart left. It took me a long time to realize, but I've been pouring myself into a glass that's got a huge hole in the bottom."

"No, Finn. You can't give it up."

I crossed the room and took both of her hands in mine. "I'm gaining more than I'm losing here. The kids, our life, it comes first. Alcott is in good hands."

"This doesn't make any sense. Alcott is your dream."

"My dream was a job where I could work outside doing what I love. But I haven't planted a tree in the name of Alcott Landscaping in over seven years. I had more fun working on the yard with you than I've had here in ages. Being confined to my office, driving by and giving crews orders without actually working with them side by side, that was never my dream. The only time I've actually done much work has been loading up trucks in the yard, and look how that went. I nearly died."

She sighed. "I think we need to talk this through. An impulse decision like this, you'll regret it."

"I won't."

Molly stepped away and paced the room again. She toyed with the hair ties on her wrist. Today's were yellow and orange. "What will you do? You'll go crazy if you sit around at home all day."

"I'll find something. I don't have to decide right away."

"But your employees. They'll lose their jobs."

I shook my head. "This guy wants to keep the existing employees. He wants to be the office guy."

I'd even given him Bridget's name. As angry as I was at how she'd treated Molly, I didn't wish her bad fortune. I knew from the grapevine she didn't have another job yet, so I'd tossed her name out there as a gesture of goodwill.

"He might destroy everything you built."

"Yeah." I nodded. "He might. And I'm not going to say that won't be hard to watch. But I'm not selling this place cheap. He's coming to the table with a hell of a check. I'm thinking he's plenty motivated to keep Alcott at the top of its game."

"Oh my God. I can't believe this is happening. I'm dreaming. This has to be a dream."

I walked to my desk and picked up the contract I'd printed yesterday. "Here. Maybe this will make it more real."

She eyed the papers for a few moments then gave in and took them from my hand. She plopped down into one of the chairs next to my desk, set the contract on top and started scanning. I knew right away when she read the purchase price.

"One point five million dollars. He's buying Alcott for one and a half million dollars?"

I nodded. "We've had a good few years in business."

"Understatement," she mumbled.

"With that kind of money, we can pay off the house, set aside a good chunk for the kids and then get creative. Maybe start another business. Together."

"I don't want to quit my job at the restaurant."

"Then don't. The point is, this gives us the freedom to do whatever we want. And it gives me a chance to right some wrongs. I love Alcott. I always will. I'm proud of what we created here. But it's time to say good-bye."

"Are you sure? I mean, *really* sure? I don't want you to resent me for this later."

"This is my decision. And I know in my bones it's the right one."

She nodded hesitantly. I gave her time to think on it, to let the surprise of my announcement fade. Molly nodded again, this time with more confidence.

When she met my gaze, it was solid as a rock. "Okay. Then I'll support you."

"Good." I picked up a pen and handed it over. "Then sign on the last page."

Molly flipped to where my attorney had flagged the signature lines with yellow tags. The pen hovered over the paper as she sucked in a deep breath. Then, as she blew it out, her hand moved, signing her name.

With it done, she pushed the paper and pen my way.

I didn't hesitate to scribble my name alongside hers, not even a second.

Alcott had been the dream. I'd achieved more success here than I ever could have imagined, but it had come at a price. Molly's heart.

Somehow, I'd been lucky enough to win it back. And I wasn't going to risk losing it ever again.

The room was quiet as I set the pen down. We sat there, listening as the air whirled.

"I feel lighter," I confessed.

She met my gaze, her brown eyes swimming in tears. "So do I."

We took one last moment to look around the room, then I stood and went to her chair. I took Molly's hand and led us outside. We got into the Jeep, smiled at the kids and left Alcott behind.

The life I'd had was in the rearview mirror.

And I wouldn't have it any other way.

———

"Pretty spot, isn't it?" I asked Kali as we stood on top of the ridge we'd hiked. Beneath us the entire Gallatin Valley was spread out in a carpet of green fields and golden hills. The trees were a fall mix of deep green, lemon lime and cherry red.

"Have we ever been up here before?" Kali asked, leaning into my side.

"A couple times when you were a baby. Your mom and I used to come up this trail a lot."

"Why did you stop?"

"There were lots of other great spots to explore with you guys too."

It was a partial truth. I'd done a ton of hiking in other parts of the valley with the kids, but I hadn't brought them up here. It was a harder climb. And this trail was Molly's favorite. It hadn't seemed right to come here without her.

Behind us, Molly and Max were looking over a different part of the ridge. Max was standing on a tall rock, making funny faces as Molly snapped pictures of him on her phone.

"I love it up here," Kali said quietly, more to herself than to me.

I hugged her closer to my side. She smiled up at me, then looked behind us as Max and Molly laughed.

Then she dropped her gaze to her feet. "They worked."

"Huh? What worked?"

"The let—" Her body tensed. Then she was gone, twirling out of my embrace and hurrying over to join Max on his boulder.

"What the hell?" I muttered to the wind.

Maybe I was wrong, but my gut was telling me that Kali had just slipped up and almost said *the letters*.

I wanted to pull her aside and ask again, but I forced myself to let it go. For now. I'd ask her when we were home and alone.

After a family selfie, we made our way down the trail. The kids took the lead, setting the pace on our descent as Molly and I brought up the rear.

"That was fun." She nudged my shoulder with her own.

"Yeah, it was."

"Are you okay? When we were on the ridge, you looked upset. Is it Alcott? Because we can rip those papers up when we get to the Jeep."

I pulled her into my arms, stopping us on the trail. "No, it's not Alcott. It was nothing."

"You're sure?"

My answer was to put my lips on hers and kiss her breathless.

"Gross!" Max shouted.

Molly smiled against my lips. "He's grounded."

"For at least an hour. Kali too. Long enough for us to shower together when we get home."

"You're brilliant. I love you."

"I love you too." I kissed her again. "Race you to the bottom?"

"Oh, I don't think we should. Your first hike out, you'd better take it easy."

"No, I'm fi—" Before I could finish arguing with her, she'd shoved me away and was running down the trail. "Cheater."

Her laughter echoed through the trees as she flew past the kids. "You'll never catch me, Alcott."

Max and Kali giggled as they took off after her.

I chuckled, jogging slowly along to give them a head start.

I'd catch her, all right. I'd never stop chasing.

———

"Hey." Cole saluted me with his bottle of beer. "About time you got here."

"Sorry. We got delayed at home."

We were late for the barbeque at Cole and Poppy's place, but it had been worth the scolding from my sister. Molly and I had showered so long that we'd run the hot water heater down to cold.

"Beer?" he offered.

"Please." I followed him through the house, away from the noise of the kids playing and the adults visiting in the kitchen. He kept his stash of beers in a mini fridge in the garage, as well as the car he was currently rebuilding in his spare time. "How's the 'Cuda coming along?"

"Great. It's going to take a year or so to finish, but it's been fun to tinker on. My dad's been helping too. I heard you're unemployed."

"News travels fast." Though it came as no surprise that Molly had already told Poppy.

"What are you going to do?" Cole asked.

"Enjoy life." I sighed. "Buy Molly a diamond ring. Drive the kids to school every morning. Mow the lawn in the summer. Shovel snow in the winter."

"Good for you. I'm glad for you guys."

"It was the right move." I took a sip of my beer. "I owe you."

"For?"

"The letters."

Cole tried to hide his grin behind his beer bottle. "I don't know what you're talking about."

"We went for a hike today and Kali almost slipped up. She caught herself, but it was enough to get me thinking."

There was no way my daughter could have done it alone. There were no dates to put them in order without more context to our relationship. There was no way she could have timed their delivery to the mailbox just right. But if she'd had help, if she'd been the mailbox delivery person, that I could believe.

There were few people in the world Kali trusted. Her uncle Cole was one. My guess was that he'd found the letters, and Kali had become his little mouse, helping him sneak them into the mailbox.

"When did you get them?"

"Remember that year we played city-league softball?" he asked and I nodded. "You forgot your cleats. You were working and didn't have time to run home, so I stopped to get them."

"That was . . ." I mentally tallied the years. "Four years ago. You've had them all this time?"

He nodded. "I was just waiting for the right time. When you broke up with Brenna, I decided it was now or never. You'd been so hell-bent on dating someone for so long. Every relationship was a disaster. Poppy was pushing Molly to date her neighbor, and I thought I'd give it a shot. I asked Kali to keep a secret. She was more than happy to be my minion."

"Did she know what was in them?" *Say no.*

"No," Cole promised. "She never knew. I just asked her to deliver some letters that would be good for her mom to read. She never knew they were from you, just that I hoped they'd make Molly happy."

They hadn't at first. But in the end, they'd been the catalyst to heal our hearts. To mend them together.

"Why?" I asked him.

"I'll do anything to make my wife happy."

My jaw fell open. "You did this for Poppy?"

"And for you." He shrugged. "When Poppy and I first got together, it was right after you and Molly divorced. You'd just found kind of a truce and you'd decided to start dating again. Poppy told me it was because you wanted to find happiness again and love, like she had with me."

"Not my smartest move," I muttered.

"Honestly, at the time I thought it *was* smart. You and Molly were divorced. You were moving on. Eventually she would too. Poppy had such a hard time with it. She knew you both still loved each other and thought you were wasting love."

And for a woman who had lost love unexpectedly, it was no surprise Poppy had taken it hard.

"Our opinions swapped, Poppy's and mine," Cole said. "At first, I'd thought it was a good thing. Poppy struggled with it. Then she started to accept that you and Molly were through. The more I was around you both, all the years you'd look at each other across the room and smile, forgetting for that split second you were divorced, it started to make me crazy. But I didn't want to get involved."

"Then you found the letters," I guessed.

"That's right. I found those and took a wild guess that Molly had never seen a single one. I figured, maybe if she did, you two would stop fucking around."

I chuckled. "Quite a gamble."

"Nah. I knew you two wouldn't let me down." He brought his bottle to his smiling lips. "How'd you figure out it was me?"

"After Kali said that today, I knew it had to be someone close. I started thinking back to all the times Molly and I confronted you guys about the letters. Everyone denied it. Over and over. Everyone except you. You evaded."

Cole had acted shocked. He'd had alibis for his where-abouts every night. But he'd never actually come out and said *No, it wasn't me.*

"I don't know what to say," I admitted. I set my beer aside and stretched out my hand. "Thanks."

"Do right by Molly. And by yourself." He shook my hand. "That's all the thanks I need."

The door to the garage opened and Poppy poked her head outside. "Cole, you can start the grill."

"Okay, beautiful."

Cole and I left the garage with fresh beers. While he went to the grill, I found Molly standing in the kitchen, eating chips and salsa.

"Hey." She took my beer away for a healthy swig. "Poppy and I were thinking of throwing you a party to celebrate your 'retirement.' We could have it at the restaurant. You could invite anyone from Alcott. What do you think?"

"I'm game."

She smiled. "Good. We'll get planning."

The kitchen was buzzing with activity as people gathered around the spread of appetizers Poppy had laid out. My parents were here. Cole's were too, along with his sister's family. It was guaranteed to be a fun night, but before we got to the good times, I had to talk to Molly.

I had to tell her that Cole had been the one to send the letters. For that, I didn't need an audience.

"Come with me for a sec." I grabbed her hand, threading our fingers together as we snuck away to the front porch. Then I told her about how Cole had sent the letters and how Kali had helped.

"A part of me wants to hit him upside the head for putting us through everything. But I'm grateful. So very grateful."

"Me too." I pulled her into my arms, resting my cheek on the top of her head. She gave me her weight, settling into the embrace like we'd done a hundred times. Like we'd do a thousand more. "I'm not going to stop."

"Stop what?"

I held her tighter. "The letters."

From now until the end of our days, Molly would get my letters.

*Darling Molly,*

*I just might have to marry you. Again.*

*Yours,*
*Finn*

# epilogue
## Molly

T*en months later . . .*
       "Finn, would you *please* slow down?" It was the third time I'd asked.

"I'm going the speed limit."

"It feels faster." I couldn't see the speedometer, but from the backseat of the Jeep, it felt like he was practicing for the qualifiers at the Indy 500.

He grumbled something I couldn't hear before shooting me a glare through the rearview mirror.

"Eyes on the road!"

"Molly, we're going to be late." His hands tightened on the steering wheel as he fought to keep his patience.

I was in a bad mood today. Everyone in the car knew it. Kali was sitting up front in the passenger seat, doing her best to avoid my wrath by blending in with the leather upholstery. Max was next to me, his gaze aimed out the window to avoid all eye contact.

"I'm sorry, guys." I sighed. "I'm just tired. And I really don't want to do this today."

Finn's eyes softened as he looked back in the mirror. I gave him a small smile.

The last thing I wanted was to go to this memorial today. They weren't fun to begin with, and today's would be doubly miserable considering the week I'd had.

On Monday, I'd spent twenty hours in labor attempting to birth our son. And when the baby just wouldn't come out, my obstetrician had wielded her scalpel and sliced me in half. That was on Tuesday. Wednesday, Thursday and Friday had been spent in an uncomfortable hospital bed because at thirty-seven years old, my doctors were worried I might have complications from the C-section. Finally, after a mandatory seventy-two-hour postop hospital stay, they'd set us free on Saturday morning.

Finn and I, along with James Randall Alcott, had been able to go home. What I wanted more than anything for my Sunday was to laze around on the couch enjoying our new baby. Instead, I'd shoved the watermelons that were my breasts into a nursing bra. I'd showered, done my hair, put on makeup and dressed in my most nonmaternity maternity shirt with my pregnant jeans.

And we'd all piled into the car to go to a memorial service for Randall.

I wasn't sure how I'd summon the energy to stand by a tombstone for more than twenty minutes. The last week had exhausted me completely. I didn't remember feeling this tired after having Kali or Max, but with Jamie, my age had become an issue.

"Is this going to take a long time?" Max asked.

"I hope not. I really hope not."

"Let's make the best of it, okay? After we're done at the cemetery, we'll go to the restaurant and you guys can run around."

We were closed today for a family function. That was going to be my saving grace. I only had to make it through the service, then I could hide away at the restaurant, where everyone wouldn't care if I sat in a quiet corner to nurse the baby. There'd be plenty of people to bring me things.

It wasn't my couch at home dressed in my ratty maternity sweatpants, but it was the next best thing.

Plus, it would give everyone a chance to fuss over Jamie.

Finn and I hadn't planned on another baby. Two weeks after he'd moved in, I'd found a letter on the bathroom counter. Underneath was a diamond engagement ring.

I wasn't wearing it at the moment because my fingers had swollen into sausage links during my pregnancy. But the second I could make out knuckles again, it was going back on my hand.

I toyed with the chain around my neck. It had the first engagement ring Finn had given to me in college along with my first wedding band.

Finn wore the wedding band from Marriage Part One, as he'd been calling it, on his right hand. The band from Marriage Part Forever was on his left.

We'd opted for a destination wedding, jetting off to Hawaii to get married on the beach with our families close by. My parents even made the trip, despite my mother's irritation that I was remarrying Finn.

In the last ten months, she hadn't gotten over it. Maybe she never would. But if she had thoughts, she kept them to herself and that was all I could ask for.

Everyone else was ecstatic to see us tie the knot again. Finn wore a simple cream suit. I opted for a tea-length chiffon dress. We partied the night away with tiki torches and loud music. We enjoyed the beach until the weekend was over.

Finn and I stayed for a honeymoon while his parents took

Kali and Max home. We spent a week exploring Maui, hiking in the jungle and relaxing on the beach when we weren't busy in bed.

It was a rainy day that we think I got pregnant. I'd missed a birth control pill somewhere along the way and had hoped it wouldn't matter.

It mattered.

I wouldn't change it for a thing. Jamie was the piece of our family we hadn't realized had been missing. And Poppy was over the moon that we'd asked to name him after our departed friend.

As Finn turned off the main road and into the tree-lined drive at the cemetery, my irritation with today amplified. "This is so stupid."

"I'm not going to argue with you," Finn muttered. "But let's just get it over with."

We pulled up next to a curb and parked behind a short line of familiar vehicles. I wasn't used to packing up a baby, so we were the last ones to get here. Our friends and family members stood under the shade of a tree to avoid the scorching August sun. It was only eleven in the morning, but as soon as I stepped out of the Jeep, my sweat glands opened.

Finn hooked one arm through the handle of Jamie's car seat and put the other around my shoulders. "You look beautiful."

"I look awful." I looked up at him and smiled. "But thanks for lying to me."

"We'll get through today. The kids will be gone at camp tomorrow. And you, Jamie and I are going to get some fucking sleep."

I was taking a few weeks off from the restaurant, just managing the books from my laptop at home, and Poppy and Rayna had the rest covered. Finn had taken on a few freelance landscape-design jobs this spring but didn't have any looming deadlines.

"You won't hear me argue." Tears welled in my eyes and I leaned into his side, sniffing them away. "I'm so, so tired, Finn. I don't know if I can do this."

"I'm right here." He held me tight and kissed my hair. "I'm right here."

I nodded, blinking the tears away as we got close enough for everyone to converge.

MacKenna and Brady approached first, wanting to see their new cousin again. One of the cutest pictures I had from this past week was of me in the middle of the hospital bed, holding Jamie, and all the kids piled around me, staring at his button nose.

"Hi. How are you today?" Poppy asked.

"I'm good."

She frowned. "You're dead on your feet."

"Yeah," I admitted, still using Finn as a crutch. "But we'll get through today and then I can take it easy."

"We're making this short," she declared. "It's stupid anyway."

"Hey," Jimmy snapped. He'd been hovering over the kids to get a look at Jamie. "Let's be respectful. Randall wanted this as his memorial service. We owe it to him to carry out his wishes."

A chorus of groans filled the air. Every one of the adults rolled their eyes.

"Let's get started," Cole said. "Then we can get out of the heat."

"I hope this isn't the attitude you'll have at my memorial service," Jimmy grumbled as he led the way to the newest tombstone in this section of the cemetery.

He was the only one wearing all black today.

As we circled the tombstone, Jimmy pulled out some reading glasses from his shirt pocket. After they were perched on his nose, he unfolded a piece of paper that had been in his pants pocket.

"Thank you all for coming here today," he read. "We are here to celebrate the life of Randall Michael James, a beloved friend."

Jimmy went on to read about Randall. He recited a list of Randall's accomplishments. He talked about those qualities we all loved most about our dear friend. And at the end, he dried a tear from his eye.

"Randall and I, well . . . I couldn't have asked for a better friend at this stage in my life. The fights. The competitions. They were all in good humor. I'll miss you, friend."

The air was silent as his words echoed across the green grass. We all stared at the grave's marker, until finally, MacKenna broke the silence.

"Mommy?" She looked up at Poppy. "Why is Great Grandpa going to miss Grandpa Randall? Isn't he standing over there?"

*Bless her little heart.*

MacKenna pointed past us to a tree on the far side of the cemetery. A tree Randall was doing a poor job hiding behind.

Cole was the first one to start laughing. Finn, David and Rayna joined in next. Poppy broke last, causing Jimmy to toss the piece of paper in the air and mutter, "I give up."

I tried to stifle my laughter but only because it hurt. Unfortunately, it was no use. I clutched my stomach and the medical band wrapped around me to keep the stitches contained.

Poppy laughed. "I'm going to pee my pants."

"My stitches are going to split." Still, I couldn't stop. Even the kids had lost it.

"It's good to see you're all taking my death so seriously," Randall said as he joined our group. "You're all standing on my grave. Laughing."

"You're alive!" Poppy cried, throwing up her hands. "You wanted us to have a memorial service for you while you're still alive. Of course we aren't taking this seriously. It's a million degrees outside. We're standing over a tombstone that isn't even complete because—again, you're alive. And we're not standing on your grave. Because, I repeat, you are alive."

The laughter turned to howls that lasted much longer than the speech Jimmy had tried to give. Finally, we all pulled ourselves together, drying eyes and letting the muscles in our cheeks relax.

"I was doing this for you," Randall told Poppy. "So you wouldn't have to sit through a memorial service after I'm gone. I don't want you all crying over me."

And that was why we loved him so much. That was why we'd miss him so terribly when his time did come. Randall had the biggest heart of any person I knew, even when he hid it deep.

Poppy and I shared a look then went to him and pulled him into a three-person hug. Really, it was more of us hugging each other with Randall in the middle because he was still pouting.

"I love you," I told him.

"I love you too," Poppy echoed.

He sighed. "I know."

We stood there for a few moments until it was too hot to share the body heat.

"Let's go get some lunch." Poppy looped her arm with Randall's. "You can have as many desserts as you want today."

That perked him up. "Jimmy, did you hear that? No dessert limit today. Bet I can eat more apple pies than you."

Jimmy scoffed. "We'll see about that."

The two of them set off toward the cars, the kids and Finn's parents following, which left Poppy, Cole, Finn and me. In unison, we turned our gazes to the far end of the cemetery.

To where Jamie was buried.

Poppy looked away first, smiling as she took Cole's hand. "Today is the first time I've been here and laughed. Maybe Randall's crazy scheme wasn't so crazy after all."

"Maybe not." Cole bent and placed a kiss on her cheek. Then he led her toward the cars, to where their children were laughing.

I didn't look away from the opposite end of the cemetery. Jamie would have loved having a nephew with his name. He would have loved teaching him bad habits and how best to prank his older siblings. He would have loved to know that his wife was so cherished.

He would have loved to know that Finn and I had made it back together.

"He would have been so proud." Tears spilled from my eyes again. "Ugh. I'm so emotional."

Finn simply smiled and took me under his arm once more as I fought to suck in the tears. Then he led me and our baby across the grass.

"Jamie," Finn said quietly to our son, still asleep in his seat. It was a miracle he hadn't woken up during all the ruckus. "One day, I'm going to tell you the story of how in college, your mom and your uncle Jamie locked themselves in a trunk."

"Oh my God." I smacked Finn's stomach, my tears disappearing into a happy smile. "You can't tell him that. It's humiliating."

"Maybe not tomorrow. But someday. Someday, I'm going to tell him all the funny stories. The ones about you and me. About Poppy and Cole. About Jamie. I want him and Max and Kali to know how blessed we've been and how much I love you. Because that's our story."

It wasn't perfect. But it was ours.

———

True to his word, Finn told the kids our story. He waited until our twentieth wedding anniversary, when Kali and Max had families of their own. When Jamie had grown into a young man.

That was when he shared our love story with them.

One letter at a time.

———

Read Poppy and Cole's story in *The Birthday List*.

# acknowledgments

Thank you for reading *Letters to Molly*! I hadn't planned on writing this story. When I finished *The Birthday List*, I had truly planned on that story standing alone. But with so much excitement and demand from my readers for Molly's story, I opened my mind and her book came pouring in. Divorced couples who reunite isn't a wildly popular trope and this was a unique writing experience for me. It's a different take on a second-chance romance. So again, thank you for reading. I hope you loved Molly and Finn's happily ever after.

Special thanks to my family and friends for all of their encouragement. This is my eleventh book and their support as I chase my dreams never waivers.

Thank you to my team for all the work they do on each of my books. My editing and proofreading team: Elizabeth, Marion, Julie and Karen. Because of you, I never have to learn how to use a comma. My cover designer: Sarah. And to the team at Brower Literary, thank you for promoting my books all across the world.

Thank you to each and every blogger who takes the time to read and post about my stories. Thank you to the members of Perry Street, who are the best group of super fans I could have ever asked for. And thank you to all of my author friends for being so supportive and willing to collaborate. The book world truly is the best world.